The Opera Ghost Unraveled

Michelle Rodriguez

DEDICATION

For every phan who wished for a happy ending for our
beloved, masked hero.

ACKNOWLEDGEMENTS

A special thank you to Jessica Elizabeth Schwartz for your amazing photography, for being a wonderful friend, and for constantly inspiring me with a Phantom obsession that may rival my own!
Also a thank you to the wonderful cover models, Ryan J. Mulrenin and Caitlin Kerling. You brought the story to life!

Chapter One

Twilight, and the world glowed in pinks and violets as shadows elongated their sinewy fingers until they swallowed any brightness lingering behind. Christine gave no thought to the dark or the watching shadows. Not a single one could dim the smile upon her lips. As she entered an iron gate that resounded in an annoyed whine after her, she contemplated that this was the first time she'd been able to enter such a sacred place with lightness in her heart. Typically, there were tears and a hollow pain in her chest that ached with every step between marked graves, but this time nothing could steal her elation.

Crickets chirped an early summer song, and she paid close attention to their pitch and timbre. For the first time, *everything* around her seemed like music, from the distant coo of an owl in an unnoticed tree to the rustle of her footsteps. A song when it all came together, a song to capture this moment in time. Her whole life was music! Every glorious detail, and how she adored that her ears had finally been opened to hear its sweet strains!

Her laughter filtered above in its own counterpoint as she scampered between more headstones, seeking one in particular. She halted before its permanent marking and stared at the letters carved into its stone, letters that came together in words that tried to pull at her light heart. And yet

1

even reminiscence could not darken her spirit as she quickly knelt on the chilled ground before the grave of her beloved father. Was it wrong that she felt no urge to cry when tears would usually be half the words spoken at this spot? But she had no need to mourn what extended beyond death and its limits. Yes, her father was gone; she was not foolish enough to believe the dead still walked the earth, but his soul had proven to exceed its eternal rest and bless her one last time.

"Oh, Papa," she softly bid as she touched her palm to solid stone. "Thank you. You sent him to me, just as you promised. I never doubted you would, but it's hard to hold onto dreams in a cynical world. I was so alone and lost, but you saw me. My darkest moments without a path as my own, and you gave me an angel to inspire my heart once again."

Merely the word brightened her glow until it beamed like sunlight in her eyes. *Angel...* And hers was everything she had ever hoped to have as her own.

"You would be so proud of me, Papa," she continued, forcing away echoes of an ethereal voice in her ear. It was just too easy and preferred to fall into her mind and daydream that voice into corporeal existence. "The Angel of Music is teaching me. He says I have an extraordinary talent, and...," she lowered her voice as if she spoke a secret, "Papa, he says I shall be the prima donna. He truly believes it and insists I must as well. It's as if he knows my every dream and is bringing them to life for me."

Her excitement laced every word, and as her eager eyes glanced at appearing stars, it seemed like they were within her reach, like any dream she could ever have would be given to her by her devoted angel and his adored presence.

"The Angel of Music," she breathed to herself, eyes still on twinkling stars. "It must be wrong to carry such affection for a holy being. It must be," she asserted. "My head keeps telling me not to love him, that it can never be and I will only destroy my heart, but... He is *everything* to me. I barely survive the day until I am once again in his presence. Just a word spoken from his beautiful voice, and my knees shake. How ridiculous to tremble at a mere hello! But to know he's there and speaking a greeting to *me*, as if I deserve such brilliance, ...it overwhelms me."

Her smile only then dropped its corners. "And yet I realize my heart must eventually be broken in two. He's an *angel*. I can't see him, can't touch him even if I long for those very things. To know he exists and hear his voice must be enough, but my heart selfishly yearns for more. It must be a sin!" she decided again. "I have tarnished the innocent beauty of his existence in my life, but...I love him."

With such a heavy admission, her eyes lowered to earth and headstones as impeding dark made them little more than silhouettes. "Papa, you didn't want me to be alone, so you sent the angel, and it is ungrateful of me to want more. But...can you ask God to make my angel real? A man with a heart and a soul to love me in return. He speaks of the music, and it would seem to be all that matters to him, but I've caught longing in his voice and words an angel must not indulge or feel. If he were a man, he could love me without restriction and tragedy at our end."

She shook her head and insisted, "I know I'm asking for too much, but...I'm terrified someday, he'll leave me and return to heaven. An angel can't stay forever, but a man... If he were real and tangible, we could be together always. How selfish I must seem! You sent me the Angel of Music as you promised, and I *had* to fall in love with him! But...my heart knows where it belongs. It yearns to be only his forever."

Her voice broke off, and yet her smile slowly returned as she rose with one last touch to the name on a grave. "I must go. It's getting dark, but...I know I have an angel to watch over me, and I'm not afraid.

No, I say, shadows come near if he will swoop down from heaven to protect me." Suddenly laughing aloud, she decided, "I am such a fool! I must be to fantasize such a fate! But I see it in my mind's eye: an angel with brilliant white wings, the most beautiful creature ever to exist flying from heaven and taking me from this world... If you were here to hear such a thing, Papa, you would call me melodramatic and tell me how wonderful my talent at exaggeration will translate to the stage. You always said the most overdone people make the most believable actors. Well, the stage is my destiny. You were right, and I love you for it."

Pausing one final breath, Christine dared to bend and set a solitary kiss to the top of the cold tombstone as if it were a daughter's duty. "Goodnight, Papa, and thank you...for not forgetting me."

And there were the tears she thought gone, gathering in the corners of her eyes despite her smile. But to realize that not even death could sever her father's love was humbling. She hardly felt she deserved the gift her father had sent. *An angel...* It had to be wrong to wish for more. But fantasy held no boundaries, and it encompassed her in its pictures, creating visions of a beautiful, white-winged man.

Giggling at her own ridiculousness, Christine ran for the cemetery gate, her cloak billowing behind her like its own set of matching wings. Throwing her arms out, she embraced the night and its transcendental power of illusion as if only in shadows could dreams be real. The night played its music, over laden in promises, and with hasty steps, she hurried to savor every one and wish on spying stars for a hundred more.

The instant the iron gate whined closed behind her, one of the shadows watching shifted its shape, transforming from a seeming part of an elm tree's base into the distinct form of a human being. He chose to be unseen, spying like the stars always from the background, typically only touching lives if violence and consequences were involved. But...this was the one life he touched with nothing more than tenderness and a certain reverence for her very existence, as humbled by her presence as she was by an angel's. He was so careful in every interaction with her, making music the most important thing when he felt too awkward and terrified to speak about much else. Music was his passion, and it seemed a fitting disguise to assume the role of her yearned for Angel of Music, as if it were a vacant spot waiting for him to fill it. And now... She said she loved him.

No, sense argued. She didn't love Erik, the flawed, corporeal man; she didn't even know he existed. She loved the angel he'd created for her, the intangible, bodiless voice. She would never be able to fathom that her heaven-sent guardian was really a flesh and bone man, watching her, loving her, lusting after her from behind the mirror of her dressing room. That was a sin far greater than loving an angel could be. Loving an angel, ...loving a monster was more accurate. The reality dulled every vivid hope taking root in Erik's heart. Her innocent, little fantasies showed her a beautiful angel; she could never accept the true horror of the creature she had allowed into her life. Such a nightmare was beyond the limits of her imagination. Her angel love was a disfigured murderer...

Silent as the graves surrounding, Erik followed her trail, always keeping beyond her sight. No idiom needed to exist for the plain fact that she *did* have a guardian angel ready to rush to her aid if necessary. He would never allow any harm to come to her. He might be the furthest thing from beautiful, white-winged angel in existence, but he would protect her like one. He already felt so sure that she was *his* to guard and cherish. *His*... It should have been impossible and improbable. She asked for a transformation into a living, breathing man; would she be able to accept a flawed carcass over the perfection in her mind?

The question would not quit haunting him, not as he saw her safely home, not as he kept a silent vigil outside her apartment, not even after he surrendered his post and wearily trudged through the abandoned, nighttime streets of Paris.

She wanted her angel as a man to love her. He could give that to her, but at what cost to both their hearts? Weeks of lies and fabricating a heavenly existence, and when reality meant shattering her dreams, it left him hesitant. If he did this, he would be thrusting her out of her childhood; he would be stealing naïveté and trust, and he might lose her in his hope to win her.

Without a decision as his own, Erik slipped back into the darkness that led belowground and out of sight. Alone, secluded, separated from life, he'd accepted that fate long ago. Why then with one glimpse of an innocent girl with blue eyes that pierced his soul did he suddenly want so much more? Why was the mere idea of ending contact and leaving her to her life inconsiderable? Such a path held nothing but cold emptiness in its details. To never see her beautiful face again, never hear her sweet voice sing so brilliantly or call him 'ange' as if he could be suited for the title, to never hold the hope of appealing to her as a real man and a life with her that could be his if she were willing... No, he couldn't possibly. It was the equivalent of ending existence and never breathing again. She was his future. Amidst every fear in between was that one certainty, and if he were brave enough to seek her heart, then he might have his every dream spread before him.

With a full head, Erik entered his underground home, already scheming how he could weave himself into her reality without destroying it to pieces.

*****

Disappointment was a common emotion for a

tortured life. Erik was victim to its bitter sting over and over again from days of childhood. *No,* always *no,* always raising hopes to have them shatter in every detail of his tragic existence. Attempts to be normal and fit into a world that only ever denied him were hopeless and pointless and never with an ending that did not involve violence and regret. So the world rejected him, and he took to living on its outskirts. Belowground, buried like the corpse they'd called him. Disappointment did not touch one who didn't hope. Perhaps it would have been merciful never to know hope again. But...hope came with big blue eyes and dark curls, with sweet porcelain features and the glorious curves of an artist's creation.

Christine... She had changed every detail of his world in his first glimpse of her. For the first time in Erik's existence, he was resigned not to settle with disappointment as a finale. No, he would fight for her, no matter what it took, until every bad emotion and heartbreak must be snuffed out of existence and turned into bliss.

Lingering behind her dressing room mirror, Erik waited impatiently for her to return from rehearsal. How many hours had he spent in this place? Pining for her presence when she was onstage, longing for her even when she stood so unwittingly before him. Was he meant to have only yearning, and was it to be enough to tide over a passionate soul? Love had seemed inconsequential when it was nothing but a word to a blind heart, but now that he understood its possession, he had rewritten his world in hopes of capturing it.

And yet he watched through mirrors... Huffing his discontent, Erik stared into the world on the opposite side. This dressing room had been an unused storage closet until he had manipulated his wishes out of the managers. As the omnipotent Opera Ghost, he had quietly had the room renovated and made ready at the same time that he had had

Christine pulled out of a gaggle of ballerinas and given small, insignificant roles. Nothing too auspicious...*yet*. This was only the start. Soon enough, he had great plans for her to be the headlining prima donna. But for now he settled with getting her heard, building her confidence, and putting her in a place where he had redesigned a full-length mirror to a transparent boundary between their worlds. Since its construction, he had not dared to set foot through its threshold. That was all about to change.

Like a fantasy that betrayed reality's grip, the door on the other side of his protective glass opened, and his beautiful muse glided inside, closing out the world and as eager for his presence as he was for hers. Of course, to her, he was a *voice*, intangible, never a threat if hands and faces were only imagined. She could never know her image made his heart skip madly against his ribcage and his hands tighten to fists with their unconscious need to touch her. Or how he suddenly ached in a way only a living, breathing man could ache, ...a way angels would be damned to dare.

A smile curved her pretty lips. Oh, how often had he witnessed its brilliance lately? It stole away his first impressions of a crying, broken child without father or friend. This was a light-hearted, euphoric woman before him; ...this was a woman in love.

"*Ange*," she called, and the appellation tugged at his heart. How he longed to be worthy of its title! "Are you here?"

Erik paused a long breath, racing one more ravenous stare along curves accentuated by her simple, dark blue gown. His eyes lingered on her eagerly expectant face with that ever-present light in her blue eyes before he answered, "Good evening, Christine. I trust your rehearsal went well."

At his first word, Erik watched her smile brighten until it was a beacon all its own. It touched him like a caress and made him press a wanting hand to the glass between them. Had he ever mattered so much to anyone?

Beyond her elation, Christine didn't comprehend his words at first, amusing him with her unhidden admiration. It was so powerful as it overcame her that he once again had to push, "Rehearsal? How was your arietta in scene two?"

"Oh..." Sense suddenly seemed to appear with an abrupt return to reality. "Well enough, I suppose. I could have done better, but I was a bit flustered. La Carlotta stood in the wings staring daggers at me for the entire piece. It was distracting."

Erik did not heave the curses playing in his head. He already knew the cause for Christine's mediocre performance, having watched every moment hidden in his box. He rarely liked to leave her alone and carried a worry that one day she would finally break under Carlotta's poorly-concealed jealousy. The reigning diva's lecherous envy was thickly cast in cruel insults and taunting, and his poor Christine had been its victim ever since the managers *suddenly* gave her a minor role. Considering his own ambition had put her in the crossfire, Erik felt entirely responsible for what she endured.

"As I've told you again and again," he said, his flaring temper only revealed in tense letters, "you need to put Carlotta out of your mind. There will always be a dozen like her, ready to tear at your spirit and shred your confidence at every note. *You* need to believe they don't matter. I could insist it is only petty jealousy fueling her, but until you believe you *deserve* to be on that stage, it will mean nothing to you."

She put weight in his every declaration, and he half-regretted being so blunt when she dutifully lowered her head and red-tinged cheeks with abashment. But no. Didn't she need to learn such things? It was equally for his sake.

"Christine," he breathed in gentler tones and

watched her lift eyes eager to please him at every moment, "your heart is so pure, so untarnished by this cruel world. If it were up to me, I would protect it and block every atrocity from ever touching it, but...I can't be with you forever. You must learn to be strong."

They were empty words. He had no intention to leave her, but merely the threat brought his desired response as her eyes widened and she clasped desperate hands in frantic beseeching.

"Oh, please don't leave me yet, *ange*! I've disappointed you with my childishness. I promise to be stronger, *anything*. Just please don't go!"

Erik's fingertips touched the glass at the level of her cheek, wishing with whole heart that he could touch skin instead. "No, Christine, you are *never* a disappointment to me. You are the only one... But you *must* be strong, *petite*, more than you've ever been. I have such plans for you, so many glorious goals I know you could surpass, but if you let the world tell you what to think and what to feel, you will crumble. ...You want to please me, Christine, don't you?"

"Of course, *ange*. More than anything!"

"Then tomorrow when you sing your arietta, I don't want you to consider Carlotta or the daggers in her eyes. Only consider *me*, Christine. My voice, my guidance. Sing for *me* alone, and the rest of the world will mean nothing. ...Will you do that, *petite*?"

The answer was already vivid in blue eyes. "Yes, *ange*. Of course. I will *always* sing for you."

"Then let's begin."

This time was Erik's favorite, as cherished as time spent composing, more so because it was shared. It was easy to forget everything when music was the sole purpose in the room. Even the mirror doorway became nothing but an ignored piece of glass, no longer acknowledged as a boundary between worlds. How could it be when it did not hinder notes from pouring in and streaming about him, lighting the darkness that shaded his backdrop?

He could love her so simply in the music, love bound in a certain respect that prevented overdone compliments. Her training was his most imperative task. He never considered that Christine pushed herself and posed such a diligent work ethic for him alone. He'd seen her as a ballerina, practicing to exhaustion until every step was accurate and every graceful motion elegant. It was a point they had in common and something that made his adoration soar. She put all aside but a determination to learn and perfect her technique, to exceed herself.

Their role of choice was currently occupied by La Carlotta. How uneasy Christine had been when he had first presented it to her! As if she had no right even to learn it! He had insisted against her wary concerns until full tones had come from her lips and she had shown exactly why she was destined for greater things. She was claiming the title of prima donna without ever realizing it and had no idea that her perfect and brilliant rendition would be the one seen on that stage. The plan was already underway, and Erik was adamant she would be prepared.

They worked well into evening, and even then he was loath to end and lose her fixed attention and the companionship shared through staves on a page. How preferred it was to make music their world and be swallowed in its wonder!

"We shall stop there," he finally found the will to say. All at once, he felt dropped back into the body of a mortal man, as if he truly had been an angel when teacher; now desire surged to overwhelm any moral notions. *Desire*, ...his eyes ravished her, desperately memorizing for the unending time of her absence. One more vision to tease his eager mind.

"*Ange*?" Christine could not keep the reluctance from tainting her voice, her gaze wandering the corners of her familiar dressing room as if he would materialize. "Will you...?"

"Speak freely, child," he urged.

She hesitated, finding the words upon her tongue and collecting bravery before she could mutter, "Will you stay a bit longer? ...I don't want to leave you just yet."

This was new, and she grew anxious when no answer to her request came. Silence. She had a growing terror that she had crossed from a considered sin by secretly loving an angel to a committed one.

"Stay," Erik breathed without sound, shifting uncomfortably on his feet. *Stay*, have a real conversation as he had only created in his inner ear... The idea was so terrifying he wasn't sure he could concede. *A role*! He would play a role! Erik the mortal man had never had a decent conversation with another human being, but his other personas carried the confidence he couldn't. Angel, Opera Ghost, neither would hesitate. They would know words and exact phrases to capture her interest. And he adopted the façade as easily as ever, burying fear beneath feigned bravado.

"All right, Christine, I will not leave you yet. Shall we discuss the next piece we shall work on? I already have dozens of ideas in mind."

"No, no," she nervously insisted. "No more talk of music. Our every word is always about singing and my future, a career on the stage."

"But...that is our most important goal."

"Of course, but...will you tell me nothing of yourself, *ange*?" Her voice trembled to ask such a bold question.

Erik was once again shaken beneath his countenance, and he stammered distantly, "What...what would you like to know?"

Relaxing with a sigh as if she had been expecting anger or rejection instead, Christine suddenly flounced down in the center of the room, arranging her skirts about her shape. "A...a name. Have you a proper name, perhaps an appellation before you became the Angel of Music? Or have you only ever been known by such a revered title?"

"Erik," he breathed before he could think better of it, but the mere idea of hearing his name spoken in the glorious timbre of her voice was too great a temptation. "My name is Erik."

"Erik," she repeated, and he shuddered down the length of his spine. Dear Lord, it was a more beautiful sound than he'd imagined! It made his name into a legato lyric as soul-stirring as the renowned librettos of the stage.

"Of course it wouldn't be appropriate for me to call you such a name," she mused, "but...I like knowing. It almost makes you seem mortal and less like a spirit beyond my reach."

"Never beyond your reach," he was compelled to correct. "You make it sound as if I am above you, and I cannot bear to consider being so far away."

Christine could not dim her smile, shying it beneath dark-fringed lashes and a pretended concentration on the wrinkles in her skirt. "And yet...you *are* so far away. You fly to heaven every night and leave me alone on earth. I am no angel; I cannot go with you or even be in your ethereal presence. To me, you are only a voice."

"And...that isn't enough for you?" he inquired idly, focusing on crescent-shaped lashes of half-closed eyes.

But instead of an answer, she posed, "You're the omnipotent Angel of Music. Surely you bestow the gift of your presence to other deserving mortals as well. When you are not here teaching me, ...are you teaching others?"

Erik almost laughed aloud, replying with the undeniable flutter in his voice, "What an absurd question!" Jealous, ...she was *jealous*! And he adored her at that moment.

Blue eyes flew up, roaming random spots in the ceiling as she bid, "I'm sorry. I'm being too forward! I didn't mean to upset you, *ange-*"

"No, no, I'm not upset. I simply find your question ridiculous. When I spend every moment watching over you, there is no time for anyone else, nor do I have the ambition to seek those who can only be disappointments. *You* are the *only one* worthy of my presence. You have so much talent."

"Talent," she softly repeated. "You watch over me to make certain I am meeting my potential. But...is that the only reason?" A blush tinged her cheeks, and she bit her lip as if regretting her question.

"If only it were!" he replied on an exhalation. "It should be. I should watch you with only your future in mind, but..."

"But..."

An admission he wasn't sure should strike the air was on the tip of his tongue, and he denied its urging. "You should be on your way home, Christine. You need to rest."

A dutiful nod, and Christine reluctantly rose on shaking knees, eyes downcast as she slowly collected her cloak. Another visit from her adored angel over, and now she would have to endure the long set of hours in between until she could be back in this place. But could she dare let this conversation go so quickly? Never to be mentioned again?

She was a step from the door when she paused one final instant. Hesitant, she concluded, "It's because of what you are, isn't it? If you say you care, will you be punished? Will you be tossed from heaven? It's a sin, isn't it?"

"Yes, it's a sin," Erik somberly admitted. Beyond a sin, it was a crime. An angel falling from grace for loving her; no, a man burning in hell for lying to her.

She didn't speak another word about it, but he could read her hurt. In a small voice, she said, "Goodnight, *ange*." And with that, she was gone.

Erik stared at the final close of a door, and every bone in his body ached to pursue, to appear as a man, take her away. But he knew the sick reality. He'd be a stranger to her, no matter the countless hours they had savored each other's company. She would look upon a man in a mask, and she'd be afraid. And he might utter words, convince her through his voice that he was one and the same with her Angel of Music, but she'd hate him for his deception. He would lose every sweet smile, every anticipation, every hope. She could never understand that when she asked for a mortal man, she'd be getting a monster.

It was that moment that he decided he could love her all he liked from behind a mirror's protective doorway, but nothing more. He was acquainted with the sting of disappointment; he would not teach her the same thing. Disappointment... Disappointment was returning to his world alone and knowing he was doomed to remain that way.

Chapter Two

Crystal clear high notes resonated off the meager walls of the dressing room, bounding to the ceiling and within a mirrored doorway to tease Erik with their brilliance. He was astounded. How could Christine not realize how gifted she was? But true to his thoughts, the instant the last pitch faded, she lifted questioning blue eyes to her invisible audience.

"How was that?" she asked with a worried cringe.

And though a stream of gushing compliments played on his tongue, all he indulged was, "Good. You sang it well. Now onto your next entrance. The duet."

Limited praise, and yet he saw her unease calm with his favor, as if his opinion was the determining factor in her own.

"The duet," Christine repeated as she flipped pages in her score. Scanning staves, she hesitated. "I...have a difficult time finding my starting note. It would be easier to hear it with the tenor lines that precede. Could you...could you sing it with me, *ange?*"

It was an unconscious desire. How often had Christine fantasized that very thing? Her angel had entered her life with a soft song to announce his presence. Since then, no more than corrected vocalises had boasted the beautiful, golden timbre that sang in her dreams. To sing with him was almost too blissful to consider!

"I shall give you the pitches, Christine. The tenor line before your entrance." The melody sounded in the high strains of a violin as Christine hid a frown. But she could not make the request again because within a breath, she was singing as if only music made up language.

Sing with her... Did she know how great the temptation was? But Erik preferred self-denial, certain if he heard the sheer brilliance that would come from voices entwined, he'd be addicted to the sound and never be able to live without it again. It would prove more an obsession than even her presence in his life. He treated music like an intoxicating drug, one he could not survive without. Love, desire, such things were farfetched and beyond his grasp. To sing with her, to have that intimacy of joined voices and passion in notes and legato melody would be too much bliss for a man who couldn't deserve it.

As the tenor line rose to join her in harmony, he continued to play his violin with hands that had no time to tremble. It was a minor consolation and a lackluster duet when it took two voices to truly make it beautiful.

Christine sang impassioned lyrics with emptiness, as if every word had its center hollowed out and was nothing but a shell. How could one sing convincingly of love when it felt like walls surrounded the heart? She wanted to love, but it felt leashed and stifled, kept at arm's length from where it yearned to be.

Voice and violin reached the end of the piece, and as silence overruled, Erik flatly declared, "We can end there for the day."

"It was terrible," Christine decided for him. "You'd rather not say, but I already know. I didn't sing it well."

"No, you didn't," he replied honestly. "Oh, of

course, the pitches and rhythms were correct. But what sets a pretty voice apart from the throng? It is not an *accurate* rendition; it is a *memorable* one. If you sing the way you just did, you're no better than a soprano in the chorus." Erik saw his comments make harsh strikes, but he did not recant a single one. "Music comes from the soul, Christine, not the vocal cords or an instrument's strings. Every note must carry a piece of yourself in its timbre. You have to *feel* it to sing it."

"Sing it with me," she impulsively pushed again. "If you were to sing with me, I know I could do better."

He huffed a sigh loud enough to be overheard and decided, "Not tonight. It is late. Consider what I've said, and when you are less tired, you will have another chance."

No argument came as Christine closed her score and sought her cloak with shaking hands. She remained quiet and pensive, losing herself within dark material as if it would make her vanish from sight. That suddenly seemed a preferred fate to standing in place but being just as unseen.

"Perhaps I'll never be able to live up to the standards you've set," she softly said, shaking a desolate head.

From behind the mirror, Erik studied her solemn expression with the desperate need to steal the frown from her lips, to smooth the furrow of her brow, to *touch her* and make everything into happiness again. If only he could! But he had to settle for insufficient words, and words had no fingertips. "No, you will exceed them. I've no doubt. But to do so, you must be able to open heart and soul, to stop holding back, to yearn and want something more."

"But I do!" she suddenly protested, raising adamant eyes to search every shadowed corner as if willing him to appear. "I *want* so much more!

But...as you've said, it is a sin. You want me to open my heart, to *love* the music. ...How could I possibly?"

"I am the music," he contended half to himself.

"What will you have me opening heart and soul to, *ange*? The notes on the page...or you?"

Erik watched her every expression and glimpsed the hope in her eyes. Her innocent little heart loved a lie, and when the truth would shatter it, how could he dare? "And...if I merely said the words, would it be enough for you? Would it make any difference when language is all we have? I cannot belong to your world, Christine. I cannot be an ordinary man who takes you into his arms and kisses your beautiful lips, who holds you and dares to touch your skin." The bitter reality cut into flesh and bone. "Perhaps it was a mistake to come to you this way. An angel... I don't deserve to be an angel, especially when an angel has no right to touch you. If you only knew..."

"Please," Christine bid, and without a thought, she knelt on the carpet as if in prayer. Tears filled the corners of her eyes, and as she blinked, they dared to tumble free and cascade down her cheeks. "Please, Erik, don't leave me. I'll never speak beyond music again. Just please don't go."

Erik... And did she know the sound of his own name would unravel of any shred of nobility he had? Sense told him not to listen, to go and not look back. How selfish was he that he refused to listen to it?

"Christine," he breathed tenderly and poured every ounce of emotion he possessed into the simple letters of her name. He saw the way she savored the sound, closing her eyes for the briefest instant, and on a will of its own, one little hand extended as if reaching to touch him. How he ached to feel its caress! "I won't ever leave you, *petite*. I can't. It is far too late to limit ourselves to music alone. There are too many other desires breathing in this room."

"Then...come to me, *ange*," she begged. "Love

can't be a sin."

Love... His heart ached to hear her say the word, and when better judgment commanded he refuse the only thing he'd ever wanted, he instead vowed, "Soon. I promise you, Christine. I will come to you soon enough. But you must make your own promise to me."

"Anything," she immediately declared, smiling in spite of tears.

"The music must be all that matters to you. The music, ...*me.* You cannot run off or put other priorities or anyone else first. Music...must be all you breathe and think, your sole purpose for existing. I will promise to come to you if I know your heart is only mine."

Oh, that voice! Its timbre washed through Christine with every glorious word she'd been waiting to hear, and shivering delight, she replied, "Yours, *ange.* I promise, only yours."

The glow about her enamored Erik as he decided with finality, "When I am certain you have proven yourself, I will come to you, Christine. I vow it on my very existence." It might very well be the final nail in the coffin, but his mind was spinning with how he could turn an inevitable tragedy into a love story instead.

*****

Christine raced down the long corridor toward her dressing room with frantic steps. Too many thoughts were reeling her mind, stealing concentration and replacing it with the conviction that only her angel could steady her shifting world on its axis again.

Almost there, mere inches from reprieve, and a small hand caught her arm and nearly made her jump out of her skin as she flipped about with a flustered cry.

"Oh, Meg! You startled me!" Christine exclaimed as she met the equally wide, green eyes of the little golden-haired ballerina. Meg was the nearest to a friend Christine had ever had. How many ballet rehearsals had only been survived with each other's constant whispered giggles? But since Christine's escape from days of toe shoes and pirouettes, conversations had been fleeting and spoken in broken phrases between scenes.

"My goodness, Christine!" Meg exclaimed. "You look as though you were expecting a ghost! I thought you could only carry fears of the undead if you were in a tutu! Once you move up the ranks, things like ghosts and phantoms aren't supposed to scare you; they're supposed to make you heave violent curses in Italian, or so La Carlotta has taught me."

But Christine paled at the joke. "And look where those curses have gotten her! I never truly believed all that ghost nonsense. I only gasped and feigned frantic with the rest of you, but *this*! Meg, Carlotta was practically killed! That falling backdrop barely missed her!"

"And I would be the first one screaming and near tears if it were anyone *but* Carlotta," Meg admitted with rolled eyes. "In this instance, I can't fully pin blame on the ghost. There are quite a few stagehands that wouldn't regret a little accident to befall the diva. She's humiliated practically every person in the cast, and I truly can't say I'm upset she stormed out of here and refused to sing. But...well, she isn't my concern; *you* are."

Pale became bright pink as realization began to settle in. "I can't do this, Meg. I'm not a diva."

"Not yet," Meg decided with a bright smile. "Oh, Christine, this could be your dream come true!"

Though she tried to nod agreement, all she could consider was her dream included a white-winged angel carrying her away from the world.

"Are you really so nervous?" Meg demanded with a little laugh. "You said you were taking lessons with a great teacher. So what's the matter?"

Christine was about to reveal blatant truths when her dark brow suspiciously arched. "Wait a minute. You dare ask? *You*? You, who can't keep a secret if your very life depended on it? Anything I tell you might as well be said to the entire cast of ballerinas!"

The fluttering laughter in Christine's voice was echoed in Meg's. "I never said the word *secret*. No promise to keep silent, so therefore I am not at fault if the words tumble out in conversation with others. But...for *your* sake, I will attempt a buttoned lip on the issue. *Attempt*, I say, just in case of failure. I've never claimed to be anything but what I am. You've known from the first day that my personality does not include restraint."

"Oh, yes, I know it well!" Christine decided with another giggle.

"So...? Are you going to tell me? Who is this teacher of yours?"

Christine hesitated another moment, clasping the words inside and holding tight before she dared let go. "He's...a great musician, a genius. He is pushing me to a talent beyond myself. When I sing for him, ...it isn't the same as when I'm on the stage. ...I can't say more, not when he'll be expecting me; I'll be late if I don't hurry."

Meg's huff of concession spoke her disappointment, but she added with an unavoidable grin, "Your eyes light up when you talk about him. Did you know that? That alone reveals *far* more."

With a final giggle, she scurried back down the hall, leaving Christine to stare after her. Evidently, secrets did not need lips to tell them. In love with her teacher... And it was a transparent truth.

No more interruptions meant she was finally able to close herself in her dressing room, locking the door with shaking fingers before her nervous eyes scanned the small quarters. "*Ange?*"

A pause, and then that heavenly voice

answered, "Yes, Christine. I'm here."

"Oh, *ange*," she breathed, and her expression fell with the weight of her dread, "what am I to do? Something awful happened, an *accident*. La Carlotta insists she will not sing the opening in two days, and the managers...they decided *I* will take her place. I don't know why they presume I could! All the girls in the chorus were staring at me with such spite as if I'd done something immoral to earn the managers' favor. I didn't ask for such an honor. They chose me, ...and I really wish they hadn't."

Chose, Erik considered silently, or rather were threatened by the resident Opera Ghost. Give the role to Christine or the accident befallen the reigning diva would not be *just* an accident the next time. Jealousy from others who felt more qualified to take Carlotta's place had been expected. What hadn't been anticipated was the terror in the girl standing before him.

"Christine, but...this is your chance to show them what you can do. This is what we've been working toward."

"I don't want it! I don't want it!" she suddenly exclaimed, wringing trembling hands before her. "The arietta was frightening enough! But the lead...? I can't do it!"

"You can," Erik stated, firm and sharp, and he immediately regretted the hint of his temper. It shook Christine and made her curl limbs into herself. Temper, another flaw, and if she had any idea how near to the surface it always was, one spark from erupting into an inferno, it would likely be the very thing to drive her away.

"Christine," he sought a gentler tone, "you were born to perform on the stage. You are only afraid because you haven't had the opportunities that should have been yours."

"But all those people-"

"Forget all those people!" he snapped without

regret this time. "None of them matter! Every scornful look is laced in envy." He hesitated, knowing what card to play but pondering every ramification before he dared. "Your arietta... I told you to sing it for me, and when you did, you showed them a glimpse of what you can do. You were brilliant and unafraid. So...sing for me, *petite*, *only* for me. Your voice, every note made to be mine."

"But, *ange-*"

"No," he harshly insisted, and every idea fell into place. "Sing for me. *Please me*, Christine, and I will come to you the night of the premiere. I will sing, and you will know my voice. After the show, I will appear to you, but *only* if you please me."

Both their desire, and he was using it to an advantage and saw the intended response in the growing smile upon her lips, the bliss flickering in the back of awed blue eyes. Nerves would no longer be an issue, not if she had something greater worth singing for. He found the door into her life in one attested command. She would sing and shine as she was meant to, and then after she awed the world with her performance, she would be his.

*****

Final dress rehearsal had most of the cast and crew anxious as if awaiting the next so-called accident. Christine hardly paid them more than a passing glance; she had far more important things to occupy her mind.

Her angel would come to her! It was a dream she couldn't fully believe true! He watched her through every rehearsal and every moment she spent onstage; she could feel the power of his stare, but instead of faltering beneath it, she grew more determined. Her mind spun with vivid fantasies, imagining him in his ethereal beauty gazing upon her, loving her, wanting her... A secretive grin upturned the corners of every vowel passing her lips, and though she expected a chastisement later about the effect such things had on her technique, she couldn't find the will to dim its glow.

It was the end of the final chorus. Christine's anticipation was already dragging her ahead to her dressing room with her angel's voice sounding in her inner ear when she was abruptly jerked back to awareness. A couple of gentlemen entered the theatre doors and took seats in the back row as if this were a performance and not only a rehearsal. Typically, such a thing might go unnoticed and without a care on Christine's part, but one of the gentlemen had eyes fixed on her with the sweetest smile upon his lips. So familiar, so long unconsidered, and the recognition caused her to falter and break character.

How many years had it been? At least a decade, and yet every memory came flooding back as if lived anew. The Vicomte de Chagny by title, but to her, he had only ever been her Raoul. They should never have been playmates. Affluent aristocrats did not associate with children of poor violin players, but Raoul's kind heart had requested the company of a lonely little girl. He had first seen her singing on a street-corner for coins while her father played his violin, and he had told her later he befriended her because he'd never known a real performer. At her every insistence that she was no such thing, he'd laugh the way that made his eyes twinkle and say, not yet, but she would be.

Christine tried to keep her attention on her role, but her eyes kept drifting to meet her observer's as she sought every change in him since their last meeting. Their unacceptable friendship had been short-lived. Try as he might to distance himself from his family name, to sneak off for games on the countryside and suppers with her and her father, his status was always a cold reality. As soon as his own father had learned where Raoul was spending every free moment, he had had the young Vicomte sent off to the finest boarding school in the country. It was never said aloud that the deportment was to separate him from Christine and blooming affections that could not be permitted, but they'd both known it. She had not seen him again...until this moment.

How odd! Her childhood crush, real and tangible before her with visible fingers and hands, eyes that lit upon her. A living, breathing man! And how vastly different to long for an incorporeal being!

Rehearsal ended, but rather than race to her dressing room, Christine lingered amongst the throng, trying to seem inconspicuous as she cast a few glances out of the wings. But Raoul was gone, and she actually knew a rush of disappointment that he had not tried to speak with her. Well, ...it was for the best, wasn't it? His title was the same barricade it had been a decade before, and conversing with opera singers was certainly a faux pas.

Tucking a fallen lock of dark hair behind her ear, she wearily began to walk toward her dressing room. Modesty insisted she must hurry and change out of her costume before her angel arrived, and a disconcerting thought appeared on its heels, a curiosity if he'd glimpsed her dressing before. Certainly, an angel of heaven understood privacy and did not ogle like the stagehands Christine caught watching her during quick costume changes in the wings. The idea alone was a perverse transgression, and yet...she felt her cheeks heat with a blush, half sure she'd make every gesture a bit more graceful just in case.

She was so engrossed in the thought and the tingle trailing the surface of her skin that she suddenly bumped into an approaching body and lost her balance, swaying on her feet.

"Oh, I'm sorry. I...," she stammered and halted as she met the amused elation in two familiar blue eyes. "Raoul, ...I mean...Vicomte. It...it's been so long."

"Such formality!" he exclaimed with a laugh.

"You've *never* used my title before; I'm entirely certain you forgot it when we were together."

"Yes, and it was inappropriate," Christine protested and yet could not help but match his smile. "But a little boy with a handkerchief tied about his head insisting to be called Captain Scoundrel the Pirate steals a level of formality, wouldn't you agree?"

The memory made Raoul chuckle harder. "Ah, yes, Captain Scoundrel the Pirate. I pillaged the Seven Seas, didn't I? But always with my loyal first mate, Little Christine. We had such splendid adventures together. We spent that entire summer practically living in one another's shadow."

Sighing reluctance, Christine reminded, "Until make believe was shattered by the rest of the world. They never understood pirates and ghost stories and the games we played. Titles got in the way." Christine knew she was being rude, but she could not keep from studying his every detail, taking in the features she had once known so well now without their childish innocence. No, this was a man before her, and she still felt like an awkward little girl in comparison. "We're not children anymore," she continued in the train of her thoughts, "and it is an indiscretion to discount titles, ...Vicomte."

His smile never faltered as he teased, "And what shall I be calling you then? ...La Christine perchance. Prima donna. Diva. How often did I insist you were destined to great things with that voice of yours? And you've done it, Christine! You are the star soprano."

"Temporarily."

"It doesn't matter. They'll hear you, and your name will be recognized after this. I'm one of the patrons of the opera house, and when the gossip began to brew about La Carlotta's exit, I felt the world shift beneath me to find out the name of her replacement. I had to see it for myself, and now to look upon you again after so long..." He trailed off and returned the study she'd given, running his eyes over her every detail. It was little different than the way the stagehands leered, and yet she wasn't disgusted because there was more than just flickering wanting in Raoul's eyes. There was affection, caring, and the charm to make desire seem unthreatening.

The corners of her lips were a smile, but she scooted a few steps away and quickly replied, "I really should be going, Vicomte. The premiere is tomorrow... You will be there, won't you?"

"Of course!" Raoul gushed. "As if I would miss it! I am so eager to hear you sing; it's been ages. But if you dare call me Vicomte again, I shall rush about proclaiming you as La Prima Donna. No titles, Christine. I don't want to be the Vicomte with you."

"And yet you are," she reminded with a doubtful shake of her head. "This isn't like when we were children; we can't denounce the rest of the world."

"Why not? Let me be the Vicomte for them," he gestured to the empty theatre beyond, "but not for you. As children, we stared down propriety and never cared. Let it be the same."

Christine meditated his words, reading the sincerity in those familiar blue eyes. How well she recalled their every sweet expression! It was the rest of him that still felt a stranger. Her smile returned, and she bid as her answer, "Goodnight then, Raoul."

"Until tomorrow," he corrected.

She held his eye a moment more before reluctantly taking her leave, but one glance over her shoulder showed him lingering, watching her and granting a wave to meet her gaze. She ducked her smile out of his regard. It was just so easy to be enchanted by him! Charisma had always exuded from every nuance; obviously, that had not changed. He made everyone want to be in his presence and long to be the focus of his attention. A little girl had fantasized elaborate scenes of marrying him, of a mansion house with every luxury she'd never had, of a devoted husband, handsome and wonderful and always ready to make her laugh. A little girl's very own fairytale, but now that fairytale had transformed and the mansion house was a version of white-clouded heaven and her husband, an angel divine.

So many complicated thoughts, Christine's head felt heavy as she entered her dressing room, already reaching for the clasps of her elaborate costume. Only one came undone before her hand halted and fisted fingers into its palm.

"*Ange...*"

"Why are you late returning?"

The question was sharply heaved, and Christine shuddered as she glanced about the warmly lit room, wishing she had an expression to read the way she had been able to read Raoul's. Sound alone insisted anger and practically goaded her to lie.

"I...I stopped to speak to someone." It wasn't untrue, but she could already tell the matter wouldn't be dropped so quickly.

"Someone? *Who*, pray tell?"

More questions thrown viciously. She felt them bite at her skin. *Oh God, what had she done*? "A...a friend."

"A *man*," he corrected. "Or were my eyes mistaken? Because I saw a shameless suitor, and by your own promise, such a thing is forbidden, is it not?"

"He...he's not a suitor," Christine quickly insisted. "He's an acquaintance. I knew him when we were children. He just...came to say hello-"

"Acquaintance? And do all acquaintances lust with their eyes? My God, Christine, are you naïve not to see how blatantly he desired you? He was practically propositioning you!"

Her arms weaved about her waist as the flames of embarrassment painted her cheeks in pinks. He was right, and it disgusted her to realize she had not only allowed Raoul, she had encouraged him as if it were acceptable.

"I...I'm sorry," she whispered, tears filling her eyes. "It will *never* happen again."

From behind the glass, Erik had the urge to call her a liar, so sure promises made would not be kept, but the image of her, so penitent and crying those beautiful tears, tugged mercilessly at his heart.

"No, it won't," he agreed, unable to drain the harshness from his voice. "You are not to speak with that Vicomte ever again. He is a cad, Christine, after only one thing, and you are too innocent to realize it. He will destroy you and every dream we've built together. ...If you see him again, I will leave, and I won't come back."

"No, please!"

"If you see him again," Erik repeated, "it will tell me that you are undeserving of everything I've done for you, and...I can't permit that."

"I won't see him again," Christine vowed, heart and soul pouring from every glistening tear. "I promise. Don't leave me, Erik, please."

He gave no answer. All he said was, "Go home, Christine. Get some rest for tomorrow. If you please me and sing for only me, I will reward your loyalty. I'll come to you, and then none of these games will mean anything anymore."

"I will," she fervently bid. "I will sing for you, *ange*."

"Well, we'll see, won't we? Goodnight, Christine."

It was a final goodbye, and Erik had every intention of honoring it and storming below to his home in the depths. He even spun about with ferocity tainting every motion, but...one look back at her tear-stained face and trembling body had him lingering in suspension.

How it tortured him to know he'd hurt her! He longed to be the one begging *her* for forgiveness,

30

especially when he placed all blame on that damn Vicomte. Yes, the Vicomte was the one at fault with his perfect, unflawed face. Erik despised his very existence! Jealousy stole every urge to comfort Christine and recant his harshness. How could he possibly seek a gentle tone and words of peace with so much rage twisting in his gut?

This sort of sense-altering fury was dangerous. He was no stranger to crime; oftentimes murder seemed a valid choice. But he was calculated about it, planning the details like a scene in a well-directed play. He was in control. Now the power of overcoming anger threatened to slip out of his clutches. And what consequences would come? Likely, a dead Vicomte and showing Christine her angel was a monster before he could ever explain himself. *Damn*! Rationale needed to remain intact, and the Vicomte needed to remain alive. But Erik was suddenly impatient for the next night's events, to take Christine away and give her a flesh and bone mortal before that Vicomte had the chance to speak to her again and sway affections that were supposed to be his.

A silent sigh had Erik forcing his focus back to Christine as she lingered with solemn tears. That girl... What would it take for her to realize he could love her more than a dozen vicomtes combined? That though he bore the burden of sin and ugliness upon his shoulders, she could transform him into a creature worth loving with the gift of her heart? Only her...

"Ange?" Christine called hesitantly, eyes glancing about an empty room, but Erik didn't reply. What more could be said? He regretted his temper and burying Christine in his rage and self-loathing. What could he say beyond profuse apologies that would mean nothing when the Vicomte returned to incite his wrath all over again? No, he couldn't ask forgiveness for what he was, especially when he already knew he was destined to fail her.

One more survey of her silent surroundings, and as Erik's eyes widened, her little fingers reached for the clasps of her costume. A gentleman would have left the scene at that point, or rather, a gentleman with a regard for privacy and possessing any moral fiber whatsoever. If the Vicomte were in his place, Erik doubted *he* would turn away. And that was the thought that kept Erik in place. This wasn't his right either, but he was already a monster on every scale, bound to be a disappointment when compared to the perfect Vicomte. If this was all he'd ever have, he could not regret.

Nimble fingers released one clasp and the next to her waist, the thick, beaded material creating a deep chasm that revealed pale white satin beneath. His footsteps made not even whispered sounds as Erik crept close to the transparent doorway, racing feverish stares over every curve. He stared, intent and ravenous, and watched the gown plop with its heavy weight upon the carpeted floor.

He'd purloined this vision before. The love of his life in only white undergarments with every feminine line and feature of her beautiful body like shadows against flimsy material. He ached so badly for something he was sure he would never be able to touch, never know or shower with the sheer adoration bursting in his soul. And why? All because he was no handsome Vicomte. He could spout the same flowery sentiments and gush endearments, but if the mouth producing them was misshapen, it was undesirable. By vision alone, it was condemned. How unjust was that?

The girl on the other side of the glass was oblivious to his presence, and yet he noticed how her gaze roamed the room again with a certain curiosity attached, her hands hesitating in motion at the waist of a thick-layered petticoat. A pause and then it was discarded as well to pool on the floor.

His beautiful girl. Erik set trembling palms to

that infernal barrier in between, slowly curling wanting fingers into fists as the need built. The need to touch, to feel, to grasp with urgent hands, to never let go, to rip fabric and hear its shrill tear, to seek warm, silken flesh instead, to forget every looming detail in between this moment and having her in his arms. It was far beyond a physical ache. There was desire, but there was also a necessity to be that close with another human being. For once in his life, he wasn't content with being alone. Not when loving her felt imperative to his existence.

Blue eyes cast one more look about before she reached for her gown and began to dress, and white satin became hidden with a layer of dark plum. It felt like his secret to carry when everyone else would see dark plum and never know what existed beneath.

The softest sigh fell unbidden from his lips, practically inaudible, and yet as Christine fastened the last button of her gown, she suddenly lifted flustered blue eyes. But she never said a word, never called for his presence, perhaps preferring not to know if he was spying. He held his breath and waited for her to leave, watching her rush out with staggered steps.

Oh, yes, Christine, a part of him longed to answer, *your angel is no angel at all, but a devil who spies upon you at every moment and aches with the flames of hell in his veins, who fantasizes about your mouth upon his body, who longs to bury himself within you and find fulfillment...*

Erik cursed his own thoughts. Admitting such things only further convinced him that she shouldn't be his. ...*Shouldn't*, and yet he was determined she *would* be his. Perhaps he'd never have his fantasies, but he'd be damned if that Vicomte would be the one in his place!

Chapter Three

Nerves were inconsequential as the performance began and Christine awaited her entrance in the wings. Her only nerves existed in her anxiousness to please her angel. She wasn't a fool; she understood there was more to his command. Focusing on him made a full audience of strangers no more than backdrop to her scenes. Though she would have otherwise considered a few hundred people each with their own thoughts and fierce opinions in their heads, her mind made them into one coagulated body of hollow shapes.

Not even the Vicomte held sway. Behind the eyes of her character, she took note of his presence in his family's box and glimpsed his enamored stare, but that was all. She noticed but did not care. He was only a part of the mass, nothing important or distinctive.

Erik... She sang for Erik; every note that passed her lips and resounded to the rafters belonged to an angel. She was proud in that fact, longing to impress him and exceed his expectations. She let music pour through her body, one with every glorious pitch until her soul was indecipherable from legato melodies and brilliant cadenzas. She *was* music in the way her angel insisted, and she felt his admiration caressing her skin. Her angel, and what better reward to await her than his tangible presence? It felt like she was fighting to win exactly that, and she knew she would have victory.

Too quickly, the final chorus sounded, and the smile curving the corners of Christine's lips was her own and not the role she played. A smile, a triumph, utter elation, and she beamed to realize she'd finally have her dreams placed before her.

The instant the final curtain fell, she raced into the wings, pushing past cast mates that filtered offstage and barely acknowledging kind compliments from random voices. There was only one she longed to hear, and she was impatient for its every word.

Above a sea of heads, Erik equally rushed through the rafters, glancing down at every chance for peeks of his heart's desire. His adoration felt like a physical thing tonight; he wondered if she could feel it exuding out of him. He could not contain it when she had glowed bright as a star for him alone. Hurrying on two separate levels of earth and yet destined for the same place, Erik could only rejoice in the realization that she would be *his*. His limbs shook with a potent dose of anticipation and fear as he slipped into one of his secret passages and hurried toward a mirrored doorway that was about to be opened for the first time.

Well wishes were nothing but a nuisance to Christine; they meant slowing her pace and bestowing fake, empty smiles. It was a relief when at last her dressing room came into view, and she did not hesitate to rush inside and lock the door.

"*Ange*?" she immediately called, quivering inside and out to expect an answer. "Oh, say I pleased you! Every note, every melody, they were all *yours*. Tonight and always. Please say it was enough..."

Soft at first, she heard her answer. A beautiful legato line in gentle hushed pitches, and it wrapped warm sensation around her body. Her eyes drifted closed to savor the brilliance, a shiver racing her spine at his voice, tender and so glorious. Tears choked the back of her throat and gave her away as her eyes opened again and urgently searched for a source when echoes were all she had.

"*Ange,*" she whispered breathlessly, terrified that spoken words would add harsh ugliness to such pure sounds. "Please..."

His voice steadily grew louder, laden with more emotion at every pitch. There were no lyrics, just long, unbroken lines of melody that carried heart and soul. Christine could feel everything: pride, admiration, ...love, all so thickly woven into every note. Of their own accord, her arms extended, reaching, seeking something to embrace when they'd suffered empty for too long.

All reverberation seemed to settle in one place, and with curious eyes, Christine fixed her attention to her full-length mirror. The prima donna was what sense tried to see staring back, a persona she had yet to accept, but its facets hadn't mattered tonight. She'd given little thought beyond this moment and the promise of an angel's presence. The portrait before her blurred the longer she watched as if the glass grew hazy...or shifted. Suddenly, her reflection vanished, and all that lingered was darkness, a seeming entry where beautiful music poured out to greet her.

Without regret, Christine approached, suddenly impatient to join the world inside, but before she could claim its sanctuary, a sharp knock at her dressing room door shattered the dream.

"Christine? Are you in there?"

Raoul... There was no mistaking that voice, and her frantic eyes glanced back as if he would break through locks and bolts and find a way in to witness the transgression she was about to commit. Her cheeks tinged pink with a flicker of guilt. ...*What was she doing?*

But she had no chance to contemplate. All of a sudden, a gloved hand caught her wrist, and as she gasped, it jerked her into darkness.

Music had ceased in the shadows. The only sound to meet her ears was a soft click, and quickly looking over her shoulder, Christine saw her dressing room, a bit opaque and fuzzy at the corners.

"Christine?" Raoul's call and more knocks were muted and dulled, and she had an impulse to shout back and beg for help, for anyone to pull her out of the dark. She was afraid.

"Christine..." A soft, enticing whisper beckoned her back to her surroundings. She focused first on the black, gloved hand still on her wrist. Long fingers curved about and easily overlapped upon her narrow bone. A hand, corporeal and real, the indiscretion of an un-allowed touch.

But before she could dwell upon its details, the song rose again. *That voice*! She had no doubts when it filled her ears, and fear was insignificant in comparison.

Oh, to have her so close! Erik was overwhelmed with so many nuances he hadn't prepared for. Her scent, her natural heat, the loosely-defined contact they shared through a clasped wrist. Loving her through barriers had always seemed cold, a love without a center; *this* was warm and flowed through his veins, seeping within the boundary of a glove as if she herself filled every gap he bore within his own being.

He continued to sing, feeling her resistance fade with every pitch. He might have seemed a frightening, dark silhouette, but his voice was recognized and craved. He knew she would not deny him.

On the wings of wordless song, Erik guided her in slow steps. He was accustomed to sight in blackness and was unhindered, and it astounded him that though she was blind, she trusted enough to follow his gentle tugs, to already be certain he'd never let her trip and fall.

Deeper into dark, dank passageways they went.

He never quit singing, making his song an anchor for her. Every glance back showed him curious eyes and the hint of an undimmed smile. No fear, *never* fear again. His beautiful Christine was within his grasp and not separated by barriers and guilt. Here with him, far beyond her world where no one could interrupt or corrupt the beauty of this moment, not even her overly eager Vicomte. There were no vicomtes here to steal her away. No, here they could go unfound and untouched.

The underground house came into view with scant rays of light escaping cracks in its entry. Light should have been an enemy. It was about to reveal secrets the darkness masked and did not dare utter. But it was time for the games to end. He needed to give her more than disembodied voices to hold as hers.

The instant they entered the door, peeking beams became a bathing glow, and music died in his throat as he brought her to his sitting room and released her wrist, condemning his own touch before she could.

No words, never an explanation as he faced her for the first time without manipulations in between. Keeping a modest distance, he stayed fixed in place and simply let her look upon him.

As the last echoes of pitches faded from her consciousness, Christine felt the tingling return of trepidation skitter the surface of her skin. A man, ...a man in a mask, gazing upon her through hesitant eyes, one so brightly blue and one deep emerald green. A man dressed formal and pristine like an elegant gentleman, another patron of the opera perhaps, and yet...had she ever seen any man in a mask? It glowed stark and white, concealing most of his face, and stealing her focus with its odd, encumbering presence. All she could define was one high cheekbone, so vividly pale, the line of his jaw, and the hint of a pink lower lip, and it was so unusual that it left her unsure what to say or think.

Angels were supposed to be pure white with feathered wings and halos, resting in heaven not a dim, fire-lit, but rather cozy house. Realizations were close, but she longed to forget every one and ignore the suspicion that brewed in common sense. *An angel...* It suddenly seemed a bitter fantasy.

Erik watched the changing emotions upon her face, *terrified* what sort of conclusions were forming. He hated the feeling; it made him weak, and for a man who kept control of every situation in his existence, it was unacceptable.

Lifting to a confident posture and refusing his body's deceptive tremble, he forewent propriety and simply asked with hope he could not hide, "Shall I play something for you?"

A gesture from those long gloved fingers, and Christine furtively eyed a piano in the far corner of the room. Music was a preferred dream she chose with a flustered nod. He held her gaze a moment longer and then strode with utter grace to the instrument. From his seat on the bench, he could regard her at his will, and though she kept back, she did not recoil. Why would she? Music had never held a threat.

Within a breath, beautiful notes sounded from the piano's striking hammers, and a soft sigh passed her lips unnoticed. Such gloriousness! It left her shutting out rationale, for how could any mortal man create such ethereal brilliance? An angel, ...yes, he *must be* an angel.

Erik only looked at her every so often, focusing most of the time on the music spread before him, ...music to a different piece altogether, but black notes on white pages made sense, much more so than enthralled blue eyes. He played one piece and then another and another, seamlessly tying melodies together so that silence or explanations could never breathe.

Eventually, a hasty glance showed that at some

unknown point she had taken a seat on his plush couch. It was foolish, but he could not help but think differently of that familiar piece of furniture now that she had blessed it with her presence.

More melodies, melodies to gently lull her to sleep, and he watched as she laid her head upon soft cushions, curling her legs beneath the skirts of her costume gown. Meeting her enraptured stare every few lines, he saw comfort and ease. She felt safe. He read it clearly the moments before her lashes fluttered closed and she fell asleep.

The hint of a smile curved his lips to stare at her undisturbed and play onward. Night hastened by in its minutes, but all the while, lullabies kept nightmares at bay and let dreams reign.

*****

Music played in her sleep as a soundtrack, and Christine dreamt of angels, beautiful creatures with golden voices flying so gracefully through heaven's sphere. As she stirred to awareness, she half-expected to by lying on a downy cloud. But no...

She peeked from slit lids and saw a cozy sitting room with the embers of a dying fire dancing shadows along the walls. Music was no longer legato lines, but was instead flustered chords, dissonant and uncertain with the occasional rustle of pages and the scrawl upon staves. By the dim glow, she could decipher the shape of a man, not an angel, ...a man in a mask.

Reality appeared with that one memory. A man in a mask, and it was pointless to keep arguing the naïve fantasies of childhood. She *knew*. It was a lie to continue to deny it. This was no angel, and they were not in heaven. The deception weighed heavily upon her shoulders and twisted in her stomach. *She knew...*

Silent as a ghost, Christine lifted shaking limbs from the couch's soft cushions, casting furtive glances at her companion, but he was too engrossed in pitches and finding correct fits for chords to realize she was there. It took little effort to creep near. Near when sense bid her to run, to escape while she had the chance. But...she had to see. Doubt would always linger if she didn't.

Tentative tiptoes brought her behind his piano bench, and her eyes took in a very mortal being, shoulders not overly broad, a thin stature, a *body* and no evidence of wings. Echoes of his heavenly voice teased her memory with every fabrication. *The Angel of Music*, he'd said, and how much a fool she was to believe him! She cursed herself as viciously as she cursed him. Christine knew only one creature in a mask. A legend, a story because the few who saw the truth disappeared and were assumed dead. Angel of Music, no, ...*Opera Ghost.*

Movement felt heavy like the dream continued somewhere in the periphery as Christine lifted a trembling hand toward the corner of the mask. She no longer considered what she did or why; it was necessary.

One motion, quick and abrupt, and that damning mask was in her hand. She stared at it for a long held breath, observing its foreign construction and trailing frantic fingertips over the white surface. The interior was warm, warm because it had been against skin...

Before the thought could spiral beyond control, it was dragged from her mind and set before her in a violent growl as her deceiving angel flipped about to face her.

"Oh God," Christine moaned, tears immediately filling her eyes at what she saw. Nightmares boasted monsters, but they had the advantage to exist in the boundaries of the subconscious. This was *real* and a horror story brought to life.

Dying cinders in the hearth flickered shadows along a damaged canvas. A *corpse...* That was her first thought, a dead body but with fire and rage in his mismatched eyes as if the dead were walking instead of hollow. No nose, barely any flesh, those eyes were set in deep sockets of bone, *so much* bone exposed when it should have been cushioned by skin and tendons. Her frenzied gaze halted on his mouth as heaved breaths passed those misshapen lips. *Misshapen?* It seemed an inadequate description when the upper lip arched high and swollen, the predominant collection of any flesh on a face that was a distorted mess.

"Damn you!"

Tears fell faster, and Christine stumbled backwards, unable to tear her stare from that monstrous face. No, she couldn't look away and protested in only a whimper when those hands, bare now and reminding her of a skeleton in their boney length, approached. They caught her shoulders and dug pointy fingertips into her skin with their taut grip as a whimper became a soft cry.

"Please!" she gasped.

"Yes, beg me, Christine!" the Opera Ghost roared. "Scream! Plead for your pathetic life! Give me all the drama I saw you put on that stage and make it another glorious performance! Sopranos typically toss their most emotional moments in high notes. So go on! Sing to the stratosphere for me! This will be as full of heart and soul as the premiere. You sang for an angel then; will you do the same for a demon?"

"Let go," she insisted, but struggling made him grip firmer until she cried out, sure he'd leave marks. "Please! I'm sorry!"

"Sorry! You deceiving, little viper!" he shouted, and a vicious jerk pinned her against him, her every curve forced to his body and her face inches from the horror of his own. "Go on! Look upon the true face of an angel! Take your fill! You ruined *everything*! Every dream shattered in your damning, little hands! *Look at me*, Christine! Don't you dare try to lower your eyes! *You* did this! You couldn't leave it be! I would have adored you! Damn you!"

He released her shoulders but only to catch her face in his cold palms. It was almost gentle, and compared to the undimmed flames in those mismatched eyes, it erupted confusion within her. She trembled, and yet she felt mirrored shivers leaving him, the hands against her cheeks quivering as if it took a great effort to remain tender.

"You ruined everything," he repeated, but this time anger was overcome in desolation, and as she watched through an unblinking stare, she saw tears flood his eyes and stream from their deep sockets along that distorted face.

"I'm sorry," she insisted again, her own tears captured in his cold hands. "Please, *ange.*"

The appellation brought a violent sob, and with its power, he suddenly released her and slid to his knees at her feet, covering his face with hands stained in her tears. "No, no, I'm no angel," he moaned, the admission alone torturing him. "I've never been an angel. I'm a monster, only a monster. But I wanted to give you more than that to love. Oh, Christine..."

Her guilty eyes traveled from the mask still clutched in her hand to the man, crumbled and broken at her feet, her gaze lingering on the thin, dark hair covering a corpse's skull. She didn't know what to feel as too many emotions fought for supremacy. Pain, betrayal, anger, fear, pity, disgust. None of them were pointed enough to push through the muddled haze, and so she remained rooted in her place, numb and awaiting something to shake her back to reality.

On the verge of another sob, her unmasked angel suddenly caught the hem of her skirt in his bony hand and bent to lay a hesitant kiss to its manmade material. She went stiff in her spot, unable to breathe. She recalled dozens of stories of the demon Opera Ghost and his sinful crimes, and though she had never heard mention of rape, her addled mind reminded her that she was locked in his home far away from any aid. He had proven he was strong enough to keep her submissive if he chose. She had already made herself a victim.

But his hand only remained curved and clutching the hem of her skirt, never daring to venture beneath, and though she stayed rigid and suspicious, she let herself take necessary, shallow breaths and listened as her mind sought a way to escape.

"Christine." That beautiful voice made her name into a prayer for absolution; she felt its effects tingle her skin. "This is a monster before you, but he adores you more than any mortal man ever could, more than any *Vicomte* ever could."

The Vicomte... She remembered her so-called angel's tirade against the Vicomte's presence. Oh, how foolish she suddenly felt!

The broken man before her bent in supplication, his forehead pressed to her clutched hem, and his voice escaped in fragmented phrases that burned her ears. "I am a horror, Christine, ...a repulsive freak, ...a corpse. I'm sorry this is all I could give you. I wanted to be more. I wanted to be...ordinary, a normal man *for you*. I *tried*, but I couldn't. I'm not enough. And now...I disgust you. You are appalled by the monster. I...I'm ugly, and you could never accept the heart of an ugly beast."

Ugly... The word alone hurt her; it stung in a merciless bite, and yet...she knew just what to do with it. "No, ...no," she softly bid, her voice cracking with tears that would not cease their fall, "No, *ange*, you...you're beautiful."

"...What did you say?"

She caught the hint of hope, so subtle and afraid, and she encouraged it without hesitation. "Yes, ...beautiful."

"But...you were disgusted."

He still would not look up, and she was grateful. He never saw her cringe with the memories and never found the telltale hints of a lie. "No, I was...surprised. I wasn't expecting... But it wasn't disgust. I...I think you are beautiful, ...so very beautiful."

"How could you possibly? I am...*deformed*."

"As you said, ...you adore me." She used his own words against him, but she couldn't hate herself for it when she desperately longed to be free. "If...if the heart is beautiful, how can the man bearing it be anything but beautiful as well?"

"I do!" he suddenly exclaimed. "I adore you, Christine! So much! I've never cared for anything the way I care for you!"

"I know, I know," she whispered back, tears stilling on her lashes before their fall.

"Love can make this face beautiful?" he said as if realizing it himself. "It must! Oh God, if you could look upon it and see the heart beneath... Christine, ...please don't lie to me."

"I'm not."

"No...?" His mistrust did not diminish, and he tilted that face upward, forcing it into her line of view. "Beautiful, you said," he taunted as he slowly rose, making her anxious with his full, towering height. "Beautiful, Christine?"

"Yes, ...yes," she stammered, shaking and frantically trying not to avert her stare.

Erik did not hesitate as he caught her arms again and pulled her close, even when he felt her tense and shudder. *Beautiful*...and was he to believe her on words alone? When her every nuance screamed horror? He kept his face inches from hers, denying a rush of shame that begged him to hide it away. No, she brought this upon herself. She wanted to see.

"Prove it, Christine," he commanded, tears halted in his eyes and glistening by the light of flickering ashes. "Prove your own words. ...Kiss me."

"K...kiss," she stuttered, shaking her head urgently.

"Yes, a kiss. If you are not disgusted, then it should be of no consequence to you. Vicomtes indulge in dozens of kisses with never a second thought. I ask for *one*. ...I've never known a kiss. Surely if you see my heart and its adoration, you also see this is the first time I've ever wanted such a thing. A kiss, these misshapen lips against yours..."

It hurt him to take the image of something he yearned for and use it to taunt her and sway her lies. But her gaze locked on his mouth and spoke far more than words, her entire body racked with a shudder.

"Beautiful, Christine?" he provoked yet again. "I wouldn't have expected such cruelty from you. Lying as if it means nothing at all. You selfish child."

His tone was deceptively apathetic, and it frightened her as she watched anger building once again and felt his fierce grip pinch her skin.

"Go on!" Erik snapped. "Lie again! Tell me how *beautiful* and *perfect* I am, that I am the answer to your very dreams! Spout more sentimental rubbish about my heart and twist my emotions about your fingers! Make this seem so pure and untarnished when I feel it like a fire in my veins! You truly believe hearts and love are all that matter? That dangling your affections before my eyes will leash me at your side like a trained puppy? Then you have no idea how completely you've bewitched me. As if your lies alone would save you!"

Without a chance for regret, he abruptly captured her hips between his frustrated hands, deafening his ears to her cry of protest. The mask dropped from hands that sought to push him back, but he would not be deterred as he forced her flush to his body and let her feel the protruding extent of his ache, grinding the hardness of his need into her soft shape.

"How I want you!" he could not keep from gasping. "It consumes me!"

One hand pressed firmer to her lower back, and

he dared to lift the other to her face, racing desperate caresses along her porcelain features as if this would be his only chance to touch her. She was shaking so hard, tears slipping between his tracing fingertips, and he suddenly accused, "But you're afraid of me, aren't you? You're afraid right now as I put my repulsive hands upon you. Every bit of me is repugnant. Tell me, Christine. Tell me that you're afraid."

"I'm afraid," she admitted in a sob, wanting to look anywhere else, but he was too close. She had no choice but to become lost in malformations. *"Please let me go!"*

Christine watched the changing emotions upon that face, like the transforming pictures of a kaleidoscope, and without warning, he hastily released her, dragging fisted hands to himself and recoiling. Without his strength, she wearily sank to the floor, tears coming quicker as her deceiving body betrayed her and still felt the lingering imprint of his form pressed to every curve.

A rustle of motion met her ears, but she refused to look. She knew he was collecting his mask and replacing it to hide what she found most repulsive. ...As if with his face covered, he wasn't a monster but was an angel again. A part of her actually wished it were true.

"Come on," Erik stated flatly. "I'll take you back."

She did not question his motives or why he had changed mind, not with freedom so close to her fingertips. Only a fool would take that risk, and she was determined never to be a fool again.

Erik led the way back with a lantern in hand this time, never offering a single touch when too many taken had been sins. Only a few careful glances were granted back, but Christine kept eyes lowered to the stone floor and gave nothing away. He didn't need to see to know what she was thinking. Of course, she was afraid, betrayed, ...disappointed. He shared that burden. The one who wasn't supposed to be a disappointment to him, and now...he cursed his own naïve optimism.

No words were uttered when every one felt insufficient. Erik left her on the opposite side of her mirror with only a single look shared between them. He saw pain and terror that seared its vision into his memory, proof why she could never be his; he forced his returned stare to be resentful and devoid of his own hurt. Hating her was preferred to a broken heart.

Christine refused the pull of more tears, not with his witness. She waited until he vanished into the shadows behind her mirror, until only her reflection stared back, ...until she was truly alone without a man in a mask, ...without an angel. *Alone...*

Her heavy eyes landed on a nearby clock, and it was another shock to find it was the middle of the night. Deep in an underground home, time had seemed irrelevant without starlight to make it mean something. The opera house would be empty. The Vicomte would have returned home hours ago, believing himself rebuffed, and by now the city streets would be quiet and unable to disturb her melancholy. The idea convinced her to seek solace; she knew right where to go.

Quickly yanking a long cloak around the beaded costume she still wore, she lifted the hood over disheveled curls and fled the opera house with frenzied steps. A chilled rain tumbled from the clouded night sky and dampened her skin as she ran through the vacant streets, only her clanking shoes to create sound. Faster and more determined with every step as her body shook inside and out. Her heart felt cold, beating in erratic pulsations against her ribs. Oh, what had she done...?

Without pause, Christine shoved the cemetery gate open and continued between tombstones, her heels sinking into the muddied earth as she went. The raindrops wet her cloak and started to seep inside as she walked the worn path to the grave she wanted. No moon, no stars to cast glows, and the letters etched in stone would have been definable only by touch.

"How could you?" Christine gasped, sliding into a heap upon the cold, muddy grass. "You were supposed to watch over me and keep me safe. You said you'd send me an angel, and I ignorantly trusted. What a fool I am! To truly believe you could have found a way to conquer death and send me a blessing!"

Between shadowed headstones in the same place he had lingered at her last visit, Erik watched with an ache in his heart. Her every word was a dagger driven through skin to bone. He had done this, taken a child full of hope and innocence and thrown her into the cruel, garish world of adulthood with never a consideration beyond his own desire. He truly was a monster.

"An angel...," Christine softly sobbed, her tears mingling in raindrops. "But there was never an angel. He wasn't real. He was a man, only a man. No, ...a monster."

Erik stiffened at the word, considering how different it was to hear it from her lips. Ah, of course, it had always suited him better than angel, but it sounded like an unusual contortion from a voice he adored so much.

"You left me and gave me a monster to love. I am truly alone..."

"Never alone," Erik softly called and watched her lift her tear-stained face. There was no surprise in those blue eyes; no, he only saw anger.

"Leave me be," Christine retorted, desperate to appear strong. She was no longer chained to the underground and this time let conviction remain.

"No," he stated simple as that and took calculated steps between headstones until he could stand before her. "How quickly you forget that you asked for an angel, Christine! Do you recall it? You cried and pleaded for your father to send the angel he promised. I was only giving you what you wanted."

"You deceived me," she insisted back. "It was a lie."

"And which of us begged for it to be more than that?" he countered, and though the fire flickered in his glare and tightened his tone, he kept a fraction of control this time. "For weeks, you have teased me with what I've wanted most of all. It wasn't enough to be your intangible teacher, not for either of us. You *loved* an angel, Christine."

"An angel that didn't exist."

"The only lie was in a title, a *word*. I never could have approached you any other way. You would have looked in horror as you do now. Terror and pity for the disfigured creature. Isn't that what you feel?"

"I don't *know* what I feel," she admitted in another sob, curling tightly into her cloak as if seeking a warmth she could not seem to find.

Erik dared to step closer, noting how intently she scrutinized his every movement, and as he extended a tentative hand, he had an answer in her impulse to recoil. "Fear, disgust," he spoke with necessary detachment and then chose anger. "You wanted an angel; I *gave you* an angel. Am I now to be blamed for waking you from the land of fairytales? Perhaps the story could have continued, but you had to peek behind the curtain and destroy the illusion, didn't you? An angel, you said, but it wasn't enough. You wanted a body to touch, a man to touch you back, and I gave you that as well. But apparently, you were expecting perfection, and what I have to offer is a disappointment."

"But you're a monster-"

"No!" Erik roared and did not care when she shrank back in her place. "No, I am a man with a heart and soul! I offered everything to you, laid it at your feet, but you are far too fixed on mourning what didn't exist to realize what always has!"

Fear was vivid in her eyes, and though her limbs trembled, she gave one unavoidable argument. "But you're the Opera Ghost." She didn't need to elaborate and accuse. It was reason enough, and she watched him grow silent to accept it.

Long moments extended, and the only sound was the oddly serene patter of raindrops upon tombstones.

Finally, in a soft breath, Erik bid, "You knew last night. I wouldn't have denied it if you had asked, but instead you sought to destroy us both and dared remove my mask as if you had a right. You sought retribution for my deception by stripping me of my dignity, and I would argue you deserve what you uncovered. You will be punished forever because I won't let you go, Christine. The Opera Ghost usually takes the lives of those who see his face." He noticed her pale even though no moon lit its shade, and he wondered if she truly believed he was monster enough to kill her.

"Why can't we go back?" she desolately whispered. "And...pretend."

"Pretend? That is impossible! And how will you forget this face, Christine? How will you bury the visions of its ugliness that will torment you?"

"But if you were an angel again-"

"And hide behind your mirror still? Only a voice to you? Have you any idea the longing I've suffered, the ache to be a part of your life, ...to touch you?"

"To hurt me," she somberly added. "You touch me with violence in your hands."

"I'm accomplished at causing pain," he replied laden with self-loathing as he recalled the softness of her, the fragile details, and he'd so viciously clasped her, likely left marks behind. "I've never touched anyone unless it was out of violence. Forgive me for knowing nothing else."

Her eyes locked on his hands and watched nervously as he fisted them in the open air between. When concealed in gloves, they had been another part of the allure; now they were too pale, too thin and long, too *real*. "If you were an angel again, you couldn't hurt me."

"Couldn't *touch* you," he corrected bitterly. "And so much the better, isn't that right? I am abhorrent to you. The lie is preferred to the truth." Before she could reply, he crouched on the wet ground near her, and even though she tried to draw back, he ignored her attempt and crept closer. "I hurt you, but it doesn't have to be that way. It wasn't what I intended, ...none of this was. Let me show you, Christine. Let me touch you without violence in my hands and show you why being an intangible angel can't be enough for either of us anymore."

She recoiled; she couldn't help what felt like a natural instinct, but he still extended one hand toward her, fingers blooming out of a fist until threats evaporated to trembling instead. To her, a fist had spoken pain, but perhaps a fist had been only to hide weakness. Curiosity kept her in place and staring inquisitively at that hand with a wonder how it would feel upon her again. Her skin seemed to recognize his before her mind could, and by its impulse, she tilted into his touch and let his palm curve about her cheek. His flesh was cold; inside and out, she was already cold. Why then did one touch sear her with a heat that was not even present? Penetrating within her very being and branding her? This touch could be gentle, and yet she felt sure it would leave as much of a lasting impression as bruises and scars.

Erik did no more than caress her cheek, his un-tensed fingers grazing the silkiness of her hairline as delicate as he'd ever been. One touch, and it only led to an ache for dozens more, for a permanent molding of skin to skin that could never be broken again. He had no doubt that despite the consequences, this simple bliss was worth ending facades of invisible angels. To touch her, to feel the smoothness of her skin, to know that though she was wary, she permitted him and was in that moment with him, sharing the only good memory he'd ever known.

"I won't hurt you," he softly vowed, but the skepticism never abandoned her constant gaze. "Never again, Christine. Here is the truth finally laid before you. I am no angel; I am only a man, a monster by your own assessment. I won't deny it. I am Erik, only Erik. But, Christine, you *know* me. My heart was always before you in the music. The music held the truths I could not say. ...I won't hurt you," he repeated firmly and wondered what it would take to steal undimmed suspicion. He wasn't sure he had enough words. He tried one last time. "I'm sorry." An apology, sincere and honest, and he watched more tears flood her eyes. "Christine?"

In the midst of a sob, she spoke an accusation that pierced his heart with its pain, "You were supposed to be an angel..."

Nothing existed to wipe the lies clean, and all he could do was solemnly nod and accept every bitter rush of blame. Yes, he was supposed to be, and even pretending it, the dream was gone.

Drawing his hand reluctantly away, he bid, "Come on, Christine. It's late, and I won't have you taking ill in this rain. ...I'll help you home."

Her tears would not cease as they meandered already wet cheeks with their descent, and shaking a weighty head, she softly insisted, "I'm so tired."

"I know." Tired, empty, lost, and though he felt the same, he picked up the strength between them. Vowing again as if it excused his actions, he reached toward her, saying calmly, "I won't hurt you."

But she was too exhausted to offer arguments any longer and did not struggle or even cringe as his arms came about her tightly-curled shape. So heavy, and in the next breath, so weightless as he lifted her off the cold ground. She ducked her head out of his view, pressing her temple to the inconstant, stammering beat of his heart. He insisted they could not pretend, but like this, with his mask out of view and only the comfort of his strength, it was too easy. It was preferred. And a broken heart did not have to feel broken when she was cradled so gently in his arms.

Erik purposely chose a slow, languid pace, delighting in holding her far too much. He strolled in the rain with never a thought of tomorrow or the number of tears cried this night. He merely concentrated on the girl in his arms, her shape and warmth, the weight of her head against his chest, the curls that had fallen free of her hood and tickled his jaw at every gust of wind. He was so attuned to every nuance that he knew the instant she succumbed to sleep. It seemed such a great achievement and certainly a blessing that in spite of the horror he'd placed before her, she was calm and safe enough in his presence to rest.

Maybe he was being foolishly optimistic again, but he did not bring her back to her apartment or even her dressing room. No, he took her with him as if she was his to keep and carried her through the damp catacombs to his home.

This time he brought her past the vacant sitting room where a nightmare story had played out an hour before and down a narrow corridor to a bedroom. *Her* bedroom... He called himself a fool again and was shamed by his boldness, but at first thoughts of entering her life weeks before, he had transformed his music room into an elaborately decorated bedroom for Christine, meticulous down to every last detail. More optimism and a fantasy, but when all he had to offer was his own bedchamber in the dark hues of a funeral parlor or a decently cozy couch, neither seemed acceptable. He wanted her to have a place of her own, to make her feel like she could belong in this life with him and not overwhelm her completely. And considering he knew she lived in a poorly-furnished, hardly adequate apartment, he wanted to spoil her in a luxury she'd never known.

Peaches and pinks, the room was decorated in warm colors that completely contrasted every other shade in his life. Erik brought his sleeping angel to a canopy bed, accented in billowing chiffon curtains, and gentle so as not to rouse her, he disentangled her damp cloak, unraveling black material and tossing it aside before he lay her within the thick covers in her dirt-smudged costume. It was the very portrait his mind had created and drawn over and over again when he had arranged the room: his Christine peacefully asleep in the bed he'd picked for her, content to be in the depths of the earth with him. It was so close to being his.

For a long time, Erik stayed in that place, watching her sleep and contemplating how he could make this permanent. Finally sometime after dawn, he lit an oil lamp in an otherwise dark room and silently crept back into the house, utterly determined in his plan.

Chapter Four

Blue eyes fluttered open with an ache to remind Christine of tears cried. Her first coherent thought was she felt deliciously warm, and it was odd when she was so accustomed to waking in her cold apartment with a flimsy blanket granting no heat. But instead she felt like the proverbial princess waking in a fairytale story. Perhaps that was exactly his intention...

She was reluctant to sit up and face reality, but a bedside clock showed her that it was well into the afternoon, ...or was it the middle of the night again? A time on a clock, but she had no windows to confirm. Afternoon was her conclusion only because she couldn't imagine sleeping an entire day. Afternoon, and here she was in an unfamiliar bedroom, locked in the underground with the Opera Ghost. With that thought, a fairytale returned to a nightmare.

Shaking from anything but cold, Christine left the cocoon of her bed and nervously wandered the room, observing the elegant, carved furnishings and the random objects arranged purposefully for her use: a brush and comb, a bottle of perfume, a pale pink gown draped idly on a vanity bench, a vase overflowing with fragrant roses on a nearby end table. Sense and suspicion insisted Erik had done all of this for her. She wasn't sure if she should be grateful or upset.

She had no choice but to play into the fantasy when her only possession was a dirt-smudged costume gown. Anxious eyes glanced about with a lingering fear of invisible opera ghosts. She still couldn't fully accept that while she had yearned for heavenly presences, a flesh and bone man had been watching her every motion, ...a flesh and bone man who had made it vividly known he carried lustful desires. She was suddenly terrified to think she'd tempted them to life and equally afraid to encourage them further.

She couldn't be sure no one spied, but with trembling hands, she quickly changed into the pale pink gown, disturbed by how perfectly it fit. ...As if created just for her. Grabbing the brush, she worked through tangles in disheveled locks and tied them back in a matching pink ribbon. Readying herself for the Opera Ghost... The very idea left her uneasy and apprehensive as she finally left the sanctity of her room and crept into the dimly lit corridor.

Before she even arrived in the sitting room doorway, that masked face was raised and expectant, and lingering back, she held his mismatched stare and refused to cower under its intensity. Details were absorbed since so many from the night before felt hazy and dreamlike. Now she pensively studied her once angel with a certain, necessary disengagement, noting that he seemed to be doing the same, as if neither of them knew what emotions were permitted and which ones were sins. But she caught one brief lapse in his apathetic façade with the rush of his gaze surveying her from head to toe. Then she saw the briefest hint of flames and a blatant longing to touch her that went un-indulged and wasted.

"Good morning," Erik greeted with enacted civility, "or I should say, good afternoon. Morning has come and gone already." His hands seemed desperate for some task to busy them, and he resigned to lift his teacup from an end table, cringing when it rattled upon its saucer and gave anxiousness away. "Would you care for something to eat? I laid breakfast out in the dining room for you. It will likely be cold by now, but I was unsure when you would arise. I thought after you ate, we could make use of our time and return to your lessons."

"Here?" she posed skeptically, eyeing the piano and recalling its glorious timbre as it played her lullabies.

"It's as good a place as any; perhaps better if I may judge your technique without barriers to hinder."

"And...you mean for my lessons to continue?"

"Well, of course," he proclaimed as if the answer were obvious. "I told you last night. There were never lies in the music. Your potential, Christine, your future. Surely, you realize now that the premiere has past, we must work twice as hard to secure your rightful place."

"Rightful?" she inquired with a doubtful shake of her head. "La Carlotta would argue against that. If news of the premiere is spreading, she must be furious and out for blood by now."

"Exactly! And what would you do? You'd duck your head and apologize for your existence to her yet again as if your performance was a fluke," Erik insisted, and his stern expression did not crack and show his delight to see a spark of protest in her eyes. "You played the diva for one night, and the vast majority of it was a façade spurred by my own devices. We need to work on your bravado, and I think courage will come if you are forced to face one of your fears on a daily basis. You may have the Opera Ghost as your ally, but it is worth nothing if you crumble at every chance. Imagine how much courage it will take to stand face to face with the Opera Ghost every day. My reputation puts La Carlotta's to shame."

It was partly a jest, an uncommon and slightly awkward attempt at lighthearted humor on his part, and he was pleased the result was the tinge of a smile on her lips, however meager and lacking the glow he'd grown accustomed to glimpsing. He only prayed full, unhindered smiles would eventually be his again, ...and this was how he would try to win them: by dulling harsh edges and controlling emotions at their point of inspiration, by taking the threat and the pressure away. Trust reconstructed from its base, and if she could learn to endure his presence without the trepidation he could feel pouring out of her at present, then he still had hope.

But there was one facet he had not considered in his great scheme, not until she brought it to light. "And...do you expect I will stay here with you as well? That room... Did you arrange it for me? Was it intended to be mine?"

Erik cursed his ignorance and suddenly lashed out, "That is a rather presumptuous claim, is it not? Did you never ponder the more logical conclusion: that it is a guest room, and I simply collected some items to make you more comfortable? That since you destroyed the costume you wore last night to the cemetery in the rain, I was being considerate in finding you something to wear? Why is the logical answer denounced over the devious one?"

He was so careful in his words. No more lies, for he'd never admitted to anything. This was not the time to present his uncontrollable obsession and reveal the lengths he'd gone to in hopes of her presence. No, not when merely his retort had her trembling and nervous.

"I...I'm sorry," she stammered, kneading flustered fingers into the soft material of her skirts. "I don't mean to seem ungrateful. Thank you for the gown..."

He was apprehensive as he admitted, "I took the liberty of filling the wardrobe for you. I only thought to make you happy. That is all. There is not always a sinister motive to my every act, and I apologize if it seemed otherwise." Heaving a sigh when she did not calm, he insisted, "You are not a prisoner, and I am not your jailer. You are free to come and go as you please. After all, you have rehearsals to attend; I understand that. I am only presenting the option. You may stay if you like, or you may leave. Your choice. Now go and fetch something to eat so we may tend to your lesson. We have a lot of work to do."

Christine eyed him doubtfully, but she used his command as her escape. Following the direction of his gesturing hand, she mercifully fled to the dining room and felt her body release its tension the instant she was beyond his stare.

Violent curses played in Erik's head as he found his own relief in her absence. How he wished to know the right words to put her at ease and squelch her suspicions! *Were* there even right words? He had done this with deception. There had been no walls between her and an angel, only a transparent mirror that never hindered the connection of hearts. Now...they could stand in the same room and yet never be further apart. The voice in his head insisted he stick to his plan, build trust and desperately try to rein his temper all the while. As impossible as it seemed!

*****

It took the majority of her lesson time just to acquaint them both with the new situation. Erik was more agitated than usual, stuttering when he usually flowed in every word. But he was oddly shaken to have her standing in the bow of his piano, facing him with those demanding and uncertain blue eyes at his every command. It was a frustration!

Christine did not attempt to make it any easier for him. She read his distraction and knew a strange enjoyment for it. How long had she endured lessons so nervous to please an angel, terrified he'd eventually leave her for good? All unqualified fears. She was the confident one between them because *she* now had the power and option to leave. Yes, now he needed to please *her* as she had so desperately sought to please *him*. It was a meager compensation, and yet it was something.

She wanted to tell herself that she would no longer seek to make him proud and earn his praises, but as she executed a flawless cadenza, the notes flowing smooth and gliding to blossom on a high note, she met the unhidden awe in his mismatched stare and her heart urgently skipped against her ribcage. How often had he stared with that expression behind the mirror where she couldn't revel in it, only giving reserved appreciation when she'd longed for more? And here it was, blatant and unreserved for the briefest instant before he re-established his calm façade. It was so much more than any words could say; it proclaimed a deeper adoration than she realized or wanted to acknowledge. But for the first time, she was happy barriers were gone and a mortal man was the one watching her.

"We can end there," Erik decided, trying not to show disappointment, but when everything was unsteady and fragile, it was preferred to go on in the new peace they found in music. Hesitant to utter the question, he softly bid, "And...do you intend to stay, or will you return to your apartment?"

Christine knew the answer he wanted. ...To stay with the Opera Ghost in his underground home, this time by her own choice... She longed to ignore the hope in mismatched eyes as they held her stare and made her shiver. "I...think it best if I return home. I can't stay here... How could I possibly? You are a stranger to me."

"My face is a stranger to you, my body, and the nuances, but...you know me, Christine, better than anyone ever has, I daresay. It is your decision which holds more sway: the corporeal being before you or the soul I've given since the first moment." The desolation in his voice felt like a betrayal to his heart, and he quickly transformed it into detachment. Rising abrupt and determined, he bid, "I will take you back. Get your cloak. It should have dried by now, and...the catacombs are cold and damp, unpleasant. Go on. Hurry up."

She hesitated one last moment, knowing she hurt him. She wasn't sure how to take the regret welling within, the urge to beg forgiveness. But she did not give him more than a set stare before rushing to comply, burying her emotions and doing a better job at it. She gave nothing away, not as they abandoned the warm coziness of an underground home, silent and without a single touch, not even as he brought her through her mirror.

"Tomorrow you have rehearsal," Erik reluctantly told her. "When it is over, I shall meet you here and take you below to your lesson. Is that acceptable?"

A solemn nod was her reply, and then he was gone. Within the breath, she was moving with rushed steps, eager for fresh air and welcoming breezes. Sunlight played upon her face, and it was the most delicious sensation that she closed her eyes and let it wash over her, not caring that passers-by on the busy city street cast her odd stares. It felt like freedom, as if every dimly lit detail in between couldn't be real. The sun, the blue sky, and how often would they remain hers? How long until she was confined to the underground? ...The real question was: would she fight consumption or be eager and willing the day she surrendered? Even her better sense could give no answer.

*****

Christine suffered nightmares, cold and alone in her bed that night, shaking and rousing with unconscious tears streaming down her cheeks. Not even sleep gave reprieve for the ache in her heart; it was as poignant as ever.

Somber was her chosen mood, as she dressed

in one of her old gowns that looked pitiful when beside the pale pink one from an angel. She found her fingertips adding an unconsidered caress to its pink silk where she had draped it so tenderly along her vanity's bench. The loveliest gown she'd ever had as hers...

Her mind tugged thoughts back and forth between longing and abhorrence and twisted her feelings until she wasn't sure she could trust herself. She was actually grateful to have rehearsal as a distraction. ...Grateful until she arrived at the theatre amidst sharp curses and heaved insults that filtered out to meet her in the lobby. La Carlotta was raging to the managers, the stage director, random cast and crew, anyone with ears, ...and all about Christine. Oh, how she had dreaded exactly this scene!

"There she is!" Carlotta shrieked, pointing frantically at Christine the instant she passed the doorway. "The little usurper! How dare she!"

"Signora," one of the managers, Monsieur Firmin, gushed in pacification, "Mademoiselle Daaé did her best to fill your place, but, of course, she cannot touch your talent and charms."

"Of course!" the diva agreed, narrowing a glare on Christine that she shrank back to endure. "*No one is my equal!* And now that I have returned, I insist you toss the little imposter out!"

Christine's eyes widened with a thought of how Erik would react to such commotion, but thankfully, before she could find out or have to plead for her employment, Monsieur Firmin replied, "Signora, tossing her out is a bit hasty. She made a favorable impression at the premiere, nothing near your accolades, but enough that she would be missed if we let her go. She will be put back where she belongs, and you will reign as diva again. Surely that is a reasonable compromise."

Carlotta fixed her seething on Firmin and hissed, "If I have to hear one more word about the little tart and her performance, I will leave and never return. You will lose every patron you have without me to fill your seats. You cannot *afford* to have La Carlotta as your enemy." Straightening to an elegant posture, the diva cast one more glare at Christine before turning to stalk backstage, calling over her shoulder, "I expect a bouquet to be delivered to my dressing room with a note of apology."

"As soon as possible," the other manager, Monsieur Andre, replied in sugarcoated tones before turning to Christine. "Mademoiselle, you had best take care until things settle back to normal. But...you did well at the performance. I received quite a number of compliments from our patrons. The Vicomte de Chagny even insisted on increasing his family's usual contribution. That is a great honor."

The Vicomte... She had never gotten to hear his opinion. Obviously, his contribution declared his enjoyment, but...it would have been pleasant to hear the compliments on his lips.

Rehearsal felt like a moment plucked out of the past with her prima donna performance as a delightful fantasy in between. How could it be real when no one wanted to cross Carlotta and acknowledge it had ever happened? Everything picked up where it had left off before Carlotta's untimely exit, and Christine wondered if it were better that way.

Finding herself offstage in the wings, Christine listened to Carlotta singing the aria she had performed, resisting the urge to hum along. It felt like hers now that she had performed it, and it was a sting to know she never would again if Carlotta had her way.

"Christine!"

The soft call was the prelude to a little hand upon her arm, pulling her further from the stage. "Meg, aren't you supposed to be practicing?"

The little ballerina gave an idle shrug and

rolled eyes to declare how much she cared about such news. "I told Mama I was on the verge of fainting, and she gave me a moment to 'collect myself'," she proclaimed with exaggeration. "Her maternal care is secondary to her ambition, and sad to say, if I *had* fainted, she likely would have yelled at my comatose body and made the other girls continue dancing around me."

A genuine smile lit Christine's lips, and she was grateful, recalling that it had been days since she'd found any need for happiness. "And were you truly faint, or was it a fabricated excuse to escape your mother?"

"Well, how else would I get a conversation with my dearest friend in the whole world? Christine, where have you been? You vanished after the premiere, and no one heard a word from you. What happened? There was a very flustered Vicomte racing about backstage after the show seeking you out, but you were gone. ...A very flustered but *very* handsome Vicomte." Golden brows arched suggestively. "What haven't you been telling me?"

Christine's smile was enough to insist she carried secrets.

"Oh my goodness!" the little ballerina exclaimed with frantic giggles. "Are you courting a *Vicomte*? Christine, tell me! I will burst with excitement if you don't!"

"No, no, not courting," she quickly corrected, holding up her hands. "Quieter please! I have enough animosity tossed at me. If anyone thinks I'm courting a Vicomte, any shred of a reputation I still have will be lost."

Green eyes widened blamelessly. "Oh, it's already a well-known topic of the gossip chain, and that is *not* my doing. It was justifiably concluded when your Vicomte rushed about the corridors with a full bouquet of roses calling you very improperly by first name. *And* he was crushed not to find you."

"Oh?" Such news left Christine a wave of guilt and a queer hope that she hadn't ruined her chance. It was just so *ordinary*. Raoul, enamored by her, bringing her flowers to gush over her performance; perhaps he'd wanted to take her to supper afterward. *That* was how things were supposed to be. Not a masked man dragging her into darkness and rewarding her achievement with presented emotions from a corpse's face and too many tears to recall.

"You aren't denying it!" Meg insisted. "Oh, you *say* you aren't courting, but you know him, don't you? There's more to the story, and I *need* to know!"

"Don't you mean the *world* needs to know? Once I say a word, the gossip chain will be ringing," Christine reminded, and Meg made a face.

"Ha, ha," she sarcastically taunted. "I told no one about your little liaison with your teacher. That must account for something! ...A love affair with a genius musician or a love affair with a rich and handsome Vicomte? Good Lord, Christine, how lucky you are to have such a choice! The best offer I've gotten is that scrawny stagehand who follows me around like a stray dog!"

"But you love teasing him."

"Yes, but I doubt the projected outcome. You have two fabulous propositions before you, and which will you choose?"

Huffing her apprehension, Christine shook her head and asked her own question instead, "Meg, what do you know of the Opera Ghost?"

Meg arched a brow. "Oh, fine! If you don't want to be interrogated until you decide, I'll let it go, but pretending an interest in the Opera Ghost to distract me is pointless. I already know your aversion to the topic. You *don't believe* in the Opera Ghost."

If only she didn't... "No, I didn't believe in the other ballerinas' constant screeching at every misplaced stocking or bump in the hallway."

"And you suddenly changed your mind?"

"Not to frivolity, but...the night of the premiere I saw a shadow in my dressing room, and...well, my mind has been corrupted by enough shrieking ballerinas to assume ghosts are a logical explanation." It was the nearest to the truth she dared go, and it left her to nervously scan the silent corridors around them, hoping futilely that Carlotta's high notes onstage muted any less than acceptable conversations. "Is...the Opera Ghost a mortal man?"

Meg giggled as if her question were absurd. "He's a *ghost*, Christine. People see him on occasion in the form of a man, but he's omnipotent. He can come and go without anyone glimpsing if he so chooses, and he can commit his crimes without ever being caught. He's a specter. ...Makes it extra frightening, doesn't it? You never know where he is or where he'll appear."

Christine deciphered which parts of the story were facts. "*Omnipotent*? Hardly. But...people have seen him?"

"That's the most terrifying part of all," Meg replied with a shudder. "He's a *monster*. He haunts the opera house in a mask because his face is *distorted*. Perhaps *that* is what killed him or perhaps it is a result of decay!" She grew more frantic with every phrase, and Christine had to raise hands again to remind her to be quiet. "Anyone who sees him usually disappears," Meg continued softer this time. "But once a nighttime janitor happened to get free of his clutches. He caught a glimpse of the Opera Ghost's true face beneath the mask. He told everyone what he saw, the horror of it all, but a few days later, he vanished just like the rest. No one ever saw him again. That was years ago. Everyone else has been intelligent enough not to willingly test the stories."

"And the accidents around the theatre?"

"Well, I may be the first one to shout Opera Ghost at every noise, but I don't actually believe he does *everything*. It's just fun to fuel the fire! But everyone knows better than to utter a word against him. A single curse or denunciation, and the one who says it tends to suffer some sort of trauma. The last I recall was a prop boy who claimed the Opera Ghost wasn't real and then fell down a ladder from the rafters."

Christine wasn't sure how much was conjecture. Meg had a talent for overdoing details, but she nodded as if she believed and tried to decide if she could imagine Erik pushing a boy out of the rafters. It only left her to shudder.

"So?" Meg pushed urgently. "Do you really think the Opera Ghost was in your dressing room?"

"Maybe..."

"You better take care, Christine. They say once the ghost sets his sights on you, he won't quit and give up so easily. I couldn't bear to consider that he might come after you." Nervous glances were indulged to every corner, and Meg quickly insisted, "I must return to rehearsal before Mama comes after me. A fainting spell will seem like a luxury compared to what she'd do. Will you be all right, Christine?"

"Yes, go on, Meg. ...Be careful," she felt compelled to add the warning with an anxious twist in her stomach, and as Meg scampered away, she saw why. One look to the rafters above her head, and her eyes locked with the mismatched colors of blue and green fixed on her. The blatant pain she saw on his masked face said he'd heard every word. But just as quickly as she saw him, he was gone in the softest rustle, disappearing from sight as if he'd never been there at all.

Chapter Five

Christine expected anger; she was almost anticipating it by the time rehearsal ended. Anger in heaved curses from his temper, but as Erik appeared before her in the mirror's glass, he was stoic and apathetic. *She* was the one left to carry the anger between them.

Emotion seemed a sin in the days to follow. Every evening as rehearsal ended and Christine conceded to go with the Opera Ghost to his underground home, he was only teacher. Nothing showed through his chosen professional demeanor, and it bothered her to no end. No affection, no hints of the heart she had known as an angel's, *nothing.* It struck her bitterly, for she felt as if she could have been anyone at all and it wouldn't have mattered.

He might have chosen detachment, but she was still jarred by face to face interaction, unable to keep from fumbling simply because of his eyes and the intensity of every stare. It was disturbing that he could rattle her and tie her up in so many conflicting emotions that she'd leave with a head swimming in confusion. *Leave* because she never stayed the night in his underground home, though every evening he offered the proposition. Perhaps he hoped enough inquiries would one day lead to her agreement. But when even that intimate request was muttered without a heart beneath it as if he were indifferent on the subject, it took little effort to refuse.

And so every night she returned to her apartment, half-convinced he followed her home and half-convinced she was growing into paranoia for the very thought. The instant she locked herself safely inside and mercifully alone, apprehension that built during her time with her once angel cracked and fell to a longing that disgusted her with its presence. She only excused her self-betrayal with the insistence it was an *angel* she longed for, an *angel* she missed and ached to have as her own once again. She couldn't want the mortal man. No, she *wouldn't let* herself. No matter that too often she found her mind drifting, fantasizing about a night that had spiraled in a tornado of emotions and getting stuck on his cold touch upon her cheek, on the hard planes of his body against hers in the moment he'd forced her to him, ...God help her, on his *face*.

It was a vision in her dreams down to every last horrifying detail, and it shamed her to admit how many nights she awakened to find her arms reaching to a figment in imagination. That face... To close her eyes meant to recreate its malformations behind her lids and see it in stark precision. Curiosity was an inherent trait, and she blamed it for an urge to touch a monster's face, to learn what it felt like against her fingertips. It looked smooth; she wondered if that was how it felt. Obscure oddities, ones she had no comparison for in her own existence...

Would it hurt him if she dared? Was it as sensitive as an open wound, as tender and easy to inflame? ...And how would he react to such a bizarre situation? Would he assume she was mocking him or that she was perverse to long for such a thing? Considering his rage the last time his face had been exposed, she reasoned he would only be upset. But she had an inclination to ask and at least break him out of apathy even if anger would be his emotion of choice. *Anything* to make him seem to care again.

How upsetting to realize how much his avoidance bothered her!

Another rehearsal ended, and Christine dreaded her lesson to come. She had the urge to tell Erik that he wasn't nearly as good a teacher when he treated her like a task and no longer a pleasure. Imagining his reply to such bold words created an odd sense of mischief that twinkled in her eyes. Perhaps it was time she pushed *him* a bit. When he was adamant to make her miss a nonexistent angel this much, it seemed qualified.

She was about to escape to her dressing room, devising the safest way to stir Erik's temper without permanent repercussions when the idea evaporated mid-thought. "Raoul?"

The Vicomte de Chagny, looking uncomfortably nervous beneath an attempted charming grin, rushed to block her from leaving. "You don't mind that I'm here, do you? I know it isn't proper to be wandering backstage, seeking you out, but...well, I had to see you."

She understood his apprehension as a glance showed random cast and crew eyeing them and whispering. If gossip existed simply from his fruitless search after the premiere, both of them now together screamed as proof. "I...I'm pleased for your company," she stammered, trying to ignore too many eyes.

But Raoul was equally attuned, and lowering his voice, he asked, "Is there someplace we can go and talk for a few minutes without the constant audience to eavesdrop?"

Her dressing room was not an option. Gossip would become excited squeals, not to mention the worse reality of an infuriated ghost spying every moment. But...she had another idea, and nodding to the relieved Vicomte, she gestured for him to follow and led them away from watchers.

A doorway at the end of the hall opened to a

narrow staircase, and without pause, she guided the way. An angel had brought her downward in darkness; she was determined this time to go up to the light.

They emerged onto the vacant rooftop as twilight colors left ribbons of pinks and purples and stars began to blink in its furthest dark blues. Cool breezes with hinted warmth at their center surrounded and welcomed their company, and Christine breathed deep and calm. It felt freeing as if every gust could carry her away if only she'd let it.

"It's lovely up here," Raoul said after a moment of silence extended too long.

His voice broke her contemplation with its timbre; to her ears, it sounded wrong. It wasn't the voice she expected to hear. "Yes," she distantly bid, trying to hide disappointment, "up where dark means night, and shadows can't reach us."

"Shadows?" Raoul questioned. "More ghost stories, Christine?"

"Perhaps, but when we were children, they never seemed they could be real. It was a game, to scare one another with exaggerated tales." As she spoke, she idly wandered to the edge of the rooftop and sat on the surrounding ledge. "I believed less as a child than I do as an adult."

"Oh?" The Vicomte took her admission as a joke, and grinning wryly, he came to sit beside her, seeking to keep her dwindling attention. "Are you haunted by ghosts, Christine?"

Christine met his eye solemnly, but instead of an inconsiderable answer, she asked, "Why did you come to see me, Raoul? Surely you realize it isn't wise to be here."

"I've never much cared for wise choices; I prefer to follow my heart instead," he admitted and avoided her anxious stare. "I wanted so badly to find you after the premiere and speak every praise playing in my mind for your performance, but you were gone."

"I was with my teacher," she answered before she could think better of it.

"Your teacher?"

"Yes, he..." Her gaze suddenly scanned the vacant rooftop, intently scrutinizing every shadow. She *knew* someone was observing every word of this supposed betrayal. She knew, ...and she had a mind to make certain he heard something worthy of a decent reaction. It was an earlier plan, only better, and she wondered if she was a masochist to be so eager to incur his wrath.

Her attention fixed on the awaiting Vicomte, and she suddenly declared, "My teacher would do anything to win my affections."

"Your...affections?" The Vicomte's disappointment was unhidden. "Oh, he...he loves you, does he?"

Christine scoffed in reply. "*Love*? I don't think he knows what that means! His version is too restraining to be love." She cast a furtive glance to watching shadows as she told Raoul, "He is *incapable* of real love."

She wasn't certain she didn't mean it.

"Oh, Christine, that is awful!" Raoul caught her hands in his, and she wondered if he believed her fool enough to consider he acted out of solace. Solace was not warm thumbs tracing delicate circles along her knuckles as if her lack of struggle gave him permission.

"And why do you indulge him as your teacher if he has overstepped his boundaries? You should sever ties with him."

"As if I could!" she exclaimed sincerely. "He won't let me go, ...and I'm not sure I want him to." Before he could infer a truth she did not want to ponder, she claimed a weak excuse instead. "Because...he's a genius, a musical virtuoso. My talent and skill come from his instruction."

"No, your talent is your own God-given gift. Do

not grant credit to anyone for it. You were born to shine on the stage; I told you so at our very first meeting. Christine," he paused until she finally dragged her eyes from a shadow she could swear breathed with life and forced her focus on his compassionate face with its every well-sculpted feature. "You tell me this news of your teacher, and I must worry. How could I not? You are already so dear to me, as if all the years in between never existed. A little girl knew my every detail so well; I long for the woman she became to do the same. That's why I came to see you. I won't depreciate the truth with pointless excuses. Since the instant I saw you again, I've thought of nothing but being with you."

Her blue eyes grew wide with such admissions, and though she finally sought to break free, he wouldn't let go. "Raoul, but my teacher-"

"Tell me plainly. Do you care for him? Does he hold your heart?"

She hesitated, glancing frantically at shadows again. "I... He's my teacher, and I..." Jerking hard so he had to release her, she scampered to her feet and insisted, "I have to go. I have a lesson, and I can't be late."

"Why?" Raoul demanded, huffing a soft curse beneath his breath. "Is he cruel to you, Christine? Does he hurt you if you upset him? I can protect you; you need not live in fear." Extending a hand, he pleaded, "Come with me."

Staring at that hand, she wondered how much of his offer was out of pure jealousy, an urging to try and make her choose. He seemed so sure his suit would win, and to compare his flawless features with the distorted ones in her memory, he *did* seem the favorable one between them. But the shadows beckoned with their own unuttered proposal and tugged her heart in their direction.

"I...I can't," she stammered, creeping back toward the staircase. "I'm sorry, Raoul. I...I have to go." One last shared look, and she darted through the door, even as she heard him call after her.

Oh God, ...she'd wanted to inspire emotion within Erik; she now regretted the plan a thousand times over. Tempting the Opera Ghost was surely not a good idea. She'd be lucky if he did not abandon every affection he carried and strangle her deep in his home where no one could save her!

Quickly locking herself in her dressing room before Raoul could pursue, she trembled inside and out to eye her mirror's glass. The girl staring back looked like a traitor.

Within the minute, the glass disappeared through his little trick, and she was faced with the overwhelming aura of the Opera Ghost, permeating the air even before he became a tangible silhouette. She was on guard, rigid in her place and ready to cower and cry if need be, but he gave nothing away...as if he'd never been a shadow on a rooftop.

"Good evening, Christine," he called in the same formal tone she'd been subject to all week; this evening felt no different than any other.

"I'm sorry." The words tumbled past her lips before she could catch them, and she cringed at her own ridiculousness.

His expression never changed. "It is I who should be sorry. I am late to meet you. I was working on my music. I can become quite engrossed sometimes, and I forget the rest of the world exists. Have you been waiting long?"

"N...not long," Christine bid and hastily insisted, "Shall we go below then, *ange*?"

She noted how he tensed at the appellation, but he nodded and moved aside with a gesture, inviting her into darkness with never a dared touch. As she passed him, her eyes momentarily caught on his gloved hands with a memory of his skin's chill. And Raoul was so warm to the touch, *alive*... It bothered her to even consider the word.

Her lesson time was repetitive and no longer enjoyed. To her, it seemed they were more strangers now than they had been the night an angel had been unmasked.

As they finished for the night, Christine lingered in the piano's bow, expecting Erik's question and wondering when the day would come that she'd say yes and stay the night in his home. She had a feeling she was fighting an inevitable fate to keep refusing.

But instead, she watched Erik close his score and shift it aside with slow, calculated movements. "Christine, ...I wondered if I might seek your inspiration for a moment."

"Inspiration?" A dark brow arched inquisitively. "I'm not sure I can be much help to you, Erik. You are the virtuoso between us, you know."

"Of course, I have notes and melodies. They play in my ears at every moment. I never need aid when it comes to composing. It is in the other, more ordinary facets of mortal life that I am deficient. My opera," he gestured to a stack on manuscript paper upon an end table. "I've been working on it for years, writing, editing, re-editing. It is a tiresome process. But...I long for it to be realistic, and since at its essence, it is a love story, I am after your opinion."

Petrified in place, Christine anxiously muttered, "And...my opinion matters so highly to you?"

"On certain subjects, ...and considering the fact I am 'incapable of love', your answer will hold more sway."

His expression never changed as he sat, poised and stoic, awaiting an answer, ...awaiting a *confession* she was certain her wide eyes already gave. But to her surprise, he appeared like her words on a rooftop meant nothing. ...Well, if he was going to play the game, she could as well!

As composed as she could manage despite

telltale, shaking hands, she asked, "What would you like to know, Erik? I am hardly versed on the topic of love, but I will do my best to answer."

He scoffed his disbelief. "Surely a girl such as yourself has known the pleasures of love! So, tell me, Christine. Tell me what it means to love."

"Love is putting someone else's well-being and desires above your own," she suddenly blurted out with sharp blame in every word. Oh, let him hear it and realize his own follies! "Love is sacrifice."

"Sacrifice?" He mulled over the term, and Christine saw the quickest flicker of despair in his distant eyes. Guilt swelled within her veins to realize she was the cause. "I don't wish to hear more. It is late, Christine," he decided in somber tones. "Perhaps I should take you back."

"And...you're not going to ask if I'd like to stay?" she demanded, surprised by her own boldness but she was suddenly desperate for the semblance of a routine that seemed to be shattering beneath her.

"It is a wasted want. I'm tired of asking."

"Ask me, Erik," she begged urgently and leaned her trembling body against the piano's bow in a meager attempt to be closer. "Please, just ask me."

Though he eyed her oddly, he did not interrogate her bizarre mood as he obeyed. "Would you care to stay the night in my home?"

"Yes," she answered almost before he finished the request. "Yes, I want to. I want to stay with you."

Christine called her eagerness a residual effect of her guilt, refusing to acknowledge she was actually *terrified* never to hear the question again, ...to never have the chance to accept.

Her hesitant eyes watched the flash of emotion upon his masked face. Awe so quickly lost behind confusion and a skepticism she knew she well deserved. But he did not speak doubts and instead replied, "Well, ...go on to bed then. Your room is just as you last saw it."

Yes, it was *her* room, and beneath flimsy explanations, she was certain that room had been arranged just for her. The thought should have scared her; why didn't it scare her?

With a dutiful nod, she softly bid, "Goodnight, ...Erik," and held his pensive stare one last breath, reluctant to sever its connection.

But finally, she turned with flustered footsteps and scurried down the nearby corridor.

She never knew Erik watched her go and kept a locked gaze on the empty hallway after her in a turmoil of emotion. Elation, despair, anger, longing, all twisted into an indefinite bundle that rotated around one inarguable fact, and he almost smiled with an odd sense of relief. She was here, beneath his roof, by choice and not coercion this time, and in spite of every pain, that was something to be grateful for.

*****

Christine took her time readying for bed. It was odd, but she felt strangely snug in the underground house, tucked away from life. A week ago she would have cursed that very reality. Perhaps it was only coming to light because the option was almost taken away. This room was *hers*, more so than her apartment or her dressing room above. This room reminded her of a fairytale.

She indulged in a luxurious, hot bath in an adjoining bathroom and dressed in a nightdress so soft to the touch that it seemed to caress her skin before slipping beneath the warm covers of her bed, every detail savored and appreciated. As she turned the bedside oil lantern down to a subtle flicker, she let her mind wander into a fantasy where this was always hers. The idea should have darkened with a thought of her companion, but...it didn't. It seemed an added pleasure to have a presence in the next room. When she had grown accustomed to being alone and on edge at every creak and settling of her apartment's old room, she felt protected in Erik's company. Foolish,

78

she dubbed herself, and certainly underestimating who Erik was and the things he'd done. But...in fantasy, she could easily forget such things.

Not long after she curled beneath her covers, her mind still wandering in and out of imagination, she heard the smallest creak and peeked out of half-closed eyes. A shiver raced her body. Faint light tiptoed in from the open slit of a door she recalled closing, and casted in its meager glow was a silhouette.

Her heart halted its constant beat, breath trapped in her lungs as she waited with a queer thrill of anticipation. For the longest pause, all she had was a weary exhalation, not even a sigh when it would have created ripples of sound. She sought to seem unaffected, feigning sleep even if not very convincing, but then she felt his approach and every sense locked on him.

She never refused, not a struggle or a cry. She simply waited, curled on her side, frozen in place, but her eyes fluttered open the instant her shadow visitor climbed atop the mattress with her.

It felt like a dream. Hazy at the edges and too odd to be reality. A silhouette became a body laying tentatively atop covers she was cuddled beneath as streaks of intruding light illuminated only some of the details in its meager capacity. The white mask, so stark, mismatched eyes laden in longing so poignant that it seared through her skin and branded a path inside.

"Sacrifice," he whispered into the hush of silence. "You said love meant sacrifice."

She choked back a reply when lips would not cooperate and simply stared with wide eyes as he lifted a trembling hand and caught her cheek in its cold, bare palm. She had the urge to whimper in unacceptable delight.

Every breath he took was strangled and half a gasp as he fervently insisted, "Sacrifice is *not touching you*." His free hand joined the caress, trailing her hairline and sliding into her loose curls without hesitation. "It's having you before me day after day and aching so much simply for a touch. All I've wanted... Oh, Christine, it is *torture* after touching you once; it's denying what feels like instinct. How I've wanted only to *feel you* all these empty days!"

Never a protest, but never the frantic agreement floating through her mind. She concentrated on his hands and every flustered caress they granted as they trailed so innocently along the features of her face. Her lids felt heavy with the weight of sensation, and so she watched through half-closed eyes and found every emotion she had been seeking for days, all vivid on that masked face.

"Incapable of love," he repeated her own words, and she regretted every syllable. "If only I were! It would make this easy, and it wouldn't cause such pain to see you with *him*. You ran from me, Christine; you tried to hide on the roof. ...You dared to tell him of me, and you dared allow *his* touch. He took your hands..."

On the memory's recollection, Erik's hands slid beneath the edge of her blankets and sought hers, catching and weaving fingers as he lifted them out and clutched them between their bodies. "He touched you like this, and you did not shun him as you've shunned me. You did not know disgust. I don't understand... My face is abhorrent, but my hands...they're not scarred, not that different from his, and yet it is a transgression for them to graze your skin. But he...he does not even need permission."

Forcing her voice to comply, she abruptly reminded, "I am not shunning you now, am I?" Her fingers tightened at knuckles to make a firmer grip.

"And why, I wonder," he suspiciously bid. "You told your Vicomte that I do not know what love is. You called my heart's attempts 'restraining', and yet *you* clasp my hands and make your own unbreakable hold upon me."

Never loosening her grasp on hands she knew could be deadly weapons for anyone else, she admitted "I knew you were listening."

"And yet you spoke such hurtful things?"

A tentative nod was her answer.

"*Cruel*, Christine," he accused with a hint of sharpness even in whispers. "You meant to cause me pain."

Another nod, and she never released his hands, trying to focus on the way his skin felt against hers, palms flush as if molded that way. It was pleasant when compared to the flickers of betrayal in his eyes.

"Your Vicomte thinks I've abused you. You've given him plenty of assurance without ever agreeing, and now...now he'll do everything in his power to take you away from me."

"I won't let him," she suddenly vowed. "You are my teacher, and it is *my* choice."

"Teacher...?" Erik eyed her with such ravenous longing that it left him aching as his fingers matched the ferocity of her grasp. Daring to edge closer, he intoxicated himself on every detail, inhaling her into his lungs and praying to be drugged on scent alone. "And is that all I am to you, Christine? Your teacher?"

"It is better than calling you the Opera Ghost, isn't it? Or the phantom?"

Pain laced his sigh. "I always preferred angel. It felt like I meant something when I was in that role."

"But you are no angel," she reminded, and he glimpsed a flash of sadness in blue eyes, a mourning for a creature he'd never been, ...a mourning for a lie.

Nodding acceptance, he posed, "And you wanted me to pretend for you, to allow things to settle into their past boundaries. Do you now see why that can never be?" As proof, he drew entwined fingers nearer and pressed the backs of her hands to his chest, knowing she'd feel the immediate skip of his heartbeat.

Christine acquiesced, never pulling free as she replied, "And yet you've been less than angel to me these past days. You've been so cold."

"Cold? And that is only because I burn so intensely within that I am terrified to frighten you from me again," he admitted, spilling the secrets of a ruined plan. "I hoped distance would show you that I can behave like a civilized man, ...like your Vicomte. And yet *he* was the one to cross boundaries and practically profess love and desire in one conversation while I have had to censor every word and every dared touch. It hardly seems fair. You don't push *him* away at every turn. He can openly want, and it pleases you to hold his heart in your hands while mine is an abomination."

Erik studied her as he spoke, memorizing details he'd refused to distinguish in the past days of forced indifference. Had he ever been so close to her, near enough to notice every flawless inch? To truly admire the spectrum of blues in her eyes, the dark curved lashes, ...the fullness of pink lips?

As his eyes lingered on their arched shape, she suddenly stated, plain and inarguable, "You want to kiss me."

A *kiss*... He ached merely to hear the word from those coveted lips. "And...is that a sin in your eyes?"

She didn't reply, instead insisting, "You can't kiss me with your mask on."

"But is it a sin?"

Her mind recalled the fantasy, imagining its facets, and as her cheeks tinted pink, she decided, "I will make it one, and I will tell myself that it is a sin over and over again until I believe it."

"Why?" he demanded, and a firm grasp of her hands became painful fists. "Why must it be a sin? If your Vicomte kissed you, would you say the same? A sin, Christine? I want you! Why is that a sin?"

"Because you're the Opera Ghost." Her voice

trembled with rising dread. "You've killed people. I'm supposed to call you a monster."

"No, I don't have to be a monster to *you*. I can be more; I can be the same man as your Vicomte if you'd let me. This is your choosing, Christine. You decide what I will be. Make me a monster if that's really what you wish, and you will have a monster before you: heartless and cruel, with never a regard to anything beyond selfish desires. But seek a man worth loving, and that is what I will be. A heart, vulnerable but loyal to adore you forever. I can be a man; why will you not let me prove it to you?" With a fierce growl, he abruptly released her captive hands and rose from the comfort of her bed.

Christine missed his nearness the instant it was gone and stifled an urge to reach for him, to find hands again with hers as if their grip was meant to be a soldered connection. But it was the glow of rage in his eyes that kept her frozen and reminded her why separation was necessary. Never joined, never soldered. He could not be her forever.

Looming at her bedside a moment longer, he flatly declared, "I will not bother you again. If you don't believe me, lock the door after my exit. But be forewarned, Christine, if I knew without doubt that you wanted me, no lock would keep me from you. No, ...if I knew, I would face hell and condemnation, whatever obstacle attempted to stand in my way to have you. But...as I said, until I know, I am no threat... Goodnight, Christine."

She made no reply, only watched with unblinking eyes as his shadowed shape faded back into the intruding stream of light and took its illumination. Fantasy dimmed back into the darkness with him.

Christine never locked the door. She simply drifted off to a contented sleep, oddly relieved with his anger and rage. They meant his heart was still hers; if only she knew whether or not she wanted it.

83

Chapter Six

Erik found a peculiar delight in rising at dawn and knowing Christine was once again in his home, asleep in her room as if in the place she truly belonged. She had chosen to stay, and despite every uncertainty and a stubborn Vicomte who felt it equally his right to have her, Erik appreciated his minor victory. She wasn't forcing him away, convinced he'd destroy her. It was definitely a start.

Taking great care, he readied for the day eager to be in her presence once more. Instinct begged him to peek into her room and gaze upon her as she slept, but he did not dare indulge the whim. Not yet... One day soon that luxury must be his, but for now, he kept restraint and instead focused on cooking an elaborate breakfast, determined to give her so many memories that she'd yearn to stay again if only to relive them.

By the time he heard a stirring in her room, anxiety was twisting within him and stealing every pleasant emotion with its voice of doubt. He could awaken to her presence with joy, but would she feel the same? Perhaps she had spent the night terrified he'd return and regretting her decision to stay. The notions built upon each other more and more until he started to believe them. In their clutches, every sound from her room seemed rushed, as though she was impatient to dress and leave. ...Leave and never return, maybe run to her Vicomte and beg his protection from the madman who dared accost her in her bed. ...Oh God, perhaps he'd already lost her!

As the soft creak of an opening door announced her approach, Erik attempted a nonchalant pose on his piano bench, desperately trying to read notes on the pages spread before him. Music suddenly seemed a foreign language. He had to settle on running simple scales, cursing beneath his breath to sound like a novice warming up to play. Why could she make him feel like a fumbling fool with barely a glance?

As she appeared in the doorway, shifting uncomfortably on her feet and as apprehensive as he feared, he abruptly ceased and forced his hands to fist and steady as he sought an aloof façade. "Good morning, Christine. Breakfast is in the dining room. You should eat something before I take you back for your rehearsal."

That was all he said, and his mind insulted every contrived phrase as he pretended to focus on music again, not on *her*. No, ...nothing but a quick glance at her pretty features, at the perfect fit of a lavender gown that defined her curves, at eyes locked on him expecting something more he could not decipher.

She didn't move from her spot, and growing more agitated with every breath, he pushed, "Go and eat, Christine. I won't have you late for your rehearsal."

"And...is that all?" she softly questioned, and his surprise thwarted his mediocre attempt at avoidance as he fully met her stare.

"What more would you like me to say?" he replied sharply. "I'll not fall at your feet, apologizing for my behavior last night if that's what you expected. I do not regret it even if it was a lapse in my better judgment." He anticipated fear, perhaps a touch of anger, not the hurt he received. "Christine, ...what's wrong?"

"We've returned to pretending emotions don't

exist and being distant strangers." The assessment was quiet as her eyes lowered and focused on nervous hands smoothing patterns on her lavender skirts.

"And what would you have me do?" he snapped before he could think better of it. "Would you rather I gush endearments? Fill your ears with every thought in my mind that you would deem unacceptable?"

"Yes," she insisted, lifting eyes again.

"Ah, you want a pathetic lover who vies for your heart even as it dangles miles away," he concluded, "like your dashing Vicomte. Fine then. Instead of making you tolerant to my presence, let me shame us both with my offensive and improper thoughts. Perhaps they will teach you to stop asking for more when you cannot accept it yet."

He paused and this time did not hesitate to let desire leap rampant and dangerous in the gaze that languidly observed her every detail. "Emotion is what you want, but all I feel right now is longing. You are the most beautiful creature I've seen in all my life, and even though I know I am unworthy of you, I still *ache*. It never goes away. And upon your entrance this morning, I yearned to tell you so, to whisper adorations and insist I burn to touch you again. My God, Christine, you are temptation! And to speak such things now makes me pitiable, doesn't it? You claim to want emotion, and now that I've indulged you, I seem as repugnant as any unrequited suitor. Your Vicomte could spout his desires, and if they were reciprocated, they would seem blessings. When my very existence disgusts you, it seems wise to seek companionship first and not pity for the worthless creature that lusts after your every breath. Do you now see why I prefer indifference? You blush and tremble before me and leave me to regret every word."

Blush and tremble, ...did she? Pressing the backs of quivering hands to her cheeks, she felt the heat within her skin. Such details said more than she wanted to reveal. "I didn't realize... But tell me how I should reply. Shall I pick up your role and choose feigned apathy? As if not a single thing you said affected me? You are punishing me with your pretense."

"Punishing? No, punishing would be forcing you to acknowledge my heart every instant we are together."

"How do you know that? How quickly you've decided my innermost thoughts and secrets for me!" Shaking her head, she did not stop herself from admitting, "I told the Vicomte that your idea of love was restraining. It may have been the one truth in a bundle of lies. You've decided how I should feel and why, and I am not permitted to argue."

"You felt *disgust*," he coldly reminded. "I am seeking to avoid the same mistakes again. I had too much faith in you the first time. I was a fool and far too optimistic for my own good. I was so sure the rapport you shared with an angel could be recreated. Now I know it can't be, and I'm seeking to build something substantial, even if that means settling for your tolerance over your love. And so if I choose not to utter my every desire, count yourself fortunate you don't have a pathetic waste, pleading and crying for your heart. Be glad that I *do* practice restraint."

Christine refused to cower to his temper, holding her ground with only shaking hands to tattle the truth. All she spoke in return was, "And if I prefer to denounce restraint, what then? A game of pretending couldn't be enough, you said so yourself. But neither can this. We will always want more."

Biting back any more words, she shared one final, adamant stare before turning and heading for the dining room. Rehearsal waited, and she was yet afraid to push the unstable temperament of the Opera Ghost.

*****

Restraint was practiced on both their parts as he brought her back to her world with only a curt

87

parting and a command to await him for her lesson as soon as the cast was dismissed for the day. She could already guess his train of thought with a memory of an unanticipated visit from a Vicomte the evening before.

This time unanticipated had an earlier curtain call, it seemed, because the instant the cast was given a break for lunch, she noticed the Vicomte lingering in the back of the theatre, seeking to catch her attention.

As she cast him a little wave in reply, Meg grabbed her elbow and softly exclaimed, "One of your heart-struck beaus! He's quite charming, isn't he? It would seem impossible for you to refuse such a man."

She nodded agreement. Refuse Raoul? And for what? The resident phantom who sought to win her heart by keeping her at arm's length unless his temper was involved? Could she truly be blamed for finding appeal in the Vicomte's sweetness? *And yet...* Her gaze wandered the empty theatre for Erik's invisible presence with a twinge of guilt.

"Christine, he's coming onstage!" Meg's excitement forced Christine's attention, and before Raoul could reach them, she clasped Meg's hand tight and kept her from scampering off.

"Oh, Raoul, ...what are you doing here?"

A polite smile was the extent of Raoul's greeting to Meg before he focused solely on Christine. "I've been sick with worry since you left last night. I wanted to make sure you were all right."

Before questions could be asked, Christine quickly filled space with flustered words. "Raoul, this is my dearest friend, Meg Giry."

"Mademoiselle," Raoul properly greeted, and even though his eyes kept drifting to Christine, he spoke with a measure of eloquence, "Christine and I are old acquaintances. I feel so fortunate to have found her once again."

"Oh, I'm not asking, Monsieur," Meg assured with a little giggle. "You do not need to explain yourself. I find it all too adorable."

"But it's true," Christine insisted.

"Yes, we spent our childhood playing pirates and chasing ghosts in my attic." Catching Christine's eye, Raoul grinned so bright that she could not stifle an echo of it upon her own lips.

"More ghosts?" Meg inquired. "I thought your belief in ghosts was recently acquired, Christine. And did any ghosts of your youth hold a candle to the Opera Ghost?"

"Opera Ghost?" Raoul bid, mischievously arching dark brows. "Indeed! So little Christine still plays ghost stories in my absence?"

Christine paled, desperate to hide her rising anxiety as Meg replied, "It's no game, Monsieur Vicomte. The Opera Ghost is *real*. He haunts the cellars and occasionally causes accidents about the theatre. He's dangerous! And anyone who sees him meets a terrible end. You think I'm teasing! Tell him, Christine."

"It's true." Christine tried not to tremble, but unease fell loose as a giggle when Raoul made an unconvinced face. Such an expression on anyone else would have been unpleasant, but he had a way of making it so boyishly attractive.

"Opera Ghost who haunts the cellars?" he dubiously posed. "Well, I say let's hunt him out!"

"No!" both girls shouted in unison, and their outburst only made Raoul chuckle harder.

"You little, scaredy cats!" he taunted. "Come on. You have a break. Let's explore the cellars and hunt for the ghost."

"And risk never coming back?" Meg shrieked with wide, green eyes.

"We'll be together," he countered. "And I promise as the gentleman among us to protect my lady companions. All right? It will be a fun adventure."

Christine continued to regard him as if his suggestion was absurd. Wander the cellars? And what would happen when Erik found them? She had no guarantee he wouldn't *kill* the Vicomte on the whim of his annoyance!

"Christine," Raoul sweetly grinned and captured her hand in his for a quick squeeze, "come on. You don't want to deny me this wonderful excursion, do you? Our ghost hunts as children were fruitless. Maybe this time we'll find something extraordinary."

Extraordinary? She felt inclined to argue, but Raoul still had her hand, encouraging with entwined fingers.

"All right," Meg decided, "if I can face my fears, so can you, Christine. Besides, you've already been in the Opera Ghost's presence, and he didn't hurt you. You said he was only a shadow that night in your dressing room."

"Your dressing room?" Raoul inquired, lifting teasing brows. "And must I vie for your affections with this Opera Ghost as well?"

He chuckled, but Christine never softened her somber expression beneath the weight of the truth.

"Christine?" he pushed, regarding her oddly.

"Let's go," Christine suddenly insisted, desperate to be out of his focus. Agreeing to his absurd game seemed more acceptable than forming more lies. "Let's explore the cellars and find the ghost. You can berate him for haunting my dressing room."

Making light of serious doom... Christine prayed in a terrified mind that Erik was locked below in his home, perhaps engrossed in his music and not watching her. After all, it was *hours* before they were to meet. Maybe a jaunt through the cellars would be enjoyed without a ghost's presence. ...Certainly he couldn't be spying on her all day, could he?

She was already regretting her choice as a flustered Meg led them to the cellar door. No one from the cast or crew lingered about, intelligently

accepting the freedom of a lunchtime break, and
Christine wondered if enough overdone flirtations
could convince Raoul to take her to a café instead of
the dark, cold cellars, chasing deadly phantoms. It
seemed a fool's crusade! Taunting a very real ghost?
People with an ounce of sense knew better than to
dare such a thing!

Meg collected a lantern that hung alongside the
stairwell, and holding it out, she guided them down by
its meager glow, muttering in nervous giggles with
every step. "You best say nothing to my mother about
this."

"Of course not!" Christine agreed. "She would
be more terrifying to face than the ghost if she knew!"

"Indeed?" Raoul glanced over his shoulder and
caught her eye in the dim light. "You girls are an
anxious pair, aren't you? Scared of ghosts? Scared of
mothers? What else do you find frightening,
Christine?"

Matching his wry grin, she decided,
"Enthusiastic Vicomtes." Giggles poured down the
stairs ahead of them, both girls delighting in the
Vicomte's smirk. Their laughter cut the dark and the
reality that the only other sounds were their footfalls
on creaky stairs.

"How humorous you are!" The Vicomte sought
sarcasm, and yet chuckled as he held her eye. "If you
did not make even insults seem something to live up
to, I might be heartbroken right now."

Thankfully, she did not have to form a reply as
they reached the last stair into the first level of cellars.
Everything was forgotten as Meg suddenly grabbed
her hand and squeezed tight, gasping, "Perhaps
...perhaps we should go back."

"But we've only just arrived," Raoul insisted,
taking the lantern from the shaking ballerina and with
it, the lead. "Now you have no choice but to follow if
you can't see your way back up."

Meg let out a little shriek, and Christine

couldn't contain her laughter as she pulled a petrified ballerina after Raoul, calling, "Any ghosts, Monsieur Vicomte? Or will we have to entice the spirits to show themselves?"

Shining the lantern here and there, Raoul glanced between haphazard stacks of boxes and wrinkled his nose with the unavoidable scents of age and dust. "This is unimpressive. I was truly hoping for spider webs and haunted shadows. This is more boring than my attic."

"This cellar is the only one that's used," Meg offered in a small voice. "The others are where no one dares to go."

Raoul lifted a mischievous grin that looked spooky in the dim glow, and Christine chastised herself for finding him appealing, most especially while dragging a terrified Meg behind her.

Without pause, the Vicomte led them to the furthest wall, casting the light ahead to illuminate the entry to another stairwell.

"No, no," Meg muttered, curling tight to Christine's side. "Not good, Christine. The ghost!"

"Oh, no worries, Mademoiselle," Raoul assured. "I shall protect you both to my own demise should any ghosts materialize. You are perfectly safe."

Down again, and the cellar at the bottom of creakier stairs was exactly what Raoul had described: over-laden with spider webs and dilapidated boxes in uneven stacks whose sides were crushed inward from damp decay.

Meg clutched Christine with quivering arms and buried her golden head against her shoulder. "The ghost," she whimpered as Christine gently smoothed her hair.

"Meg, it's all right. Don't worry."

Raoul met Christine's eye with a little smile, and catching Meg's arm, he carefully pried her free. "Stay with me, Mademoiselle. I will deter every ghost from a single look at you. As Christine told you, I played a convincing pirate back in the day, and pirates know no fear. They battle without hesitation and are always brave. I will guard you by the hilt of my swash-buckling sword."

"But a sword can't kill a ghost," Meg whined. "And...you don't even have a sword! You're a Vicomte! You carry nothing beyond a pocket-watch and a handkerchief!"

Making a face, Raoul insisted, "It can be a debilitating pocket-watch if swung with enough momentum. Just trust me, Mademoiselle."

Meg whimpered again, but conceded to let Raoul pull her further into the cellar.

Christine called her own fears ridiculous when witnessing Meg's, and on the verge of giggles, she lifted a hand and disguised them as a cough instead. *Fear?* She was too amused to remember to be afraid!

The light of their lantern created more shadows at the edge of its beams, and as Raoul made a circle to uncover the details of their surroundings, Christine only saw more boxes and the occasional spider. She cringed and kept her distance from their dark, little bodies. Some lolled in their webs, watching the intruders to their domain with a territorial sense of malevolence; she could swear she felt little eyes crawling on her skin.

It happened the instant Raoul stepped ahead with Meg curled to his side, and in some unconscious way, Christine had been expecting it. An arm caught her from behind, slithering about her waist, and a long, white hand splayed flat against her stomach as she was drawn into the darkness. Never a cry left her lips as she felt the erratic beat of his heart, the hard plane of his chest, and she did not hesitate to press back against him and yield to his abduction.

Christine could see nothing once beyond the immediate beams of the Vicomte's lantern, and nerves tensed her limbs and made her shiver with unease. To her surprise, though her abductor uttered no assurance, his free hand rose to tenderly caress her hair. It was the sweetest touch, and she leaned closer to its delicacy. Instinct begged her to touch him back, but before she could dare, he halted their escape and spun her about to face him. He was not even a silhouette in such blackness. She could only *feel* his presence, and nearly gave a cry as he edged her back until she bumped into a stack of boxes. Trapped, and yet willingly so.

Contemplating his intentions left goose bumps along the surface of her flesh and stilled the breath in her lungs. With blinded eyes, she felt his approach, but he only hovered close, his lips lingering above her ear as he rasped out words that made her shudder.

"Erik must practice restraint, but the Opera Ghost...the Opera Ghost knows no boundaries. The Opera Ghost can devour you like a demon of hell and know no remorse. As far as I'm concerned, you brought this upon yourself by wandering the dark with only your noble lover to protect you."

Erik deciphered her every detail, and the reaction she gave to what should have been deplorable and damning surprised and intrigued him. She wasn't cowering, and though she trembled, she inched closer to his body with never a protest.

Pushing temptation, he lifted a hand that only he saw in its awkward shaking, and never blinking for fear he'd miss the disgust he searched for, he grazed a subtle caress along the exposed line of her collarbone. Disgust... But *where* was it? He felt her shiver again and had the softest gasp tickle his ears, but all he heard in its utterance was longing.

"Christine...," he whispered, falling in and out of his own posed game as he desperately sought to understand. A firmer touch along the same path brought a muffled cry, and as he desperately wondered if it was finally in disgust, he bid, "Scream for help. Call your Vicomte to save you from the opera demon. Beg him to come and stop me from touching you."

Determined to show her malice, he grabbed her wrists, yanking them behind her and binding them in one of his larger hands against the small of her back. And *still* she gave no struggle! He was astounded, wondering if fear kept her silent. ...But he couldn't find fear either!

"Christine, beg me to stop," he commanded. The hand at her back jerked her against his body and bluntly insisted the potency of his desire. "Dub this an abomination, and call for your Vicomte."

"No." It was only a whisper into shadows. "Don't stop, Erik."

Every breath trembled in his lungs as he gazed at her in astonishment. Slow and careful despite the dark, his free hand discarded his mask, tossing it away unneeded and exposing lips that ached so badly to taste her.

A kiss... He pondered how desperately he yearned for such a trivial intimacy, stating to his rampant paranoia that she was ignorant to his scars. Blackness washed them away, and he wondered if she had forgotten their presence. As if *he* had such a luxury! Hide them away, and they didn't exist. He couldn't bear the idea of kissing her blind when light's intrusion would steal pleasant sensation and return disgust.

Instead, he settled for tasting skin, and with only the slightest hesitation, he bent and followed her collarbone with delicate, uncertain kisses. Every one was a light grazing, and yet she whimpered and arched closer. How amazing it was to know *he* was causing such a response!

He lingered at the hollow of her throat, daring to let his impatient tongue free to steal a quick taste. He wanted more, *so much* more, and yet as expected, the moment shattered.

"Christine! Where are you?"

The frantic calls were a distance away, far

enough that earlier attempts had gone unheard and unheeded, but they were now undeniable. As expected, he felt Christine go rigid against him and drew back to watch her eyes widen with reality's return.

"Are you now prepared to shout for help?" Erik taunted sharply as disappointment stung him. "Sense returns, and this is a transgression once again, and you are ready to denounce *me* for everything *you* feel. But recall this through modesty's little chastisement..."

His gripping hand at the small of her back forced her flush to his hardness as he purposely arched against her and gasped, "I've *never* wanted *anything* as I want you. This is not some fleeting attraction as your darling Vicomte would claim. This is eternal."

"Christine!"

With an angry huff, Erik released her and collected his mask to hide what could only be undesirable behind its shield. His eyes studied her as she quivered and wearily leaned against dusty boxes.

"Christine! Where are you?"

Scuffling footsteps and a lantern's glow were growing near, but Christine made no attempt to announce her presence, still huddled in the dark with arms that crept to hug herself. Erik knew he could not leave her there with only a hope the Vicomte would find her. One last look to tide himself over, and creeping back, he shoved a large box and listened to it topple before he disappeared from the rushed approach of revealing light.

Lurking as constant guardian, Erik heard the grateful cries of Meg Giry. He peered from between boxes and watched that damn Vicomte cup Christine's cheek and search her eyes.

"Are you all right?" he demanded urgently. "Why did you venture off in the dark?"

"Was it the ghost?" Meg frantically bid, jerking

Christine's sleeve with shaking hands.

"Of course not," Christine stammered. "I...I thought I saw a mouse."

"And you ran *into* the dark?" Meg doubtfully asked.

But Raoul did not question as he tucked his arm about her shoulders. "My poor girl! You're shaking so hard! So you'll chase ghosts wholeheartedly, but rodents scare you? Oh, my sweet girl!"

Rage twisted in Erik's gut to watch her, a part of the Vicomte's embrace and without complaint for it. No, she *allowed* and even *leaned into* him, and it took every bit of effort Erik possessed not to give them a real ghost to fear. How dare she!

It was pure torture to let them leave without consequence or at least another story to add to the library of Opera Ghost tales, but the idea of having to witness Christine play the role of scared and cowering from him yet again held absolutely no appeal.

Damn that foolish, meddling Vicomte! His presence gave Christine an excuse and an escape from the valid emotions in her heart. And what were Erik's options? He couldn't kill the boy and give Christine another reason to push him away. Idle threats would make the Vicomte appear a hero. Stealing Christine away for good would make her hate Erik. His only course was to win her heart legitimately before the Vicomte stated his claim. What a torturous path for a man who preferred control! This was chance and hope, and dear God, it made his stomach sick with merely the consideration that in the end, she could choose the Vicomte and Erik could lose her forever. *Vulnerable*, this was so very vulnerable, and Erik despised every second of it!

In the world above the cellars, Christine sighed relief when sunlight pouring from the rooftop windows chased shadows away and bathed her in its protection. Before she had a moment to clear her head, Raoul caught her hand and demanded her focus.

"I will come for you at the end of rehearsal and take you to supper. How does that sound?"

"But I have a lesson-"

"Nonsense! As if I'd leave you here alone in an opera house full of ghosts and your mysterious teacher! I'm sure you could miss one lesson, and after this, I'll talk to your teacher if you'd like." Abruptly changing his mind, he asserted, "I'll find you a *better* teacher, the best money can buy. Then I won't need to worry over your safety. I know you have an affinity for your current teacher, but if he's overstepped boundaries, it seems foolishly naïve to keep humoring him simply because you respect his talent. I promise, Christine. I'll get you the best teacher in Europe. All right? And I'll meet you here after rehearsal. No frowns. This is for the best. You'll see."

Before she could argue, the Vicomte released her, rushing off the stage and out of the theatre. She wondered if he knew she was a breath away from declining his every invitation.

"Oh, Christine," Meg bid as she crept closer. "Well, ...he's dashing. I'll grant you that. And he genuinely cares about you. All wonderful points in a potential suitor...if that's what *you* want, of course."

"*He* is convinced it's what I want," Christine replied, still staring after him.

"And it's not? I mean he *is* a Vicomte. It's astounding he's jeopardizing his reputation to come here and be seen speaking with us." As if memory just caught up with her, Meg's green eyes widened, and she gushed, "And he protected *me* from the ghost! Oh my goodness! He had his arm around me! Just wait until I tell Jammes! She's going to be so jealous! I mean...well, of course, he's *yours*, Christine, but to even be able to say I *touched* a *Vicomte*!" She broke off with an excited squeal.

"And you recall that *now*? He explored the

cellars with you practically attached to his side, and you only remember it after the fact?" Christine demanded with an unavoidable giggle.

Meg made a face. "Well, of course, I was too petrified to think straight! You had me looking for *ghosts*, Christine!" she whined. "You know how that affects my temperament! In fact, I practically repressed the whole scene already, never to be remembered or recalled under penalty of an episode of anxiety. I'm going to forget every unpleasant detail and only remember the ones I like. And...can I tell Jammes about the Vicomte," she sighed, "*touching* me? Please!" She caught Christine's arm and bounced up and down in her anticipation.

"Of course," Christine decided. "All the better. The less ties Raoul has solely to my name, the safer for us all. Leave the gossipers confused over the Vicomte's intended target. It might preserve my reputation." In her mind, she added that it also might quell some of Erik's suspicions. Even if she was yet unsure she wanted to rid herself of Raoul's presence, if murmured gossip left doubts, she might be saving herself. ...And now if she only knew how to handle two suitors expecting her company at rehearsal's end. That problem was far trickier to solve!

Chapter Seven

The stage director, Monsieur Reyer, was giving his final notes for the day when Christine noticed Raoul slip into the back of the theatre. Careful to remain an anonymous body in the crowd, she crept alongside Meg, who arched knowing brows.

"Distract him," Christine quietly begged. "I have to go to my lesson, and he can't possibly understand that."

Meg's green eyes lit. "Does that mean you've made a choice, Christine?"

Had she...? She quickly shook her head. "No, I just prefer to keep the peace. Between the two of them, my teacher is the one who would react hastily if I abandoned our plans."

Her words, though carefully chosen, still inspired Meg's worried suspicion. "What do you mean? He'd be...upset with you?"

"He puts my education first," Christine assured, "and one does not simply skip a lesson to have supper with a Vicomte if one wants to sing lead roles on the stage. Now *please*, Meg, keep Raoul busy long enough for me to get away."

Reyer waved a final cue to end, and as Christine waited with desperate eyes, Meg nodded concession. With a quick squeeze of hands, Meg headed for the edge of the stage through the dispersing throng while Christine rushed the opposite direction toward her dressing room. Anxiousness made every step barely touch the ground, convincing her that Raoul would be only seconds behind despite Meg's best devices. It was with a sigh of relief that Christine closed herself inside, locking the door with abrupt and shaking fingers.

"Don't bother."

Flipping about, she came face to face with an open mirror and a furiously pacing Erik, his eyes gleaming fire from behind the mask the instant they settled on her.

"Erik, I...came as soon as rehearsal ended as you wanted. You have no reason to be angry."

"Oh, don't I? And yet tell me, how much of you would rather be with *him*? The bastard! Making offers and propositions! A new teacher, the '*best*' in Europe! Is that what *you* want, Christine?"

He halted his steps before her, raging as she fought an instinct to recoil and tried to stand firm. "Please keep your voice down. If he hears you in my dressing room-"

"Oh, we can't have that, can we?" Erik retorted, never any quieter. "Yes, because he will pursue, come to the *locked* door, and hear a *man* in your room, shouting his jealous rant. And he will break the door down, the gallant hero, and come to your rescue from your brute of a teacher. Isn't that so? He will conveniently forget that my current bitter mood is caused solely by his infernal existence and his dared propositions. A new teacher? Damn him! Has he no respect for what I've done for you?"

She could not argue what she agreed with. "I didn't concede to his offer, *ange*. *You* are my teacher; I don't need or want another, even if it is the so-called 'best' in Europe. Erik, ...you are unrivalled as a teacher. Why would I ever want another?"

"As a teacher," he repeated, eyes narrowing on her. "Yes, as a teacher, I am acceptable in your life. Right, Christine? As a *teacher*!"

He muttered a bitter curse beneath his breath that she cringed to overhear and abruptly demanded, "Well, shall we get to your lesson? It might be the only right I have to you, but at least it's something."

Christine gazed at him somberly a long moment, reading a pain he would not share, but all she was granted was a cold gesture to the mirror doorway. Without a word when consolation felt too bold and definite, she obeyed and led the way into the catacombs.

He did not speak during the journey below, and thoughts were all she had for company, memories of an excursion in a cellar. She was unwilling to reveal how they had tormented her during the afternoon's rehearsal. If he had been watching, perhaps he had an idea that her distraction was his fault. She had even missed entrances in her bemused reverie.

Now to be in his company again with dark, inviting shadows at the edges of his dim lantern, she felt haunted by a scene that was almost a dream. His fingers upon her skin, his *lips* upon her skin... One consideration made her shiver.

"Are you cold?" They were the first words he'd said, and they burst the bubble of her fantasy so abruptly that she swayed on her feet. As reality returned, she noted he'd obviously been watching her quite closely, ...close enough to notice her shiver. ...It was a bit disconcerting.

"Cold," she repeated, grounding her wayward mind in the act of speaking. "N...no. I'm not cold."

He regarded her oddly, but shook his head and led her onward.

Christine tried to focus on the present as they arrived at his home and a lackluster lesson. *Focus!* she reminded every time memory threatened. But her eyes were betrayers. They had their own agenda. His hands captivated their stare whenever he played an interlude and left her to fumble entrances. Then as he halted and chastised her mistake, her disobedient eyes kept catching on the shape of his bottom lip and desperately tried to recreate a full image of that mouth, filling in the vision upon the white of the mask.

"Christine!" he snapped once again for attention, and she cringed at her folly.

"I'm sorry!"

"Where is your head? Amateurs perform better than you are tonight," he sharply stated, and embarrassment lit her cheeks pink. "It's that damn Vicomte, isn't it? You are dwelling over *him* and the thought of him waiting and realizing you abandoned him."

"No, I'm not. I-"

"Perhaps you *should* find a new teacher!" he shouted as he slammed shut the score before him.

"No!"

"Discipline! I have told you from the start that music must come first. Before *everything* else, Christine. Before Vicomtes and their charms. Before heartstrings and your little daydreams of happy endings. Before even this nameless game we are indulging between us. And if you dare to stand before me during time that should be spent learning and are too busy regretting choices and fantasizing suppers with Vicomtes to concentrate, then I am through! I will not teach someone who treats their talent like a hobby!"

Christine had no doubt there was far more to his outburst than a few missed entrances, but she simply said in appeasement, "I'm sorry, Erik. You're right. Our time together is precious, and I shouldn't waste a single second."

Her words struck him with their validity. Precious, ...*every* second with her was precious. If only she realized how much! Calming to melancholy, he suddenly inquired with pleas in his eyes, "Will you stay tonight? ...Or are you only too eager to be out of my company?"

She hesitated, and he wondered if she sought words to refuse. "...Yes, I'll stay."

Erik's surprise and gratitude were vivid, but he never drew attention as he simply stated, "Well then...it's been a long day. Go and get some rest."

She nodded and obeyed without protest, and he missed her the instant she was gone, replaying every detail in his mind and becoming lost in regret.

*****

Christine took her time readying for bed once again, enjoying the new sense of home already attached to this place. Home...with a masked Opera Ghost far beneath the earth's surface... Unconventional, but then again if the heart was content, what was the difference? If only things were easy and sense didn't need to become involved and recall truths she'd rather forget.

As she sat before a vanity mirror combing through curls still damp from her bath, heart and sense waged war within her. She was no longer certain which she wanted to win. Sense insisted an incident in the cellars must be a sin and should fill her with terror. Being devoured in utter darkness... A good and modest girl would denounce the very idea, but Christine found herself craving it. It was desire, she had no doubt, but desire at the hands of a disfigured murderer. Yes, reality was the cruel voice that shattered every daydream and created shame to fill the place of longing.

Christine felt as confused as she had been the instant she'd unmasked an angel and started this wayward game, and with uncertainties pirouetting their paths in her mind, she slowly rose and crept out of her room with silent footfalls. Taunting the Opera Ghost was a bad idea to the rational side of her, but when her heart posed instead that she was seeking Erik's company, it seemed satisfactory and wanted.

Timid tiptoes brought her to the sitting room doorway, and staying back in shadow, she peered inside. Erik was pacing fitfully, almost angrily, back and forth in front of the hearth as if fighting his own internal battle. Every so often his churning thoughts surfaced in muttered words that her ears fought to decipher. "She" was the predominant one, and Christine was doubtless what his rant centered upon.

"*Ange?*" she called softly and saw him start and jerk about to face her. It was almost amusing. Had she ever snuck up on the almighty Opera Ghost? ...Well, once, and since a scene of unmasking, he was usually extra attentive and diligent to catch her presence even a mile away.

"You're supposed to be in bed," he sharply replied as an excuse for his failure. But almost immediately, his expression softened as his gaze ran down her body and up again.

She shivered, overcome as she always was when he regarded her in such a manner, and her cheeks flushed pink with one consideration that she wore only her nightdress. White and soft, it felt far too revealing when she was accustomed to layers in between.

"Come in here," he suddenly commanded, and though she hesitated to take a steadying breath, she slowly wandered into the sitting room on legs that shook to hold her weight. Firelight bathed her in its warm glow, but it was not soothing when it meant it also illuminated every detail. She cursed her own foolishness not to have grabbed a wrap.

Forcing herself to remain stable on her feet and endure his intent scrutiny, she sought her composure and asked with a slight waver, "What were you doing? You seemed upset."

"It's nothing to concern you."

"Tell me," she pushed. "Are you still angry with me? ...Or is it something else?"

A sigh left his lips as he hastily faced the fire. He couldn't seem to speak the thought and know she heard, but he finally replied, "I can have you as I wish when darkness is about to hide what you'd rather not recall. How bittersweet is that? As long as you can forget the unacceptable parts, you can be mine. Last night in shadows, today in blackness. But your Vicomte... He comes to the theatre and walks among the cast in broad daylight. He wants to take you to supper in crowded restaurants, beam with delight as you turn heads with your beauty and your laughter, dance with you and hold you close as every other couple watches in envy. His perfect life is my daydream, but I...I have shadows and dank cellars. It hardly seems fair."

Christine watched him and saw hands that fisted and un-fisted at random moments. She wondered if it was intentional motion, preventing impulse when she had no doubt he wanted to touch her. Keeping eyes locked on that denied urge, she softly replied, "And yet I didn't go with the Vicomte to supper. I came home with you."

"Yes," he snapped, "because you were terrified of the consequences if *I* were the one left in the Vicomte's place. Hurt feelings are all you need worry about from a dejected Vicomte, but a dejected Opera Ghost... You said it yourself. I am a murderer and a monster, and you're terrified to incite my rage. ...Terrified. Is that all you'll ever be of me?" He shook his head with feigned apathy and stalked closer to the fire, refusing to look at her. "And I must wonder if that is why you permit what you otherwise call a transgression. My hands upon you... Do you only allow me because you are afraid to deny me? Do you think I will *force* you if you refuse? ...Those are the thoughts that torture me, Christine. They seem to hold validity if you are continuing on with your Vicomte at the same time that you twist my affections about."

"*He* came to see me," she reminded.

"But did you shun him or insist he leave?" he retorted in a growl, spinning about to face her again.

"No! You smiled at him! The perfect coquette! And you brought him into the cellars as if to flaunt it to me. To make it clear *exactly* what you were doing."

"I don't *know* what I'm doing," Christine suddenly admitted. "Raoul is my friend. I don't want to hurt him."

"But you don't denounce his illusions of love either. You allow him to think he has a chance to win your heart, and you use his presence to hurt *me* instead!"

"Erik," she softly bid, fighting a rise of tears.

Before she could form apologies, he abruptly approached, halting before her with never a dared touch as he begged with frantic eyes. "Tell me why you stay with me, Christine. Why did you consent to remain under this roof? Was it only out of fear to refuse? Have I damaged your heart so much that pity and terror are all it can know for me? ...And my God, am I so delusional and desperate that I've *imagined* desire into existence and made it seem you actually *wanted* my touch in the darkness?" He was shaking in his spot, those hands once again fisted tight, and in a whisper, he asked, "Is fear the only emotion you carry for me?"

That was the only question she could answer with certainty while the rest held too many doubts playing between letters. "No."

Mismatched eyes searched her with wariness, and it bothered her that even her honesty was suspect. She could be candid and sincere, but he couldn't simply believe. Not without proof.

While the question hung in the air and created an unbroken web of tension and idle unease, he surpassed every woven thread and suddenly extended an open hand. Her eyes traced the long smoothness of his palm and every finger with firelight to remind her if she touched, it would be real and not another half-dream in the dark. She'd considered a corpse at first glance of that hand; now she only saw something coveted and wanted, ...the longing hand of a man. Dragging her eyes to his awaiting expression, she stated a silent question of her own.

"Will you dance with me?" he bid, and in that one request, she heard fear. It seemed to take such a well of courage to offer even that mundane desire, and beneath enacted boldness, she saw a timid, little boy, terrified by her very existence. That image made the choice for her.

Holding his eye, she tentatively set her palm against his and did not waver even as he closed his fingers about hers in an unbreakable hold.

Erik was unable to stop the shiver that raced his limbs, certain she felt its reverberation, but he gently drew her to the open space before the hearth. Slow and unconfident in every motion, he guided her closer. How odd that in darkness he could act without trepidation and assume the persona of the Opera Ghost to fill his own inadequacies, but here with her eyes on his, knowing she acted willingly and not blindly, he was reminded that aside from fleeting embraces, he'd never held her tenderly, never with the depth of his adoration in plain sight. And never had he danced; it was another mystery in a life full of denials.

Near enough that her scent teased his nostrils, he nervously rested his free hand at the curve of her waist and shuddered to feel its perfect shape with barely a barrier in between. He was overcome, and as she set her little hand upon his shoulder and branded him through clothing and skin, imprinting on bone, he stifled an urge to cry. A willing touch, ...un-coerced. Even in its miniscule contact, he felt wanted.

With unhurried steps, he began to lead her in a dance. It was without pattern, no set beat or distinctive meter, and yet every movement was graceful as a waltz or minuet. A dance, ...no, an excuse to hold her as the Vicomte would have done. A conventional and allowed embrace in a room full of people, and while Erik had to settle for an underground kingdom with no one to spy, was it not a better situation? Only he and Christine as she let him act the way a normal man would and learn the pleasures of life offered to the fortunate.

Daring to push his fantasy, he asked, "What would you say if I made a similar proposal to your Vicomte's? What if I asked you to go to supper in a restaurant amongst Paris' finest patrons?"

She tilted her head thoughtfully, and he was captivated to watch her dark curls stir and tumble over her shoulder. "Is that truly what *you* want, or would you only ask because that was what *he* wanted?"

"Existing in public, daring to walk among the masses. Would you dub me a liar if I said *I* wanted such a thing?"

A furrow lined her smooth brow, and he yearned to touch it and learn how it felt against fingertips. "I have been granted the impression that you are not fond of the general public."

He could tell she was choosing her words carefully, afraid to stir his temper. But he only gave a light chuckle and watched her eyes widen in astounded surprise. "And why would you think that? Perhaps because I spent so many days behind your mirror, gazing from afar, watching you from shadows about the opera house, and now I choose to abduct you to the underground to share your company?"

She did not reply, only continued to stare through bewildered eyes, and Erik conceded to admit, "I am not fond of the general public. I am accustomed to too much cruelty, bitterness, and violence to think any better of the world. But...there is an appeal to suffering its snares with you at my side. Then I think they wouldn't hold as much sway." He studied the features of her face again, savoring every finely-shaped nuance. "Well? Would such a request be listed another abomination? In that world, they'd stare at us, Christine, whisper obscenities behind fake smiles and pretended tolerance, perhaps even toss insults. With your Vicomte, you would be a source of envy; ...with me, you would only be pitied."

Meditative again, the furrow did not leave her brow until she decided, "I don't want to be envied. I'd have to play a part to endure it. But pitied...? Then I could be myself and prove through smiles and happiness that I am not a case to be pitied at all."

Her words inspired his hope, but rather than speak it aloud, he gently drew her closer, a dance now no more than forgotten footsteps. "But...would you be strong enough to suffer such condescension? You who cannot even endure the beating of my heart against yours? How would you face the world at my side?"

Christine knew he sought assurances, but rather than granting words that felt too binding, she softly said, "Teach me to be that strong."

"Love me, and it won't matter."

He said it so simply that she would have believed it an easy task. *To love him...* That seemed the only point worthy of real fear.

She made no reply as heart and sense returned to their battle, building only more uncertainty in their toils. Love him... Her heart wanted that so badly. Her fingers tightened their hold on his shoulder, curling into his jacket as if a fist alone was inseparable. Hold tight to the fantasy, and why did reality have to mean so much?

His gaze roamed her face, still desperate for the answers she would not give, but as his attention halted and locked on her lips, he instead declared, "I want to kiss you. ...Last night, it was a transgression. Will it be the same now?"

"It was a transgression because of who you are," she insisted in a voice that shook as much as every inch of her. "That hasn't changed. You proved it in the cellars. You are the Opera Ghost."

"And you *want* the Opera Ghost," he accused. All halfhearted dance steps ceased, and his arms dared to weave about her waist, his hands digging fitfully into the soft material of her nightdress.

Oh, to feel her! To have her body against his, devoid of layers and corsets, only feminine curves! It made him ache and throb. "Oh, Christine," he breathed, sharing her quivering breaths. "Say it. Tell me you want me."

"Why?" she demanded with a gasp as his restless hands wandered her spine. "It doesn't change anything."

"You want me," he asserted again as his tensed fingers curled in frustrating material and pulled it taut between eager hands.

Christine wanted to deny his words, but her body answered in passionate affirmations, arching nearer as if it recognized its mandatory match. In the release of an exhalation, she breathed, "Why do you make me feel this way?"

"You want me," he repeated as his reason, "and it amazes me! You respond to my touch as if you *crave* it!" Clutching in fists, he guided her to move with him, pressing his one bare cheek to her temple to be tickled by silken curls. "Oh, Christine, let me have you. Please, Christine, just let me love you. It can't be a sin if you allow it. It won't be forced or manipulated. Love me of your own free will."

"But it *must be* a sin," she gasped, and yet she leaned closer and nuzzled her brow to his cheek. "What you make me feel steals sense-"

"Let it," he begged, his restless hands delving into her curls and twining. "How I want you! Christine, ...it is *your* choice. For the first time in my existence, I yearn to rid myself of this infernal mask, but I won't dare if it will make disgust out of desire."

"Desire? Is this desire?" she breathed.

"I will give you so much more," he vowed fervently, rubbing his cheek to her temple again and wishing he could devour skin. "You said it last night. I cannot kiss you with the mask in place, and I *ache* to kiss you. ...I know my face is abhorrent, but I can make you forget. I can give you such passion that the heinousness of my scars won't matter. Please, Christine, ...let me make you burn."

She wanted to succumb. Lord help her, how she wanted nothing more as his claiming hands made paths along her back and kept her flush to his body. Love him... Desire him... She wanted to remove his mask, to form kisses against those misshapen lips, and she hated herself! Good, moral girls wanted vicomtes, not disfigured murderers!

That one thought broke the spell, and so sudden that he had no choice but to release her, she struggled and broke free, creating a distance that felt necessary.

"No," she decided and yet her trembling body contradicted her conviction. "I can't love you, Erik. I can't... Not when I must hate you for the things you've done."

"Hate me?" he posed with a sarcastic chuckle that put her on edge. "How long do you intend to keep lying to yourself and insisting such falsehoods? Hate *me*, you little hypocrite! You hate *yourself* because say what you will, you want me anyway. And it is such a disgrace to you that you will use any excuse to hide your secret."

"No, I-"

"I am not a fool!" he roared, and she shrank back in her place. "I feel you, and you come alive in my arms. It terrifies you, doesn't it? You want what you've always been taught was wrong. Good girls don't desire opera demons with mangled faces. Isn't that right, Christine?"

It was as if he had taken the thoughts from her mind, and her returned expression proclaimed her guilt. "No, they don't," she agreed. "Can't you understand how this is tearing me apart?"

"*You!*" he shouted and caught her forearm before she could try to escape. "You selfish child! And I am the consequence of your fears and indecision!" This hold was different; it was angry, and in his desperation, he pleaded, "Tell me what you want of me, and I will do it. *Anything*! Do you want explanations, apologies, regrets? Do you want my life story spread before you? What will it take to make this acceptable?"

Tears filled her eyes as she shook her head somberly. "I don't know. Please, Erik, just stop."

"You like this, don't you? Teasing and tempting me to violence and all because of the little game you won't quit playing. Perhaps it amuses you to believe you have the Opera Ghost twisted about your fingers. You have the power, and you're *searching* for a valid reason to fear me."

His eyes bore into her with every bitter accusation; she never denied a single one or flinched as he leaned near enough that if no mask stood in between, he could have kissed her. But his words were daggers instead and made kisses seem an inconsiderable notion. "You can't accept who you are. You are *not* the good, dutiful little girl, daydreaming of vicomtes and mansion houses. No, I have you fantasizing shadows and craving something so much darker that it's unfathomable to admit you want it. And so you will dangle me at arm's length and dally with your Vicomte in the wasted hope that you will one day find him to be enough for you, and we will all suffer for your weakness."

With a suddenness that made her stumble, he released her and coldly commanded, "Go to bed, Christine. I'm tired of playing tonight."

It was as if he dismissed her, and he strode to his chair and threw himself into its stiff cushions with a fixed stare on the hearth. Never another glance, never another word, and Christine was resigned to obey. Perhaps with daylight she'd have a chance to fix things, but now... Too many tensions and unfulfilled desires hung thick in the room to push any more.

In a timid tone, she called, "Goodnight, Erik," and wearily returned to her bedroom. That night she locked the door, but she couldn't decide if it was to keep Erik out or to preserve herself and her dwindling control. For if he came to her, she wasn't sure she'd resist, and with so many bends in the path of right and wrong, regret and guilt must follow.

Chapter Eight

Erik barely spoke a single word as he returned her to the world and left her for the day. Nothing beyond another brusque command to be awaiting his presence at rehearsal's end. Though it stung to know she was the cause of such coldness, she was uncertain how to mend things besides conceding to what he wanted. And she wasn't sure she could do that yet.

He wanted and needed her to be strong, but strength did not seem to be an inherent trait. It was just too easy to cower and seek to please others if strength meant creating ripples in an otherwise smooth pond.

Tortured by her thoughts, Christine could endure little more upon her shoulders, and as if a cruel test of fate, she once again spent her day the scapegoat of La Carlotta's vindictive nature. It was too much, and as the cast was finally granted a break for lunch, she ran to the sanctity of her dressing room and collapsed in tears. Strong meant standing up to the diva who never shed her own tears for her victims. Strong did not mean crumbling beneath the weight of the world; it meant facing it without regret or second thought. Why couldn't she do that?

"Christine..."

Like a scene from the past, he was only a voice that floated through the room and immediately soothed her with merely the sound. A girl who'd once been naïve had believed the sound came from heaven. Knowing better now, she locked her eyes on her reflection in the mirror's glass and fantasized images of masks instead of halos.

"What happened, *petite*?" the voice called so temptingly, and as every golden letter raced the surface of her skin, she could not suppress a shiver.

"Nothing...nothing. Are you going to come out? I must be back to rehearsal soon." Swiping leftover tears from her cheeks with the backs of her hands, she fought to portray the strength everyone wanted, and yet all she saw staring from the mirror was a façade. Evidently, pretending strength wasn't as valid as genuinely feeling it.

"Tell me what happened, lest I devise heinous details and torment myself. If someone hurt you... If this is because *I* hurt you..."

The amount of self-loathing in his tone shattered her halfhearted bravado, and tears tumbled anew. "Oh, no, no, Erik, this isn't... I mean you didn't hurt me."

"Then please tell me, Christine." He paused before quickly insisting, "Here is your game of pretend. Even if it isn't real, you once spoke so candidly to an angel with never a fear of consequence. Speak the same now. Pretend nothing has changed...at least for a minute, and tell me what happened to upset you."

He'd won her over with merely the concept. How she missed an angel that had never even existed! It was so wanted to play the game that she readily complied. "It was...La Carlotta. She enjoys making me miserable, but this time it was too cold and spiteful to bear." Hesitating only a breath, she kept eyes on the mirror when heaven seemed ridiculous and told him the story and its every humiliating facet.

"We were being fitted for costumes. I was being measured when Carlotta came in for her turn, and...she laughed at me. We're fitted in only our

undergarments for accuracy, of course. She looked
me over head to toe and insisted before all the others
awaiting their turn that I was such a little girl. And
how could any man, especially a Vicomte, want me
when I bore no womanly curves or graces? She said
the stagehand boys are more endowed than I am.
Everyone laughed, and I...I was so embarrassed. I
couldn't even get dressed and end her tirade because I
was still being measured. I had to stand there,
exposed while they all laughed and listened to
Carlotta insult my every feature."

She ducked her head as her skin flamed pink
and let her curls cling to her cheeks, feeling ridiculous
to have told him.

"Insult you?" Erik demanded back doubtfully.
"Such things spoken by the squealing pig herself!
Really, Christine! Not a single word out of her
oversized mouth holds any ounce of credence. She
delights in preying on those weaker than she is
because she knows you won't fight back. You need to
be strong-"

"Strong," she interrupted in a shout, abruptly
tucking her curls behind her ears. "Strong, strong,
strong! That is all you can say! The world wants me
to be strong; *you* want me to be strong! Perhaps I am
not built that way."

"Christine." His voice softened, and she caught
a hint of amusement. "You are stronger than you
realize. It is there with such potential to be something
great if only you'd let it. How quickly you forget that
you conquered a legitimate fear already to stand face
to face with the Opera Ghost everyday. *That* is
strong!"

Shaking her head sadly, she reminded, "But I'm
not strong enough to give you want you want."

"Well, ...not yet," he conceded, and with a huff,
declared, "I am impatient. I want too much too
quickly and don't praise you for minor victories. You
tolerate my presence without cowering. That alone is

a feat most could never match. *That* takes strength."

"But what Carlotta said-"

"No," he interrupted inarguably. "Strength means confidence, Christine, and that is one point you often lack. You need to be convicted in what you know to be true and not let pettiness sway you." As he paused, she envisioned him in her mind's eye and could practically see him shake his head with his disappointment. "But that's just it, isn't it? You *believe* her. For as callous a woman as Carlotta is, you hold a modicum of respect for her. After all, she reigns in the place you dream to be. And so, she tears you apart at every turn, and you have an unqualified fear she's right."

Lowered eyes were enough to tell him that he was right, and he sighed. "Christine, ...my God, you truly are naïve. Carlotta is sick with jealousy for every detail of you. Why don't you see that? ...Shall I fill your ears instead with what *I* see when I look at you? Surely my opinion is more important than hers. You once so diligently clung to every praise I granted. My assurance gave you the confidence you needed for the premiere. If I transform her cruelty, will you make my words be your sense of truth?"

Part of her questioned what could come from it, but she dutifully nodded and fought to forget it was anyone but her beloved angel speaking to her. Not a man with skin and bone, with arms to hold and lips to kiss. No, a cherished angel who reverently adored with never an insistence for a more she could not give.

On a held breath's exhalation, that golden angel's voice said, "You are the most beautiful woman I've ever seen in all my life. Every detail is perfection. How often I just stare and marvel over you! Every expression that crosses your face, every gesture and movement you make. Your very existence is a wonder to me. And you dare let that woman tell you otherwise! Listen to one who...loves you instead. Because I look at you and see my dreams brought to life. ...Is any of this making an impression upon you? Do you believe what I say?"

'*One who loves you...*' Her mind stuck on those meager syllables and every meaning they held beneath. Of course he'd said such things before, but to truly forget every other detail and listen to him speak about her as is she were something exquisite... She had only dreamed such words from an angel's lips. Now to remind herself there was no angel felt like a disappointment all over again.

In a small voice, she replied, "I believe you, ...Erik." Not '*ange*'. No, there was no angel. There was a man, and he wore a mask and hurt people on his whim...

"Do you?" he inquired doubtfully. "You're still sad. Carlotta is not worth tears."

She did not correct his assumptions; she simply let the tears fall. Let him think Carlotta had broken her heart...

"Well, let me finish," Erik insisted. "She dared to mock your body, and that is distasteful and malicious. You *know* such things are not true. My God, you feel it every time I hold you. It isn't as if I can hide it. I desire you. I'm unashamed to admit that I barely have to look at you, and I want you." Intimate musings, and he seemed at ease to speak them when out of her line of sight. Their powerful reverberations tainted his voice with a hinted huskiness, and in spite of the shy blush on her cheeks, she silently savored every word. "Last night when I held you... Oh, Christine, you were so soft and warm against me. I traced your curves, and I dubbed them as mine. I burn merely to imagine touching them again. ...Will you not put such truths above the ranting of a jealous diva? I am a man who desires you and aches to know and possess your every detail. That must mean more."

It did, but she didn't tell him, trembling with the intensity of his implications. Love, desire, and she was suddenly terrified. She played a dangerous game with the Opera Ghost, and here was her proof that it was no game at all.

"Christine?" he questioned when she had yet to reply.

"I...I have to return to rehearsal." A meager excuse, but she was suddenly desperate for air.

"Are you all right? ...I've upset you," he concluded somberly, and she did not lie and claim he was wrong as she smoothed her skirts and wiped away tears.

"May I ask you a question, and will you answer honestly?" she demanded instead even as her heart begged to keep silent.

"Of course."

"After what I told you, ...are you planning your own punishment for Carlotta?"

Hesitation, uneasiness, and finally, he justified, "She needs to be put in her place. That infernal woman has a way of overstepping the boundaries any decent human being possesses, and if not for me, she'd get away with it. No one else will dare speak against her."

"If not for you...," Christine sadly repeated as the pieces came together in her mind. "And the last time? It wasn't an accident. You did it. You dropped that set piece and frightened her off so that I could sing the premiere." With a desolate shake of her head, she insisted, "You could have killed her."

"Nonsense! If I had intended to kill her, she'd be dead. I don't make mistakes. That was only a little trick."

He said it with disregard and no regret, and she flatly demanded, "And this time? Would her transgression warrant death? She hurt me, and you claim to love me. Is that how you'd justify murder?"

"Perhaps not murder. Perhaps another warning, but my patience only goes so far with heartless divas who have no talent worth preserving.

Her death would be no great travesty. Why are you denouncing my methods? You were just in tears from her villainy. One would think you'd be grateful if I defended you."

"Defended? …You speak of murder as if it means nothing," she gasped. Without a mask before her to make threats, she forgot how easy it was to light the fuse of his temper. "It is a *sin*, Erik, and you hold no remorse for its inception. You forget that you are not God. You don't have the right to choose who lives or dies and punish insolence because you are upset. Forgiveness and tolerance, that is what we are taught. That is what makes a humble heart and a pure soul."

Scoffing his disagreement, Erik retorted, "And what makes a flawless face, Christine? What magic quality do I lack that transforms reality? You so quickly cast off what you can't possibly understand. I feel I have a right to enact my own vengeance if the need arises. Call it compensation for too much of a life endured as a victim. I was broken and destroyed by all those humble hearts and pure souls you speak of. How innocent you are to the cruelty of mankind! The vast majority of this world does not practice tolerance or forgiveness, at least not for someone who does not fit the mold of what a human being must be and must look like. I am a monster, and humanity punishes me for it. If I fight back, I feel it is warranted. I *will not* crumble to their brutality again!"

"Do what you will, but don't presume to act in my name," she insisted, trying to sound convicted, but his words affected her façade. It hurt her to imagine the injustices he'd suffered, and her own compassion felt like a sin when she was letting it validate murder. "I don't want you to hurt Carlotta."

"A warning," he insisted, "an accident to remind *her* to be tolerant. If I do nothing, it leaves her prone to continue. It isn't as if *you* will seek retribution; you would rather be her victim again and again."

"You don't know that." Standing tall and straightening shoulders, she decided, "You insist I must be strong. Well, let me learn, and stop fighting battles for me. It is not your responsibility."

"Christine, I want to protect you. Why is that a sin?"

"Don't. If you care for me as you say, then you'll leave Carlotta be. I will not be your excuse for your transgressions."

Before he could argue it further, she hurried for the door and fled her dressing room. Part of her was afraid he'd open the mirror, and she was suddenly anxious with the thought of being in his presence. He'd just admitted to thoughts of murder not a few minutes after he'd reverently spoken words of love and desire. He could make sin sound acceptable, and her conscience swelled with guilt for wanting to believe him.

Consequences were not being considered; all she could think was that she'd suffocate if she didn't break free. A note slipped to one of the stagehand boys while she awaited her entrance in the wings, a coin to deliver it in secrecy, and a rendezvous was arranged before she could dub it a mistake. She never second-guessed, not as rehearsal ended and she fled like a fugitive into the night, not as she ran and purposely molded into the crowd on the Paris streets, not even as she inconspicuously headed for a brightly lit café instead of a home in the dark underground. Part of her wondered if Erik would figure out her plan and find her despite her attempts to remain unnoticed; part of her didn't care.

"Christine!" Raoul rushed from where he'd been lingering beneath the café's awning to meet her. Before she even uttered a greeting, she clasped his hands and yanked him inside, out of the open watch of strangers. "Christine, what is it? You seem anxious."

Anxious? She felt *terrified* and anticipating a doom that must follow, but she feigned a weak smile and bid, "I'm glad you came."

"Of course! I was elated to receive your note!" His smile was genuine. "But if it were up to me, I would have taken you to the finest restaurant in Paris and not a simple street café."

"Oh..." She glanced about their rustic surroundings and then at Raoul's grimace of distaste, and declared, "You'd be too well recognized in a restaurant. Here...well, we can be anyone we'd like and no one would know better." The excuse was equally hers. To be someone else, ...someone who knew the right path and did not crave the touch of a sinner as if it were the route to salvation instead of damnation... "Come on. Let's find a table...away from the windows, if that's all right."

"Whatever you wish," he breathed, grin only growing as he led the way to a vacant table.

Supper was pleasant enough. Christine found that if she did not allow her mind to wander and think of Erik awaiting her, upset with her, hurt by her abandonment, she could enjoy Raoul's company as if he were all that mattered. Why couldn't he be? This was simple. This was a fairytale romance most girls could only dream to have as their own, and if she only lived for the moment, she could almost pretend she wanted it.

As supper plates were cleared and they sat together with cups of coffee, Raoul studied her, finally letting his concern shine through. "You haven't said much. I've done most of the talking, and while most gentlemen appreciate a rapt audience, I enjoy being your equal far more. So...tell me what is truly the impetus for this clandestine meeting away from windows. As much as I'd like to simply delight in it, I know better, and it's bothering me to consider you arranged this to avoid being somewhere else."

Her breath deflated her lungs and her

halfhearted façade with it. "My lesson," she filled in for him. "I was supposed to be there right at rehearsal's end, and instead, I snuck away."

"And I'm grateful. You know how I feel about this teacher of yours. I worry with every thought of your time spent with him."

Raoul's version of protectiveness was as jealousy-based as Erik's, and yet Christine wasn't sure his brand of revenge would ever include sin and murder.

"Erik won't hurt me," she vowed to unspoken implications. "He loves me."

"You told me before that his love is controlling."

"It can be," she admitted, "but he knows no better. It scares him to leave things be as they are and not narrate the story."

"But," Raoul grew solemn as he posed, "do you love him, Christine?"

"I don't know," she answered honestly. "Sometimes I think I could, but then my mind reminds me all over again how impossible it must be. To truly love him... He...he's done terrible things. It's difficult to forget them when forgetting means condoning sin."

"Christine," he sighed and caught her hand in his, entwining fingers upon the table. "I am not going to pretend it doesn't bother me to hear you speak of another man. I care for you; it isn't as if I've ever tried to hide it. If I knew this man was worthy and he was what you wished, I would step back and let you be, but to hear your words and know he has a tainted past leaves me certain I can't allow you to go to him without a fight of my own. You deserve better than that."

Shaking her head miserably, tears rimmed her eyes as she admitted, "I'm so confused; it is ripping my soul apart. I once knew what I wanted without a single doubt in my heart, and then without permission, my world turned upside down and nothing makes sense anymore. ...I can't give him up; there are too many ties that hold us together. To sever them might destroy us both."

"I think you're afraid to give him up," Raoul decided for her. "To walk away would mean to be stronger than you can be alone."

Strong again... Christine resented him for his words. It was the exact opposite of Erik's claim. Erik believed *she* could be strong; Raoul seemed to think she needed *him* to make her strong. In a way, it was insulting.

"I...I should go," she suddenly declared and yanked her hand free of his grasp.

"And what will you do? Will you run back to him at first chance and beg forgiveness? Christine, please stay away from him. This man is a sinner by your own words, and if he has hurt others, he could hurt you as well. I only want you to be safe."

Though his sincerity was real, she did not doubt he wanted more than that. It was written with the affection in his kind blue eyes.

The slightest smile tugged her lips as she suddenly asked, "And what if I told you that the Opera Ghost was in love with me? Would you call me crazy, or would you seek to protect me from ghosts equally as gallant? You can't fight every threat for me, especially when sometimes like ghosts in the shadows, the threat isn't even real."

"You and your friends are a bit preoccupied with notions of ghosts. Ghosts may not be real, but gentlemen with sinful pasts and evil intentions are. You foolishly discredit one in playing games with the other. We're not children anymore, Christine. Not every person in the world is good just because you hope they are." One hand rose to brush a fond caress across her cheek, and she did not pull away. "I wish I could preserve your innocent view of the world, but I'm also afraid if you don't learn otherwise, you're going to be hurt before I can save you."

She didn't tell him that her innocent view already bore cracks inspired by a faux angel and his guise. No, she just permitted his touch and once again considered how warm his fingers always were, warm and inevitably strangers to her skin when their caress felt empty.

Raoul walked her to her apartment. It took a concentrated effort not to insist on returning to the theatre instead, but part of her was doubtless once out of Raoul's gaze, she would end there anyway. How could she not as her betrayal sank in and reminded her that no matter excuses of fear or reservations, Erik must only be hurt?

Raoul held her arm like a gentleman suitor the entire trek, and she didn't protest. It was normal and yet uninspiring. Perhaps if every encounter with Erik had not taught her to want something more, then this comfort with Raoul would have been enough to please her. But...she couldn't help but wonder where the sparks were, the anticipation, the tingle beneath the skin without even a contact to ignite it. Why had she ever learned such sensations? And why were they for the wrong man?

As Raoul halted and prevented an immediate escape outside her door, he said, "I don't want to push you, Christine, but I must take it as fate that the little girl who once fascinated and thrilled me reappeared in my life. But...in the end, it's your choice, and if you want me to step back and leave you be, I will. Is that what you want?"

But that meant choosing Erik without doubt or hesitation, without undiminished trepidation. His idea of winning her heart was to murder every adversary. The Opera Ghost, she wasn't certain she was brave enough to love him or that she'd ever be.

Attempting a smile, she sincerely admitted, "I don't want you to leave me for good, Raoul. Everything else may yet be a blur, but I do know that."

Despite the ambiguity of her answer, he took it optimistically, and with only a brief pause to watch her reaction, he slowly leaned close. Her heart shrieked at her to duck away, but...it was just so *ordinary*. Once again she was caught in the illusion of what should be and what was right, and lost in its false fantasy, she stayed in place and waited with a modicum of curiosity.

His lips barely touched hers, a grazed kiss, but...they were warm, and warm seemed to mean *wrong*. One single brushed kiss, and before she dwelled on the fact that she felt *nothing* inside, better judgment insisted he kissed her with no barrier. There was no mask that needed to be removed because ordinary men did not wear masks. They could indulge in a kiss without a million other implications attached. It could be so simple.

As Raoul drew away and met her intent stare, he softly bid, "I apologize if that overstepped my boundaries, but...you're so beautiful, Christine. It's hard to recall propriety when every instinct I have tells me to kiss you."

She did not scold his behavior. She merely gave a slight smile and concluded their indiscretion, "Goodnight, Raoul."

"Goodnight, Christine."

With a quick squeeze of his hand, Christine slipped within her apartment building and closed him out, relieved the instant she heard retreating footsteps. Guilt choked her with its overwhelming power, striking her heart and strangling its blood supply until she felt dizzy and sick with shame.

But she never had the opportunity to succumb. An arm suddenly caught her about the waist, and a hand clamped over her mouth, ...a *cold* hand. Shivers, tingles, bolts of lightning raced her spine and electrified the surface of her skin with its contact. She did not struggle, almost crying out in relief as he drew her back against the hard wall of his chest.

"Sshh," Erik bid against her ear, and she lost a gasp with the delicious tickle of his breath. "Not a sound. If one scream calls that Vicomte back here to play savior, I will kill him in front of you without a qualm."

There it was, the danger that frightened her, and even though she would have conceded without a threat, she now conceded with a twinge of fear and hated him for inspiring it.

Lifting her gracelessly, he brought her to her apartment door and stole inside. She pondered how long he'd been awaiting her return, long enough to find a way to surpass locks, long enough to turn up lanterns that had been unlit for days spent underground, ...long enough to potentially spy a kiss under the moonlight.

Erik released her in the center of the small one-room space, and as he backed away, his eyes shot fire and venom through a single glare. "Well?" he demanded coldly. "Where are the heartfelt apologies and tears? Unless you aren't penitent. Was all of this an intentional means of cruelty on your part?"

"No, of course not, I wanted-"

"You wanted to continue to keep the Vicomte from losing interest for the day you decide to run heart-first into his arms."

"He's just a friend-"

"Friend!" Erik spat. "And do friends indulge in parting kisses? ...You let him kiss you, Christine, as if it were the most natural thing to do. While I...," he trailed off with a huff of self-loathing before admitting in pain-laced tones, "I wanted to believe it wasn't real, an illusion my mind created to torture me with what I want and can't have. But no, ...it was *real*, and you allowed him to kiss you. From my vantage point, it looked like perfection: a beautiful woman, a handsome gentleman, sharing the pleasures of first love. The storybook ending."

Rage became desolation, and Christine's heart

ached in reply. "Yes," she finally agreed, "and with Raoul, it is mundane. It's easy. I never need worry he will make me a casualty of his temper. I'm not afraid of Raoul..."

"Is that it?" he softly inquired as tentative steps brought him closer. "As if you mean *nothing* if you aren't the pretty porcelain doll ready to bend to my whims." Shaking his head, he demanded sharply, "Are you afraid I'll force you? That I'll become desperate enough to steal what isn't mine? ...I put up walls, and you denounced my restraint. Now I destroy them at their very foundation, and you run to another man. What is the answer? What do *you* want?"

"I don't know," she insisted.

"It must be ideal to have a Vicomte to hang upon your every word and promise you stars and moon if only you'd have him. How amusing that he can appeal to you as a man and within days, assume kisses and caresses when I spend months as your only ally and am subject to suspicion at every attempt. You forewent your lesson tonight to be with *him*," he snapped. "You snuck out of the theatre as if the devil himself were after you, nipping at your heels, and you deceived me with your cruel, inconstant heart. So what am I to do? Hate you for it? Leave for good and never return? Should I wring apologies from your lips and hope to God they are not lies? Tell me, Christine. How long do you intend to punish me for who I am?"

"I'm not punishing you-"

So abruptly that he never gave her the chance to react, Erik caught her shoulders in his tight hands and leaned close enough that she had nowhere to look but his eyes. Blatant and straightly put forth, he asked, "Do you love the Vicomte?"

She turned the question in her mind, and her answer was honest. "No."

"Then why?" The desperation for answers played wildly in his eyes. "You *want* to love him, and you're hoping if you try hard enough, you shall. But love doesn't work that way, Christine. You can't choose what your heart wants. Do you think *I* would have chosen *you* if I had the power of decision in my hands? The selfish child who unwittingly *breaks* my heart at every turn?"

She flinched beneath his words, and yet he refused the tug of remorse with one memory of her arrogant Vicomte. That vision left him to pinch her shoulders tighter in his grasp and pretend it didn't matter when he knew he must be hurting her. "You truly are cruel, Christine. You let him kiss you," he hissed the accusation and did not quell a burst of fire. "As if it was his right to do so! All *I* have wanted and pined for, and you gave it to *him!*"

Every statement increased anger and a grip so fierce that he had the fleeting consideration he'd leave marks. If only they were permanent! But even bruises faded, and what would he have left? Nothing to prove she was his.

"I'm sorry," she softly said.

"Just tell me why," he begged shamelessly. "Why do you run to him? Why am I not enough for you? Let me prove your hesitations are unwarranted. Is this...is this because of my face?" It was the question he was terrified to ask and endure an answer, and when she tried to look away, he felt certain what it meant. "No, look at me. So the Opera Ghost and his tainted life scare you, but not nearly as much as his mangled face. Is that so, Christine? The Vicomte is allowed to kiss you, but his lips are perfect. Mine are an abomination in comparison."

He expected to be correct. It surprised him when she grew adamant. "You make me sound so petty as if your face alone defines you in my eyes."

"Doesn't it? You cowered from it, Christine. You were terrified and disgusted, and you still carry its heinous image in your mind. One mention of a kiss from these lips, and you pale and shudder. I am only good enough when my face is covered from sight." ...Covered from sight and hidden away, and he suddenly commanded, "Close your eyes."

"Why?"

"Always curious," Erik commented with undeniable affection before insisting again, firmer this time, "Close your eyes."

And though her brow arched in a dubious question mark, she obeyed, and her dark lashes lowered, her lids like curtains dropping at the end of an act and ceasing the play of drama upon the stage.

Erik did not pause. The Vicomte hadn't; why should he? Haste kept the act of removing a mask from holding the significance it otherwise would have. But he was so convicted not to lose his opportunity that when the air touched his scars, he did not dwell on the vulnerability or the sense of baring his innermost soul with its every demented plane. He simply kept the mask clasped in a fist, ready to be replaced if horror appeared, and fixed his attention on full, pink lips and the upturned features of her beautiful face.

It was the answer to his prayers. Erik pressed his lips with their bloated arch and irregular shapes against hers with a suddenness that made her sway on her feet as he clutched tighter to keep her in place. A kiss, and he was so determined to make her feel it that he almost didn't feel it himself. He wasn't confident. Not even acting a role made such an intimacy less of a mystery. He kissed her firm and hard, always questioning in his mind. Could she feel the distortion of his mouth? Was that her only consideration despite his every attempt to make her forget? Was she wishing he'd stop this unacceptable assault? But no! He wanted this; this was *his*, and by God, he was going to claim it.

His lips moved against hers with less pressure, encouraging her to respond. His first kiss, and he was so afraid his inadequacies wouldn't please her that he never took the chance to engrain the sensation in his memory. It was fleeting, and almost suddenly, he jerked away, clamping the mask back in place with hands that shook violently and extended their tremble down every limb as he recoiled, curling into himself as if broken.

"Please, Christine," he begged, keeping fingers fisted to prevent another touch. "Don't denounce this. Don't break my heart in your callous hands."

Christine didn't want to open her eyes. Why face reality when the dream was so exquisite? She felt altered inside and thrown from any stability she'd ever had. A kiss, a simple token of affection, and she felt as if it had changed every aspect of her life.

But she finally looked and saw the desperate man before her, the man who had already stolen those lips, covering them with the mask as if they weren't permitted to be hers. He spoke desire and then ran from it just as quickly as she did. And what could be said when her body craved and could still feel the sensation of his lips to hers?

It seemed he carried the same apprehension, for before she could find a coherent reply, he beseeched, "Let me have the dream a little longer."

She didn't deny his wish, giving the slightest nod and wondering if there would be more kisses. But he never dared touch the mask again as he tentatively held her eye and swept her into his arms. She could feel the erratic pace of his heartbeat, throbbing like a drum against her, the shivering of his body, and it astounded her that though he'd initiated the kiss, he was left even more shaken than she was.

Christine never found nervousness. Perhaps it was lost somewhere beneath the power of his; she merely acquiesced with a twinge of intrigue and permitted him to carry her to the narrow bed in the far corner. With all the delicacy he seemed to possess, he set her upon the mattress and lifted the tattered quilt over her as if putting a child to bed. She watched his dark shape wander her apartment, turning lights down to miniscule flickers before returning to her side as a shadow again, once more hiding in the dark.

Erik knelt beside her bed as if in reverent prayer, and with the smallest sigh, he rested his forehead to the mattress, never regarding her as he admitted, "I'm sorry I disgust you, that I am not the handsome hero you've wished for, but, Christine, I can't let you go. Call me selfish if you will, but you are *everything*. Can you not see that? ...It will only frighten you further if I threaten the Vicomte's life and place ultimatums before you, so instead I shall ask, ...beg if I must. *Please* stay away from him. You said you don't love him; then stop encouraging his affections. Stop using him to hurt me. Christine... Is it so awful to love me instead?"

His voice was thick with despair, and curling onto her side to face his penitent pose, she extended trembling fingers and tenderly stroked the crown of his head. His entire body stiffened, but he never pulled away. The longer she continued with never a hinted danger, he started to relax and allow her without trepidation, even leaning ever so slightly up to her caress.

Not another word was spoken. Eventually with her guardian angel beside her, she drifted to sleep, and just as he had requested, the dream played on and carried her to a place where things like masks, faces, and sinful pasts did not exist or matter. It was much more pleasant than reality and exuded its bliss in the hint of a smile upon her lips as she slept.

Erik tilted his face to watch her, never disentangling from the warm hand still resting against his crown. And when the horrible scenes of the evening yearned to come to the forefront and play out again in his mind, he forced them away and concentrated on her, on the fact that at the end, *he* was the one at her side, gazing at her as she slept. *Vicomte be damned*!

Chapter Nine

Christine was disappointed to wake in her apartment alone. Her single room felt stark and cold compared to Erik's home as if the natural glow of sunlight streaming in was an unwelcome intrusion and enemy.

Under the weight of a heavy head, she rested on her pillow and let her gaze idly wander to the spot where Erik had knelt, conjuring his image in her mind's eye. She wondered how long he had remained with her. Had he spent the entire night in that sacred vigil? Perhaps he had only left because of sunlight's cruel appearance, unwilling to risk wandering the city streets with its bitter illumination to give him away.

Erik... He had kissed her and changed some necessary component of her very makeup. She recalled it in vivid detail. Mask-less, but he had ordered her eyes closed and wouldn't let her see. Only sensation, only the pressure of oddly-constructed lips with their foreign texture and irregular shapes. It should have disgusted her to fantasize them into existence and remember the horror of bloated, unnatural flesh, but Christine's mouth tingled as she delicately touched her lips with tentative fingertips and tried to recapture a feeling.

That kiss and its inspired wanting spun endless webs in her head. All during the never-ending span of rehearsal, incessant fantasies played and pulled her into their pictures. She was impatient to be set free and take the path she'd desperately avoided the previous night.

How different everything suddenly was! She had been taught to adore an angel and fear an Opera Ghost, but the creature that had kissed her carried no omnipotence or grace. He was only a man, vulnerable and weak, timid in his indiscretion and so dear to her because of his inexperience. For once, fear had been inconsequential and epithets had been suffocated out of existence, and she was left to wonder which she would be faced with tonight: man or myth.

The instant the cast was dismissed, Christine vanished backstage, never lingering with a worry for the Vicomte's appearance. No, not tonight. Tonight, she knew what she wanted and had no patience for indecision and its temptations.

She burst into her dressing room, anticipating Erik's voice and his presence. A grin was already curving her lips, but...she found nothing but a girl staring expectantly back in the mirror's reflection.

"Erik," she bid softly, approaching the glass and hoping it would give that familiar click and part to the secret doorway. Not a sound, not a single sensation that anyone was nearby watching. No, she was alone...

Oh God, had he chosen to leave her? He had threatened such a consequence, of course, but she never thought he would act on it, ...especially after a kiss and its life-altering repercussions. ...Unless he believed he'd committed a sin, forcing it upon her as he claimed he never would. She'd given him no reason to think otherwise. She had only made walls, every one seeming insurmountable and permanent. If he had given up and left, it was her fault, and she wasn't certain she could fix it.

Christine pressed desperately shaking palms to the cool surface of the mirror, but a push would not open it. To anyone who did not know the secret, it

135

was nothing but a piece of glass mounted to a wall, and she seemed crazy to be leaning her weight against it and becoming urgent when nothing happened.

"No, please," she softly begged, unable to quell the rising tears in the back of her throat. "Please come back."

But no answer came, and as the desolation overwhelmed her, she set her forehead against the glass and cried. She had done this, and now...he had chosen to punish them both. Tears tumbled free and struck the reflective surface, smearing wet paths as if the glass itself cried with her.

Minutes dragged, one to the next, and even though tears eventually ceased, Christine crouched at the base of the mirror and huddled limbs close, unwilling to give up and leave. Her distant eyes stared up at the evidence of a broken heart, fingerprints where she had touched, stains where tears had fallen. It was as if in sorrow, she had sought comfort from cold, inanimate glass and had been granted an empty embrace in return.

She had no idea how long she stayed in that spot. Gradually, sounds of bustling beyond her dressing room door faded as everyone left for the day until only deafening silence remained and tortured her with its presence. Alone, and her mind created stories of a future without Erik, what it would mean never to have him in her life again, to lose his voice, his music, his touch, his attempts to capture her affection. His kiss... Was one to be enough to last eternity? ...And what would she do? Consent to Raoul's courtship, perhaps one day wed him, and have nothing more than a heart caught in suspension that would never truly beat again...

A bleak ending that felt as much like death as going to the grave. The idea to exist without feeling held no promise and certainly no anticipation. It was a future worth dreading.

She was falling further into melancholy with

too much quiet closing in around her, and the sudden yearned-for click of a secret entrance made her jump as she abruptly scampered to her feet. Smudged glass became a door again, and as it opened, a dark silhouette appeared in shadows.

Christine did not pause or hesitate. In flustered steps, she rushed to him and threw quivering arms about his neck, hugging herself to his body as though she would never let him go.

Overcome by her forwardness, Erik remained stunned in his place, rigid and fearful with arms flexed tense at his sides. A physical assault he would have known how to deal with; this unthreatening contact confounded every one of his senses until he could hardly reason in coherent terms. Christine, ...his Christine, embracing him as if it were only so natural, as if they'd shared such intimacy enough to make it standard. Her body was warm and soft against his, her every tremulous breath and unsteady heartbeat like a syncopated symphony with his own and equally as erratic. She seemed afraid, and he longed to remind her that between the two of them, he was the one foreign to such advances and with more to fear if he made a mistake and did not please her.

Momentary shock faded enough for him to realize an embrace should be reciprocated, and he forced arms that felt awkward and uncertain to carefully weave about her and hug her back. Her loose curls tickled the surface of his skin, twining about his knuckles. He repressed an urge to chuckle with an odd sense of delight at their silken, unwitting caress. Why was every bit of her such a wonder?

Erik was reluctant to break the serene of silence, but he feared the longer it stretched, the more likely she would pull away with regret. Gentle and tentative, he asked, "Christine, what's wrong?"

"Where were you?" she demanded, clutching for one last breath before to his dismay, she drew apart from him. And yet...he saw no rejection or even a blush upon her cheeks. It was a meager consolation.

"Did you worry I'd left?" he posed in reply, humbled by her little nod. "Oh no, ...no, of course I wouldn't leave you, Christine. I apologize for my tardiness, but...I have something for you. I was delayed finishing it. Will you come with me?"

Without a second thought, he extended a gloved hand, inviting the touch he so wanted. Perhaps her boldness had inspired him, but he felt eager to try. He never saw hesitation as she complied and weaved her fingers between his, pressing palm to palm. It left him to wonder if the world had changed overnight without his knowledge.

He dallied only to close the mirror again, and his eyes locked on the telltale prints marring the surface of the glass. Casting her a look, he only then took note of the subtle hints to tears. She'd been crying for him; ...he savored such knowledge.

He never spoke a word about it, still nervous to lose what felt like a fragile connection. He only focused on her nearness, her shoulder gently brushing his as he led her into the passageways, her hand burning him even through leather material. The only doubt he received was in a quizzical look when he deviated their usual path. Not down tonight, not underground and buried. Tonight he led her up.

He did not offer explanations as they emerged through a hidden entrance out onto the opera house roof and the cool breeze of night engulfed them in its fresh, billowing rush. Stars twinkled above by the dozens, over-filling the black sky like sparkling diamonds and appearing within reach this close to heaven. And arranged in the center of the vacant rooftop were a small table and chairs, an elegant supper with only the flickers of encased candles to vie with the beauty of moonlight.

Erik nervously glanced at her, desperate to read her reaction as he stammered, "I know this cannot rival supper in a café or an elaborate restaurant as the Vicomte would offer, but...I've never made a genuine attempt to court you, to play the role of gentleman instead of the others I've tried. Is this...? Do you like it, Christine? Does it please you?"

The smile she lifted to his worried regard held an answer in its every brilliant curve. "This is beautiful."

"*You* are beautiful," he corrected before he could think better of it, but her smile never faltered. Subtle encouragement, and without another word, he led her to the awaiting table.

Supper was...easy, and Christine was surprised. She had expected unease to linger, a hesitation to words and smiles, but in the midst of a single kiss and an earlier fear of abandonment, she stopped ignoring intuition and let things be. A mask went unacknowledged beyond a brief thought that it seemed a hindrance to eating. Logical considerations, not dwelling on what lay beneath or the appellation added to such a face. No Opera Ghost. She refused to recall the title, and as such, they fell into a comfort she had only known with an angel. It reminded her why it had been so simple to fall in love with a voice.

They spoke of mundane topics, of the opera and music, of the warming weather and springtime. Only when the meal ended did words gain depth.

Christine gazed at the night sky and softly asked, "Do you ever miss the stars when you spend all your time below? Or the moon or sun? I think I would miss such things if I rarely saw them."

His eyes traced the lines of her upturned face, following the gentle curve of her jaw. Eyes could not caress, and he was distinctly sure not even fingers would be enough; no, not until he could trail that perfect line with lips instead. Then it would feel claimed.

With an inaudible sigh, he fought to recall her question and form an intelligible answer. "It isn't as if I've gone my entire existence without them. I have enough memories to fill the void of loss. Such trivialities can be recalled, and it is sufficient. You don't mourn them in the way one would mourn losing a person. I could survive without ever seeing the stars again and not be shattered to a million pieces for the sacrifice, but...if I never saw *you* again, now that would be a genuine loss worthy of bereavement."

Her focus lowered from stars to his intent stare, but she never blushed or ducked her observance. Meditating his admission, one dark brow arched inquisitively. "But why? I must wonder. Most of the feelings shared between us have been of an unpleasant vein. I seem to have brought you quite a bit of pain and disappointment."

"And yet the fleeting moments of bliss and pleasure far outweigh every heartbreak. Have you any idea how often in my life I've shared conversations, touches, ...kisses? Never, Christine. Not even cordial friendship. You speak to me now as if I am not the monster I've always considered myself. I never forget what I am, what I've done, and I don't expect you to. But if I can convince you to see beyond it instead of dwelling on it... Well, I hope I showed you this evening that it doesn't have to be painful between us. It can be wonderful. ...I would do anything for you, Christine. Surely that means something."

Christine watched him carefully, denying an instinct to look away, and the loneliness she could decipher when he spoke of his life tugged at her heart. How many times in the past weeks had she denied her compassion and insisted his suffering was inconsequential because of who he was? It seemed a sin worth condemnation when she now looked and saw only a fallible man, not an Opera Ghost on the level of a god. This was a man who'd never known a good emotion until now, and how cruel of her to punish him for it!

"Anything...," she repeated. "You'd do anything for me? What if I asked you to stop being the Opera Ghost? Stop hurting people and controlling lives to get your way? Stop controlling *me*?"

"I don't-"

"Yes, you do," she somberly insisted. "You're trying to keep my heart without ever letting it beat."

Erik was silent, and she wondered if he would refuse as she waited impatiently for his response. Finally, he stated, "It isn't that simple. None of this is. Do you ever wonder why I am afraid of you as much as I am in love with you?"

"Because I can hurt you."

"Because you can *destroy* me. I am half the legend itself. The almighty Opera Ghost, and no one dares to trivialize such an ascendant persona. I spent my lifetime weak, tormented, beaten into submission because my face dubbed me as different, as a freak. I became a ghost to transcend such atrocity and never let another thing touch me...until you appeared. You have inspired such hope. I never knew it could exist. You look at me, even if it's a masked face and never mine, but there is no animosity in your eyes. You seem as if you want to be in my company and in my life, and I can't imagine giving that up. If I lost you, every good feeling would go with you and leave only the bad. And then I'd truly be nothing more than a monster."

"But...as the Opera Ghost, you've killed people," she protested, refusing to relish his affectionate admissions. "They say you murder those who've seen your face."

An idle shrug never even hinted at remorse. "It isn't a common occurrence. I'm usually careful enough not to be caught, and these days, they only see my face if I will it. I use it as a weapon; how pitiful is that? The face that condemns me, and I purposely frighten people with its ugliness. When I take off the mask, they scream. They react...like you did the first time you saw. And in that moment amidst revulsion and terror, I strike. You want regret for my actions, apologies perhaps, but being sorry doesn't change reality and certainly does not transform my face. It may purify the soul, but what good is a clean soul in a blemished vessel? Being penitent won't put me one step closer to heaven. Curse salvation! *You* are my salvation. If *you* can love me, I'll be sorry. Is that what it will take? Then I will act contrite and beg mercy for my deeds and sinful indiscretion, but I cannot apologize for what I am. All the prayers in the world won't change it; I know that better than anyone. I used to pray until my tongue twisted with the words, and I never was heard. Perhaps *you* should try. Pray I become a prince with a perfect face, and see if you get what you want." He shook his head in frustration before adding, "I try to control your heart, but it is only because I know my limitations. Fate alone would never let you be mine. Fate never smiles upon a cursed man."

"You're so certain the only way you could have my heart is to steal it," she stated and wondered how much blame was her own.

"You don't know what you want," Erik accused. "If stealing it guarantees it will be mine, it seems warranted." Even though he fought to seem aloof, his gaze was drawn to the subtle motion of her dark curls in the night breeze. The silver strands created by moonlight named her a luminescent goddess. "Christine, ...last night I kissed you. I've never...," he trailed off, looking away from deep blue eyes with a rush of embarrassment. Instead of admissions, he asked, "Did you feel anything? Was it only disgust to remember my misshapen lips were upon yours?"

"Not disgust," she replied, and when his expression never softened, she concluded, "You don't believe me."

"Jealousy spurred that kiss. It was as much a damning offense as murder, more so because I never need to look the corpse I've wronged in the eyes afterward. If you want apologies, that is where you should start, and I will offer a dozen."

There was the regret she sought and a self-loathing interspersed, so potent she wondered how anyone could carry its weight. On shaking knees, she rose from the table and approached, timidly kneeling on the cold, hard ground at his feet.

"What are you doing?" Erik asked, hesitantly eyeing her every motion as she edged near enough to brush his leg and lightly rest a trembling hand on his knee.

Never an explanation or an answer. She simply inquired with a nervous waver, "Will you kiss me again?" Before he could speak, she closed her eyes and tilted her face expectantly.

Kiss her... Her awaiting, pink lips captivated Erik, slightly puckered as if in invitation, and his memory filled with a fleeting recollection of their softness, their taste, their delicious and addictive warmth. Sense wondered why she was attempting this and subjecting herself to his improper advances a second time, but desire was intoxicating and urgently reminded that he had been longing for another chance since the moment he'd entered her presence. She was willing, and he felt desperate.

Hesitating only long enough to catch a breath, Erik slid to the ground, kneeling with her, eyes riveted to her, but she dutifully remained in place and never dared peek. The slight curve of those pink lips said she knew she won and would receive the kiss he yearned to give. Her anticipation inspired his awe.

It was far more difficult this night to remove his mask. The previous attempt had been fueled by impulse; this time jealousy was dulled in the background, and all he knew was wanting.

Inching closer, he stifled thoughts that his disfigured face did not deserve to share the same air with her beauty, that it was a transgression merely to be so ugly and expect her to accept it. No, *she* had requested a kiss. *She* wanted it, eager and willing despite the horror of his disfigurement. *She* wanted to prove herself, ...and he had a seemingly perverse urge.

Timid as could be, he grazed her waiting lips with his in a most delicate caress, but then instead of pressing a misshapen mouth to her kiss, he dared press his disfigured cheek. She started, a soft gasp escaping lips that were no longer forming a kiss, and he knew a warm rush of regret, jerking away in shameful terror.

"I'm sorry," he stammered, his shaking hands lifting his mask and trying to hide away. "Oh God, I'm sorry."

But her hands stilled his movements. His gaze darted to her in fear as intruding moonlight illuminated his unmasked face, but her eyes were yet closed, her grip unsure and clumsy. As her palms pressed to the lapels of his jacket, they seemed to find their guiding compass and moved tentatively over his shoulders. Those small hands gripped the crown of his head with never a touch to his face, and as her fingers weaved in his hair, she brought him close to her again.

Erik's breath stilled in his lungs, never exhaled, never another as he permitted her, urgently curious to her intent. Her lips found his, warm, gentle, overwhelming him so that when his breath finally slipped free, it was a soft cry swallowed between touching mouths.

Christine felt his entire body tense with her boldness, but she only clasped tighter, unwilling to let him change his mind and end this just yet. Her mouth moved delicately against his, a constant question present yet never asked, and the flood of sensation she recalled and ached for swept through her every limb, leaving her to tremble as hard as he was. But he wanted strong, and she was determined not to cower, especially when he seemed a moment away from faltering completely. He could choose to be the omnipotent Opera Ghost in every other detail, but a kiss threw him from his throne. Such a revelation made her adore him.

Tenderness kept him as her willing victim, and as she urged him to kiss her back, she found her senses swimming in the odd thrill of his lips with their unordinary details. Cold, foreign shapes and textures, why did abnormalities that should deter her only make her more eager? Leaning up on her knees, she scooted closer and sighed her delight when he hesitantly slipped his arms about her waist, drawing her nearer yet until she was flush to the frantic beating of his heart.

She had asked for a kiss, and Erik felt sure he would burn alive if he didn't have more. Her motion was gentle, and he broke its boundaries, pushing it to fervent instead. More pressure, more desperation, and shuddering down the length of his spine, he dared to part her yielding lips with an eager tongue longing for a taste. Sweetest intoxication, he drowned in its spell, and to feel her hands fist in his hair and her body arch into his blotted out reality and taunted him that this must be a dream.

His tongue tingled with every taste, entwining with hers, tempting her to lose herself just as willingly. He wanted more, ached for more, but as one of her gripping hands loosened its hold and slowly trailed his forehead and temple, barely caressing his scarred cheek, he suddenly cried out, breaking away and scooting beyond her reach.

Christine held only empty air in place of a fevered embrace, and her brow furrowed with unwanted rejection as she listened to frantic fumbling and knew he replaced his mask. She waited until silence returned, silence except for un-quieted, harsh breaths before she dared open her eyes.

He knelt on the ground a fair distance away, masked face lowered and refusing a glance at her, and her gaze caught on gloved hands, fisted tight at his sides as if should they un-flex, they would betray him and give up control, shake, reach for her, every weak impulse he didn't want to show.

"Erik," she whispered, afraid her voice would shatter his meditation and remind him to be angry.

"What was that, Christine?" he suddenly demanded with never a look. "Was there disgust? Was it just well hidden so I wouldn't see it? ...Was that an act of pity?" Shaking his head, he somberly bid, "You seem like you want it, ...want *me*, but... Pity and a good performance are a more realistic conclusion."

"Pity? And is it pity that keeps me in your company as well?" she asked with a modicum of hurt.

"No, that is a lingering effect of your attachment to an angel. You permit my presence because I remind you of those peaceful days of illusion."

He spoke so matter-of-factly, trivializing her heart in one decided point, and it inspired an uncommon burst of anger within her. "Illusion?" she insisted and hoped he noted her annoyance. "And do you perceive me fool enough to still wish illusion would return?"

"You once asked exactly that. You wished me to be a voice behind your mirror even when you knew I was a man who wanted you. Reality is cold and a nightmare in comparison. But I tug on your compassion. Humoring my affection isn't beyond your capabilities. A kiss or two for the pathetic monster to pacify his crude desires. ...It makes as much sense as your disgust."

"Disgust is irrelevant," she persisted to argue. "And so is pity. They don't exist in the space between us, not anymore. All that lingers is fear, and it isn't even mine. ...Erik, are you even listening to me?"

"Wait. Sshh." His head tilted as if seeking indecipherable sound, and she wondered if he was purposely ceasing an unpleasant conversation. She heard nothing but the patters of hooves from the city street below and the occasional hum of passers-by, nothing to warrant suspicion or concern.

So sudden that she jumped, he got to his feet and crept to the open skylight in the opera house ceiling. Curious, she followed on tiptoe after him.

Light filtered from the theatre below, but that was hardly uncommon. Though the cast had been dismissed for the day, the crew often stayed late to finish up. Anyone else might have been spooked and claimed lingering noise meant the Opera Ghost was haunting, but Christine had his company. Those below could not hold a threat in comparison...or so she thought until a familiar voice resounded.

"You must know where she is."

Christine glanced at Erik, feeling him tense before shooting her a glare of bitter blame. She yearned to yell back in indignation that this couldn't possibly be her fault.

On the stage in the vacant theatre, Raoul was stalking fitfully while the exasperated managers Andre and Firmin chased behind him.

"Monsieur Vicomte," Andre appeased, "perhaps she left while you were unaware and has returned home."

"No," Raoul snapped as if the suggestion were absurd, "I checked her apartment before I started scourging the opera house. It's as if she vanished into the air. Do you mean to tell me that you have no clue what is going on right under your noses? People disappearing? Accidents happening frequently enough not to be coincidences? Christine stolen away?"

"Stolen away?" Firmin doubtfully shook his head. "She likely went off with friends for supper. We respect your concern, Monsieur Vicomte, but it is a bit too soon to leap to horrific conclusions. She was at rehearsal earlier. She's barely been missing a few hours."

"Fool!" Raoul shouted, and Christine shrank back with an irrational fear that he would overhear the gasp she gave in reply. "She's taking music lessons. Do you know who her teacher is?"

Andre exchanged a look with Firmin before replying, "Many of our cast take lessons, Monsieur, but it is in their free time outside of our watch. We can't be expected to keep track of every teacher in Paris."

"But perhaps that's where Mademoiselle Daaé has disappeared to," Firmin offered. "Perhaps she is attending a lesson."

"That's what I'm most afraid of." Raoul's anger faded to dread. "What do you know of your resident Opera Ghost?" he abruptly demanded, and both managers recoiled with widened, fear-fringed eyes.

"The...the Opera Ghost?" Firmin stammered. "Why...do you wish to know about him?"

"Because I don't think he's a ghost at all."

Christine lifted nervous eyes to Erik, but found his attention only on her, gauging *her* responses as if they were far more important than any of the Vicomte's dangerous revelations. That mismatched gaze flickered with betrayal, and she shook her head urgently. "I didn't...," she whispered before he held up a hand for silence.

"What do you mean?" Andre asked, and she averted her gaze back to the scene below, desperate to deny the appearance of tears. No, she couldn't cry, and certainly wouldn't let Erik see it if she did.

"It's too convenient," Raoul explained, casting random glances about the theatre at its many shadowed corners. "One of your stagehands claims the ghost is nothing but a man, a *monster*, he said. He insisted this creature murdered his friend, and all because it was seen and the secret was learned. *Murdered*, Messieurs. You have no incorporeal spirit wandering your theatre and its cellars. It is a flesh and blood man."

Both managers absorbed the Vicomte's assertions and took them as fact. "But," Firmin replied, "ghost or not, he's *dangerous*, Monsieur Vicomte. We dare not cross him. If you hoped humanizing him would make a difference, I'm sorry to say it doesn't. He's laid enough threats with proof they will be carried out if we don't comply. We may seem like puppets while he pulls our strings, but it is for the good of everyone in the company. Too many lives depend on us for protection; we can't put them in jeopardy."

Though Andre nodded agreement, he latched onto one unexplained point. "And Mademoiselle Daaé? How is she involved in this?"

Raoul's bravado faltered and crumbled to genuine despair. "I think this so-called ghost is fixated on her, obsessed even. Enough pieces have come together to scream such a truth. Her *teacher*," he grimaced over the word, "is not a teacher at all, or at least not a legitimate one. Your Opera Ghost has practically chained her to him and is controlling her every action. He seems to have her convinced she cannot leave him."

"She told you this?" Firmin asked.

"I figured it out; she has given me enough hints to put it together. She is at risk, Messieurs, and he has corrupted her to defend his presence. I'm beside myself with worry that she is with him as we speak, and I'm terrified to consider what that means."

Another glance at Erik, and Christine caught the briefest glimpse of pain before he buried it beneath a scowl. As if a kiss suddenly meant nothing...

"What would you like us to do, Monsieur Vicomte?" Andre inquired.

Raoul pondered a moment, shaking his head. "What I want I can't have at present. It isn't as if you could make Christine appear and prove to me that she is all right." His concern tainted his voice, more evident than he wanted to show as he quickly regained his composure. "Just...keep this news to yourselves for now. I need to devise a way to handle this situation, but it wouldn't do any of us good to spark a panic through your cast and crew. Leave it be, and leave a ghost as a ghost. But...I won't let him steal Christine. I *will* protect her, no matter what I have to do."

That was all. With such a vow, the Vicomte rushed out of the theatre without pleasantry as the managers called out saccharine farewells after him.

Christine was reluctant to shift her focus to Erik. As she finally lifted her eyes, she saw rage, jealousy, possessive fire, directed first at an empty theatre then heaved coldly at her.

"I didn't-" she began again, but he immediately interrupted.

"What do you want?" he suddenly hissed. "Do you want to return to your apartment, or do you want to stay the night here? Make up your mind. I haven't time or patience to deal with debates."

Time... Oh God, what did that mean he intended instead? Stuttering over words, she declared, "Here. I want to stay here."

A brusque nod, and he got to his feet and stalked toward his secret entrance, leaving her no choice but to silently follow. She gave one last look at the remnants of a pleasant evening and a supper under the stars. It now seemed a bittersweet fantasy.

As soon as they entered the underground house, Christine wasted no time. She practically ran to her room and readied for bed with hastiness, jerking her nightdress over her head and tying it in place with shaking fingers. No, she couldn't give him long alone, not minutes enough to ponder an option to rid himself of the nuisance in their background.

Leaping onto the bed and tossing the covers over her lap, she suddenly called in high-pitched hysteria, "Erik! Erik!"

With barely a pause in between, he rushed into the room, his wide, frantic eyes seeking her out and searching her every feature for a cause of his obvious panic. "What's wrong? Christine, my God, you gave me a fright!" Annoyance became blatant and biting now that he saw she was unharmed. "Why in the world would you scream like that?"

She shrugged innocently and attempted to seem calm as she requested, "Will you stay here with me? I...I slept so well with your presence last night. I...don't want to be alone."

A kiss earlier was never an act of fear or second-guessed; what she asked now was *solely* inspired by fear and a terror of what he would do otherwise.

"...All right," he hesitantly answered. His confounded expression insisted he did not fully trust her, but turning her lantern to a mediocre flicker, he took a seat upon the chaise beside her bed, never once making an attempt to touch her. Tonight she was oddly grateful for that.

He was only a silhouette, the shadow watching over her, but collecting her courage, she softly begged into the darkness, "You said you'd do anything I asked to have me. ...Please, Erik, don't go after the Vicomte."

Her words struck him harshly, and he sneered his contempt to no one but the shadows. Ironic or just? He could have her but only as a consolation to preserve her precious Vicomte. The Opera Ghost would have manipulated control and rid any barrier that stood in his way. She didn't want the Opera Ghost, but her request seemed to say she didn't want Erik either.

"Erik?" she called when long minutes of seething silence extended.

His jaw was clenched in a tight line, but he managed to mutter, "Whatever you want, Christine, but one mistake, one single urging of his misguided heroism, and I won't be responsible for what happens."

Shadows were never a hindrance to his sight, so he clearly saw her sigh in relief before she cuddled deeper into her covers and closed her eyes. Ignorant girl! She wanted to drain the supposed evil out of him, to reform the Opera Ghost and hope to find something beneath a malevolent exterior to pin her heart upon. Naïve, even after he'd shattered her childhood fantasies of angels! He would have denounced pathetic vows and gone after the Vicomte anyway if not for the lingering taste of her on his tongue and the recollection of her soft lips and willing mouth. He was not about to lose such pleasures, and if that meant playing by her supposed rules, he would...for now at least.

Chapter Ten

Christine was not surprised when she returned to rehearsal the next morning and saw Raoul rush in flustered steps through the corridor to meet her. This encounter had been anticipated since she had awoken alone in her room below, and though she had scripted it and run it in her mind, every word faltered to glimpse his sincere concern as he searched her face as if making sure not a single detail was altered.

"Raoul, ...good morning."

"Christine." He reached for her hand, but as she cast a wary glance at others sharing the hall, she shrank away and did not allow him.

"Don't," she softly bid and hoped he'd heed her warning.

"Where have you been?" he finally demanded the question she'd been waiting to hear. "I thought... Christine, I worried something happened to you."

"Happened to me?" She forced a convincing smile. "How ridiculous! As you can see, I am well, but I will be late for rehearsal if you detain me further."

"What's wrong with you?" the Vicomte insisted, and with never a care for her obvious unease, he caught her shoulders with his hands and kept her in place. "You must tell me. ...What has *he* done to make you behave so coldly? A couple of nights back, we were practically courting, and now you seem desperate to be rid of my presence. ...Is *he* watching us right now?"

He had drawn too many accurate conclusions, and she adopted her best façade and feigned ignorance to hide her distress. "*He*? Who is *he*? No one is making me do anything. If I seem cold, it is only because you are neglecting my every word. I must get to rehearsal, and you must leave me be."

She tried to break free, but he would not let go. "Not yet. First, promise to meet me after."

"I can't. You know-"

"Let me help you, Christine," he fervently begged. "I know there are secrets not meant to be shared, and you are terrified to betray them, but I am not your enemy. I would *never* hurt you. I only want to protect you."

"I don't need protecting."

"Just tell me. Did he command you to stay away from me? Did he pose some sort of threat to force me out of your life?"

"No," she easily lied and did not regret it as she finally broke out of his hold. "Please...leave me be, Raoul. It is for the best. You are a Vicomte, and this is not the place for you."

"That is a pitiful excuse I refuse to believe. Someone is twisting your thoughts and trying to steal you away. Well, I won't have it. I will fix this, Christine. You deserve far more than murdering ghosts steering every detail of your life."

"Raoul!" she suddenly snapped. "I made the choice, and I ask that you respect it."

"Christine..." He was on the verge of another argument, but with an aggravated huff, he flipped about and charged back down the hall amidst dozens of spying eyes. And yet Christine was entirely sure that this was far from over. It was no different than every time she ran back to Erik; once the heart was involved, it was impossible to simply sever its ties.

With a solemn stare, Christine glanced to the

rafters above her head, but only shadows looked back. No masks or mismatched eyes, but she did not need an image to know Erik lurked about. She only hoped he realized the Vicomte's obstinacy was his own transgression. She had done as she promised and prayed it was enough to save them all.

*****

Erik knew what Christine's mood would be before she met him at the end of the day, and it certainly wouldn't be melancholy for her encounter with the Vicomte. No, he had made certain she would barely recall it. He truly wished she would see that sometimes playing the Opera Ghost had only benefits.

As expected, the instant she burst into her dressing room, she halted before the open mirror and demanded without greeting, "What did you do?"

At first, he only grinned; it was far too amusing to incite that bit of temper she rarely displayed. If she could willingly indulge it even when faced with his presence, he was hopeful conviction would follow.

"Erik?" she pushed sharply, never cowering.

Chuckling beneath his breath, he strode into the room and teased, "You have to be far more specific. I can't be sure what you're so obviously upset about."

Scoffing her doubt, she flatly declared, "I am now sharing Carlotta's role? Does that sound familiar? Because I have no doubt how such a thing came to pass. So she will sing the premiere of the new production, and I will sing *her* role at the matinee the next day."

"If you would have let me play things my way, you would be singing both performances, but...I did it without violence, didn't I? You didn't want me to hurt others to get what I want, and...," he idly shrugged as he roamed the dressing room in calculated steps, "no one is *dead*, are they?"

Her expression never changed as she insisted again, "What did you do?"

Erik huffed in perturbation at a decided lack of gratitude. Sitting upon her vanity bench as if he were accustomed to inhabiting this side of the dressing room mirror, he explained, "A note to the managers with expressed commands that you would have a chance to play the lead, along with a harsh berating about the nonchalant way they've buried your talent under insufficient minor characters. *You deserve* to be the diva, Christine. How quickly they've cast your debut under the rug to please La Carlotta! All of your ovations and accolades! I'm through letting them brush off your worth and fall over themselves to please that screeching cow! No more!"

Christine eyed him skeptically, not even a flinch at his ranting. "But what did you do to convince them to follow your commands, Oh Opera Ghost?"

An undeterred laugh escaped him at her matter-of-fact assessment, and for a moment, Christine forgot why she was upset. How seldom such a reaction was indulged! Too many tears and too much pain, and to gain a laugh from his lips, a genuine one without malice or sinister plots beneath, she thought it was one of the most beautiful sounds she'd ever heard.

"I will be honest," he declared and returned her to annoyance. "I would prefer to say my obedient managers follow my commands at merely a mention, but a good threat is insurance. Oh, don't look at me that way! *Threat* does not imply *action*, at least not at the moment. I've already exonerated myself from blame, seeing as how there have been *no* accidents today, and since they obeyed my orders, the threat is null and mute. I need not arrange a disaster beyond imagination to cover it, and you, *petite*, have no right to anger when I have done nothing save present you an opportunity. I am your teacher first and foremost, and furthering your career is my most important task."

Christine rubbed aching temples, shaking a

doubtful head. "And do you know what your interference has gotten me? I'm sure you can imagine how Carlotta took the news that *I* would be sharing her role. And the rumors! Dear God, do you have any idea what they're saying about me?"

"Indeed. You know I have ears everywhere." With a thoughtful tilt of his masked face, he recalled their details. "The one I found most humorous and also most absurd in the bunch was that you were bedding one of the managers or potentially *both*. I doubt either of them protested such slander, not when it must seem flattering and certainly uncommon."

Christine shot him a glare, but he continued even as his joviality faded. "The rumor I found most unappealing was that your dearest Vicomte arranged this for you, paid the managers for your role. Some believe you've already bedded him; others that this 'gift' will be the very point to win you over and get you there."

Her annoyance abandoned her to watch him speak of Raoul and glimpse a pain he was trying to hide beneath irritation. "And if you were about today," she offered in consolation, "you saw that I openly rejected the Vicomte's presence."

"Yes," Erik somberly bid, studying her carefully, "I watched you play your part and preserve the boy's life. I watched you hold your head up through the vicious rumors circulating. I watched as I always watch. It's the sad reality of it. I cannot stand at your side and endure it with you. I watch from the background, and when I try to exceed boundaries and grant you some compensation, lay opportunities at your feet, you chastise me for how I go about it. What would you have me do? Stand back and watch some more? Let your talent go wasted while Carlotta inflates her ego? Or better yet, walk into the managers' office and put my face on display to make my offers? Would you feel better about this promotion if I subjected *myself* to their cruelty instead?"

"Erik," she said with a sigh, and a smile lifted the corners of her lips. "Thank you."

Erik stared in awe of that smile, unsure how to reply to genuine gratitude beyond an awkward smile in return, but shrugging off his insecurities, he sought a lighter topic and teased, "Not a single rumor floating about speculates you are romancing the Opera Ghost in the shadows. I should feel offended no one supposes *I* am the mastermind of your seeming good fortune. One would assume I'd acted enough of a reign of terror about this place to be a primary suspect. Not even the shrieking ballerinas happened upon the truth, and they are usually the instigators of my very sordid reputation."

Christine's smile brightened, and he sought to imprint the image of its brilliance in his memory before he abruptly got to his feet and decided, "All right, let's get below. We have a lot of work to do to prepare you."

"Perhaps you need to add some lessons on self defense," she replied as she followed him into the mirror. "If it's up to Carlotta, she may have my head before this is over and put rumors of an Opera Ghost's accidents to shame."

Huffing with feigned annoyance, he declared, "If you had just let me take care of her, you'd have the role all to yourself. Another little accident to spook her and send her running. Last time she wasn't hurt. She ran for fear alone, and we were all better for it. But since we're playing it *your* way this time, I suppose I shall have to teach you some witty insults to offer in retaliation, preferably intelligent ones she won't fully understand. It will make it all the more humorous to behold." With a sudden point in her direction, he added, "Perhaps they should even be spoken in Italian. Insult her in her native tongue."

He made it seem so serious and direct that her smile broke into giggles that echoed down the dark passageways of the catacombs. Erik savored that sound; it meant hope.

*****

Christine was exhausted. It seemed a normal condition of late. Every day she endured extensive rehearsals, sometimes shadowing Carlotta, which made time seem to pass slower, as if each minute purposely lengthened its seconds just to prolong her torture.

From one rehearsal to the next, and Erik was no less severe in his attempt to prepare her for her role. The premiere was half a week away, as he diligently reminded to excuse his strict demeanor, and every moment they had in between was precious and meant to have its seconds sucked dry. She was not perceiving it as favorably and on more than one occasion had to stifle the urge the throw something akin to a diva's tantrum and insist the world did not exist for opera alone. But even beginning a protest seemed like too much effort, and so she had to hope he read the musings in her glare instead.

"Christine," Erik snapped, "you're not even *trying* anymore. ...Are you listening to me?"

Her focus had been locked on his bottom lip for the lengthy instruction he had been giving, letting words muddle to a drone in the background in favor of her mind's escape. Even now, acknowledging his irritation felt less important than mesmerizing herself on the motion of that exposed lip mid-speech. It would feel chilled to the touch; she pondered it from memory's chasm when kisses were only fantasies at present. His bottom lip was so nicely shaped, so perfectly pink, and the upper one... It was misshapen and swollen but no less desirable as an integral portion of a whole mouth. ...A mouth she wanted on hers.

"Christine!"

A mouth that was suddenly as tensed as the rest of him, and as her reverie shattered, she gave a

159

sigh of disappointment and insisted, "Yes, I'm listening to you. I've heard everything you've said."

"Have you?" he posed doubtfully. "The premiere is in three days, Christine. *Three* days! When your current frame of mind seems to include acute ennui, I am losing faith you will be ready. The cadenza was abysmal at best."

Her eyes narrowed as she protested, "Just because it did not meet your standard of perfection-"

"Yes, exactly!" he interrupted with an exasperated point from his place at the piano. "It didn't. Your concept of perfection and mine are two different things. Your notes and rhythms were precise, *too* precise. Where is the line? Where is the flow? You are treating it like another strictly measured part of the aria and are too concerned with accuracy to be saying anything worth hearing." Pounding the chord of her entrance, he sharply commanded, "Again."

Christine scowled at him, and she was driven further into annoyance as he purposely ignored it. Perhaps it was not the best idea to attempt a beautiful, lyrical cadenza situated at the top of the staff and beyond when she was contemplating slapping her teacher. ...Or so she noted as her high note went awry. Cringing her distaste, she nervously eyed Erik, dreading his response.

"What was that?" he practically shouted. "You spread the high note wide and flattened it to ugliness! You didn't round your vowel. You know better than that!"

"I'm sorry!" she exclaimed, matching his tone as she slammed her score shut and tossed it with a bit of a shriek onto the piano. "You're making me crazy! I can't sing when you're yelling at me every few minutes! Erik, you're treating this like a life or death situation! You make it seem if I don't perform to your expectations, I might as well not perform at all. I just want to sing!"

He had grown quiet during her outburst, scrutinizing her with those eyes that made her knees tremble, and though she expected retaliation, calm as could be, he stated, "All right, I concede. I have been working you a little too hard, pushing a bit too harshly."

"A bit?"

"But," he pointedly insisted, "I know your potential. I've seen you exceed it when you sang for an angel. I have no promises for you this time, no vows to make you strive for greatness. This time there is only me, and...I want that to be enough to inspire you." Shrugging off the somberness of his admission, he insisted, "Singing for angels made you a wonder on the stage. I want to surpass that. I want you to be an absolute amazement and astound even me with your brilliance."

Irritation was gone and forgotten, and with suddenly set resolve, she bid, "Play the chord again."

Sing for Erik, the mortal man with every one of his flaws, and though an angel had once inspired her, she reminded herself as the chord resounded, that angels were intangible. An angel couldn't love her in return...

Her voice rang through the small room, quick runs and a savored trill all before soaring to blossom on a high note. It was rounded and full and practically vibrated against the walls. As it faded, though she vividly saw his pride on display, she also glimpsed so much more: affection, gratitude, ...adoration.

But reining emotion with determined hands, Erik nodded and insisted, "Sing it like that for the performance. If you dare spread the high note, you will be lectured on it mercilessly afterward. I want them to see what you just did and gape, Christine. Show them what a diva truly is."

"And you?" she added, the hint of a challenge in her stare. "What will *you* do if I sing it like that?"

Her proposition intrigued him, and he smiled as he inquired, "What would you have me do? Fill your ears with compliments? Fall at your feet with pride and reverence? ...Something more... A kiss perhaps?"

"Perhaps," she conceded and lowered eyes that showed too much eagerness.

"But tell me," he pushed, and she could feel the power of his stare penetrating her skin as if it sought to read her soul. "Would it be wanted? In such a situation, a kiss would seem a prize, a gift even, and certainly not an act of pity or sacrifice. It would seem...you genuinely *wanted* a kiss."

A silent nod and still not a single look as she insisted, "But first I'll have to triumph in the daunting task of making you proud. So...shall we run the aria again?"

Erik nodded a reeling head. Too many days without a touch or a hint of affection had taunted him with doubt, insisting Christine had only been indulging him with a sense of duty and misguided compassion. To know she *wanted* a kiss, that in the midst of her own achievement, she considered such a token from *his* lips as a prize...

He played the introduction to her aria, and as she began to sing, he noted she wasn't holding back. No, she sang it as if to prove she would triumph, and though a small smile tugged at his lips, she never once cast him a glance, determined to keep the sweet secrets in her eyes as her own. But anticipation radiated through every pitch and soaked into him, and his smile only grew.

*****

It was late, and though she should have been abed, Christine wandered in wayward footsteps about Erik's sitting room. Since she had started spending her nights in the underground home, she was convinced Erik *never* slept, but finding herself alone disproved her own theory. Her initial intent in rising from a restless bed had been to distract her addled mind with his company. But...it was hardly as if she intended to sneak into his bedroom and wake him.

The house was too quiet without his immediate presence, and of their own accord, her eyes strayed to the door out to the catacombs. Common sense insisted no one could possibly find the path below, but she still felt on edge. Shadows... Here she was in the home of the Opera Ghost, and she was anxious over shadows? It seemed backwards.

Forcing attention, she tried to focus on the real reason for her unease. The next night was the premiere, and even if Carlotta would be the one to give the performance, Christine was as nervous as if it were hers. Worse than having a role to portray was having a chance *after* the reigning diva, destined to be held to comparison and criticism. She could already hear every sharp comment in her ears, suffocating and tormenting mercilessly.

Muttering excuses to nonexistent voices implied insanity, and so instead, she plopped down at Erik's piano, desperate for sounds that were contrary to ugly made-up insults. Pressing gently upon ivory keys, she struck random pitches, trying to string them together into a spontaneous song. They didn't fit as well as she wanted; she wasn't Erik and couldn't hear the pitch in her head before it resounded. It occurred to her that he practically had a span of piano keys in his inner ear and didn't need the instrument to hear it played. She suddenly wished for such a gift.

Barely a dozen pitches had rung when a voice called, "What are you doing?"

Christine jerked her hand from the keys, but as she lifted wide eyes to the doorway, she didn't find anger, only concern. "I...I couldn't sleep, but...neither could you, it seems."

Erik still wore his formal attire, not a trace of grogginess to imply he'd been awakened, and she returned to her previous notion that he didn't sleep.

"You...hadn't gone to bed yet?" she pushed for her answer.

He shook his head as he strolled into the room to join her. "I don't rest very well with you here."

"Oh?"

"I have this absurd paranoia that you'll wake and need me, and I won't hear you if I'm asleep," he admitted with feigned apathy. "I think the only real sleep I've indulged was that night I sat at your bedside. So close, I could listen to you breathe all night in my dreams and know you were all right."

His words warmed a path within her, so endearing, so genuine in their simplicity, and though she smiled, she noted he never looked up to see it. Not a glance as he timidly approached and took a hesitant seat on the piano bench beside her. Had he willingly been so near in the past week? She found herself instinctively inching closer until she could nonchalantly press her leg to his.

His eyes lingered on that contact. Fighting a telltale waver in his voice, he bid, "Why can't you sleep?"

"The premiere is tomorrow."

"Your role tomorrow is minimal, a handful of lines at best."

"It doesn't matter. My mind will be playing the lead."

"Oh, I see," he replied, casting furtive glances. "And nerves are keeping you from sleep."

Nodding, she pointed out, "You didn't see me the night before the last premiere. I wasn't yet a staple in an angel's home, so you didn't have the privilege of witnessing my hysterical tendencies. I spent most of those hours as a tightly-wound bundle of anxiety and certainly knew no real rest."

"Then let's talk through your fears and decide why each and every one is irrational. Tell me."

Christine pondered the vast jumble of trepidations calling for attention, and said, "I might forget the words or the steps."

He shook his head. "Not likely. In rehearsals, you've been more accurate than anyone on the stage and that includes La Carlotta. You are a natural performer, Christine. Even if you forgot the steps, went left instead of right, you would make it work. Trust your instincts."

"What if my voice cracks?"

"It won't if you use your technique. You know that."

She meditated more excuses and replied with a bit of a smile, "What if there is an unexplainable accident, and a piece of scenery falls on my head?"

"That can't happen because you have the Opera Ghost on your side. The Opera Ghost would protect you rather than cause you harm." Erik watched her carefully from the corner of his eyes and was pleased to see her smile only brighten. "Do you trust me, Christine?"

"Of course, but...*you* are my biggest source of anxiety. What if...what if I don't please you?" She admitted it softly like a secret.

"Now that is the most illogical fear of all," he decided. "You've *already* pleased me a dozen times over. I've watched you grow; in every lesson, you exceed my expectations. Why are you always so afraid I will be disappointed? You put my opinion before everyone, even *your own*. Why do you not strive to please *yourself* instead?"

"I like to make you proud," she whispered, gaze locked on untouched piano keys. "And...I know I've disappointed you in so many other ways, but if I can sing for you, perhaps it makes up for a little bit."

"Christine," he breathed softly, and she shivered merely at the sound. "...How can I calm you? There must be something I can do to distract your anxiety."

She hesitated, and yet she already had an answer in mind. "Will you...will you sing for me?"

165

"Sing?"

"Yes, *you* sing and strive to please *me* instead," she decided, shifting on the piano's bench to face him expectantly. "It seems only fair."

"Does it? But I am no performer with a need to practice what must be displayed onstage."

"You asked what would calm me, and when you sing... I forget everything else when you sing." Before he succumbed to his reluctance and refused, she quickly added, "And what shall I offer if you please me? You offered incentive to do the same. What would *you* have *me* do, *ange*? Would you like a genuine and sincere critique? I could assume the role of teacher and evaluate your technique as you do mine."

"No, thank you," he firmly replied. "Teaching is *my* task, not yours."

"Well..." A blush tinted her cheeks pink, spreading like wildfire through her skin as she quietly bid, "Shall I offer what you have offered? ...A kiss, Erik? If you please me, would a kiss suffice?"

A kiss... He trembled with the surge of wanting that raced his veins, but huffing his discontent, he snapped, "You'd offer a kiss as a reward, and once again I cannot approve of your impetus. Always an excuse, whether it be pity or sacrifice, now as an incentive, never just because you want it. No, Christine, I don't want a kiss from you. I cannot endure the guilt and regret that goes along with it again."

Playfulness faded to a frown upon her lips. "Don't ask for a kiss. Don't ask for anything. Sing for me, and let me choose how I wish to show my appreciation. And then...if I kiss you, it will be out of my admiration and not at your demand."

Erik wondered if she perceived her offer as a compromise. Denials were a product of sense, but he preferred to listen to an aching heart. "All right, Christine. *Your* choice. Perhaps I shall fail to please you at all and simply send you to bed laughing at my mediocrity."

He was seeking to lighten an intimacy that felt too heavy and delighted in the sweet curves of her smile as she replied, "Well, at least *try*. Give me *something* worthy of judgment."

Without an answer, he rose and took her usual place in the bow of the piano facing her, strangely enjoying this reversal of roles as he teased, "Don't worry. I don't expect you to play."

As she grinned her amusement, he began to sing. It was a lullaby, nothing overdone or showy, no classical arias or elaborate art songs. Something delicate, something beautiful.

Christine was enraptured from the first pitch. If it were her choice, she would beg him to sing to her forever. His voice! It was truly heaven-sent, and to feel the emotion he put into every note, to experience the golden timbre weave about her like a longed-for embrace, she shivered with the sensation swirling through her body and did not quell the adoration in a gaze he never even regarded. No, he was fixed anywhere but at her as if one glance would break his focus. She savored his obvious apprehension. Say what he liked, she knew he was eager to please her no matter what incentive was attached.

His lyrical tenor glided in legato lines, soft and tender, up to a brilliant high note and wrapping about to a cadence. She yearned for more the instant sound faded. How he could make music into a language more beautiful than any in existence!

Before he gave a single look as if hesitant to gauge her estimation, he approached again and knelt beside the piano bench, humbly beseeching at her feet.

"Erik," she softly breathed and waited until he finally met the unconcealed awe in her stare. "You're so afraid, but you must know what a wonder your voice is."

"And how would I know such things?" he demanded in return, desperate to understand. "I don't sing for anyone, Christine. ...Not anymore. My voice was once as abused as my face, exploited for its contradiction. Something so pure to come from a face so ugly. Its illogicality was the main attraction in a Gypsy freak show, and I was locked in a cage and forced to perform for the paying clientele. Oh, don't look at me that way. I can't bear your bewilderment. I've hinted at my unpleasant upbringing before."

But the horror would not dim as she fought to accept his revelations. Locked in a cage, ...it seemed too heinous to be truth; she was sickened merely to imagine it. And then to look at the man kneeling before her and realize that was his *life*, that he was desensitized to such atrocity because he had suffered through it... She wanted to cry and show the emotion he seemed unable to give. "You...you never told me that."

"I'd rather not recall it when I'm with you, but...you listen to me sing and call it *beautiful*. ...I can't share that sentiment, not when singing, to me, meant to the accompaniment of jeers and horrendous insults and the brutality of a whip's sting if I dared stop. A thing of beauty... *Music* is a thing of beauty; my voice is not. It is a further anomaly to an unordinary life, and it is a weapon. How often have I used it since those days to hypnotize prey? My God, I manipulated *you* with it. So please, Christine, cease regarding my voice as a wonder. You should consider it as much an abomination as my face; more so because it deceives you and makes you think of angels. ...*Angels*? I am the *devil*."

Tears cascaded down her cheeks, but he wouldn't look and did not see them. He was too consumed in self-loathing to realize she was hurting with him.

Her voice quivered and betrayed her compassion as she quietly bid, "You said if you pleased me, I may show it as I wish. ...May I still?"

"More pity," he sneered. "More sympathy for the monster. No, I don't want that, ...not from you. I once convinced myself that if you felt *anything* beyond horror, I would grab to it with both hands and never let go. I've grown to see otherwise. You'd kiss me because you want to wipe away every torturous memory from my head."

"No," she softly protested, "I'd kiss you because I'd want to make better ones."

Erik still would not look at her, and she knew she was not bold enough to remove his mask on her own, not after the catastrophe of her last attempt. And so shaking with a shyness she wanted to conceal, she bent close to his crouched form and set a soft, cherishing kiss to his masked cheek, carrying a volatile hope that its gentleness would seep through manmade material and caress his damaged face.

His eyes closed, slow and savoring before a muffled sob shook his shoulders and racked his seemingly broken shape. A tear trailed a path down his one bare cheek, and she did not stop the impulse to brush it away with her fingertips.

"Erik..."

Mismatched eyes were a more vibrant shade than she'd ever seen when tears pooled in their depths as if emotion made their blue and green hues more brilliant, and desperation made them beautiful. In a voice that was hoarse when it had just been crystal clear and golden, he pleaded, "I want to kiss you, Christine. Will you let me? I ache so much..."

She nodded her consent, hoping he glimpsed mirrored longing when she couldn't find the words to speak it. Almost abruptly, he stumbled to his feet and rushed to each lantern scattered about the room, turning their flames down to subtle flickers that left more dark than illumination. One after another as her eyes fought to adjust to dimness.

His body was a silhouette as he tentatively

returned and knelt again at her feet. No more than those blazing eyes and black and white haziness.

"I don't want to put the light out to nothingness," he breathed in thick consonants. "I want you to *know*. I'm so tired of hiding in the dark."

Christine never protested; she waited with anticipation to tingle the length of every limb. One of his hands set so unthreatening upon her bent knee, reassurance and stability as if her presence was the very thing to ground him. The other lifted to his mask. She saw it as another silhouette that trembled vividly to proclaim its trepidation. Shadows, more shadows as he lowered the mask and escaped its protection. That face... This was her first glimpse of it since its revelation. It wasn't a terror when malevolent light was muted. It was a peculiar canvas of indefinable shapes, perhaps a mistake in the ultimate scheme of creation, unusual, uncommon, ...but so wanted that she stifled an impulse to touch. Not yet, not when she was terrified to frighten him away and destroy the moment's translucent bubble.

He held his breath with his exposure, but when she gave no cry of fear or disgust, he released it in a soft sigh, every feature of a mangled face losing tension and softening harsh corners. Still hesitant, he dared to inquire, "Can you see me, Christine?"

"I see...shadows," she whispered back and waited, enthralling herself with the way dim flickers translated their meager glow across that face. It was strangely beautiful and made every detail seem like a dream.

With another sigh, this one laden in surrender, Erik lifted himself higher on his knees and found her lips before she could comprehend his intention. Her gasp was swallowed in his kiss, her entire body jolting with an overwhelming intensity that was too great to bear. She felt thrown from reality for a brief instant, awkwardly uncertain when his lips were so insistent, so urgent and possessive. He was making desire blatant, a revealing admission of what he wanted, and she refused to falter to fear. Not when it felt too wonderful and consuming to deny.

Erik's mouth devoured, lips lacking gentleness when he was afraid if he did not savor this instant, it might never come again. The hand still poised on her knee tightened its fingers to a fierce grip, his tongue deepening the kiss and inspiring a desperate groan to taste her. Why was it so easy to lose head, heart, sense when her willing victim? His face exposed when he rarely removed his mask, his misshapen mouth kissing hard as if it were his right, every abhorrent nuance unhidden. But she kissed him back! And it seemed to validate his sin.

One kiss and another and another, and when he tried to end his violation and draw back, her arms suddenly darted out and caught him about the neck in a demanding embrace as she gasped into the breath of space between mouths, "Don't stop. Please, Erik, don't stop."

Her fingers weaved in his hair, attempting to pull him back, and he did not refuse, a tinge of a smile lost somewhere in the midst of another desperate kiss.

She met every movement, and he groaned his delight when her tongue followed his and barely grazed his misshapen lips to taste him. More, he had to have *more*, but it was she who drew away this time, her hazy eyes fluttering open to meet his for one brief, unsteady breath before urgent transformed to tender. With a sense of longing he had not expected, she set that same branding kiss she had placed to his mask against his scarred cheek.

A hissed breath was sucked into uncertain lungs, but he kept frozen in place even when instinct begged him to flee. The face of a monster, and it had only ever known violence or a mask's coldness, never anything worthwhile or wanted. But she kissed it like it was hers to mark, and even though he was rigid down every muscle, his tongue twisted with an urge to plead with her never to stop.

Warm and soft, he'd never imagined anything could feel so amazing, but her lips brushed those tender kisses from one horrific detail to the next, along his pronounced cheekbone, following the cavernous socket of his eye, lightly touching his nonexistent nose. Delicate! God, she was *so delicate* with him as if terrified too much pressure would shatter him, and in spite of an oath to allow her without interference, tears slid free from the deep corners of his eyes and met the journey of her mouth. She brushed them from an undamaged cheek with fingertips and kissed them from a mangled one.

"Why are you doing that?" he finally breathed, desperate not to sob. His eyes closed as her lips touched his lids with grazed caresses.

Leaning back to gaze at that shadowed face, she repeated in breathless sound, "You said if you pleased me, I may show it as I wish."

"And you wish to kiss something so repulsive?" As she formed another kiss to its distortion, he exclaimed, "Stop! Please, God, just stop! Don't you realize what you're doing? My face...it's *disgusting*, an *abomination*. Dear Lord, Christine, stop it please!"

But though he protested, Christine noted that he made no move to break free, remaining willing when she kissed the obscure, swollen arch of his upper lip. Stop, he said, but so abruptly that she gripped his shoulders for balance, he tipped his mouth upward and caught hers again in another series of desperate kisses.

Long minutes tiptoed by without notice. Everything faded to eager mouths and gripping hands. She longed to beg him never to let go, but he stole letters between his lips, and she was left to clutch his hair as her beseeching. Taut fingers spoke a command for more, and as his hand raced a fiery trail up her spine, she shuddered and cried out into a kiss.

One more taste of bliss to tide him over, and

Erik pulled away, longing only to go back and relive every moment. But he was forced to let time spin forward instead.

"No," she muttered through hazy clouds, restless fingers clenching and unclenching in his sleeves.

"You make me forget the rest of the world," he told her, his voice thick with wanting. "But...you have a performance tomorrow. You need to rest."

Protests still lacked words and were instead murmured sounds of displeasure that grew louder to watch him replace his mask and steal away the vision of his shadowed face.

His hand lightly grazed the knee he had clutched for support, a fond gratitude to one more flawless detail of her body. "Tomorrow you must humbly linger in the background and let Carlotta purloin your rightful place, but your performance will make the sacrifice worthwhile. And...afterward, as per a promise, if you please me and sing to your full potential... A kiss, Christine? Is that still what you want?"

Her nod was without hesitation and so convicted that it was simple torture not to indulge himself and take the offered kiss now. No, he reminded himself, he must be her teacher first.

"If I please you," she replied, blue eyes still flickering with her longing, "I don't want you to turn the light out this time. I want to see you...and your face when you kiss me."

Memories flashed in his head of the last time shadows had been irrelevant, of horror and tears, of a disgust that stung as acutely in recollection as it had at its conception. But then to consider her lips against his cheek, her kisses like the most delicate adorations, ...hope convinced him to nod his concession. "Light...has never been kind, but for you... Whatever you wish, Christine."

She smiled and set her palm atop his, curving

her fingers about his knuckles for one last second before she rose. "Goodnight, *ange*." Smile never dimming, she pressed a quick kiss to his masked cheek, ending the encounter exactly as it had begun, and Erik shivered to consider the routes it had taken in between.

"Goodnight, Christine." Longing eyes watched her go, missing her image immediately. With a smile of his own, he conceded to the power of memories with fingers that touched his bottom lip in vain hope of feeling her kiss once again.

Chapter Eleven

The premiere soared by in a whirlwind.
Christine performed her part while trying to forget the
next afternoon she would be in a very different and far
more integral role. Carlotta, however, had the
opposite objective and made it a point to cast snide
glares and muttered comments every instant they
were offstage. Her latest abuse was to gloat after her
aria and sneer, "That's how it should be done."
Christine ignored her in favor of more pressing
matters, namely a constant perusal of shadows with a
hope that Erik was nearby.

He must be, of course! Didn't he always watch
her? She had to admire his control, for no accidents
befell Carlotta during the extent of the production,
even ones that might have been well deserved.

As soon as curtain call ended, Christine rushed
offstage, eager to be away and cursing the injustice
that she must waste time changing out of her costume
first. A plain, rather forgettable maid's uniform, and
how daunting a thought that the next afternoon, she
would have a lavish, beaded gown instead! Her gaze
lingered on Carlotta as she received a throng of
admirers with fake graciousness in her cold stare. *The
diva*... Tomorrow that would be her.

Before the thought sank in, a hand upon her
arm broke it away. "Christine, come on."

"W...what?" It was the meeting she half-expected and yet dreaded to the depths of her being. Raoul had been conveniently absent as of late, but here he was, clasping her arm and trying to lead her opposite of her dressing room. "Wait, no. Let go."

"Please, I need to speak with you," Raoul persisted. "Alone, where we won't be overheard. Christine, you owe me a conversation at least. I can't bear to leave things as they have been between us."

"I...I can't. I have to-"

"Ten minutes. A conversation, that's all I ask."

She allowed him because one more tug gave their destination away. Up to the roof. As she reluctantly acquiesced, he led her along the path they'd traveled once before. Up, but privacy didn't exist there either, a detail she wasn't indebted to tell him. The roof had ears and eyes, and every word spoken would be its own death warrant.

"Raoul," she demanded as soon as chilled wind and stars appeared, "are you going to tell me why you are lurking about the opera and dragging me away before I've even had the chance to change?"

"You were wonderful tonight," he told her, but his gaze only held hers an instant before it scanned every far reach of the vacant rooftop.

"It wasn't difficult to be wonderful with half a dozen solo lines in the entire show," she protested, guard raised and at the ready. "But that isn't why you're here. Tomorrow is when your kind words would hold meaning."

"Yes," Raoul stiffly replied, "tomorrow when you sing the leading role as the Opera Ghost cast the production."

The remark stung even if that wasn't his intent, and she narrowed her eyes and snapped, "The Opera Ghost? Because I don't deserve anything without his help, you mean."

"No, no," Raoul quickly corrected and rushed to her side, "Of course you are exceptional, Christine, ...more than exceptional, but we don't need to play games with this. The managers told me the truth. He *demanded* that you have the role. Did he tell you that? Did he reveal that he posed threats if anyone refused him? Or has he portrayed himself as your ally and hero?"

"He didn't hurt anyone," Christine fervently insisted, "and he wasn't going to. He's just trying to take care of me."

"And look at this! He has you spouting his lies and making sin acceptable! Can you not see what he did was wrong? Or has he corrupted your thoughts so much that you would defend him? Christine," Raoul caught her shoulders in his palms, his touch deliberately gentle, "do you realize what you are dealing with? He puts on a show as your devoted teacher, plays on your kind heart, but he's manipulating and deceiving you."

"No," she stated firmly, desperate to find that spark of bravery Erik always tried to inspire. Hold to her thoughts and her convictions, but it was easy to listen to Raoul, to falter despite everything she'd already decided as truth. She had to deny a weak spirit's instinct to bend, and her voice wavered as she tried again, "No, you're wrong. You don't know him as I do, Raoul."

"How has he managed to tie you to him, Christine? Fear? Do you defend him because you are terrified what would happen if you didn't?"

She contemplated when fear had lost its significance and disappeared. *Had it* disappeared? With one thought of Erik coming upon this scene and a reaction that must be violent, fear was a reality all over again. And did it matter that she feared for *Raoul's* welfare and not her own? It still meant doubt; she had a suspicion she might *always* doubt.

"Erik won't hurt me," she spoke the one truth she fully believed. "Why are you so determined to convince me that he will?"

"Because you don't realize the true danger you

are in." Huffing his frustration when she shook her head, he changed directions. "I care for you...so much, Christine, but I am not acting out of petulant jealousy or revenge. If your heart chose another, I would let you go. But that's just it. I don't think you *chose* anything. I think you've had fear twisted about until you were convinced it was genuine emotion. It isn't difficult to believe you care for someone who seems to love you so much he would do anything, even *kill* to keep you. Fear, a sense of obligation, misguided sympathy, and he's spun a love story for you in the midst of it."

Strong, she insisted to herself and stated again, "Erik won't hurt me."

"But what happens if you get him angry?" Raoul pushed. "What happens when his temper snaps and surges beyond control? I've heard rumors around the opera house. My God, the managers are terrified to censure him. ...And then there are the stories about his face."

Christine's eyes lowered with the mention, and she knew it gave revelations away. "Stop, Raoul. Just...forget what you've heard and let it go."

"Is it true?" he demanded, and even though she wouldn't look, she felt his blue eyes boring into her with their inescapable interrogation.
"He's...deformed?"

"Don't say it that way," she sharply commanded.

"Well, disfigured then. They say there's a valid reason he wears the mask." Reading her every telltale response, he decided, "It *is* true."

"Please stop."

"And that's why you stay with him and defend him, isn't it? You feel sorry for him."

"No," she protested, but adamancy had lost its weight and a denial sounded like an admission.

"They say he's...a freak of nature, and his face is a monstrosity. ...Have you seen it, Christine?"

A dull nod was her reply, no words when every one felt a betrayal.

"Oh, my poor Christine," Raoul breathed and suddenly hugged her. She never struggled, ashamed somewhere inside to have such a discussion with someone as flawless as the Vicomte. "And that's why I knew I had to come tonight. You need to understand I am only acting in your best interest."

"What are you talking about?" She finally found the impetus to draw away, and her brow knit to observe his solemn stare. "What do you intend to do, Raoul?"

"Tomorrow afternoon when the show is over, ...I mean to take you with me and get you away from that madman."

"No," she immediately insisted. "I won't go. You can't possibly understand him-"

"He's a *murderer*!" Raoul vehemently reminded. "Somewhere beneath his alluring façade lies the truth in its every unpleasant detail. Christine, the *Opera Ghost* with his disfigured face and sin-tainted soul, and what will you argue? That he also has a heart of gold capable of a love you yourself once claimed impossible? Will you let him steal you from the world, love him as he commits his crimes, forgive him every time he crosses a line and *hurts you*? That is preposterous! You're letting yourself be another of his victims!" Grasping one of her shaking hands, he pleaded again, "Think over all I've said. I will be here tomorrow to see you sing, and if you have even one doubt, come with me. Please, Christine, stop and consider if what you feel is rooted in pity, if you stay only because you feel indebted for all he has done for you, ...if you can truly see yourself *loving* him, spending your life with him."

Christine was silent, and this time she could not help but hear his every word. They filled her with dread because she didn't *want* to think of such things.

"Yes, Christine, consider those subjects."

Christine went numb, eyes slowly widening at the sound of that voice before she jerked free of Raoul's grasp and flipped about to face the Opera Ghost in all his glory. He strode with confidence lacing every step and came to stand beside her, glaring coldly at Raoul as if a look alone had a backlash that could kill.

Never glancing at her, Erik added, "You already know what I want, Christine. Your dashing Vicomte poses valid points that need answers. Can you love a monster even as the rest of the world tells you that you are wrong?"

"You *are* a monster," Raoul snapped, and any surprise at Erik's sudden appearance was thrown into unshakable anger. "It sickens me that you have manipulated Christine to your side and convinced her to proclaim your innocence. How dare you?"

"And what would you call a man who claims best intentions but acts because he can't accept rejection?" Erik arrogantly retorted. "She refused your courtship, and you are no better than the unrequited lover obsessing over what he can't have."

"She refused me because *you* made her do it," Raoul stated without sway.

"And have you proof of such absurdity?"

"I will when she chooses to leave with me tomorrow."

"Stop," Christine pleaded, but her meek command went unacknowledged. Bravery and strength felt empty when they bore no direction.

"As if I'd let her go with you so easily!" Erik exclaimed, looming menacingly near his unrelenting opponent. Faced with a masked Opera Ghost, and never even a twinge of apprehension, and that only made Erik more enraged. "You stupid, meddling boy! You cannot accept defeat because it is to *me*! You cannot take such a bruise to your ego."

"You are a murderer, a monster! You probably have Christine locked in a cage to keep her as your dutiful little pet!"

Locked in a cage... The fire danced in murderous flames in Erik's eyes, but Christine latched onto such cruel words and the recalled memory of a violent past. Her little hand caught his sleeve as she begged, "Erik, please, don't."

"No, Christine," Raoul yelled, "don't restrain him and plead for my life. Let him attack and show you what he is. *This* is not a man beside you; this is an animal ready to kill the instant his temper is sparked. You need to look and truly *see* for once! He's a monster!"

"Oh, a monster, am I?" Erik taunted back before averting his fiery glare to Christine. "Yes, Christine, look and see the monster in all his heinousness. Better yet, let's complete the picture. A monster? Here's a monster for you to hate and run from. I'll give you the very excuse to leave with your Vicomte tomorrow."

Before she could reason his intention, he jerked the mask from his face and exposed his disfigurement. A gasp tore from the Vicomte, disgust, aversion, and yet Erik never even glanced his way; his focus was solely on her.

"You wanted to see it by the light," he coldly hissed. "Well, look and see if it's as acceptable as it was last night. Oh, no, of course not, not with your doubts in place again. Now I'm a repulsive corpse, isn't that so?"

Moonlight streaming down, candlelight streaming up from rooftop windows, and the glow was sufficient to chase shadows from abnormalities and make them stark when viewed next to the perfection of the Vicomte's face.

"Christine," Raoul called, and for the first time, his voice wavered with his uneasiness, "you can't tell me that you want *that*."

Erik shot his glare to the Vicomte and presented a vivid view of every horrendous detail.

"Because I am ugly and abhorrent. You know, those who see this face usually don't live long enough to spread the rumors, Monsieur Vicomte."

"No," Christine spoke firmly this time, and clasping Erik's sleeve again, she commanded, "Raoul, leave."

"But, Christine, how could I possibly-"

"Get out!" she shouted, never once regarding the self-dubbed corpse smirking malevolently beside her. "Now! Get out, Raoul!"

"Christine, ...I will return tomorrow," the Vicomte vowed, staring in challenge at Erik's mangled face. "This is not his battle won. I will *not* leave you to this."

"Go!" Christine commanded again. One last shared stare, and she saw an oath in Raoul's eyes, one she wasn't sure she wanted.

As soon as Raoul vanished through the stairwell door, her posture fell, her head cradled in a shaking hand, but feeling Erik tense beside her, she tightened her hold on his arm.

"No," she bid miserably, "please, Erik, just take me home."

"Home?" he posed, the question sharp and insistent.

She nodded but never looked up at him. "...With you." No, she didn't look until motion told her that he replaced the mask, and even then her gaze was distant.

*****

Erik didn't say anything beyond a cold 'goodnight', and the next morning, one word commands announced his sulking mood. But Christine did not have time to dwell. The production had to take precedence no matter how many other traumas weighed upon her shoulders.

Up in her world, she was whisked through preparations: hair, makeup, costuming. As the last of her aides left her alone in her dressing room, the door opened without a knock. Christine jumped with anxiousness as Raoul's proposition sounded endlessly in her memory, but to her relief, he was not her current visitor.

"Christine, you look so lovely!" Meg gushed as she scampered inside and plopped down comfortably on a chaise, never a thought for the awkward layers of tulle surrounding her small shape. "You are going to put Carlotta's performance to shame! Did you know she isn't even here? She refused to make an appearance!"

"That is hardly a surprise," Christine replied as she focused on her reflection in her vanity, never her full-length mirror. No, this meager glass had an advantage of having no eyes to stare back from the other side.

"Well, I think her behavior is petty," Meg announced, picking at her stiff skirts. "If I were a prima donna, which of course I'll never be since I can barely carry a pitch, but if by some twist of an alternate universe, I sang like a lark, and you and I were dueling it out over a part, I would at least make myself look like the bigger person and make an appearance. And by *bigger*, I mean *figuratively*, not literally, although in Carlotta's case, literal is true as well." Giggling to herself, Meg only then took note of Christine's somber air. "What's wrong? You're not nervous, are you? If you are, I can put you at ease by telling you that *only* Carlotta thinks greatly of herself. No one else agrees. Her high notes last night were sharp enough to make ears bleed."

Even though she knew better than to reveal any secret worth keeping to her bubbly companion, Christine could not seem to hold it inside. "Raoul wants to take me away with him."

"What!" Meg shrieked, clamping her hands over her smile. "Where? When? Oh my, Christine, the Vicomte! It's like a fairytale come true!"

A fairytale, but if Raoul were the hero, then by

default, Erik must be the villain, and the thought alone made Christine quickly shake her head. "No, it's not. I don't even know his intentions."

"Who cares? Did you *look* at him?" she gaped. "I'd let a man like that intend *anything* he wants!"

"Meg, ...I don't love him." It was as honest a reason as any other.

"Oh," Meg pouted and nodded understanding, "and that's why you're sad. Well, ...let me be the voice of logic and point out positives." One by one, she counted them on her fingers. "He's handsome, gallant, brave, kind; he's a *Vicomte*." That one earned a longer emphasis and the merit of the rest of her fingers. "Personally, I refuse to put much credence on the concept of love. Why should the heart make all the important decisions? It doesn't seem intelligent to follow a visceral organ anyway. I think if he's a good man and he will take care of you and make you happy, those things are far more important." Jittering anxious hands, she suddenly blurted out, "Can I tell Jammes?"

"No," Christine replied firmly. "Not a word, Meg."

"Oh, you're no fun! Of course one good story won't stop the ballerinas from ogling him, but it would convince them to keep their hands to themselves."

"No, and if you dare, I will hint to your mother that your 'visceral organ' has been chasing after a certain stagehand, one you used to tease for following in your shadow...? Does that secret sound familiar? It's quite convenient how often the two of you 'disappear' from rehearsal at the same time."

That quieted Meg but left a revealing smile behind. "All right, so I'm not as opposed to love as I let on, and I'll keep my mouth shut if only to preserve my secret. ...What can I say? There is some truth to the wanting of the heart, and when it gets hold, it doesn't let go so easily."

That was one point Christine couldn't argue as

she stared distractedly at her reflection. Letting go,
...no, that was impossible.

*****

It wasn't her most brilliant performance. But
how could she give her all when every glance out to
the audience landed on Raoul watching fixedly from
his box? She blamed him for miniscule missteps and
high notes that weren't rounded or free. With Erik's
observation a mystery, Raoul was her visual reminder
of everything she longed to forget.

As the performance neared its last scene,
anxiety coiled against her ribcage for the show that
would follow the final curtain. It seemed another
production altogether. Maybe she'd feel that role
more than she felt her current one.

An emotional duet, a glorious chorus, and the
orchestra played its closing chords as applause rang
out. Before Christine could leave the stage, she
glanced to Raoul only to find him rushing out of his
box. Oh Lord, he didn't intend to come for her now,
did he?

Before she could contemplate what to do, a
collective gasp passed through cast and crew, and
turning frantic eyes, she saw the Opera Ghost, masked
and exuding power in every footstep. He strode
across the stage, his eyes only ever on her while an
audience watched in confused bewilderment. She did
not deny him or attempt an escape; she remained in
place and did not protest as he caught her hand and
pulled her offstage amidst fleeing stagehands.

Never a pause, he brought her into the shadows
beyond the chaos, disappearing within their darkness
before Raoul could arrive backstage. To everyone
else, it would seem the ghost had abducted her, and
they'd vanished from the world of reality.

Neither of them spoke on the journey below,
silence uncomfortable and thick as it permeated the
damp air. Only when Erik released her just beyond
the doorway's threshold did she say in shaking tones,

"You didn't need to put yourself on display to come for me."

"And if I hadn't?" he snapped, rounding furiously on her. "If the Vicomte had gotten to you first, would you have gone with him as willingly as you went with me?" He shook his head skeptically. "I'm convinced that you haven't made a decision, and whichever one of us claimed you first would have had you tonight."

"That isn't true-"

"Two days ago," he roared, "I would have believed you'd choose me, but the Vicomte inspired doubts I have been desperate to chase away. Now you don't know what to believe and prefer anyone else to make the choice for you. And so I did. ...Go to bed, Christine, ...and don't worry about the Vicomte. I feel no need to pursue vengeance when I have what I want right here already. The only reason I'll have to go after him is if he tries to take it away."

In the recesses of her somber expression flashed a memory: he had spoken of a kiss if she pleased him tonight. How farfetched such an idea suddenly seemed! No words of encouragement or praise for her performance, not a single kind sentiment, and as she turned and obeyed, tears filled her eyes.

Erik watched her retreat, every bit of courage gone from her posture, and his attention briefly fixed on the sparkling beads along the skirt of her costume. The opera... Had he heard a single note when his focus had been consumed forming plans? All he had seen was the attentive Vicomte and then his beloved on the stage one premature motion from being ripped out of his life. Damn that Vicomte! His need to be a commended savior had spoiled everything! Because of his interference, Christine felt further from Erik's grasp than ever before. A hope on the verge of shattering...

*****

The last thing Christine remembered that night was going to bed with melancholy weighing heavily upon her heart. Dreams were broken fragments in between, nothing concrete, moving too quickly for her to grasp hold. And then...cold lips pressed against hers with such ferocity that she jolted to awareness, heaved from dreamscape's wandering back into her body, ...a body being crushed into the mattress.

Erik... He was atop her, burying her beneath his weight as his mouth sought to make her respond with fervent coaxing. Her eyes fluttered open, but in the darkness, he was shadows again. How he seemed to prefer being the indecipherable silhouette! It was as infuriating as it was intoxicating.

No vision to ground her, and so Christine fought not to become lost to kisses that wanted to steal coherency. Erik atop her, his mouth bruising in his desperation for a response, the hard planes of his body molding to hers despite every existent barrier in between, his threatening desire arching against her belly to proclaim his wanting... Part of her wondered if this was indeed a dream, but...dreams had never been so consuming.

His mouth would not cease its violation, devouring, eager for more, and as those cold, misshapen lips parted, his tongue delved within the seam of hers, making her shiver. Tempting strokes urged her to surrender, and her soft cry was no more than a vibrated hum against his lips.

Kisses did not seem to be enough; hands grew envious for their role. They caught her face between tensed palms before making fevered caresses down her throat to curl about the neckline of her nightdress. Fingertips grazed within and traced the skin of her chest, teasing as they dipped lower to brush the space between her breasts. A temptation and yet so innocent that she was left to whimper for more with unintelligible sounds abducted in constant kisses. She instinctively arched closer to those bold hands, but they traveled up again and fisted in her loose curls.

His lips left hers longing as he made a fiery trail of kisses along her jaw and burrowed his unmasked face in the cloud of her curls.

"Erik," she was finally able to gasp, but coherency shifted in and out of focus when his hips taunted her with an arching that made her writhe. "Wait, what...what are you...?"

"I'm taking what I want," he hoarsely bid, and she cried out as his breath tickled her ear with its delicious warmth.

"T...taking?" she stuttered, unsure she cared about an answer anymore.

"Yes, that's what monsters do. They don't hesitate. If they want something, they take it."

Reality flickered into consciousness whether she wanted it or not. "Monster? What are you talking about?" She tried to pull back, determined to find his eyes in the muted light, but he would not budge from his preferred place atop her, rubbing his scarred cheek into her hair.

In husky consonants, he told her, "I foolishly tried to compete with that Vicomte on his level and woo you like a gentleman, but as I was aptly reminded last night, that is something I can never be. I will always be the notorious Opera Ghost, and my sins deem that I need not feign nobility anymore. I want you, and so I'll have you."

"Stop saying such things," she pleaded adamantly as he destroyed desire and made it seem tainted. "You are *not* a monster."

"And are you so convicted in your belief, Christine? I watched the Vicomte inspire doubts again. Everything I've done to give you something worthy of your love, and he made it sound vulgar and heinous."

Every accusation grew more biting until he was once again pressing against her, this time with anything but desire. No, he wanted to hurt her, and he ignored her soft gasp. "Your Vicomte spoke lies and his own version of the truth, and you *believed* him. Fear for the deformed monster forcing your kisses and your touch? Pity to allow me when you long to recoil? Is it true? I had concluded we were beyond such inane bases. You allow me because *I* want it? No! *You* want it, or so I thought. But you saw my face on the rooftop, and it was once again a horror with your Vicomte to corrupt your view. You let him persuade you to shun me! You let his words mean something! Why can't you be strong enough to *know me*? To quit excuses and doubts and love me even if it isn't a path the rest of the world can accept? You are so easily swayed by a moral compass that doesn't exist when it is only the two of us together. ...Why can't you just love me?"

Erik wanted anger and brutal vengeance, wanted to enact his own self-hatred upon her, but there were too many heartstrings attached. A tirade quickly drained of aggression until tears choked sound, but he still managed to demand, "Do you stay because you feel you owe it to me? Is it obligation and pity that keep you permissive of my touch? If it is... My God, I truly am a monster!"

"No, no," she quickly insisted, and her arms left her covers to wrap around his shaking body, hugging him to her. "I stay because I want to."

He shook a doubtful head. "Would you have left with the Vicomte tonight, Christine? Would you have left me?"

He knew the answer she would give, but he didn't know if he would believe her. But words were not her only persuasion. Her hand found his unmasked face in the darkness, and warm fingers caressed his scars as if they belonged to her.

"I won't leave you," she whispered, outlining every distortion. "I promise, Erik. I won't leave."

With her touch as his anchor, he finally believed and pressed penitent kisses to her caressing fingers. "I'm sorry, Christine, ...so sorry. I don't want to hurt you or force you. And I came to your bed like an animal tonight. ...Forgive me."

"Sshh," she crooned gently, and cupping his cheek in her palm, she whispered, "Just let me hold you, *ange*, and nothing else will matter."

Erik clasped her in desperate arms, terrified to let go and lose this moment. No, she was his.

He never left her bed. Words went unuttered as intruders to the stillness; they were insufficient when compared to the soft hand stroking his cheek gently at every breath.

Eventually, he lay beside her, his face pillowed in her hair, and with her curled against him, he found peace enough to sleep. When every detail finally felt permanent and not momentary...

Chapter Twelve

Christine awoke in her bed alone with only vivid memories to insist Erik had been there. All she had were fantasies of a violation that hadn't truly been a violation at all. Her innocence longed to dub his actions a sin, but her body called it a lie as it craved more. Desire...and it seemed to be swallowing her whole.

Dressing with hasty fingers, she could not seem to move fast enough to satisfy her longing. She had to see him; that was her only thought, to see if wisps of the previous night's emotions remained. She was prepared for more self-hatred displaced in anger, for sharp regrets, perhaps more apologies. What was entirely unexpected was the grin she received as she met him in the sitting room.

"Christine, did you sleep well, *petite*?"

She regarded him oddly, studying with a quizzical tilt of her head. "...Yes," she hesitantly replied. "And you, Erik? ...Did you sleep well?"

"It would be impossible not to when beside you. Your warmth and your nearness... If my very existence had ended in that spot, I would have had no regrets and only considered myself a fortunate man."

His mismatched eyes pierced her with their stare. Even his bliss harbored its own intensity, as if every emotion he knew was just that much greater than normal people. Mankind was acquainted with such feelings from birth as a human gift, but for Erik, it seemed they were too new and uncommon and must be suffered beyond their full capacity.

Still hesitant and lingering just past the doorway, she asked, "Will we have a lesson after breakfast? I have no rehearsal. Perhaps we could work on something new."

"No, not today. Today...I have too much on my mind to consider music."

"Not consider music," she muttered as if he must be joking. Did he even know how to exist without some sort of pitches playing in his head? Too often when silence ensued, she would catch him quietly humming to himself, eyes distant as he chose to compose symphonies in his mind. And now he wanted to ignore music...

"I had an epiphany I'd like to share with you. Will you please sit?" He gestured to the vacant couch and waited until she tentatively obeyed and flounced atop the soft cushions, watching him at every second. "Why are you regarding me so suspiciously?"

"Because you *breathe* music. Usually, the instant I suggest working on something new, you have a handful of scores awaiting. No lesson, no singing... Are you ill?"

He chuckled lightly, and it only put her further on edge. "No, of course not. I'm just acknowledging that there is more to the world than music and operas. I've spent my lifetime losing myself in the music because it was the only beauty I had, but now...now I have hope for something even more exquisite. Music is insufficient in comparison."

"What do you mean?"

"My epiphany," he reminded with a tinge of excitement he could not fully dim. "Will you indulge me and listen?"

"All right," she decided, but her arched brows insisted on a curiosity Erik had predicted and recognized so well. He smirked at her intrigue and took it as a benefit that she would not be assuaged until he revealed his intentions.

Sitting anxiously beside her, he refrained from an instinct to take her hand and entwine fingers. *Not yet, words first.* "I awoke this morning in your bed with your body pressed to mine as you slept, and as I marveled over your existence, I realized there is one thing that can be done to make every detail more than a fleeting pleasure."

A small smile curved her lips, and it never faded as she pushed, "What exactly?"

Eyes sparkling with elation, he bid, "Marry me."

"What?" Christine gasped. "M...marry you? But-"

"If we were married, then try as he might, your Vicomte could not steal you away. You said it last night, Christine; you promised never to leave me. Were those only empty words to pacify a monster in your bed, or did you mean them?" He scrutinized every reaction, desperate to find something more than shock and surprise. "Christine, ...you had to realize that was my purpose. I might not have planned to be this hasty about it, but I have no desire for a life without you."

"But marriage... I've already said I'd stay with you," she stammered, her voice wavering every few syllables. "Why do you need a vow to make my word have meaning?"

"Because the vow makes it permanent and binding. No man or *Vicomte* could take it away." Finally yielding to temptation, he reached to her, noting how her eyes followed the path of his hand until it landed upon hers. "You say you do not come to me out of fear or pity. ...And maybe you don't act out of love either, but there is affection between us, and it is strong enough to constantly pull us to one another. It is the most powerful connection I've ever known. It's shouting that we were meant to be together."

Her eyes were still wide with apprehension, and tracing his fingers along her knuckles, he attempted, "I would be a good husband to you, Christine. Devoted and loyal. I would adore you."

Shaking her head, she muttered, "But...you would be marrying me to taunt the Vicomte and force him from my life."

"I would be marrying you because I *love* you," he corrected, and she shivered with his blatant admission. "It...isn't such a horrid idea, is it?"

Her reply was delayed, her eyes locked on their joined hands, and he wished he could decipher the inner workings of her mind. "...Not horrid, but...where is the threat?"

"Threat?"

She still would not meet his eye. "Or ultimatum. However you choose to pose it. If I refuse, what will it be? A threat on the Vicomte's life? Something greater this time? Perhaps a danger to the entire opera house? Another accident? You threatened the managers with a catastrophe to earn my role in the opera. I'm sure you have an even more elaborate disaster to offer me. A fire to break out during the next full performance? Or...what else? Maybe dropping the chandelier upon unsuspecting innocents? You must have something dramatic in mind."

Erik glared at her insinuation. A *threat*? Wasn't he himself the greatest threat of all? "Ah, this is my own fault," he concluded. "I came to you as the Opera Ghost last night and resurrected the violence in that role. You expect nothing more. I want a marriage, and you presume I will force it upon you in some manner or another."

"Won't you?" Blue eyes finally lifted, and suspicion was written plainly in their depths. "You usually have no hesitation when it comes to getting what you want. Not even a sense of right and wrong hinders you."

"And if that were true, then boundaries crossed last night would have been *fully* crossed," he snapped, and suddenly leaping to his feet, he loomed over her. "I will give you time to consider my proposal. *Your* choice, Christine, and there are no threats to make it for you. Wouldn't it be so much easier for you if there were? You'd love to spin your own desires about and make yourself the sacrificial lamb. You could *pretend* you didn't want this and blame it all upon a futile threat: you married me to save the world. But no, I won't give you that escape this time. *You* make the choice, and *you* be convicted to follow it on your own. I am through being a victim to your weak will."

And with that, he charged out of the room, leaving her to stare after him and shiver once beyond his immediate presence. *Marry him...* His proposal held so much more importance than the Vicomte's longing to take her away. Erik's proposal churned through mind and heart. She recalled Meg's words, that a heart made its own decisions, and she knew hers was shouting at her now. But it was so simple to make the choice; it was much harder to accept it.

Her thoughts were abruptly broken as a furious piano's song poured down the hall from his bedroom and encompassed her in its rage and beauty. Every pitch stabbed mercilessly with sharp guilt. He wanted to place her before the music, but the instant she hurt him, he returned to the solace only its melodies could offer him. And she had to listen to his pain, his every emotion and rejection in a more powerful manner than words. Music...for the first time, she hated its inherent beauty.

*****

Erik kept his distance as hour after hour stretched minutes and weighed upon her shoulders. Eventually, the music ceased its aggression and dwindled into a plaintive song laden with melancholy and a loneliness she could feel as acutely as if it were her own. So much time spent listening, and through melodies, she glimpsed Erik's soul, blatantly exposed and dangled before her. It was another offer he couldn't have known he was making. His soul with its every brilliant facet and every staggering flaw. And it could be hers...

She didn't know how long he intended to linger in music's spell, and never daring to interrupt, she wandered the house's meager rooms, eventually pausing outside his closed bedroom door to listen. Pressing her cheek to the wood, she let the music sweep through her and found herself carried away in its tide. Every note made an impression in her heart, melodies modulating from one key to the next, from one *mood* to the next, never ceasing in between. Emotion knew no pause in its consumption; neither did Erik's music.

Silence finally came well into evening, and it was such a stark contrast that she jumped with a start the moment pitches ceased. By then, she had retired to the sitting room couch again and was curled upon its cushions as songs mesmerized her. Without them, she felt anxious and trembled to hear the bedroom door abruptly open and footsteps approach.

"Christine?"

"Y...yes, Erik?" She sat up tall the instant he appeared in the doorway, wondering if he'd be upset to realize she'd been listening. It wasn't as if she could help it in the small confines of the house; listening was inevitable. But she felt as if she had witnessed something so intimate and personal that she should know shame and be penitent.

But he drew no notice; the notes were already out of his head. "I want to take you somewhere. Get your cloak."

She did not question, rising and hurrying to her room. Curiosity made her obedient, but a longing to forget the reaching depth of emotion made her hasty. Perhaps an outing would steal some of the uneasiness hovering in the air.

As they returned to the world and exited onto the city street, Christine cast wary glances at her companion. The sidewalk was crowded with people, and though the shadows of a hat hid the extent of his mask, she could feel his immediate rise of tension. Fear, and fear for Erik was always answered with anger. In an attempt to pacify him, she slid her hand through his arm and kept near his side, and as per her intent, she saw his anxiety transform into pleasant surprise as he met her eye.

Acting as if it was the most natural occurrence, she led their pace, matching the strangers around them and inquired lightly, "And where are we going?"

"You'll see," he replied with a tentative smile. "I regret I have no hired coach to hasten our journey, but you favor starlight. It is a lovely night for a walk."

She agreed with that. It was crystal clear above their heads with moon and stars to glisten in their bed. Their light was muffled to the warm flickers of streetlamps, but as the city limit passed and streets grew dark, the night seemed to brighten as if someone turned up its natural glow.

Christine glanced skeptically at Erik as cobblestone walkways become dirt-lined and rural, but he only shrugged innocently without an answer. She was left to survey trees and a distinct lack of people and attempt to form her own conclusions.

"That curiosity of yours always gets me in trouble," he suddenly insisted with a huff. "Let me assuage it a little and at least assure you that behind the trees, there are residences, large houses of the wealthy class who long to keep a meager distance from city life. We are not wandering some unexplored terrain in the dark."

"What does that mean? There wasn't a single answer in your words."

He shook his head with a light chuckle that delighted her into a smile. "And I've dug myself a deeper grave, it seems. I can see the hypotheses reeling through your head. But don't worry. We're almost at our destination, and then curiosity will rest again, however temporarily."

Christine made a face, but her incessant smile made any feigned annoyance a lie.

As predicted, not much further down the dirt road, Erik turned their direction and guided her onto a gravel pathway. Her boots were unsteady, and she gripped tighter to his arm as her eyes wandered ahead through a throng of tall, old trees.

A dark silhouette appeared first, illuminated only by moonlight's aid, and as they strolled closer, it became a house, large and quaint with turrets and gables that extended to the stars. The meager light showed a spindled porch that wrapped around its shape and dozens of windows without any glow to proclaim life within.

Christine's brow furrowed with the rapid spin of her thoughts, but she kept them contained between pursed lips until they arrived at the base of porch stairs. Then before he could lead her onward, she halted and planted her heels deep into the gravel to stop him.

"Wait... What is this?"

"A house, but I thought that was obvious," he teased with a slight grin at her surprise.

"But *whose* house?"

Ignoring her bewilderment, he insisted, "Just come inside. It's lovely; you'll adore a glimpse."

"A glimpse? Into a stranger's house? That hardly seems a good idea." But her protests were weak as she lifted planted feet and let him pull her up the rickety porch. Her boots made deafening sounds on the white wood with every meager step, but, as she reminded herself, there was no one about to hear or call them intruders. ...No one as far as her gaze could see.

Erik had a key, and the thought only half-registered in her processing mind. It was an answer to a question she was afraid to ask.

But she went willingly inside with him. Moonlight streamed in from many windows and lit their surroundings. Rooms... Large, *empty* rooms.

Watching her at every breath, Erik released her arm within what should have been a sitting room with its large bay window consuming half a wall. She wandered idly to the glass and touched her fingertips to it as if testing its tangibility, and determined to push reality into focus, he took the moment to light random sconces and bathe them in warm hues instead.

Abruptly facing him, she demanded again with a slight waver, "Whose house is this?"

"Mine, ...hopefully *ours*," he admitted.

"A...a house? You bought a house?"

"Weeks ago actually. I didn't see fit to tell you until now, but...I wanted you to understand this is not some fleeting fancy or a scheme to thwart the Vicomte. When I asked you to marry me, it was because I want to spend my life with you, because I've already envisioned a wonderful future for us. ...I've overwhelmed you," he decided, reading her exasperation.

"I...I wasn't expecting... But you've always been so sure in your heart," she noted with a shake of her head. "I'm the hesitant one between us."

Strolling idly to the doorway, he stroked a hand along the carved wood trim, gazing at it fondly as he told her, "You have to understand that before you appeared in my life, I had no desire for such things: a house in the world, a family. It wasn't as though I had opportunities thrown before me, but it never seemed important. Being with you makes me selfish; it makes me long for a million more moments in your presence. Marriage is not about staking a claim over you, though I've let you believe that. If you were only a possession to me, I wouldn't go to such extremes to make you happy. I hoped this house would please you. A real home, ...neither one of us truly has that."

Her gaze lost its widened astonishment with his words, and as it roamed the room, she decided, "It *is* a lovely house."

Nodding eagerly, he took her encouragement and latched onto it with both hands. "Yes, yes, it is. May I show you the rest of it?"

She was hesitant even as she conceded and followed him to a tall, wide stairway with a spindled railing.

Room after room, and though he offered a few meager statements for each, she remained pensive, studying every nuance and never offering her opinion in return.

"The master bedroom," he told her as they entered the last and largest room on the upper floor. He stayed back and observed her silently as she wandered, her footfalls echoing as they tapped the hardwood floor. "It...overlooks a garden in the back. The last I glimpsed, it was just beginning to brim with life. Would you enjoy the flowers, Christine?"

She stared out at the so-called garden, now only brush dusted in moonlight, and as she tried to decipher species, she replied, "You've never asked me such a thing. You know me better than anyone ever has, but you don't know if I like flowers. ...Perhaps it's ridiculous to consider that."

"Mundane details," he concluded. "I know the heart of you, and that's far more important than if you prefer roses or lilies."

"Roses," she declared, meeting his watchful stare. "I prefer roses. Are there roses in the garden?"

"Yes, a few bushes, and if that's what you like, we'll plant more. Dozens and dozens until every speck of ground is laden in their vines."

But wariness did not vanish, twisting its wayward path within her, and as she averted her focus back to the darkened garden, she breathed in a whisper, "Marrying the Opera Ghost."

"No one would learn that truth. Your new husband need not be considered one and the same with the Opera Ghost. As far as anyone would know, a wealthy patron of the arts was enchanted by your performance and fell madly in love with you. Since he is an elusive and private sort, public gatherings would be unfavorable and go unattended. I could be as much a mystery in that role as Opera Ghost."

Shaking her head doubtfully, she reminded, "But the managers and Raoul-"

"The managers know better than to toy with their ghost. They will keep their mouths shut to preserve their well-being. And dearest Raoul will go ignored because it is hardly uncommon for jilted suitors, especially pretentious Vicomtes to concoct lies to save face. Let him speak one word that you have wed the Opera Ghost. It will only seem suspicious when you will be happy and over-indulged to your heart's content. Money can buy me a new reputation if I want."

He stated his plan so confidently that Christine wondered exactly how long he had been forming its facets. "And so to everyone else, you will play a new role, but what will I be left with? Who shall I be married to? The fictitious patron? The nonexistent angel? The Opera Ghost?"

"No," he gently replied, "beneath all of those roles and every disguise, you've always picked out my soul. I will not play a role with you ever again."

"You play a role now," she accused. "The man in the mask, and that is the worst role of all. It is so perfected and so natural you don't know how *not* to play it."

Temper flared in his eyes, as he demanded, "What would you have me do then? Since you are so set on unraveling me, tell me how to break my supposed role."

"Take off your mask." She spoke the command

without hesitation or regret, no matter the adamant refusal she already saw forming on his tongue. "You were to show me your face by the light," she reminded, keeping firm and stoic.

"I did!" he snapped and fisted hands in a futile attempt at control. "You reprimand me again and again for choosing shadows, but you prefer them as well. You wouldn't even look at me! That was on the roof by moon-glow and candlelight, but here...now, there is nothing to hide behind. You would see every ugly detail."

"I would see the face of the man who wants to marry me," she insisted. "Take off your mask and show me the Erik whose soul was played for me in music this afternoon. Show me that man instead." She never approached, lingering near the window and waiting, but she added, "You want me to be strong, and yet you choose to be weak and cower behind your mask. It hardly seems fair."

Impulse was to defend himself with anger as his weapon, but she was so calm before him, so convicted. Had he ever seen her that way? "All right," he conceded with a huff. "And when I take off the mask, will it assure you that you would not be marrying the Opera Ghost? That only Erik would be your husband?"

She didn't answer as she crept across the wooden floor, hearing it creak and moan with every step. By Erik's own teaching so long ago, she could hear music in every utterance, and it was beautiful because every sound brought her closer and only ceased when she stood anticipating before him. This was what she wanted: a chance to rewrite a tragedy. Life-changing events often carried a bit of regret and a wonder what difference could be made to repeat them. A second chance, and she was determined to embrace it.

His eyes were locked on hers as he lifted the mask away, but she noticed that his hand shook. It always seemed to shake when he sought to show her only bravery and cracked his façade. She adored him for it.

And then his face was exposed and illuminated in the light, and as she ran her gaze along every recalled detail, her fingertips tingled and reminded her what each felt like to the touch. For too long, she was only allowed to know him with her hands. Now to see, there was no shock left to suffer. No, all she could think was she *knew* that face already.

"You're smiling," Erik stated incredulously.

"Am I?" she muttered, inching small steps closer.

"Yes, and it's disconcerting. I know how to respond to disgust and fear, but your smile... This face repulsed you, Christine, and yet I see none of that now."

Repulsed... Merely the word made her cringe and desperate to forget its stigma, she lifted an eager hand and trailed her fingers along his scarred cheek. So delicate a caress, and she watched his eyes close to savor it, watched emotion so vibrant on that malformed face that it made her tremble. All such details finally hers. They felt like a gift.

One touch and before she could make more, his arm darted out and caught her about her waist. Dragging her yielding body close, he pressed her fitfully to him, molding every inch with fervent hands racing along her spine. Her cry gave away her longing; she was pliant and permitted him, shivering delight when his restless hands settled in the small of her back and guided her against him. Even through too many layers, she felt his wanting, and it left her knees to quake beneath her weight until she was sure it was only his strength holding her upright.

"Erik," she breathed softly, gazing into his real face. No mask, no shadows. Here was the man who professed love and adoration, vehement with almost too much passion for one body to contain and yet so vulnerable at his core. She saw every nuance of him in that face and never shied away. Her fingers were still touching, teaching her eyes what they already knew, and he tilted his head to press fevered kisses to their tips.

"Everything, Christine," he fervently insisted between kisses. "You see all I am before you, and you want me still. How can you ever question that you were meant to be mine? *No one* has *ever* touched this face; *no one* has *ever* looked upon its deformations without cowering, pleading for mercy, calling me the devil incarnate. You...you touch its every detail, and you *smile* as if it is something worthy to behold."

Without a word, she made that smile into a kiss and laid it against his cheek, relishing his gasp as he arched closer to her lips. His arms tightened their grip, and his hips pressed into hers, begging for more.

"I ache so much for you," Erik gasped against her ear and felt her shudder as if it were his own. Keeping his cheek to her temple, he declared in thick tones, "I want it understood that if you agree, I expect a real marriage and everything that goes along with it. *Everything*, Christine," he repeated and rocked his hips deliberately against hers. "That can be your excuse. You want me; you've *always* wanted me, but desire this potent and dark is shameful to you. Now you can surrender without guilt and call it your wifely duty. Only I will make sure it *never* feels like an obligation. I will make you want it so much that you plead for it."

Her breaths were shallow gasps. Every one tickled his skin on its harsh exhalation, and he silently reveled in her response, in knowing she wanted *him* and was unable to deny it.

"Christine," he whispered temptingly against her ear, "I could have taken this last night. I wanted you so much. But how much sweeter to claim it when it is truly mine to have? My face doesn't matter; you desire me in spite of it. All you have left to decide is if you can be strong enough to love me. As I said, I want everything from you. I will settle for nothing less."

Erik abruptly released her, satisfied to see her shaken and disappointed as she smoothed her skirts with trembling hands and sought to collect herself. In a confident tone as if he were not a desperate victim of desire but seconds before, he told her, "I have shown you what I offer: heart, soul, body, love and desire and every other sensation running through my veins. A house, a real home and a family, and even a fabrication to cover the unacceptable flaws for the rest of the world. *You* must decide if that is enough. You may not shun this face, but will you one day regret that it is not the perfection of the Vicomte staring back at you? Will you grow to hate me for the details I can't change? It is *your* choice, Christine. I will not vow anything to make it for you. No threats, no assurances. I am not playing a game to win you this time."

Christine listened, still unsteady on her feet, and as he replaced his mask and hid behind its boundary, she stifled an urge to tear it away and find that face again. It was so new and intriguing, and she wasn't finished exploring its oddities. But he was already leading the way out of the master bedroom and down through the house. She was reluctant to leave, and as her eyes passed one final glance into the sitting room, she envisioned it decorated and full. A real home...

But she did not share her musings with Erik, half-afraid they would be taken as a commitment. She kept silent and pensive the entire journey back.

A husband, a family, a home... Of course those were all things she wanted, had planned since childhood, but...could she see her future with Erik at her side? Why was it easier to accept when she had fantasized marriage with a white-winged angel? For as absurd as such an idea now seemed, it still played in her subconscious. One would presume it better to love a man over an angel, but when the man bore flaws that exceeded even a scarred face, an intangible angel was a dream. To love a bodiless voice, a pure soul, one that would not overwhelm her with a desire so dark and powerful that it could suffocate her in its web. Yes, it would have been simple, and yet as Erik had insisted, it wouldn't have been enough.

To love a real man with a real heart to love her back was frightening; to love the Opera Ghost was more terrifying yet. But weren't the very things in life that inspired fear and anxiousness, the most fulfilling when conquered? Her heart kept its argument that following this path might be scary, but it was destined. Something greater than she could imagine awaited her at its end. And she believed it.

Chapter Thirteen

The next day, Christine returned to rehearsal. She was anxious, considering her last appearance had ended with her abduction by the Opera Ghost for all to see. As expected, an abundance of cold stares and whispers surrounded her the instant she arrived. But strong meant keeping her head high and not breaking, and she was determined to at least pretend.

"Christine!" Meg was the only one to rush to her side, and clasping her arm, she led her beyond eavesdroppers. "What happened to you? That was the Opera Ghost! The *Opera Ghost*! And he took you with him! You must be traumatized!"

"No, Meg, I'm fine," Christine calmly replied in the face of her friend's rampant dramatics. "He...he enjoyed my performance and wanted to tell me so." A ridiculous explanation, and she suddenly cursed Erik for not devising a plausible one for her. The impatience of that man! He could have at least waited until she was offstage and out of the public eye to abduct her!

"And he didn't...hurt you, did he?" Meg nervously stammered, patting her arm. "You can tell me anything, Christine. I would *never* judge you. What did he do to you?"

Christine stifled an urge to smile. *What indeed...* And yet, how much of it was unwanted? ...And how much was she longing to do again?

"Nothing, Meg. I'm fine, just anxious for rehearsal to begin. It feels like everyone is whispering about me."

"They are," Meg bluntly declared. "You can't blame them. They're terrified of the Opera Ghost, and they saw you go with him *willingly*. You never even cried out for help, Christine."

The little ballerina was searching for a story Christine had no intention of sharing, but lying had even less appeal, especially when each lie seemed to beget a dozen more. "I have to take my place. Reyer is about to start." It was a feeble excuse that only served to make her sound guilty, but she scurried away and left Meg to draw conclusions in her wake.

Biting glares and gossip aside, everything seemed back to normal. Carlotta was cold and insulting and assigned the lead in the next production, and Christine had another futile role with a handful of lines. But she showed no disappointment as the cast list was read. She had a suspicion her lesson that evening would have her exploring the lead, a letter and a threat away from performing it. Erik's tactics might not be honest, but with a haughty, self-centered woman like Carlotta manipulating the management with her reputation and her own threats as weapons, Christine knew she would otherwise be forced backwards instead of upwards. There was simply too much politics involved in singing!

Unneeded for the first few scenes, Christine was sent to be fitted, and she accepted the reprieve eagerly, desperate to be free of lecherous stares. The corridors were vacant, everyone occupied in one department or another, and so a hand catching her arm and pulling her into a random dressing room was answered by her sharp gasp and urge to struggle. The hand was not cold.

"Raoul! What are you doing here? Are you going to make it a habit to drag me off whenever the mood arises? I am in the middle of rehearsal." She tried to seem annoyed, but in the back of her mind were skepticism and fear. He couldn't possibly be considering playing Erik's game and simply taking her away with him, could he? She jerked out of his grasp and edged a step to the closed door.

The Vicomte looked exhausted, and his haggard appearance was the one thing that kept her acquiescent. "I searched the cellars," he told her, and a shudder raced her spine.

"What? Why?"

"I was looking for you," he snapped as if she should be grateful. "When you never returned to your apartment, I was terrified that *creature* had taken you for good. My God, Christine, why do you look upset? Did you want me to do nothing and let him have you?"

"You need to stay away," she ordered, instead of a real answer. "There is only so much Erik will allow before he retaliates. You've already pushed too far, and if he knew you were in the cellars... Raoul, have enough sense not to do that again. I can't protect you if he finds you wandering where you shouldn't. He will take it as an attack."

"And *kill me* perhaps?" he incredulously demanded. "You speak these things as if they are only too typical. Killing a man for being in the cellars, and I see no condemnation for such a sin in your eyes."

"Erik would believe he was protecting me," she justified.

"And that makes murder acceptable?"

"No, but you don't know Erik. He-"

"Lives by an entirely different moral code than the rest of us?" Raoul offered. "Where murder is an anticipated and forgivable offense? Christine, what are you saying?"

"I'm saying you don't *know* him," she repeated firmly. "He reacts impulsively, and *no*, it *isn't* right. But he's been desperate to try righteousness lately *for me*. And...well, that's better than not trying at all."

But the Vicomte shook his head. "So he can murder and justify it as protecting you, but I am not allowed the same because I am not disfigured. I am not even permitted to search the cellars and hope to rescue you from danger."

"I keep telling you there is no danger-"

"Christine, I care about you! You deserve so much more than a creature in the shadows." Raoul glanced off, eyes distant with memory as he added with a cringe, "His face... I have never seen anything so vile, so repulsive."

Repulsive... Christine heard Erik's voice in her inner ear, describing himself the same with that self-loathing to taint every syllable of a degrading word. "I don't wish to discuss his face with you. It is none of your business."

"*He* was the one to put it on display, and you cannot tell me that you were not disgusted as well. It's understandable. If I hadn't been so desperate to seem a valid opponent, I would have been broken by my own repugnance. I just...I had no idea he'd look like that."

"I wasn't disgusted!" she hissed, and his brows arched with surprise. "I looked away! I admit it, but I didn't want to see his face, not like that. He was using it in anger and wanted to make me hate him for it, and I wasn't going to let him do that again."

"And guilt makes you lean and sway and give him anything he wants," Raoul concluded. "You will condemn yourself to be his ally or worse, his mistress." He grimaced with merely the word, and as she looked away, he frantically demanded, "Has he...? Is he forcing an intimate relationship with you, Christine? Dear God, is this worse than I first thought? Has he tried to touch you...or *kiss* you? Do you permit him because you are afraid to refuse?" Each query grew in anxiousness, and he didn't need a reply when her cheeks tinged pink and lowered lashes revealed every secret. "Oh, Christine... And that ugly bastard dared put his hands on you! Damn him!"

"Why are you so sure it's a sin?" she suddenly

demanded. "Only because of his face? Because he is disfigured, any attempted caress is tainted and repulsive to consider. It *must be* a violation more appalling than murder. His hands upon me... You are more *disgusted* than jealous at the mere notion."

"Well, of course!"

"And it *must be* a manipulation if I *want* to touch him."

"Yes!" Raoul vehemently replied. "How could it possibly be anything else?"

"Because good girls don't want Opera Ghosts," she decided in a whisper.

"Exactly! Do you believe me, Christine?"

"Good girls don't want Opera Ghosts," she repeated somberly. "A good girl would shun the touch of a disfigured murderer."

"Yes, yes!" the Vicomte exclaimed, nodding encouragement. "But none of this is your fault, Christine. He manipulated and confused you. But it won't happen any longer; I will help you, and together, we'll break free of this madman."

A single nod was her reply, and she softly muttered, "I have to get back to rehearsal."

"Yes, all right, but I will meet you when it's over and see you home. I won't take the chance that he'll carry you off again."

Christine remained one last breath as Raoul approached, and she permitted the kiss he brushed across her brow without a reaction. Permit the touch of one man while another's was to be shunned... Rules humanity carved into existence, and she was simply expected to follow them and never deviate from the path of ordinary people. Going against the standard was wrong, but was it a sin punishable by God or only a condemning offense to the modern elite? If being strong meant staring down every other person in the world, that was a cumbersome responsibility she had never been taught to hold. If merely a touch were scandalous, what would marrying the Opera Ghost be?

Relieved to slip out the door, Christine made a decision in that exact moment, and turning on her heel, she hurried with frantic steps to her dressing room. A locked door was a necessity and took precedence until she knew she was safe, and then she rushed to the full-length mirror and struck her fist against it.

"Erik! Erik! Are you there? Please, open the mirror!" Why hadn't she made him teach her its trick weeks ago? She felt barricaded out when she so desperately needed to be in!

She pounded her hand, watching only the reflection of her palm and never a stirring motion. What if he was at the house below and never heard her?

"Erik!" she pleaded again. "Please, let me in!"

She was thrown from her balance as the glass suddenly gave way and stumbled only to be caught in strong arms.

"Christine, what in the world is wrong?"

His voice was a subtle vibration in the chest she was held against, slightly out of breath to insist his haste to get to her, and sighing relief, she rubbed her cheek to him, adding a flustered kiss to the frantic beat of his heart. She had obviously frightened him and had images in her head of his shadow racing from the catacombs to come for her.

Drawing back abruptly, she lifted her hand to his surprised face and without hesitation, tore the mask away as if it were her right to do so.

"Christine?" he questioned again but never with anger or an attempt to look away. No, he simply regarded her peculiarly. "Whatever are you doing?"

Wide-eyed with too many thoughts, she blurted out, "Yes, yes!"

He chuckled with a quizzical shake of his head. "What are you talking about? Did something happen at rehearsal? ...You're trembling all over. Are you all right?"

Even if her entire body quivered with that incessant shaking, she smiled because he never assumed it meant disgust and never cared his face was exposed because he was too busy worrying over her. It calmed her enough to compose her agitation into intelligible words. "Yes, I'll marry you! I'll marry you!"

A soft gasp fell from those misshapen lips as his mismatched eyes stared unblinking from their sockets. She wondered if he'd been afraid never to hear such words from her. He couldn't even form a reply, and so, smiling brightly with a sense of self-pride, she cupped his face in her palms and brushed a kiss to his stunned lips.

"I've made the almighty Opera Ghost speechless," she declared, trailing her fingertips along his brow. "Oh, Erik, say *something*."

Blinking hard, he shook his head again and bid incredulously, "What did you say a moment ago? I feel I might have imagined words upon your lips that never existed. ...Tell me again, Christine."

Less flustered and more determined this time, she stared fixed and lost in blue and green depths and stated, "I want to marry you."

"You do? No more doubts or hesitations? This isn't an impulsive conjecture that will be taken back once reality sets in? If you are agreeing because you feel you must-"

"I'm agreeing because I *want to*," she insisted without waver. "You made it my choice, and I *choose* to marry you."

"Why?" he demanded sharply.

"You're not pleased? ...This was *your* proposal; I thought you'd be elated. But...you seem angry."

"No, no..." He was shivering against her caressing hands, never a smile, never anything beyond suspicion and shock. "Why have you said yes all of a sudden? I am not a fool; something obviously happened to make up your mind."

She had no intention of lying and admitted, "The Vicomte was here."

"The Vicomte?"

"Yes, and the things he said... He called your face vile and repulsive and insisted it must be a manipulation if I permit your touch."

"Damn him!" Erik hissed, eyes flashing fire, but Christine never flinched, cradling a face that resembled a monster when rage overwhelmed it. She kept a gentle touch and held his murderous gaze without doubt.

"He said such things, and it hurt *me* to bear them, as if I were equally condemned. And I realized how ridiculous it was to care over *his* opinion. He deems my behavior unacceptable because good girls don't want Opera Ghosts with disfigured faces. But what is worse: to play the role they want even though it is a lie or to defy conventionality and make the objectionable but honest choice? *I* want to marry you," she said again without a single doubt present.

"And what happens if this world you are so keen on defying learns your husband is a monster? Do you have enough courage to stand at my side and face my demons? To be shunned and ridiculed? ...To be as cursed as I am?" His eyes bore into her without softening as he sought the answers on his own. "How often I beg you to be strong! Marriage is permanent, Christine. You cannot think to appease me with a halfhearted agreement and run to the Vicomte if I fail to please you."

"Please me? Is that your worry?" Her fingers idly stroked his cheek.

"I am no Vicomte," he reminded, desperate not to fall victim to a touch so warm and gentle, making a caress into an adoration. Surely his face proved his point, existing on one end of a spectrum while the Vicomte was at the very opposite side. And yet she looked at him as if none of that mattered. "Christine,

...stop touching me that way. You distract what should be a valid argument. This face...you will be the one to look upon it for eternity, to wake up to its distortions and kiss its misshapen lips goodnight."

"I thought you wanted me to look at your face and not see its unordinary facets. To want it just the same and be brave enough to say so."

"And are you brave enough? Because I am not so sure." He fought to retain solemnity as she outlined his lips with a tempting finger. "Tell me, Christine, did you proclaim your choice to the Vicomte? Did you make it blatantly known that you do not want him?"

"No," she answered plainly, but the light in her eyes and a sweet half-smile never faded. It only grew. "He presumed to insist no more lessons and that he will escort me home from rehearsal."

"And?"

"And I let him believe I obediently agreed. I have a guardian angel that will come for me no matter where I am or what happens. The Vicomte's orders are inconsequential."

Guardian angel. His returned smile was bittersweet, but how could he dwell on past missteps with her in his arms, gazing upon him with emotions he'd only dreamed of? "Angels live a little closer to heaven, you know."

"Well then I guess that makes you even better than an angel because you are always where I am and a call away from moving mirrors to come to me."

Her playful amusement beamed, but Erik was hesitant and inquired in a voice that betrayed his fear, "And you've no doubts left, Christine? You truly want to marry me?"

"Yes," she breathed, grazing another kiss to his mouth like a vow. When lips made words and could also make kisses, having both on her side seemed to bind every detail in place. As she pulled back, it was as though a piece of her smile had remained behind to curve his lips. That was the look she'd been hoping for all along.

Just as quickly, a smile became full of flustered anxiousness. "Then I have much to do," he abruptly declared. "*So* much. I hadn't anticipated you would concede this quickly. I need to make arrangements, but...tomorrow evening, I think, will be suitable."

"Tomorrow?" Surprise was inevitable as she listed reasons. "But where shall we marry? Will it be a ceremony? ...Oh, what shall I wear?"

He laughed lightly, adoring her in his stare as he replied, "I will take care of everything. I would begin now, but I am reluctant to leave you alone."

"Why? I must return to rehearsal, and the Vicomte can make no approach until it ends. I will be perfectly safe, and truly, I should be getting back. I'm sure my scene is approaching."

"Your scene," he muttered, and his features crinkled with aversion so straightforward and vivid without the mask to shield it that she giggled. "Don't get too attached to the role; it is temporary. I have much bigger plans. The general public will not dub your new husband the Opera Ghost, but a wealthy patron making sizable donations has some leverage. That fact might create gossip, but it will go unchallenged."

"Suddenly married to a wealthy patron and mistress to the Opera Ghost," she stated with a dramatic sigh. "My reputation is as good as destroyed. Oh well."

"You don't care? Most would find being the Opera Ghost's mistress a degradation." He tried to make it a teasing remark, but she glimpsed the true uncertainty lurking beneath every consonant.

She wanted to comment in brave words that spoke a longing she could not control or dismiss, but the blush heating her skin stole boldness and wouldn't let it free. All she could murmur within its power was, "It's not a degradation, ...not if it's wanted."

That was enough to return his smile, and he turned to set a long, cherishing kiss into her palm before he pulled out of her embrace. She felt empty the instant they were apart. "Tomorrow night." He said it like an oath, and she nodded, unable to quell her timid blush.

With unwillingness, she watched him replace his mask and leave her dressing room, but just before the mirror closed, she noted a lightness to his every motion. Did she dare call it happiness? She was afraid to think the word when it could so quickly be yanked out of their grasp.

Marrying the Opera Ghost... One thought of it left her equally as light and buoyant as she returned to rehearsal.

*****

It was less difficult than fear had made it seem to avoid Raoul. Erik had too many secret entrances and exits. She slipped into the wings, and he was there, drawing her into the shadows with him.

She had anticipated his presence all day and a chance to revel in their secret engagement, but almost immediately after he brought her to his home, he insisted he could not stay. "Plans," was all he said with an adoring grin that kept her from finding anger, and with an awkwardly brushed kiss to her knuckles, he vanished and she was alone.

The next day should have been another futile rehearsal, but in the few moments she saw Erik before he once again abandoned her, he insisted he had left a note with the managers to say she was ill and would not attend. She would have argued, but was distinctly sure this illness was called by the name of a certain Vicomte. Part of her feared what sort of uproar Raoul was causing since her sudden disappearance. Abducted by the Opera Ghost would surely be his tale, but would a prisoner take time to send a note to justify her absence? Not an unwilling one anyway.

So, no Vicomte, no rehearsal, no prying eyes,

and she was left to ponder that this would be her wedding day. Anxiety kept her pacing a house that was far too quiet and cursing Erik for leaving her with nothing to do and no company save her own mind. Perhaps that was his purpose, to find out if she would crumble to hidden doubts. But she was too preoccupied obsessing over the night to come to remember anything else.

Erik finally returned to the underground in the evening. He rushed with frantic steps, urgent to find his bride. Too many hours without her and unable to be her watchful guardian made him hasty with fabricated fantasies of entering an empty house and losing every dream.

He was nearly out of breath as he burst through the door and made her jump with a start. But his presence only calmed a fraction of the agitation he saw coursing through her every quivering feature.

"Erik," she squeaked out in high pitches.

He did not hesitate. Long strides brought him to her, and he pulled her into a crushing embrace. Only with her against his heart did he believe she was real and hadn't somehow been carried out of his life. The breath left his lungs in a sigh, and he wished he had time to take off the mask and claim a kiss. But no... There would be kisses later.

"Everything is ready...if you are still willing, of course," he told her with warranted trepidation to feel her tense and go rigid against him. "But if you've changed your mind-"

"No, no, I haven't," she quickly protested, drawing back to meet his eye.

He did not question further, too afraid to find something unpleasant. She had made a choice, and he was eager to hold her to it. "Then wait here," he commanded as he released her. "I have something for you."

He was gone only a moment and returned, carrying a large box and watching that expected curiosity raise her dark brows and line her brow. Without a word, he lifted the top and exposed folded layers of white silk and ruffled material.

"A wedding gown?" she softly bid, grazing her fingertips along the flawless bodice. "Where did you get it?"

"A bridal shoppe, of course," he replied, trying to gauge her reaction.

"It must have been expensive."

Her attention was fixed on the motion of her touching fingers, and he insisted, "Money is no consideration, not where you are concerned. ...Would you rather I confiscated something from the opera's wardrobe closet? Because that seems like a costume for another role when I want a real bride at my side. Do you...like it even a little bit, Christine?"

Finally, blue eyes raised and grounded his frantic worrying like an anchor. "It is the loveliest gown I've ever seen," she sincerely answered with the touch of a grin.

"Then...if you will change, we may go."

She nodded, and he glimpsed nerves and so much apprehension that he feared she was doubting. The instant she rushed to her room with the gown, his mind sucked him into its chasm of torture and prevented him from accepting any of this was happening. All through plans laid and details executed, he had never believed it. No, this couldn't be *his* wedding. Christine couldn't possibly want to marry *him*. And now with her nerves prickling his skin, his thoughts weaved every hesitation into trauma and broken hearts.

His shaking hands fisted against his masked face, eyes squeezing shut as if to block thought from penetrating. No. She was *his*; she had *chosen* him, not that arrogant Vicomte, ...and yet did he believe her? Had he *ever* believed her? Not when he bore a lingering worry this was all a lie, a twisted scheme instigated by the Vicomte to destroy him. Oh God, would she break his heart?

Tormented by his merciless brain, Erik suddenly could endure her absence no longer and hurried to her ajar bedroom door. Not a single knock preceded him as he pushed it wide. Its telltale creak was as deafening as the gasp she gave, flipping about with shaking arms clasping around her body.

Erik halted and ran feverish eyes over her. She wore only her underclothes, a flimsy chemise and ruffled petticoat, and his gaze lingered on pale flesh, on the curves of elbows and bare arms, on peeking shoulders and more feminine graces beneath. He ached simply to look.

"Erik, what...?" she trailed off, blushing bright to be victim to such an intense stare. It was as if his eyes devoured as fervently as hands and lips could.

He was shaken, her voice thwarting desire-filled fantasy, and he sought words to justify an obvious indiscretion. "May I...may I help you dress?"

Christine hesitated, her blush deepening its pink hue. The man who would be her husband and beneath every passionate wanting, he was as timid as she was. He was simply better at pretending.

Abruptly regaining himself, he lowered flaming eyes and insisted, "I'm sorry. I shouldn't have come here. I-"

"You can help me," she quickly said in a hushed breath that cut over his self-chastisement. She shook through every limb; she couldn't have ceased it if she tried, but with a soft inhalation forced into uncooperative lungs, she lowered her arms and stood, awaiting his approach with expectant eyes.

The wedding dress was spread atop her mattress, its layers flounced and arranged with perfect care, but as he reached a tentative hand for it, she stopped him.

"I...I need my corset first," she explained and went to collect it from her vanity bench.

"Don't," he commanded. "Leave it off. It's

unnecessary and pointless when the real curves of your body are so intoxicating. And...how I'll burn knowing I could reach out and touch your softness. Christine..." The huskiness of his voice proclaimed desire blatant enough to singe her skin, and she shivered as those eyes ran over her again, languid and slower this time without her arms to hinder a real perusal. "You drive me mad. I've never wanted anything so much."

She didn't reply, but she didn't shy away either. She allowed his observation and felt heat follow the path he took, coursing within her veins and settling as an ache within her. A want... No, this felt like a *need*, something she could not survive without knowing.

Erik closed lingering distance, standing so near that her blush seared him with its radiating heat. But all he did was take the wedding gown, and though his stare smoldered with passion's fire, he carefully helped her dress. Every action was delicate and adoring, as if she were his most cherished possession.

The only sounds to fill the air were uneven breaths, and as she lifted the bodice into place, he let yearning hands capture her waist between them, his fingers relishing her softness. One moment of indulgence, and then he crept around and began to attach the clasps down her back. Brushing her curls aside was its own caress and savored as much as a graze of eager fingertips to the nape of her neck, and when her reply was a shiver, he took it as a blessing he couldn't believe was his.

With all the tenderness he possessed, he set a lace veil upon her dark curls, unable to stop his hands from shaking. ...Had they ever stopped shaking?

The perfect bride, and as he stepped about to admire her, the image overwhelmed him. This was a dream, and monsters were only meant to have nightmares. *The most beautiful dream...* Words were choked in the back of his throat, and suddenly, with emotion suffocating, he slid to his knees before her in supplication.

"Erik," she called, unsure how to bear the reverence in his stare. He looked at her as if she were so far above him, like some sort of goddess he was unworthy to have; she hardly felt she deserved such worship.

"I love you," he said, and the mixture of affection and desire in blue and green eyes was so potent it took her breath away.

Almost immediately, he composed himself and stood again, ashamed he had let so much free. "We must go. I have a carriage awaiting us upstairs."

"A carriage?" she posed with a hint of amusement. "Then we are not walking the streets of Paris this time?"

"No, of course not. As if I would make my beautiful bride traipse the sidewalk with random pedestrians. No... I'm too desperate for everything to be perfect." As he spoke, eyes still adoring at every glance, he lifted her cloak and placed it on her shoulders.

Perfect, it practically was. Now if only he could cast himself as the perfect groom.

Christine delighted in the horse-drawn carriage, and as they lurched onto the busy city streets, Erik explained, "Our driver understands discretion. I've employed him before, usually if I need something done that requires face to face meeting. I pay him well enough to keep his mouth shut, so you need not worry over rumors about the opera diva Christine Daaé traveling in a wedding gown with a masked man."

He made it seem a light jest, but they both knew his implication was solely the Vicomte. Christine had yet to decide how she wished Raoul would take the news. Every thought on the subject had a horrible ending she wanted to avoid.

But all thoughts of Raoul faded as their carriage drew to a halt. Peering out the carriage curtains, she saw the silhouette of a steeple stretching above and nothing else in the near distance. They were beyond the city and any intruders to an intimate ceremony. ...This was to be her wedding to the Opera Ghost, and her heart skipped in a peculiar rush of anticipation as Erik helped her out of the carriage. There was no going back.

Chapter Fourteen

Christine's childhood fantasies of her wedding had been as overdone and elaborate as most young girls. A fairytale in the making with hundreds of guests and gifts, lavish decorations up and down the aisle, flowers by the bouquet, and a prince, perfect and handsome on her arm. The fantasy.

But real life was a quaint, plain church, the only guests a wary priest and their carriage driver Henri, no decorations save candlelight from blessed flames, her groom a man in a mask feigning more confidence than he possessed. It was no fairytale, and yet she wanted it no other way. She was strangely content and could not keep a smile from upturning the corners of her lips.

The priest recited a condensed version of the ceremony. Every few lines, he glanced suspiciously at Erik, and it was only because of his rudeness that Christine did not insist Erik remove his mask and marry her without its infuriating presence. This priest had taken vows to his God and yet showed no tolerance, and Christine was not going to subject Erik to gawking and cruelty during what should have been a blissful moment.

Though Erik glared back and returned the rudeness, she noticed his hands were fisted tight at his sides. A potential attack? ...No, she knew he was trying to hide their shaking and never show the crack in his bravado. Without thought, she caught one of his hands in hers, feeling him flinch and stiffen before he relaxed and allowed. Strength wasn't facing the world alone anymore and enduring unjustified derision. He had said marriage meant standing by his side, and she would not take such a place for granted.

The rest of the ceremony passed in a blur: simple vows exchanged without hesitation, a ring so beautiful that Christine was mesmerized by its glint on the candlelight, and then an unconcealed cringe from their priest as he announced that Erik may "kiss his bride." Time froze in that spot, and Christine acted before her new husband could know disappointment, leaning upon tiptoe and pressing a kiss to his one bare cheek.

As she drew away, he abruptly insisted, "No, I am after perfection. We just made vows of forever. I will seal them with nothing but their rightful kiss."

Pride did not need a smile, and even as hers faltered, she nodded acceptance and watched anxiously as he removed his mask in sight of their audience. It was the most courageous act she had ever seen, and she was adamant to match his strength with her own attempt. Stand at his side no matter what, the most important part of a marriage vow.

The priest reacted with horror and abhorrence; the carriage driver intelligently looked away. And though Christine gave them each a passing glance, as her eyes settled on her husband's disfigured face and glimpsed the same candlelight that had made her ring shine beautifully illuminate scars and make them all the more hideous, she only smiled and tilted her lips up expectantly.

His returned grin beamed in gratitude, love, and everything a groom should know on his wedding day. *Perfect...* And then his lips were upon hers with gentle motion, and the rest of the world fell away.

One kiss didn't seem enough to proclaim volumes of love, but that was all Erik took, quickly replacing the mask under the horror-stricken eyes of the priest. Once his face was hidden again, the priest seemed shaken back to awareness and turned frantic eyes to Christine.

"Mademoiselle, ...Mademoiselle, I'm so sorry," he frantically bid. "I've committed you to the devil! I didn't know."

Sneering rage, Erik snapped, "That's *Madame* now. If you are to address my wife with such slander, at least do it properly." The urge to attack and punish cruelty made once-shaking hands fist with aggression this time, but Christine clasped one with both of hers and cocooned it in warm palms.

Speaking with adopted eloquence, she replied, "No apologies, Father. I've committed *myself*, and I've no regrets."

It was the air of her stage demeanor; Erik saw right through it, but it was a start. Let her feign the bravery she lacked to the petty world until it became soldered within her. As long as she never put on the same act to him, he would adore her all the more for it.

A fist of rage opened its fingers to entwine with hers, and he savored a smile that was genuine as he guided her down the aisle and out to the carriage. *His wife...* She had already faced down a first brush with a bitterness she had yet to fully imagine. One sincere prayer was in his heart: that he did not destroy her by marrying her. She was still etched in sweet innocence and lingering naïveté, and he had put her upon his own tormented path with him. *Dear God, let her be strong enough for what will come...*

The carriage rolled down dirt roads, and as Christine peeked out the window, she inquisitively stated, "We're not going in the direction of the opera house. ...Why would that be? Where are we going, Erik?"

He knew she had the answer to her own question, but to see her anticipating eyes crinkle at the corners with delight created his excitement as he confirmed, "Home, Christine. We're going home."

"Home," she sighed, catching her bottom lip with her teeth to quell an exuberant grin. He had the desire to kiss her and make that act his own, ...catch that lip with his teeth instead. He was suddenly impatient to arrive at their destination and begin a marriage he had only fantasized before this moment.

As they finally drew to a stop and she started to rise in the small confines, he held up halting hands. "No, stay here a moment and wait for me to return."

"Why?" she whined, and he grinned at her unconcealed petulance. "I've already seen the house. It isn't a surprise."

"Humor me," he insisted, unable to stop a chuckle from escaping. "I want everything to be perfect. Just wait here two minutes. All right? Or shall I take the role of dominant husband and command it?" His teasing achieved his desired reaction as she laughed, and every attempt at seriousness lost to smiles again.

"I'll wait for you," she conceded, "but not because you command it. Don't you dare think I'm bending to your superiority. I'm simply too eager to see what you've planned to spoil it with my curiosity...*yet*. Two minutes. Any longer, and I shall likely fall to its pull and come after you whether you're ready or not."

"I have no doubt of that." His smile never dimmed as he grazed a quick caress to her cheek, delicate and longing in one touch, and then hurried from the carriage door.

Two minutes was more like eight, and she sat on the edge of the carriage seat, wringing her hands in her lap. Every so often, as her fingers moved in their restlessness, her attention caught on the shimmer of her ring, reminding her in blatant sparkle that she was indeed married. This was not some opera scene acted out for his benefit; it was real and permanent.

She was too nervous to wonder if she regretted it.

A bride permitted her husband and did not cower under modesty's veil. When every memory of Erik's eyes devouring her earlier in her underclothes made her skin heat and burn, she could not help but carry anticipation in the center of uncertainty. She was afraid...and yet almost eager to succumb and finally be desire's victim.

"All right. Come on."

His call preceded a hand into the carriage to help her descend. Her tension was wound tightly within the grip of unbendable knuckles, but she feigned composure as he waved the driver off and led the way up the front porch to their new home.

Light poured out to meet them, and she guessed that was his unshared task: ridding them of the dark and revealing every surprise at first glimpse. Christine gasped her delight. The house she recalled being empty a couple days before was now a home, brimming with furniture and warm hues. This wasn't the same bare room with a bay window. Now curtains adorned that same window and details made it a sitting room ready to be occupied and filled with life.

"How did you do all this?" she incredulously breathed, setting her palm atop the back of a wingchair and trailing fingertips over its upholstery.

"Did you presume my extensive plans only went as far as a rude priest and a carriage? I have been working tirelessly since the instant you said yes, but it was certainly worth the effort to see the look in your eyes. You are pleased then?"

"Yes, of course," she gushed with a little laugh. "This is our *home.*"

"I have a few other things to bring from the catacombs. I don't favor moving the instruments, so I think I shall just buy new. And I owe you a few dozen rose bushes for the garden. That will be my next project." Even as he teased, his gaze unavoidably wandered over her as she observed their new furniture excitedly. His thoughts rushed ahead and could only be inspired when she was just so beautiful. Every line and curve of her body, all so feminine and so very soft, all merely waiting to be claimed as *his*. It was now God's truth, and any lingering hesitations accounted for nothing.

"Christine," he softly bid, knowing the huskiness in his voice told his desire before she turned and met his stare. She shivered, but she did not shrink away. Weakly attempting patience with a muttered curse, he offered, "Are you hungry? Would you like something to eat?"

Pathetic when his eyes flashed fervently and made it clear what he wanted. He was relieved when she shook her head.

"I...I'm not hungry," she stammered.

"Then...shall we retire for the night?"

A hesitant nod, but she moved with abrupt steps before him to the staircase, pausing to be certain he followed. Followed? He was practically in her shadow.

As they walked upstairs, he dared to extend his hand and rested it on the curve of her hip, encouraged when she did not start or jerk free. A gentle touch, but so possessive that he shuddered to take it. His wife, and he allowed her to lead them to their bedroom.

Like the main level of the house, he had taken care to fill a few of the upper rooms. Their bedroom now held a large, four-poster bed and carved mahogany furniture as well as little details. He always favored the nuances and arranging them perfectly for Christine: her favorite perfume, vases full of roses here and there, little trinkets he'd come across that reminded him of her including an engraved silver jewelry box. He even had the bed's posts draped in white chiffon, knowing she would love something ethereal and pure. It reminded him of heaven.

Once again, he saw the benefit of his deliberate actions in her smile. For an instant, her anxiety vanished, and it went un-indulged long enough for her to perceive his every gift. It only returned when she faced him again.

"What...what are you thinking about?" she asked, frozen in place and permitting another sweep from his desiring gaze.

Slower this time, he traced her body in intangible caresses, and she shivered as if he'd actually touched her. In thick tones, he candidly replied, "Tearing that gown from your body and every layer I must to find skin."

"Oh..."

"Yes, ...I took such care when putting it on you, and now it wouldn't matter to me if it ended in haphazard pieces when I am aching this much." Erik let his eager gaze linger on the fullness of her breasts, his hands yearning to feel their soft weight, and aching became unbearable burning with that one thought. Dragging his gaze up the pale column of her throat, he forced words past lips that only wanted to kiss. "A civilized man wouldn't speak such things and certainly would not wish to be so aggressive. Tearing wedding gowns hardly seems proper or conventional. But my God, Christine, the desire you stir in me is dangerous and tainted. It is fire's essence, and I can hardly endure burning alive anymore, not alone anyway. I want to burn with you, ...inside of you."

His every admission, husky and passion-laced, attacked her unprepared body and left her shuddering. They were each their own caress, but unfulfilling when they inspired only empty aches. She had always known desire with Erik at its source would be perilous and dark, consuming. He was man and Opera Ghost combined, and for every awkwardness that inexperience brought, the fire beneath made it provocative and arousing. She wanted him more because he didn't know how to touch her or begin, how to be what he thought a *civilized* man in the throes of desire should be. He was all wanting, and he would now have no hesitation in taking what he wanted.

Searching for her own bravery, she reached for her veil and lifted it free of her curls, tossing it upon the plush seat of a vanity's bench. "I don't want civilized or proper or conventional. I want *you*, Erik."

"Even in the midst of this dark desire?" he demanded, caressing again with eyes that sought permission to makes touches instead. "I don't want to hold back for fear I'll frighten you. I want to be consumed, and I want to overwhelm you with pleasure. Decide now that you will not cower and choose shyness."

She bit her lip tentatively before replying. "Shyness may be inevitable, but I will not cower or run away from you. This desire has always frightened me, but...I want it. I want to know what it means. Show me."

The most innocent invitation. He savored every letter as he stepped closer, circling her with confident strides to the clasps down her back. He did not tear as instinct begged, desperate to keep this moment beautiful. Brushing her curls over her shoulder, he took care to free her from the gown, admiring every detail as he guided silken material to fall in a bundle of white. It tumbled down while his fingers traveled up the curve of her back and along her spine so gently that her body shivered and leaned closer, pleading for a firmer touch.

Every flustered breath passing her lips was its own beseeching, and he splayed fingers wide against the small of her back, his palm molding to its curve. He was impatient to discard petticoats and chemise, stockings, every boundary, but unable to halt impulse, he let his touching hand shape her hip as it weaved around her stomach and forced her back to his chest.

She never uttered a sound of complaint, nothing beyond a soft cry to be clasped so tightly to the hard planes of his body. As he shared her every erratic breath, he arched his eager erection against her softness as if desperate to find its rightful place.

"Christine," he hoarsely gasped into a cloud of curls, and as he nuzzled into their silkiness, her hand rose, confident and determined, and found his mask. She stripped him of its protection as hastily as he'd stripped her of her gown and added it to the pile at their feet.

Moaning his delight, he burrowed his bare face deeper into her tresses, tickled by every strand as they danced across his scars.

Christine pressed her body back into his, and her deliberate friction made him throb. "Do you feel what you're doing to me?" he rasped against her ear. Her reply was a sharp cry that only grew louder as his lips made a partition in thick curls and found the side of her throat, covering its perfect length with heated kisses.

Exquisite bliss! To have the woman he loved, *his wife*, half-bare in his embrace and writhing with wanting. He was as much awed as aching.

Impatient hands urged his exploration, and he dragged them along the thin material of her chemise to her breasts. First contact had her shuddering in his hold, and every cry slipping past her bit lip urged more. He never hesitated, cupping their weight and marveling at the inherent softness of her every detail. His fingertips outlined the hardened tips straining against her chemise as if yearning to be set free. Had he ever touched anything so perfect? And to have his Christine arching her hips back into him, purposely provoking the harsh moans he gave in reply... It was a torture he willingly surrendered to. He had to have more.

Christine felt as if her body was one mass of sensation, so overwhelming it threatened to steal every bit of her. But every time fear threatened, she focused on Erik, on his kissing mouth against her throat, his fingers teasing her nipples, his hard body pressed to her back and every harsh breath that moved her with him. He had been right: with a marriage vow in place, she had an excuse to permit desire and know no shame for it. The darkness was frightening, but it was also so deliciously tempting. She *wanted* to be its victim.

His kisses made a path from her jaw down her throat again, his mouth trailing flames, and as he burrowed his lips in the crease of her neck and gently tasted her skin with the tip of his tongue, she lost hold of her bit lip and let a sharp cry out. She could feel his proud smile, spreading the lips devouring her, and she resolved at that moment to stop attempting control.

The thought had only just been decided when to her disappointment, he released her from his strong hold. "If I don't feel your skin, I shall go mad," he hoarsely bid, and she did not protest as he guided her about to face him, shaking harder to see the avid lust upon his unmasked face. It was all fire and pulled disfigured features into a new picture similar to the harsh tautness of anger. But she would call anger ugly upon that face, and this...this was *beautiful*.

He did not hesitate. His hands reached for her petticoat, jerking it down her slender hips into another pile of skirts and ruffles on the carpet. She could see he was growing frustrated as one layer seemed to reveal another, and stifling a smile when he huffed annoyance, she aided his plight and rid herself of shoes and stockings.

As her trembling fingers caught the hem of her chemise, he insisted, "Yes, you remove those flimsy undergarments. If I attempt, I *will* tear. Desire does not make a man delicate with lacey materials that hinder touch."

She certainly agreed, but wasn't it just as wonderful to do it herself and watch his features light and the fire surge brighter the instant she began to draw her chemise off? But desire was a wanting, and this seemed a necessity, as if he would stop existing if he didn't have this moment. It overwhelmed her as she dropped the chemise in a flutter of white and stood half-exposed to his eyes.

His hand extended, quivering in midair, but just as quickly, it fisted and was retracted. "Finish," he insisted, nearly a growl, and she complied without waver, refusing modesty. Modesty seemed insignificant when his regard held awe and pleasure. He looked at her body with amazement, and it only made her eager to show him more.

Her pantaloons were her last barrier to hide behind, and she guided them off and kicked them into the white pool. Bare, exposed, and with hazy eyes, she listened to him breathe, every shallow gasp past parted misshapen lips, and permitted the roaming stare he cast down her length and languidly up again.

That hand extended again, a fist that had to pry open its fingers before it met her skin. Oddly gentle when his gaze showed such an inferno, he made a caress down her sternum and out to cup her breast, his fingertips flicking lightly across her nipple. One touch, and it sent jolts through her as if carried by the constant paths of veins out to every extremity and back to settle at her center in liquid heat.

So sudden that she was shaken, Erik approached and lifted her into his arms, carrying her to the bed. She savored his strong embrace as that mere touch brought more burning, more wanting. When he set her upon the mattress, she immediately reached for him, yearning to burn even more, but to her soft cry of disappointment, he backed away.

"Erik," she muttered with only half a voice, and her ringed hand reached empty for him.

He did not reply or explain. Gazing at her, the fire in his stare insisting he was not done with her, he wandered to each and every light in the bedroom, turning them lower and lower until they went out.

"What are you doing?" Apprehension only returned with encompassing darkness. As the last light died out, she could see nothing as if a black shroud had stolen sight. "Erik? What-"

"Sshh..."

He was there again at her bedside, and though she wanted to yell at him for severing her view, protests abandoned her. His warm mouth caught her nipple in its cavern and choked words behind soft cries. *Dear Lord*! She knew what he was doing: hiding once again behind shadows, taking up the confidence of the Opera Ghost to conceal insecurities. Though she didn't want to allow him that escape, he seemed determined not to let her argue. No, he devoured her breast with voracious kisses she gasped to endure, and when sense insisted she push him away, desire had her gripping his hair and keeping him close.

Tenderness seemed to leave with the lights. His kisses were demanding and fevered, his tongue circling her nipple, and when her fingers threaded in his hair and clasped him firm, he only grew more fervent, sucking in a ravenous rhythm that left her shaking beneath him. His hands began to wander, caressing any inch of her skin they found. One hesitated on her vacant nipple, pinching it between anxious fingers and making her whimper. As she arched into his hand, he grazed his thumb one last time along the hardened tip before making a new path.

Though his mouth spoke passionately in kisses, his touch was deliberately gentle as it spanned the flat expanse of her stomach and slowly moved lower.

Argument and modesty fled her in wispy clouds, and when his hand timidly stroked her thigh, she parted her legs. Once again, she felt the smile he gave, tugging the lips still at her breast and making her nipple slip free from his warm mouth. He kept misshapen lips held in a frozen kiss and though she longed to beg him to continue, her attention focused on the motion of his hand. Without sight to watch, she had to wait and only *feel* his intentions.

For all his bravado, his touch was shy. It brushed her inner thigh with a telltale tremble, repeating the caress long enough to gain courage. She wondered if he was afraid she'd deny him, and eager to assuage any doubt left, she arched up to his hand and murmured, "Please, Erik."

"Oh, you want me to touch you?" he taunted, and she mewed her delight at merely the suggestion. "If that's what you want, I certainly won't object."

Language lost meaning and comprehension as his fingers granted a soft caress to her womanhood, tender, reverent, before they dared to slip inside. Her sharp cry harmonized with the moan he gave, a song of passion, and it only grew as his touch became bolder, his fingertips traveling the length of her and exploring every detail.

"Oh, Christine," Erik breathed with random kisses to her breast, "to feel you this way, so wet with your wanting! You want me..."

How often had he claimed it? And though he'd always known it was true, to have proof coating his fingers made it vivid and overwhelmed him with an unexpected rush of despair.

"How I pity you!" he suddenly insisted, dragging his fingers back and forth in languid motion.

"Pity?" she stammered, desperate to concentrate on words but failing to his ministrations.

Leaning upon his elbow, he gazed at her beautiful body, bare and spread before him, glimpsing clear even in blackness that denied her the same pleasure. "Of course, pity. You've committed your life to a monster; you will give yourself to him, not for a threat, and beyond the vow that makes this a duty. You *want* the monster. Have I truly corrupted you so much that this seems your path? If I had never come into your life, the Vicomte would be in my place." His voice tightened with the mention. As if the Vicomte had any right! The fantasy alone made Erik more possessive, and his fingers slid deep within her as she cried out and instinctively arched her hips.

Christine fought to find her voice amidst desire so potent it left her dizzy, but all she could reason as an assurance was a muttered, "And I wouldn't feel this. Erik, ...you're making me burn."

"Exactly!" he agreed amidst more vehement kisses. "Only *I* make you burn this way. Only *I* will give you pleasure. I don't deserve this, but by God, it is mine, and no one will take it from me."

Her concession was barely a nod when concentration was locked on fingers moving in and out. To her moan of disappointment, she felt him drawing away. No, he couldn't mean to leave her aching...

One breath, and when darkness gave no landmark, she had to wait in utter torment for his intentions. A startling kiss was laid to her inner thigh, held there in cherishing adoration as time stood still a long moment and etched this memory into permanent existence. And then kisses formed a path up, and only his determined hands catching her hips kept her in place and permitting when she tried to draw away.

"Erik," she gasped urgently the instant before his mouth claimed her womanhood. Kisses first, the sweetest he had given, and then as she cried out and stiffened down every limb, his tongue tasted her. It felt like a dream; she couldn't see him and had to depend on sensations that were too intense to be called real. Sensation and sound, her unbridled cries and the moans of delight he gave in reply.

His every motion was gentle, his tongue teasing with gratuitous strokes she writhed to endure.

"*Please.*" It was the only word she could manage to mutter, and she didn't even know what she begged for.

But he was yearning for an answer as he drew lips away with one more kiss and demanded hoarsely, "Please what, Christine? Tell me. ...Do you wish me

237

to stop?"

"No," she gasped urgently.

"Ah, ...do you wish for more? Are you begging me to give you pleasure, my love? Christine, ...dear God, you taste so delicious on my tongue. *I* want more of you. Answer, so I may take it."

She knew he possessed little patience, and yet he waited until she managed to whisper, "Don't stop, Erik. Please don't stop."

She felt the grin again as his mouth covered her, and somewhere beneath passion's velvet curtain, she had an urge to laugh. He was deliberately convicted to making her lost to desire, to bringing every dark wanton urge out of her, and she certainly was not fighting it. He wanted passion to match his, and she was suddenly confident she could give it.

His strokes were purposeful this time, his tongue making rougher undulations, and as she arched willingly to his mouth, he let fingertips slip inside, delving deep enough to make her cry out. The instant it became too much and suffocated her in its spell, pleasure burst with a poignancy that raced every limb and left her shuddering amidst a shout. Awareness came with its kaleidoscope eruption of color. *This* was what she had been so afraid of and ran from as if it would destroy her? It seemed ridiculous when it felt so incredible.

Kisses were being placed to her inner thigh again, and between their bestowment, he demanded, "Was that what you wanted?"

"Erik..." It seemed the only word to make sense to her addled mind, but she reached trembling hands to him and found the rough material of his jacket, weakly tugging at its intrusion.

All at once, he rose, and she heard the rustling sounds of disrobing. She could feel the power of his stare upon her, the searing brand of mismatched eyes that she wished she could share. She wanted to meet that look and consent to its claim.

And then he was there. The mattress creaked and dipped with his added weight. Eager for him, she reached an uncertain hand into the dark, seeking his shape. A touch, ...and it felt *wrong*. Her hand met a rough, unnatural texture, upraised markings, and she gasped with the brutal jolt of realization; it stole bliss with its harsh reality.

One touch, one gasp, and before she could find sense in revelation, he was gone.

"Erik," she finally forced a tongue-tied mouth to call, but she was alone. Scrambling off the bed, Christine fumbled in search of the nearest lamp, shaking as she quickly lit its warm glow. Nothing, no shadows or silhouettes, no husband with fiery, desire-filled eyes, and as tears choked her throat, she hastily yanked on her undergarments beneath a reeling head still desperate to rationalize.

Scars... He hadn't turned the light out to hide inexperience and unconfident apprehension; he'd turned it out to hide his body. Perhaps she should have anticipated such a cruel twist. A scarred face wasn't enough for Fate's bitter sense of humor.

If his face was shaming to him and met once before with her disgust, she could only imagine how embarrassed he felt by his body and how afraid he must have been to disrobe. Worse yet, because he had fled her instead of responding with rage to disguise pain. He hadn't even tried.

In only chemise and pantaloons, Christine ran from the room, searching with frantic necessity. No! He assumed disgust, and she wasn't disgusted! He said he pitied her for wanting a monster, and suddenly his every self-degrading appellation held new meaning. He genuinely *did* consider himself a monster, and it hurt her to her core that in his eyes, she had just agreed with him.

Tears fell down her cheeks, but she barely noticed as she hurried from room to room. But he was gone, the house empty. A bride left alone on her wedding night... As guilt stung in merciless attack and tainted every memory of bliss, she slid to her knees on the sitting room carpet and sobbed.

Chapter Fifteen

Cold lips pressed firmly against hers. Hadn't she had this dream before? *...No, not a dream.*

Stirring to awareness beneath the warm covers of her bed, she kept her eyes closed and *hoped* before she dared look. But the light she had left lit on her bedside table had been extinguished, and darkness swallowed images as if this was only a continuation of an earlier scene of passion. ...Wasn't it? Memory was hazy fragments when his misshapen lips were moving against hers, coaxing it out of existence.

Perhaps she would have embraced this half-fantasy without regret and believed herself forgiven, ...if not for the viable fact that her hands were pinned, her wrists clamped immobile in one of his large hands and tangled in her loose curls above her head.

Christine tried to turn and end the distraction a kiss created, but he wouldn't allow it, following every miniscule movement she attempted and keeping her mouth. It was only as his tongue dared to slip past her lips that she was able to deter him.

"Erik," she gasped, but his free hand was wandering her body, pausing to tickle her collarbone and move onward to her breast, outlining her hardening nipple through her chemise. She squirmed, recalling every earlier seduction. That was obviously his intention: to steal the unpleasant gap in between and pretend nothing unsettling occurred, as

241

if his pain meant nothing. She might have let him without consequence if not for the furious grip he had on her wrists.

He bent to catch her nipple between his lips, wetting the thin material of her chemise and teasing her through its barrier, and her unhindered whimper slipped free to reveal her surrender. They both knew she would not deny him.

Erik jerked her chemise up and out of his way, leaving it in bunched material upon her chest as he immediately captured her bare breast in his devouring mouth. His hand resumed earlier endeavors, sliding into her pantaloons to stroke her womanhood, this time without hesitation or shyness.

As his fingers slid within her, he groaned and drew back to murmur, "I barely have to touch you, and you're already so wet. Christine, ...I can't hold back anymore. I have to have you."

She didn't protest. She concentrated on his hoarse breaths so near, reasoning what little she could in the darkness. He was beneath the covers with her, but it wasn't until his hand left her wetness to yank her pantaloons down that an accidental brushing revealed he was naked. Naked in her bed, touching her but not allowing her to touch him back. She yearned to find some sort of retaliation, to insist it wasn't fair when she granted him un-argued access to her own body, when *she* hadn't been the one to flee this same intimacy hours before. But then he scooted closer and lowered his weight atop her, burrowing her half-clothed beneath him, and the breath left her in an exhaled sigh.

Oh God, to feel his bare body against her! To faintly decipher scars, too many it seemed, and odd textures to skin that should have been smooth. She ached to touch, to learn, to feel every abnormality and adore him more because of them. But she wasn't strong enough to break his fierce grasp, and she had to settle with echoes and reverberations, with shadows of what should have been hers.

Scars were her first focus and their telltale distortion to skin, but with his desperate moan playing in her ears, her attention averted to something far more significant. Scars and muscles, the broad planes of his body, and then the hardness of his desire, pressing against her. Anxiousness returned and widened her eyes in the blinding darkness.

Erik felt her tense beneath him, but every concern for her welfare was dulled in overwhelming sensation. Her warm, soft skin against him was a drug unto itself. He ached to feel her this way forever. Pushing boundaries, he rubbed his hardness against her, not daring to enter. No, only teasing, and he knew victory to feel her shiver and willingly arch closer.

"Christine," he moaned, catching her hip in his palm and guiding her against him, torturing himself to graze her wetness with his tip. He was about to give in and bury himself within her when she once again struggled in his hold.

"Let me go," she begged. "Please, Erik. I want to touch you."

"No!" he snapped harsher than intended before fighting for less cold tones. "No, Christine, I wanted this to be *perfect*. Don't destroy it by adding your compassion and pity. This is our wedding night for God's sake. I want only desire and love, not sympathy."

"I just want to touch you," she pleaded, but he would not budge.

"Not now. Please, Christine. I want you too much to keep denying it. Please give me one memory to hold that is not a reflection of my misfortune and my scars. I can't bear it right now."

Her heart tugged with exactly the emotions he didn't want, and so she conceded with a hesitant nod, instead leaning forward to find his mangled cheek with her lips and an adoring kiss.

"Don't stop," she whispered above his ear. "Make me yours, *ange*." A moment he didn't want tarnished, and yet she was certain it already was, tasting a tear as it traveled down his cheek. But she did not say a word about it; she only arched her hips to his again and urged his surrender.

She felt too wonderful to refuse, and her subtle invitation made him throb with need. Tilting his face until he could catch her lips in his, he entered her in one swift thrust and moaned deep in his chest to be so consumed. Her cry was swallowed and stolen from sounding, but he kept still and caressed her cringing features with his free hand. His fingers broke the paths of tears in their descent, and the compassion he wouldn't accept from her was his. Dear God, why did he have to hurt her to love her? It didn't make sense for this to feel so amazing, an act of wonder and awe, and yet cause her such pain. He was suddenly adamant he'd make her forget every single tear cried; he'd give her something better to remember.

His free hand roamed feather-light along her skin, slipping between their joined bodies to find the peaks of her breasts and tease them. "Christine," he gasped against her lips, "do you remember the pleasure I gave you before? I brought you such ecstasy."

She shivered against him with the memories and nuzzled her wet cheek to his scarred one, smearing tears between as she whispered, "Of course I remember. I've never felt anything like it."

"Yes, well, that was only a prelude. When I bring you pleasure now, it will be so much greater. I promise you. I will not let you regret even a moment. ...I couldn't bear it if you did." Bittersweet honesty to distract him from every sensation he longed to savor. He refused to fully consider how deeply he was buried within her heated wetness, how intoxicating it felt to be sheathed so completely and lost within her, ...one being. It seemed he had fought forever to reach this perfect moment with her.

But he was convicted to his words and drew random patterns along her features with his fingertips, guiding caresses up and down, encompassing every detail in delicate touches. Only when she began to relax against him did he dare move. An experimental motion, drawing back and sliding deep again, and he watched her intently, weighing her expression and searching for more pain.

But all she said as she shuddered and whimpered softly was, "Will you do that again?"

He smiled; he couldn't contain the elated curves upon his misshapen mouth, and pressing grateful kisses to her temple, he obeyed. Out and in, and she arched her hips to meet him, taking him deeper yet. "Do you like the way that feels, Christine?" he hoarsely demanded, thrilling as she nodded and dark curls bobbed and tickled his face. "No more than I. My God, your delicious warmth is searing me and branding my body as yours."

Every impassioned declaration was gasped into silent air, and she whimpered as she replied, "Mine. Yes, you're mine, Erik."

"*Always* only yours." Desire veiled rationale once again, dragging him beneath its curtain, and he succumbed willingly with the sounds of her eager cries in his ears. Why rationalize anymore when all that mattered was that she wanted him? He thrust harder, and she whispered his name and moved with him, urging more as she burrowed her lips against his neck and cried out into his skin.

Christine wanted to touch him. It felt imperative and necessary, and yet she denied an attempt to struggle. Perhaps she could have broken free; he was hardly paying attention to keeping her captive any longer, but she recalled his earlier fears. No, she was not going to ruin this moment. She settled for pressing fevered kisses to his throat, her tongue daring to escape and taste his skin as he moaned his delight and moved harsher with her inspiration.

Pain was gone, vanished somewhere in the power of wanting, and with his free hand teasing her in idle caresses, desire built, ebbing and swelling inside her. Her hips rose to meet his every thrust, and in a sharp cry, she found ecstasy, digging fingernails into restrained hands when she longed to cling to him instead.

As awareness poked through the lingering haze, she sighed contently against his neck and was stirred by the reverberations of his voice as he asked, "Did I fulfill my promise? Were you overcome with pleasure, love?"

She was sure he felt the smile she pressed against his skin as she breathlessly replied, "Oh yes, *ange*, very much."

It was exactly what Erik was eager to hear, and satisfied, he wove his only free arm about her waist, hugging her body close as he moved with intent. Harder, deeper, no longer holding back, and with a guttural cry that he turned into kisses against her cheek, he surrendered to an ecstasy so overwhelming that it surged through limbs and left him trembling in its aftermath.

"Oh, Christine, ...I didn't hurt you, did I?" His first thought with reality's return was drenched in worry. But peering at her beautiful face, all he saw was that same beaming smile, and he desperately kissed its sweet curves.

This felt like peace; that was all Christine could think as she eagerly kissed him back. Joined and complete, and though desire was ever-present, it was muted in its colors and dropped beneath the background of too much emotion for her heart to hold alone. She wanted every moment to feel this perfect, but to her dismay, before she could cling to it, he was pulling away, releasing her hands and leaving the bed before she could reach for him.

"No, no," she hastily cried, "don't go again. Please, Erik, don't leave."

"Of course not, silly girl," he insisted, and she could hear the smile in his tone, wishing she could see it. She was sure it was beautiful.

A rustle of motion resonated, and within seconds, he climbed back beneath the covers with her. She scooted near, but as she extended blinded hands and sought his shape, she met material, stark and cold when scarred skin had been so deliriously warm. She wanted to protest and yank his clothes off on her own if she must, but she was terrified to hurt him again. No, ...but in her mind, the topic was far from settled.

Erik wrapped eager arms about her bare body, fitting her against him as if they had always slept so close. Kisses were brushed to her brow and her temple, his chest stirring with deep inhalation beneath her cheek as he bid, "Go to sleep, my love."

"Erik," she called, never glancing up when the dark wouldn't have shown her a face, "are you happy, *ange*?"

"Happier than I've ever been in my existence." More delicate kisses were indulged, and between their sweet grazing, he inquired back, "And you? ...You don't regret your choice, do you?"

"No, never," she insisted, turning to press her own kiss to the steady beat of his heart and wishing she kissed the scars beneath material instead.

His disfigured cheek rubbed against her brow, and she arched nearer to its distorted shape. "Go to sleep, Christine."

It was too simple to obey. Closing her eyes, delicious contentment drew her to sweet dreams, and when sense tried to insist that this peace must be temporary, she didn't listen, shutting its voice out and breathing Erik's scent into her lungs. Let this be hers a little longer...

*****

When Christine awoke, she was alone in her

bed. It would have been considered no different than any other morning except sunlight poured in from sheer curtains and illuminated the room, reminding her that she was not underground. Everything felt changed. She had grown accustomed to any little transition spinning her world upside down and having awful repercussions, but this change she embraced wholeheartedly, smiling as she rose to greet the day with anticipation in every movement.

There were new gowns in the armoire. Erik had certainly taken every detail into account, and she hummed beneath her breath as she dressed, eager to be in his presence. Before she even left the room, the sound of a gentle melody on a piano's keys wafted up and announced him, and nostalgia bubbled in her soul. Home, this felt like home.

Hurrying with whispered steps, she followed music's serenade, creeping downstairs and peeking ahead with anxious eyes. A beautiful piano rested in the arch of the bay window, and she considered how odd it was to see Erik bathed in sunglow. With longing eyes, she watched his body rise and fall with music's consumption, and burned within to fantasize a variation of that motion and his body moving and arching above hers as graceful and legato as his melody. The thought alone created ripples of sensation that raced through her and settled in an urgent heat between her legs.

Wanting seemed to have a voice because all at once, he stopped playing and turned to catch her spying presence.

"Christine." His eyes lit with adoration, and as they trailed hungry caresses over her from head to foot, she shivered and felt her cheeks redden with a blush. Too many reminiscences of the previous night were candidly displayed upon that masked face.

"I...I'm sorry if I woke you," Erik stammered, feeling unusually awkward. Desire was nothing new, but after a taste, it felt as powerful as an addiction, overwhelming sense in its violent rush. Seeking a calm exterior, he hastily explained, "I was compelled to test the new piano and see how it holds a tune."

"It sounded lovely," Christine bid, grinning timidly to observe his blatant lust, unguarded and unreserved. Small steps brought her close enough to run her fingers along the piano's shiny back. "This is a beautiful instrument."

He wanted to counter and gush over her beauty instead, but he kept such musings in his gaze and answered the questions he knew her curiosity was churning. "It was delivered at dawn per my request. I had Henri, our carriage driver if you recall, here to meet the gentleman who brought it and handle the business end of things so I wouldn't have to endure the social staring. We don't need rumors circulating the city already about the man in a mask living in a mansion house with his beautiful, new wife...at least not the *mask* part of it."

The mere mention of his mask had her edging close enough to touch her fingers to its intrusive presence, and the piano was abruptly forgotten with the intensity of her passionate eyes.

"Christine," he moaned, grabbing her hips and yanking her to him. "I am barely keeping restraint intact this morning." As her hand sought to remove his mask, he suddenly caught it and held it captive. "Wait. You have a rehearsal to attend."

"What? No," she whined, every desire-laden implication dropping to an annoyed grimace. "Your note excused me with an illness. Perhaps I still have it. I could be contagious if I go. Wouldn't you rather I was here contaminating you?"

"Of course!" he sighed possessively. "Contaminate me. Destroy me. Devour me as you like. But...rehearsal first. I won't risk you losing your place because I was selfish. When the season is over, I shall take you on an extended honeymoon across the continent, anywhere you want. But for now, rehearsal, and Henri is waiting outside. He is under my orders to drive you to and from the opera house."

"You're letting me go alone?" she posed with a doubtful arch of a dark brow. "And what shall you do, resident Opera Ghost? Confine yourself to haunting *our* home instead?"

"And trust the Vicomte not to retaliate with all his stuffy bravado? Certainly not! But I can't very well accompany you and take the chance of being seen. I have my own means of travel, and you will be late if you don't start on your way. This isn't the same as walking upstairs to the theatre, you know. You now have to take the journey into account."

"Oh, all right," she reluctantly conceded with another pout that drew his focus to perfect pink lips; he yearned to kiss them into a smile, but he had a suspicion if he started, he would not stop. With an obliging huff, he made sure his disappointment was known and released her from his arms.

"Sing well," he bid. "In fact, sing as if I'm *always* listening to you; it will keep you striving to your potential. Oh, and breakfast is in the carriage. Henri is under my strict orders to make sure you eat it even if he has to watch you. You're going to need your strength and your wits about you today."

"What does that mean?" Her suspicion only received an innocent grin as its answer. "What have you done?"

"Nothing." He shrugged blamelessly. "How could I possibly have done anything when I spent the night indisposed with you? You do remember that, don't you?"

"And yet you had time to buy a piano and arrange its delivery," she countered, narrowing blue eyes.

"You have to go, or you'll be late."

"But you-"

"Go on." He caught her shoulders and attempted a kiss to her forehead before steering her toward the door. "Keep safe."

Christine made a face and delighted in his chuckle before she acquiesced and rushed outside. She knew he was right, and it was now a journey through crowded city streets to arrive at the opera house and a place that had been a substitute home for so long. And yet did she feel a loss no longer dwelling in the cozy recesses underground? She gave up one home, and yet knowing Erik was with her, she never lost the tie to her heart, the tug that insisted a house was not just a building. In that regard, she had brought her home with her.

The trip was tedious, and by the time the carriage pulled to a halt before the theatre, she was minutes from being late. She realized with an annoyed huff that she would have to allot more time tomorrow, ...and more yet, it seemed, as Henri actually obeyed Erik's order and stalled her long enough to make sure she'd eaten. Henri was not large or overbearing; for Christine's meager height, she was inches taller. But she was disinclined to pose an argument. He seemed the sort that would scold her like a chastising parent if she dared.

The little man eyed her shrewdly and stated, "I am to meet you in the lobby as soon as you are dismissed and see you home."

"The lobby? But I could come outside if you wish to wait in the carriage-"

"The lobby," he repeated. "Your husband's orders, Madame. If you care to protest, take it up with him. I was hired to do as he says."

Rolling her eyes, she replied, "The lobby then," and was grateful to finally be allowed to hurry for the door.

Her last stint at rehearsal had her the target of cold comments about her involvement with the Opera Ghost. She hoped the gossip had died down by now and actually prayed for an uneventful day spent half-lost in daydreams. ...Perhaps that was a fool's dream.

The instant she walked onstage, all whispers shot in her direction, and as she shrank back beneath the weight of crawling stares, Meg grabbed her arm and rescued her, pulling her into the wings.

"Christine! How could you not tell me? Not a single word! I had to hear the news like a common bystander and certainly not a dear friend!" The words were half-shrieked in high pitches as the little ballerina bounced up and down in her irritation.

"What news? What are you talking about, Meg?"

But Meg's stare froze, and catching Christine's hand, she lifted it to inspection, transfixed by her ring and its sparkle. "It *is* true! You're married! *Married*! And I am practically the last to know!"

"How did you find out about it?" Christine nervously demanded.

"It's announced in overly large letters across the front page of the newspaper! Everyone has seen it, and they've been talking about it all morning."

Newspaper... Well, it shouldn't have been a surprise. Erik wanted it vividly known, and if he arranged the story, he could control the details. But the front page? She could only imagine what that had cost him. The marriage of a sometimes opera diva was hardly noteworthy.

"Well?" Meg pushed expectantly. "Who *is* he, Christine? The newspaper said he's rich, an entrepreneur who tours the world indulging in the arts or some frivolous nonsense like that."

"Really?" she inquired with an escaping giggle. "What else did it say, pray tell? Did it portray him as a veritable genius and virtuoso? Because I bet he would favor that depiction wholeheartedly! My brilliant and omnipotent husband!"

Meg arched a confounded golden brow, but shaking her head, she filled in, "It read like a fairytale. He sees you sing at the opera and is taken with you to the point of impulsive proposals and declarations of undying love. ...In more formal idioms, of course. I prefer my own added detailing. But is it the truth, Christine?"

The flicker in her eyes glimmered in indulgent memories and answered even before she breathed, "Yes, that's the truth."

"So he swept you off your feet, and you *married* him? Simple as that? It hardly seems intelligent, even if it is hopelessly romantic! But what about the Vicomte? I thought you were set on him. ...Ooh, or your supposedly amazing teacher! Dear Lord, you have too many suitors to keep track of!"

Grinning to herself, Christine replied, "My heart knew the answer the instant it saw its match. No other could suffice."

"A shame the Vicomte didn't realize that," Meg commented with a disparaging shake of her golden head. "When he sees the morning paper, he's going to be here looking for you."

"Yes, I know, but that's my own fault. I let him believe things that were never true, and now...well, he won't seem to forget them." She'd told stories of murdering ghosts, and Raoul had latched onto them with eager hands. He'd *wanted* to believe, and with her own admissions as her enemy, she wasn't sure she had words enough to discourage him.

Christine didn't have to wait to find out the Vicomte's reaction. Moments after an interrogation from Meg, he was there, his expression displaying a mixture of relief and frantic concern the instant he saw her.

She was the one to approach, catching his arm and leading him beyond the earshot of eavesdroppers whose whispers grew with his arrival. She could only imagine what was spoken when she had a husband, a Vicomte suitor, and an Opera Ghost vying for her affections!

"Christine," Raoul hissed and held out the offensive newspaper to her inspection, "what is this?

You didn't...you wouldn't have married *him*."

Taking the paper, she scanned the article with eager eyes, unsure if she should be angry or grateful. As her fingers touched the black print of her own name, Raoul caught her hand and turned it to examine her ring as if tangible proof made a newspaper's words real.

"Christine, ...did he force you?"

"*I* made the choice," she insisted, jerking her hand away.

"Oh? With what collateral, I wonder. It's convenient, isn't it? Marry you and create some overdone affront to stake a claim to the world. Tell everyone you're *his* without revealing himself because if anyone knew you actually married their Opera Ghost, he'd destroy you both." Chuckling sarcastically, Raoul concluded, "You don't believe me! But you did once. I convinced you to doubt and question, and just as quick, he stole every justifiable suspicion with spells and games."

Christine's expression never changed or softened its stern lines, and she abruptly replied, "I have to get to rehearsal. Please leave me be."

"But if you would listen and stop avoiding the parts you'd rather not hear-"

"Raoul, I made the choice," she repeated, "and I won't let you turn it into a sin and make me regret. It's done now anyway; you can do nothing to change it."

"Christine-"

"Mademoiselle?" a voice broke their confrontation as a nervous Firmin glanced between them. "I mean... Madame."

"Yes, Monsieur," she dutifully replied and attempted to replace her composure as both she and Raoul focused on the elegantly scrawled letter being clutched in Firmin's shaking hand. She was doubtless they drew the same conclusion.

"Madame, I wanted to inform you that your

part has been changed; you will now be performing the lead soprano role." Firmin lifted the letter and scanned its details. "Yes, the...the lead."

"But...that is La Carlotta's role," Christine skeptically replied, avoiding Raoul's blameful glare.

"It's yours now," Firmin anxiously stuttered with an awkward, unnecessary bow. "Good luck." Though Christine continued to stare at him as if he'd lost his mind, he hurried away before she could utter another word. She caught the echo of his wavering voice calling for the stage director Reyer and guessed he was relaying the cast change to him.

The lead... As she finally lifted eyes to Raoul's angered face, she felt her cheeks redden with an unwanted blush.

"And shall we conclude why your role was changed?" the Vicomte demanded coldly. "Your husband playing his Opera Ghost persona yet again and altering the world to his liking? Is that what all this is? Marry the bastard, and he will further your career? Does your career mean as much as your freedom? Or is it only an incentive to bedding the monster? A gift for enduring his repulsive touch?"

"Stop it," Christine hissed, and the rage welling within brightened her pink complexion. "You know nothing!"

"I know he played by his own rules yet again and cast the opera as if he had a right. Surely more ultimatums were given, more threats of murder and mayhem should management refute his demands, and once again at his whim and desire, he pulls the strings and you are forced into the spotlight like his little marionette." Raoul shook his head and bluntly commanded, "Correct me if I am wrong. Go on and make this less of an abomination than it truly is. I don't think even *you* can make this irreprehensible. The Opera Ghost at his best, wouldn't you say?"

She couldn't argue when she wondered the same, but with a cold glare, she simply insisted, "I have to get to rehearsal. Leave me be." And she stalked past him before he could attempt another word.

Chapter Sixteen

In a day filled with blocking and new lines to learn, with fittings and measurements for costumes, with bitter stares in every direction and too many sharp muttered comments to endure, Christine was grateful the instant she was confined to the carriage's protection. Her shoulders drooped with her exhaustion, fake smiles and contentment finally able to release their tension. A frown felt better at the moment because it was honest.

That frown did not surrender its post even as she arrived home. Leaving Henri with a promise to be early the next morning, she wearily entered the quiet foyer as leftover streaks of sunlight chased her heels and cast late-day shadows along the floor.

"Good evening, my love. I trust rehearsal went well."

Christine narrowed her eyes as she strode into the sitting room and found Erik in the same place she had left him that morning. Then the sun had poured about his shape and given him light to play by; now a lantern performed the task though less efficiently. She wondered how he had gotten by so many years with only manmade light when she had to squint to make out details against its mediocrity.

"However did you arrive home before me?" she demanded. "I felt you watching when I met Henri in the lobby to leave."

257

"Felt?" he inquired with a bemused smile. "Indeed. Well, it seems you've always been able to feel my eyes upon you. I blame desire; it's too potent to remain silent and gives me away. You feel my wanting. Isn't that so, Christine?"

And didn't she feel it vibrantly as he trailed his lazy gaze over her and never attempted to hide his longing? He wanted her, but she wasn't about to be deterred from a few left-out details in between.

"Don't you dare distract me so I will not hold you accountable for your actions," she scolded, careful to linger beyond his reach. One touch, and she wasn't sure she'd be able to remember anything else.

"My actions? ...Ah, the newspaper article. I have no regret for that," he stated matter-of-factly. "I needed a formal announcement, and it wasn't as though I could make an appearance at the opera house and proclaim it to the world. It was a convenient compromise, and you cannot find fault. You wear my ring and now arrive at rehearsal in an elegant carriage. People were bound to be suspicious."

"Not the newspaper," she replied. "I mean your backstage tactics to get me heaved into the lead role. Playing the Opera Ghost again, *ange*? Another note filled with threats to force the management to comply? You can't keep doing that, Erik. Have you any idea the enemies I've accrued through no fault of my own? La Carlotta stomped out of rehearsal today, and I'm glad I don't know enough Italian to understand the curses she was yelling."

"Stomped out of rehearsal?" His sudden grin was full of amusement. "I missed that part. I would have loved to see it! Is it too much to hope she won't return?"

"Erik!"

"Oh, calm yourself," he gently commanded. "A little faith would be nice. You've told me time and again you don't want me to be the Opera Ghost, and I want to please you."

"But I saw a note!"

"I played by the rules this time," he interrupted, his temper flaring with the threat of confrontation. "Or your Vicomte's rules at least. A note sent from your new husband along with a *very* generous contribution to the opera house. No threats, no commands. I simply commented how much I favor seeing my wife onstage, singing the lead role. The only unjust fault you can dub is coercion, but that is the right of a patron. Money can buy you anything; such is the world we live in, and if you truly think your Vicomte wouldn't have done the same, then you are naïve."

Christine's brow lined pensively; she wasn't certain what point she could be angry about. "So...you persuaded with a donation but never outright commanded the managers to obey?"

"Exactly. Ask *them* if you don't believe me. Will you hate me for it? I didn't do anything an aristocrat wouldn't do. No Opera Ghost games. Is my word sufficient, or will you refrain from forgiving me without proof?"

His annoyance was unhidden, and she tentatively nodded and decided, "I believe you. Raoul, however, will not. He's convinced you are evil, and there's nothing I can say to change his mind."

"Oh, I don't care what your jilted suitor thinks. As long as not a single word affects *you* and your heart, then let him speak every hateful word he can concoct." For the hundredth time since her entrance, Erik raced a fevered stare over her, savoring every detail of a body he ached to admire bare. It was with a reluctant groan that he concluded, "Your lesson. We have much work to do if you are going to be prepared. Your role is deceptively simple because it isn't simple at all. I need to drag the soul out of you to carry this character from one end of the opera to the other. No more holding back. After last night...I'm convinced you can completely surrender with the right molding and motivation. Then you held nothing back. Now I just have to get that commitment onstage."

Her skin flushed pink with his provocative implications, and though she lowered blue eyes, he caught her grin and clasped it as encouragement. Ah, what torture patience inflicted! More minutes before he could have her writhing beneath him again! It seemed not even music could satisfy him now that he had found something far more exquisite.

Her lesson required full concentration and a certain level of detachment, and though Erik kept up his pretense well enough, on occasion, his desire peeked out and hinted the things he wanted to do instead. He glimpsed her shiver in reply and cursed patience all the more viciously.

Finally, he felt satisfied enough with their progress to cease work, and as soon as he carefully covered the piano's keys, he was on his feet and seeking her with urgent arms.

"Wait, wait," she commanded, holding up stalling hands and skirting his grasp.

"Why? I want you."

"No," she firmly stated, and he tilted a doubtful head.

"No? Need I remind you that *you* enjoyed what we did last night as much, perhaps even *more so*, than I? Will you deny it when I have vividly recalled feeling you find pleasure all day long? I ache to give you ecstasy again and again until you can barely endure anymore."

Erik saw the effect his erotic words had on her, the subtle squirm, the tremble, the flash of shared memories in her hazy eyes. But the instant he moved to claim victory and grab her, she jumped back and shook her head.

"*No*," she commanded again, her adamancy suddenly unbreakable. "I won't let you. That...that's not what I want."

Observing her oddly, he consented to fist impatient hands at his sides and demanded, "Then tell me what you want. Forcing your compliance under the title of wifely duty holds little appeal when I know you want me with as much vigor as I want you. So tell me what I must do to have you, Christine. I'll play your game if that's what it takes."

She obviously had something in mind, and through a brighter blush, she innocently bid, "Let me...let me undress you, Erik."

"No," he replied simple as that, and to his surprise, her anger flared.

"So for the rest of our lives you intend to make love in the dark and pin me to the bed so I may not touch you?"

Her suggestion had an undeniable appeal and only enhanced his aching as he attempted a nonchalant shrug. "You didn't complain last night when you were crying out beneath me."

She made a face at him and snapped, "So *you* are allowed to touch me at your whim, but *I* am not allowed the same? That isn't fair!"

"I'm not a fair man," he retorted, "and I don't feel a need to be in this situation. You don't know what you're asking. Subjecting you to the horror of my face is bad enough, but this... No, you don't know what you're asking," he repeated, harsher yet.

"I do!" she insisted in a shout. "I *felt* it last night, not with hands and fingers but pressed to my body. Every scar, everything you don't wish to share. I *felt* them against my skin, and I don't see why it is any different than baring your face. I've proven your face doesn't matter. Why won't you let me do the same now?"

"It is *completely* different!" he roared, and though she started with his abruptness, she did not recoil. "My face is a heinous atrocity, but I can use it as a weapon. I can detach my heart and put it on display to frighten and terrify. I can make it a strength even in its ugliness. But my body...that is only weakness. That tells a story of being a victim instead. It is a degradation far more than what the mask conceals. I was beaten, tortured, abused, and I can find nothing worth your acceptance in it. You would pity and realize how damaged a creature I truly am, and I'd rather take you in the dark and know only the music of your desire. I never want to wonder what lies beneath it. You can offer no protest when your first response to the sight of my face was disgust; you'd be a hypocrite to try."

Christine almost sighed her defeat, aware of his obstinacy, but she also knew *she* was the very key to swaying it. She had won this match before and convinced him to take off the mask. This might be a more difficult battle, but she refused to accept it as un-winnable.

On the wings of her thoughts, she firmly declared, "I want to touch you. I won't spend the rest of my life denied the right to touch my husband, and *you* would be the hypocrite between us if you said you didn't want the same. My hands upon your body, caressing you, exploring every detail, adoring you more because of the damaged places."

Her words had her desired reaction as she heard him inhale a harsh breath, but his reply was sad instead of fervent. "You think very highly of yourself, but I know better. I've seen you falter often enough. No, Christine, I *will not* bare my body to your pretense and watch it crack and crumble to dust."

"Then I say the same," she glibly declared. "I *will not* bare my body and allow your touch, not willingly. If you want me, you will have to force me, and I will struggle and fight you and perhaps truly consider you a monster if you dare."

"You teasing vixen!" he snapped in a growl. "It is hardly the same thing when *you* are perfection. I can tear every garment from your body, and though you will be angry and perhaps bear shyness, you will not know *humiliation* or the shame of being unattractive and hideous. *You* are beautiful."

"And I am trying to show you that you need not feel humiliated, not with *me*. I am not going to judge you or abhor you for things you can't change. I've learned better than that."

"Have you?" he skeptically inquired with a dubious shake of his head. "You speak it with such conviction, as if one night in my bed has suddenly sparked your strength."

"No, choosing to marry you did that," she corrected. "One night in your bed convinced me that *you* are not as strong as you'd have me believe. So *I* must be the strong one this time. Let me prove to you that I can be." Her tentative hands extended in the air between them, slow and without threat as she bid again, "Let me undress you."

He wanted to refuse; she could practically hear the bitter argument as it played in his head, but with an irritated huff, he replied, "Do as you please. I know that infernal curiosity of yours too well. I fear if I object, I will one night awaken stripped in bed without my consent, and I enjoyed sleeping beside you too much to keep my guard up and distance at every moment. Go on, Christine. Shame me further by once again proving why I am unworthy of you."

Words were a pointless waste of breath when it came to Erik; she knew he'd doubt every letter and search for hidden references that did not exist. So instead, she waited until he threw seemingly apathetic arms out at his sides and took that as permission.

Christine's fingers trembled; she couldn't control such a natural response and knew he would believe it was a symptom of weakness. Weakness? No, she was about to spin his theories upside down.

Her hands found the lapels of his jacket, and with tender care, she began her diligent task, removing one layer at a time. Jacket, vest, tie, always formal attire. She wondered if he did that purposely to hide behind another role. The pretense of perfect gentleman even if the mask was a poor substitute for a flawless face. A guise as unfitting as Opera Ghost, and yet this one was the most heart-wrenching. This was the one role he wanted most and could never have.

Her fingers stilled at the buttons of his shirt, and glancing into mismatched eyes, she found him watching her intently and fighting to remain aloof, as if coldness could hide anxiety. But she wanted it all, every nerve, every apprehensive fear, and her hand lifted instead to his mask first, quickly removing its barrier and admiring the warm candlelight's glow upon his scars. That face couldn't hide, not without its security. She was suddenly adamant to relieve him of every barrier he wished to cling to.

Taking his mask brought trepidation to the surface, and he shook to stand before her as she began to unclasp buttons. But never was a refusal spoken as they both regarded the motion of her nimble fingers, moving one button to the next from throat to waist before skin was uncovered.

Christine held her breath as with one last glimpse into eyes that showed sudden terror, she yanked his shirt free and tossed it to the floor. Scars became her sole focus. So much damage, a canvas completely destroyed, and it tugged unwanted tears to her eyes to behold it. He didn't want compassion, but she couldn't stop its swell, and her tears betrayed her.

Her gaze flicked to his, but when she saw pain poorly-concealed by invalid rage and a jaw clenched so tight she feared what words would fall out once it loosed, she concentrated on skin instead. The scars on his face were an affliction that made a living, breathing man appear as a corpse half a step into the grave; the scars on his body were not the same. They did not stir up appellations of demon or monster; this was not the body of some nightmare creature, distorted and half-animal as horror stories portrayed. This was what torture looked like.

Upraised marks were a darker color than the natural paleness the rest of his flesh held, lashes criss-crossed, some long, some barely strikes, all once deep enough to leave evidence behind. Whipped, he'd once been whipped...and burned. Oddly-textured patches insisted heat was their cause, spread in more unnatural hues along his abdomen. Dear Lord, his body was the story of his cruel life. Was it any wonder that he could not forget the details and clung to their burden and the grudges they incited? He had to *see* the memories on a daily basis. She suddenly understood why he preferred to play the omnipotent Opera Ghost. Beneath was a fallible and broken man, terrified to be a victim once again and desperate to act first, to kill before he himself was hurt.

Crying silent tears, Christine lifted a quivering hand and brushed an idle caress along one brutal mark. He jolted and shrank away as if he couldn't possibly bear even something so gentle. But she was undeterred, and creeping closer, she pressed both palms flush to his chest, feeling him fight an instinctual urge to back away. It seemed to take all his effort to remain fixed in place and allow what she considered to be mundane contact, and it hurt her to consider his body's first response was an expectancy of pain, more torture, more agony, being a victim at *her* whim this time.

"Don't touch me," he suddenly begged, breathless and violently shaking against her palms, but she did not obey.

"Why? Am I causing pain this way, Erik? Are you truly afraid I shall leave bruises and injury when I touch you so gently? Not every touch need be an act of violence, and yet that is all you have known, isn't it?" Tears fell faster with her conclusions, and emotion bound so tightly that she shook as hard as he did. "You are waiting for me to hurt you," she accused on the verge of a sob. "You're so certain that is all that can come from any touch. Pain and humiliation."

"Yes, pain," he agreed against his own tears. "Hurt me, Christine. Make your own damage. Leave bruises in your wake. ...No, bruises fade from existence; they have no permanence, and if you are to hurt me, I want its evidence as mine forever. Make something beautiful on this ugly corpse."

"Erik, stop," she commanded sharply, blue eyes flashing bright. "I will *never* hurt you. Never."

"Yes, you will. Your damage will be that fading bruise, but I never forget bruises; their scars are hidden within, everlasting patches of purple upon the heart itself. And I'll carry yours forever as a wound against my heart."

"Why are you so certain?" she frantically bid. "Why am I destined to cause you pain?"

He fixed his stare on the hands held to his chest and declared matter-of-factly, "Because one day you'll have to wake up from the dream and realize I am not the noble hero and prince. I am a monster."

Tears tumbled faster to witness the depth of his self-loathing. "You've scripted us such a bleak ending. I'm here now, touching you, and you won't believe it because if you do, then you are no longer the monster you constantly dub yourself." Her open palms slid slowly up his chest until she could cup his face between them and force him to hold her eye. "You are no monster; you are no Opera Ghost; you are no angel or devil or corpse. You are Erik, my husband, and that is enough to claim my heart. You are worthy of love and happiness. You are worthy of a future at my side without shadows and hiding. Won't you believe me? Erik, please."

Her hands released his face if only to find skin, and with the tips of her fingers, she followed the meandering path of his scars, starting at the base of his neck and continuing along his torso. Some were little hills in their remnant, and she crossed their humps to the valleys in between where skin was yet pale and untouched. She made her caresses into an exploration, finding smoothness and lingering over rough spots, outlining the sculpture of muscles beneath the curves of his ribs, pausing over his heartbeat.

Glancing through her dark lashes and catching his stare fixed upon her hands, she dared to inquire, "Do you like when I touch you, Erik? There is no pain in my hands, not in a single caress, and no shame, ...and no disgust. Please tell me that you believe me."

Erik didn't reply, but as her hands grazed his stomach, he closed his eyes and shivered with his wanting. Had anything ever felt so exquisite? His skin held its own memories as vividly as his mind, and it expected the sharp sting of a whip's lash instead or the sear of pokers held to its surface. It tingled across every inch, but her soft hands redefined the concept of sensation. Every surge through his veins was a lesson in desire, a swell, an ache, until he longed to beg her to keep touching him forever.

She took her time, and he suffered lust's ebbs and crests with forced patience, burning from the inside out. Along his blemished back, she was attentive to every flaw, and when she leaned close and pressed her lips to a distortion upon his shoulder, he could not suppress a moan. Subtle encouragement when words jumbled in his head. One moan became many as she formed more kisses, raining them across his shoulder blades and back around to scars she had already blessed with her fingers. Now they were granted lips as well, and Erik shuddered and cried out, fisting his hands to refrain from grabbing her and ending this blissful torture.

Her warm mouth touched the top of a scar, and her tongue traced its length, following it to his hip as she knelt at his feet. He was eagerly pliant to her every endeavor and did not stop her as she drew his pants down, leaving only his undershorts; they did little to conceal his telltale desire. He knew no shame for its revelation when she was the reason. His only apprehension came with the hushed sigh she gave to trail her fingers along more marks upon his legs. Her lips found evidence of a once-brutal gash along the muscle of his thigh and covered it with kisses that left him desperate not to writhe with his ache. No, not yet. He didn't want to cease her healing caresses, not when her hands curled about his calves and her mouth gently nipped his skin without hesitation. To never know a touch and then have this as some sort of reward... He hardly felt he deserved it.

Christine kissed his knee and was gently brushing her lips to his inner thigh when he slid to the floor with her. Urgent arms abruptly encircled her clothed shape as he hugged her tight, burrowing his scarred cheek against her chest and thrilling to feel her consent and wrap her arms about him, her hands taut and gripping his bare back.

Oh, to hold her and fit her to his body as a necessary half! To know no other could be his perfect match and be fortunate enough to have her! His adoration brought tears to his eyes, and he blinked them away before she could see, nuzzling his cheek to her small, soft body as though she was salvation.

"I can hear your heart." He whispered the words for fear his voice would crack under emotion's weight. "It's so strong in its every beat. ...It plays its own music, more beautiful than any I could compose. I could try and try and never capture anything near its essence. How I underestimated its steady, unalterable pattern! It isn't racing and hoping to flee at first chance with its aversion. No, it is constant and as unchanging as my own. Oh, Christine, ...your heart is a symphony."

She set a kiss to the crown of his head and gently bid, "I want you, *ange*. Scars won't change that."

"Truly, Christine? You desire this body despite its damage and imperfections? You've burned as you've touched me?"

Drawing back from his embrace, she tentatively grabbed his hand and guided it beneath crumpled layers of skirts. A pink blush tinted her cheeks and only deepened its hue, spreading heat along every inch of her pale skin as she pressed his fingers to the spot where she ached.

Erik could feel her wetness even through the flimsy boundary of her pantaloons, and it tempted him to caress further, deeper, slipping fingertips within her silken folds and groaning to be seared by her heat. "I've been aching to touch you like this all day," he huskily admitted. "It has been the core of my every fantasy. For the rest of eternity, *this* is mine. Only I will touch you this way and feel you grow wet and hot. Only I will taste you and tease my tongue with your flavor. Only I will claim you and find ecstasy within you. ...You can imagine the fever I've suffered all the long hours without you."

"Please," she whimpered as his fingers stroked the length of her.

"Please what, love? Tell me, Christine."

"Touch me," she quietly replied, blush still present.

"Oh, but I *am* touching you," he teased, grazing his fingertip to the epicenter of her desire and feeling her shudder. "How do you want me to touch you, Christine? Tell me."

"Inside," she breathlessly whispered, her gaze on his with that lingering innocence that made him throb. He didn't deny her, reaching further beneath skirts and finding a path within her pantaloons. A groan rumbled in his chest to slide his fingers deep and coat them in her slick wetness. She was ready for him, arching her hips closer to his, and he marveled that her desire stemmed from touching his scarred body.

His free hand tugged restlessly at her gown, and she eagerly helped him, unclasping and yanking it off. Caresses had to cease, but when passion was this torrid, he could think of nothing but having her bared to him. The last remaining barrier was his undershorts, and he jerked them free with the same hastiness. She was the one to halt his endeavors, her wide eyes perusing his hardened manhood with that curiosity he recognized at first glimpse. It triumphed over any looming trepidation as on instinct, her hand extended.

Erik did not stop her, watching those small fingers and shivering the instant they stroked a hesitant caress up the length of his shaft.

It was impossible to be shy when she was so intrigued. Christine tentatively curved her fingers about his vast width and stammered with unavoidable awkwardness. "Is this right? ...Is this how I should touch you? Teach me, *ange*."

He shuddered, and the fire in his mismatched eyes dulled her shyness. "Touch me as you will. There is no method. Do as you desire."

"I want to please you," she stated, caressing up and down as he throbbed against her palm. His moans grew louder, his breaths harsh, and eager to push him further, she suddenly bent and pressed a kiss to the tip of his erection.

"*Now!*" he suddenly growled, catching her shoulders and dragging her bare body to his. "I have no more control for games. You're driving me mad!"

She would have giggled at his fervor, but he abruptly lifted her hips, fitting her onto his lap, and plunged deep, transforming laughter into sharp gasps. His mouth found hers, starved for her kiss, and as his tongue mimicked motion and slipped within to taste her, he rocked his hips and created a gentle rhythm.

Christine met every thrust, running restless hands over his scarred back. She was already melting and succumbed without reservation as he found her breasts and his thumbs teasingly flicked across her nipples. Tearing her lips from his, she gasped, "Don't stop, Erik."

"No, never," he vowed, and nipping her ear with his teeth, he hoarsely insisted, "This body is damaged and scarred, but it is *yours* to do with as you please. Find pleasure for me, Christine. I want to watch you surrender."

She did not hesitate to obey, arching her hips harder into his and changing their pace to her liking. His body rubbed where she most ached, his skin so arousing pressed to hers at every possible inch. The mere consideration that he was hers and that every scar and flaw would bear only her touch for eternity pushed her to her peak. She buried her overwhelmed cry against his scarred collarbone, trembling with the power of her pleasure.

"That's my girl," Erik breathed, kissing her temple and rocking her faster with him. "Such dark desire shrouded in lingering innocence, and I am going to inspire it to new heights. You are exquisite, Christine. To watch you be overcome with pleasure is a blessing I shall never take for granted."

Lifting a shy grin, she replied, "And may I watch the same? I want to see my husband be overcome with pleasure."

Such a request! After a lifetime lost in shadows, to glimpse the adoration in her gaze, as if a face as disfigured as his was only beautiful, enticed him to give an incredulous nod. He never looked away, transfixing himself on the blues in her eyes. Moving harder and deeper with every thrust, he felt ecstasy approach. One more vicious jerk, and a desperate moan tore from his lips as he leaned close to press his forehead to hers, never breaking their stare. And he saw everything in those depths that he'd ever longed to be his.

"Oh, Christine, Christine," he murmured, cupping her face between his hands, "I love you. I love you so much."

He was certain he saw a reflection of his sentiment in her eyes, but the words went unspoken and only drifted like vapors in the air around their embracing shape. Though he longed to demand more, to push for the heart he already knew was his, he chose to be patient and simply revel in her body against his, her gaze never brushed with disgust or regret. No, he saw happiness, and it was enough for now.

Chapter Seventeen

Being the prima donna did not just mean singing one's best onstage; it meant playing a role every moment in the public eye. Christine was on the verge of exhaustion at each rehearsal's end, tired of scrutiny from every direction and far too much pressure for one person to handle. Perhaps had she climbed the ranks and legitimately earned the place, she could claim the right to play the diva as Carlotta did and make everyone bend to her will. But with her advancement under question and snide whispers in the background, she had to instead choose graciousness and keep her head high no matter the drama around her.

By week's end, Carlotta returned to the theatre with her own act of civility in place, however temporary it might be. Christine learned from the gossiping ballerinas that Carlotta had attempted to find a new company, intending to throw it into the managers' faces as an attestation to her talent and worth, but not a single theatre would hire her, not even for small secondary roles. Her only choice was to return and put on a courteous façade long enough to be certain she hadn't lost her only employment.

Carlotta's congeniality lasted no more than half a day. As soon as it was evident no one would be about to request her termination, she returned to bitter remarks and cruel taunting with Christine as her favorite scapegoat. Resentment made cruelty vicious, and though Christine tried to shirk off every biting word, too many penetrated her shield and stung.

Her saving grace in the midst of such chaos and adopted smiles was Erik. Every day as she returned home fatigued and a step away from defeat, he picked up the pieces and put her to right again. Her lessons were an anticipated staple as he treated his role of teacher no differently despite every change in between. Challenges were placed on her shoulders that pushed her talent as he encouraged in his reserved way, but she was growing to know him too well and now saw right through to the true extent of his adoration. He might prefer not to fill her ears with praises, but she glimpsed them in his eyes. And she sought to inspire his pride as much as she once did for an angel.

That was the routine required to prepare her for the opera. But as soon as the last note was sung, every detail transformed, and the role that had possessed her entire day fell free so that she was only herself and the diva was forgotten in the background. Erik had once vowed to be a good husband in his attempt to win her acceptance; he was obviously seeking to prove every word as truth. He treated her like his most prized possession, doting upon her from the moment he no longer played teacher. He never stifled a single compliment or refrained from placing heart and soul at her feet, and how she adored him for it! No more walls, no more barriers constructed in between.

Elaborate meals awaited her lesson's end, shared in their newly-decorated dining room. From the moment they entered its sacred space, she removed his mask as if a necessary action, and it stayed off for the rest of the night, its presence forgotten and now an odd sight when replaced with morning's light. She would have insisted he never wear it again, but he favored it when he was teacher as if a costume to separate such a role from that of husband and lover.

Supper was easy conversation and jovial lightness that was both new and savored, but before they were even finished, stares would grow longer and telling, an anticipation for what was to come next. Half of the time, they barely made it to the bedroom before succumbing with groping hands and desperate lips. She could hardly believe she'd ever lived without the feelings his touch inspired. They felt imperative to survive and so potent that she never wanted to exist without them again. He was careful and tender, but then sometimes when the desire sparked too violently, he ravished and swallowed her in a passion so fervent that she surrendered and begged for more. It was addictive and intoxicating, leaving her to ache and feel incomplete every moment his scarred body was not pressed to hers. No, it was as if every breath taken when not in his arms was a mistake.

Her devoted husband, and after her lesson one night, he grinned with secretive curves as she approached him where he was seated at the piano and lifted the mask away to find his face.

"I have been impatient to do that since I arrived home," she admitted. "And tell me, what is that smile? You've been keeping something from me all evening."

"A surprise," he explained, grin only growing as she trailed caresses along his face. "Shall I give it to you now? Or are you intent to tempt me to other things?"

His brows arched suggestively, and she laughed as she insisted, "Surprise first, and I hope it includes supper because I am utterly famished."

"Too much exertion in high notes. Well, come on then. I won't keep you waiting." He caught her hand and entwined fingers as he pulled her after him with a smile cast over his shoulder. How Christine adored that look! So many smiles lately, and considering how many tears it had taken to get to them, she appreciated every single one.

Erik brought her out the back door as a few stars spied and twinkled in the late evening sky. A cobblestone walkway led their path into the garden, and she laughed as he hurried their pace through a vine-covered trellis. Green surrounded in every direction, beds of stems and hundreds of buds not far from blooming.

"It may not be much to see," Erik told her, "but it will be. Another week or so, and there will be more flowers than you can count."

"You did all of this?"

"Well, not all of it. I had it cleaned and weeded, and if you will observe, I added a couple dozen rosebushes. When they bloom, they will be in every color imaginable. Does that please you, Christine?"

She beamed her delight as her gaze roamed and picked out rosebushes aglow in the final rays of twilight. "Very much. Oh, Erik, this will be lovely."

"And...," he enticed, drawing her further between flowerbeds, "for my hungry, little diva." A gesture to the pathway's end revealed a white-spindled gazebo with supper waiting, spread upon its wooden floor.

"A moonlit picnic in a garden *you* arranged and had tended," she posed with a proud smile. "I think you are growing quite accustomed to being in the world and no longer underground. It isn't so abhorrent, is it, *ange*?"

"Not when I consider sharing it with you. Then everything looks different. The stars, the garden, the night." His gaze met hers as he pulled her into the gazebo. "Would you believe not so long ago, such things held their own anxiety and embedded fear? The very idea of being outside with the chance to be noticed was a scene of terror. I did everything possible to avoid the world, but now you are beside me, looking at my face as if it is ordinary, and nothing else matters. The world is suddenly beautiful." Erik lifted her held hand to his lips and grazed a kiss to her knuckles before releasing her. "Supper, my love?"

They ate as more stars peeked out and joined night's bed, and watching her, Erik felt drawn to her every detail, too intrigued by the graceful motions she made, every genuine smile, every unguarded affection etched beautifully upon her face.

"Christine," he softly bid and burned as she scooted closer upon the gazebo floor until she could set her cheek to his shoulder. With a kiss against her brow, he said, "I have abandoned the underground, and I have no regret for it. But I am far from being a part of the world. Usually, such a point would be deemed a blessing, but I'm growing tired of watching from shadows and keeping distance. I want to be at your side, claiming my place as your husband."

"Your isolation is your own fault," she reminded. "The Opera Ghost, *ange*? You were quite diligent to carve yourself a reputation, and I daresay the sight of a man in a mask will give your secret away. Everyone will realize who you are and pin your sins upon you. I would rather not be a widow when I've only just become a wife."

Stroking her hair possessively, he proposed his idea. "A man in a mask would stir accusations unless, of course, the mask was not suspicious."

"Not suspicious?"

"The Masquerade Ball is at the end of the week. The annual excuse for genteel people to parade about and blamelessly engage in debauchery, and I want to escort you."

Christine lifted her head and eyed him skeptically. "Are you joking?"

"Of course not. A mask is suspicious; you said so yourself, unless it is the accessory of choice. Mine would just be another in the crowd. Never a whisper of Opera Ghost, never a doubt the face beneath the mask is as ordinary as anyone else. It is an ideal situation." Erik studied her intently, gauging her reaction. He had been expecting a touch of enthusiasm, at least a smile, certainly not the disdain he received. "Or perhaps you like the mystery too much, letting them concoct their fantasies about your wealthy, handsome husband. I suppose reality would be a disappointment, mask or not."

His sharp words shook her. "It isn't... I didn't mean..." With a huff, she bluntly declared, "This seems foolish. It is an unnecessary risk. Do you realize the Vicomte will be there? He could spread the truth through the entire party."

"And the Vicomte is what you are so worried about?" he retorted in a snap. "His opinion of you, of *us*, and subsequently, the views of every other. I was determined to keep this quiet so no one need know you married the Opera Ghost, to *protect you*, but perhaps the secret should come out. Games of pretend are only temporarily enjoyed, you know. Eventually, we all have to grow up and face reality."

"Pretend?" she demanded. "I *married* you. That *was* reality."

"Yes, but a marriage behind curtains where you can be the devoted wife and accept my atrocities within closed doors. How often you claim I choose shadows! Do you not do the same? I don't see you eager to appear with your husband on your arm, even when I give you the very excuse to make it presentable."

"Stop it, Erik," she commanded, and he hid an undeniable amusement to catch the hint of her temper.

"Then agree to allow my presence at the ball, on your arm, holding you on the dance floor, my rightful place at your side."

"I could say no, and you'd still come if you wished. My permission is inconsequential to your manner of doing things."

"True," he conceded, hiding the full extent of a smile. It was too difficult to stay angry when he found her continued indignation adorable. "But I'm attempting to be a gentleman and request it. Well then? The Masquerade, Christine? I am not going to allow the Vicomte to decide how we will live our life together. Let him proclaim whatever he wants. No one will believe him if my wife is looking at me in complete adoration and exuberant bliss. For what woman in her right mind would wholeheartedly embrace a future with a disfigured freak at her side?"

"I would," she replied in solemn honesty, bringing his hand to her lips and setting a kiss in his palm. "Without regret, and I will state it again and again before anyone who dares question. I married the Opera Ghost, and I am not ashamed by it, Erik. I chose you."

"You did," he insisted back, fervently capturing her waist and dragging her close. "You chose me. You're mine, Christine, and no one will steal you from me ever again."

"Yours?" she inquired with teasing skepticism. "Oh, am I? I forgot. Well, I think you shall have to prove that, *ange*. Make me remember I'm yours." Her command was a hushed breath, and he shuddered to glimpse her longing as he pressed her back against the wooden floor and leaned atop her.

"The Masquerade?" he pushed, sliding eager hands over her breasts and seeking her nipples through her gown. "Will you be the willing wife on my arm, or will I have to appear as the Opera Ghost in all his glory and claim you in front of a room full of people?"

"You would once again make me gossip's victim?" she demanded, losing a gasp as his impatient fingers wandered beneath the neckline of her gown.

"All the better! The scandal will drive up ticket sales! Every patron will be desperate to attend the premiere and see the Opera Ghost's beautiful mistress!"

His palm cupped her bare breast, his hips arching his desire against her, and in the midst of succumbing, she muttered, "All right! I prefer to choose morality and attend with my husband."

"Wonderful! I can hardly wait to play an equal with those hoity-toity patrons and garner their envy for my beautiful wife." The hand at her breast pinched her nipple sharp enough to make her jump as he decided, "Now, however, I think you need to be devoured by the Opera Ghost. Will you deny me, love?"

Mewing her delight, she yielded and buried tempting kisses against his throat.

"Christine," he moaned, shivering when her tongue tasted his skin. "Keep doing that, and I may change my mind. The Opera Ghost at the Masquerade need not follow propriety. He could take control."

"Show me," she taunted in breathless syllables that teased his ear, and with a growl, he covered her in kisses and proved the Opera Ghost was as desirable as he was dangerous while night cast its spell in a newborn garden.

*****

"What was that?"

The sound of Erik's voice the instant Christine burst into her dressing room startled her to a sharp cry, and she quickly slammed the door, praying no one overheard. "What are you doing in here? You scared me out of my wits!"

Erik sat bemusedly at her vanity, leaning back against its drawers and regarding her with unhidden annoyance. It was the first time in weeks he'd appeared in her dressing room. She had grown accustomed to separating theatre and home life, for even though she knew he was at the opera every hour she was, he did not disturb her and saved his comments and criticisms for lesson time. Obviously, today's faux pas was horrible enough to warrant an immediate scolding.

"Good!" he decided with a sneer. "That is the most emotion I've seen out of you all day even if it is the wrong one! Well?" A frustrated hand gestured for her continuation. "Explanations? Excuses? There must be *something* you can tell me to subside my avid disdain. You *know* that duet! It's engrained in your mind, and yet you sang it no better than an amateur on a street corner performing for pennies. It was empty and pathetic!"

She didn't argue her lackluster portrayal, yet her cheeks flushed pink with chagrin. "I was flustered," she hastily insisted. "The Vicomte snuck in the back of the house right before we ran the act, and I was distracted to see him."

"You know better than that!" Erik snapped. "What have I always taught you? Never break character, and if anything, you should have exceeded yourself and made it clear exactly what you can do. That's being a *diva*, Christine, and not a chorus girl playing a game of dress up. You are under scrutiny from everyone at every moment right now. You *cannot* let a single detail make you waver. One crack in your veneer, and you'll have them leaping at you like vultures. I've admired the way you've handled La Carlotta and ignored her every crude word, but I *refuse* to allow the Vicomte to be the one to break you instead. You deserve this too much to lose it so quickly."

She hated when he chastised like she was a child, especially because every word was true and warranted. "But...why do you think the Vicomte was here?" she posed the very question to blame for her poor rehearsal. How it had twisted its way through her brain and stolen thoughts that should have been on a heart-rendering duet!

Erik rolled his eyes in irritation, but Christine

pushed, "Tomorrow is the Masquerade Ball, and it seems rather peculiar the Vicomte de Chagny is lingering about the theatre during rehearsals the night before."

"Perhaps his very intention *was* to distract you, to prove he still has an effect on you," he replied with undimmed annoyance. "You practically shouted his suspicion was right, and he need but show his perfect face and you'll falter. The bastard won't just give you up. Of course not! Because then he would have lost to a disfigured madman, and that is unacceptable! A Vicomte always gets what he wants, and he wants you."

"He's *worried* about me," she corrected.

"No, he *desires* you. Oh, of course he'll use the virtuous excuse to pursue, play the noble hero, but in the end, what do you think he's after? *You* are the prize, love, and Vicomtes never lose."

His assessment of Raoul's character stung her, and she shook a doubtful head, insisting back, "Raoul is a friend. He doesn't trust you, and you've given him no reason to think any differently. You portrayed yourself in a bad light that night on the rooftop."

"Oh? Because I took off my mask? Yes, a demon face *would* make me a monster, don't you agree, Christine?" Erik harshly demanded. "It must have shamed *you* to have dearest Raoul learn the truth. When I was only the masked Opera Ghost, I was ambiguous; seeing this face puts the degradation on display and steals speculation."

"This isn't about your face, Erik. You were a step away from *killing him* that night."

"If this face were unflawed and we were simply two ordinary men fighting for your affection, do you think he'd be as adamant in his suit? He wants you and won't concede defeat to an ugly monster." Leaping to his feet, he pointed an accusatory finger and insisted, "And *you* have proven to him that if he tries hard enough, he has a chance."

"How?" Christine refused to back away and kept a defiant posture. "I've done nothing to encourage him."

"You faltered onstage," Erik reminded, eyes boring into her. "If you had no concern for his presence and appearance, you wouldn't have missed a single beat. But you let him get to you."

"And you're so certain he will *always* get to me," she stated for him. "That he will *always* break me and eventually convince me to fear you."

"He will be the catalyst to destroy our life together," Erik predicted, so surely that it hurt her. No matter every impassioned declaration and every fervent embrace, in the recesses of his mind, he still believed it was only temporary.

"I'm not going to leave you, Erik," she assured, and putting no consideration to his bad mood, she hugged herself to him and felt the shaking he'd been trying to hide. "Why won't you believe me?"

His arms slowly came about her, hands weaving in her curls and clutching tight. "Because I am predestined to be alone and ordained for a life of melancholy and loneliness. Monsters don't get happy endings, Christine. I feel as if I am simply waiting for you to see reason and run away, and it seems the Vicomte is sharing the same thought. He wants to *make you* see reason."

"*His* version of reason," she argued. "*Mine* is not the same."

"Yours doesn't have a solid foundation; it was built on lies of heavenly angels. *I* lied to you from the first moment, and that deception will always be the finest crack along a porcelain surface. If he pushes on it hard enough, everything must shatter." His premonition was thick with foreboding, and he gripped her firmly to his body, molding her like an irremovable part. "But even if you falter, Christine, if he spins tales and gives you cause to doubt, *I* won't let go. I will steal you away and make you love me again, anything I must. I will not give you up."

Though she nodded against his chest, she refused to believe it would ever come to that. No, she knew what she wanted and where she belonged, and Raoul was not going to change her mind. She carried a fear that if cracks were ever made into holes, it would not be by Raoul, but by Erik himself with his doubts as the hammers.

"But equally as important," he continued, drawing back to meet her eye. "The music. I can't let you get by on that performance today. You're much better than that. When we arrive home, I expect you to sing it as it should have been done."

"Home?" she inquired with a burst of inspiration. "No, let me prove myself now. We have an entire stage at our disposal, and...if *you* will sing it with me, I can show you how I should have performed it earlier."

"No."

"But the theatre will be empty. No one will linger with the Masquerade tomorrow. Everyone was too eager to be dismissed." She shrugged idly, and a slow smile overtook her lips. "And if anyone should happen to lurk about, they can hear me singing with the Opera Ghost, haunting the theatre with him, and spin more tales for our love story."

He chuckled beneath his breath. "If only ghosts could make such glorious sounds, but you, my love, are an angel not a ghost, and you don't favor being dubbed the Opera Ghost's mistress."

"But I *am* exactly that, and I will be proud of it. ...Oh, please, Erik, won't you sing with me?"

"You know I don't favor singing."

"But it will be with *me*," she reminded, eyes glowing expectantly "You have to admit it holds some appeal. You've shaped and molded my voice; you must have a desire to join its song."

"A fantasy," he admitted, "but farfetched. I'd rather not tempt myself with what can never be. If I sing with you, I might want to do so always, and it isn't as if I will ever perform fervent duets on the stage."

"You can right now," she encouraged, clasping his arm eagerly with both hands. "Our own performance. Please, Erik. What if I told you it was my own fantasy as well?"

"All I've given you for inspiration these past weeks, and *that* is your fantasy?" he teased, caressing her cheek with his fingertips.

"It's one among many, and if you fulfill it, I will be obligated to fulfill one of yours in return. *Anything* you want, Erik."

"Anything?" Her provocative implication enticed his grin. "I suppose it would be foolish to reject such an offer. All right, Christine, but I expect the performance I should have seen earlier: confident, full of heart and soul. Make me believe you."

With a dutiful nod, she led the way to her dressing room door, peeking into a deserted corridor before letting him follow. It was just so odd. How often had she tread this path from dressing room to stage and back again, but never with Erik as anything more than a guardian shadow secretly watching. It felt as if she were bringing him into her world this time.

The theatre lights were still aglow, and though she wondered if anyone lingered, she acted confident and unaffected. Determined strides brought her center stage with rows of empty seats stretching back as their invisible audience.

For as familiar as she was with the spot, Erik felt a stranger and imposter to the role, and he glanced about with a swell of anxiety. This was a place he avoided, keeping as far removed from the limelight as possible. Even a nonexistent audience brought to mind too many instances of forced performance, of threats and taunting, of a captor with a whip ready to coerce compliance by any means necessary.

"Erik?" Her gentle voice broke into his reverie and reminded him that awful place of nightmares was no longer real. He wasn't alone and ashamed, locked in a horrific cage with never a hope for something better. No, he'd *found* something better. *She* stood before him with hesitant eyes, waiting for him to begin, and her persuasion was not pain and violence; it was a promise of pleasure and completion in her arms. How fortunate he suddenly felt and how grateful for her existence in the world!

With never a word of the thoughts playing in his head, Erik began to sing. The reverberation startled him and almost made him falter. To hear his own voice echo and return, filling the space so many others had sung at practically an equal in strength and resonance, overwhelmed him, and he glimpsed a similar response from Christine, her eyes briefly closing to savor, her smile full of absolute adoration. She listened and heard beauty.

Christine was impatient for her own entrance, desperate to be one with that voice of her dreams. Her eager eyes watched him use the stage and move in the scene as if he'd acted it a hundred times, so precise and yet so laden with emotion. Every gesture and motion had purpose, and when his eyes met hers, she saw a reflection of the character, of himself, of inherent talent.

He encircled her, and she shivered, teased in every direction. Her skin tingled, wanting his hands and fingers, caresses along the surface. The longing pulled within until her clothing felt heavy and overbearing, wrapping her up and tying her down when she yearned to be free.

Finally as he came alongside, she took a necessary breath and let her voice escape. The first note in harmony and blend was perfection. Her mind conjured a fantasy and wove it about them: her angel singing with his ethereal voice and at last she was allowed to join him as if she were another angel eternally bound as his in their own heaven. It was better than any fairytale she'd ever heard.

Every line sung together was exquisite, vibrating through the theatre up to the crystal chandelier and down to the cellars. As his hand traveled the space of pulsing air between them, she noticed how it trembled, a revelation of amazement that flickered in his mismatched eyes. She met him midway, catching that hand and weaving fingers together. Up and easy, gliding over a high note with legato grace, and every time their parts broke apart, it was exquisite torture that burst into euphoria when they came together again. All she could think was this was how performing was meant to be. She never wanted the music to cease.

One more line, and Erik guided her to him by joined hands, tempting and teasing with pitches and making each its own adoring, intangible caress. How long he had sustained his existence on music alone, and yet he suddenly felt as if he were truly feeling it for the first time. Had it ever held such brilliance? Only with her.

The last note faded to echoes, and he tilted his head inquisitively as he bid, "Why do you regard me that way? You look as if you've just found some exquisite realization."

"I have," she replied breathlessly. "The world starts and ends in this place. Don't you feel it? You first enthralled me with music, Erik. And now...for the first time, I feel as if it is finally mine. I am not chasing your heels, falling short, your *student*. Right now, I feel like your equal."

"Sing it that way, and it will be *you* who exceeds *me*," he predicted, stroking his fingers along her cheek. "You are meant for greatness, Christine, far more than you know, and if I were a good man, I would let you free to follow the stars instead. But I am selfish and can't imagine living without you. A life without you is no better than death."

Apprehension furrowed her brow. "All this talk of separation. You're afraid, *ange*, and I don't understand why."

Erik shook his head sadly. "You've always sought to live up to my potential and placed *me* on some pedestal that shouldn't exist. I told you, Christine: a lie is our foundation. Your affection for me, your respect and the reverence you carry, all of it stems from images of angels. You longed for an angel; is that why you've settled for me? Because I am as close to the fantasy that you believe you will get?" Before she could reply with assurances he could not accept, he insisted, "I wonder these things sometimes, but as I said, I'm selfish. If I must keep you without ever being sure the answers, I shall. You deserve Vicomtes with perfect faces, but you chose a disfigured murderer. Perhaps someday we'll both be certain it isn't a mistake."

"Erik-"

"Come on. Let's go home," he abruptly commanded. "This masochism is killing me."

She allowed him to tug her off the stage, staring solemnly at his shape even though he refused to grant her another look, and a fantasy of singing with angels felt broken into fragments. He doubted; she wondered if he'd *always* doubt, if every time happiness was close to his fingertips, he would force it away for fear of claiming it. He'd heard beauty on the stage and was so terrified of losing it that he refused to accept it. And she was hurt because she knew he thought the same of her.

As Erik led Christine away and they disappeared behind the curtain, a shadow elongated its shape in one of the vacant boxes. The Vicomte de Chagny peered at the stage, fixating on the spot where Christine had stood. His Christine married to that murderous monster, ...the thought alone sickened him.

What had he just witnessed? Enough to give him hope. He pieced together a puzzle of details, finding enough deception and doubt to warrant his case. A naïve child, alone and only too willing to let demons with mesmerizing voices into her life... The monster preyed on her pity and fear until she could not fathom a life without his presence, dependent on him and his illusory music. If it were any other girl, Raoul wouldn't care, but this was Christine. He'd counted himself lucky to find her again; the hell if he'd lose her to a corpse! The demon had played by his rules to win her concession, and Raoul was determined it was time for him to do the same.

Chapter Eighteen

Christine stood before her vanity mirror, adding the final touches to her ball-gown. Pale pink with a tiered skirt and cascading bustle in the back, embellished with rosettes and inserts of cream lace. She had chosen it specifically because it was beautiful, and she knew the sort of scrutiny she would endure tonight. The opera house patrons would be in attendance, those who supported the arts with their donations and inhabited the elite boxes at the theatre, and many were partial to Carlotta. After so long as reigning diva, Carlotta had them fawning at her feet with barely a word, and despite her recent triumphs, Christine wasn't certain she could win the same ovation.

And then there was Erik and the buzz they were bound to stir with their appearance. Her wealthy husband should fit among a crowd of masked faces, but risks posed threats and left Christine to anxiously fist shaking hands in her skirts. Why did this evening feel like a trauma waiting to happen?

With a huff at ridiculous nerves, she forced her hands to release silken material and reach for her pale pink mask, lifting and securing it in place. This last article turned a regular ball into an adventure of romance and mystery, making it suitable for adults to play a child's game of pretend. Yes, for ordinary people, a mask was a trinket for jovial gaiety. How bitterly ironic that Erik would join the festivities! For him, a mask wasn't liberation from the world of reality; it *was* his reality, a fettering cord to a life of cruelty. The realization made her suddenly abhor the very idea of masquerades.

As she stood at the mirror still pondering her appearance, Erik's reflection seemed to materialize beside her. He'd given nothing of his approach away, and she wondered just how long he had been watching her. His costume only pushed irony further. The Red Death, complete with a mask etched to resemble a skull and so similar to his own features that he practically did not need the mask to portray the character.

As she turned to face him, she arched a dubious brow before realizing it wouldn't be seen behind the mask. Dear Lord, how had she spent months accurately reading a single one of Erik's emotions when a mask stole every telltale expression? She wondered how many times she had guessed what he was feeling and equally how many times she had been wrong!

"You look stunning," Erik breathed, his mismatched eyes racing caresses over her every curve. "But your costume lacks creativity. A beautiful lady in a mask. There's no story."

"I play stories every day of my life," she reminded. "Attending with my husband at my side, I'd much rather be a masked version of myself."

His gloved hand lifted, and he granted a touch to her masked cheekbone. She didn't feel it, nothing but subtle pressure, and decided she hated masks with one thought of how many of her touches Erik's mask had denied him. A night of fun in a mask felt oddly like a lesson in humility and compassion. She was bound to compare every moment of a temporary experience to the permanence of Erik's life, no matter how hard she tried to forget.

"Then I'll write you a story," Erik decided, and

only the tone of his voice told her that he was smiling. "A beautiful lady in a mask, but you are no ordinary lady. No, you are the Opera Ghost's mistress to be sure. How could you be any other? You wear a mask for a reason; you are as damaged and scarred as he is, a perfect match for a corpse."

And there was the game of pretend: pretend to share Erik's fate. How the very thought cut through flesh and pierced her heart! "Is that what you'd prefer?" she felt compelled to ask. "If I were scarred like you? Would that be the only thing to fully convince you that I am yours? Or would you reject me as I once rejected you and denounce me if I were not beautiful? You are a man who dotes on perfection in every aspect of your life that you can control. You've always longed for me to fit the picture in your head, but what if I wore scars beneath this mask, Erik? Could you love me the same?"

She saw how deeply her words affected him and gave herself credit. Perhaps she *was* well-versed at reading him even when a mask shielded nuances because she glimpsed somberness and an abhorrence for her proposed concept...and most of all, stinging hurt.

Staring at her so intently that she trembled, Erik abruptly lifted her mask and removed it as if it were necessary to find her features and make certain they were unchanged. With a sense of relief she couldn't understand, he caught her face between his gloved palms and ran fingertips along every feature.

"So you couldn't love me," she concluded sadly, "if I looked like you."

Tears he couldn't fight made their appearance at the corners of his eyes, and his reply was exhaled in a rush of breath. "That is my *nightmare*, Christine. You, bearing a face like mine, enduring the life I have led. What if *you* had been made to suffer the atrocities I have...and I couldn't be there to protect you? You would have been broken before I ever found you. ...And what if I couldn't fix you again?"

He shook his head, and the tears broke free to slip beneath his mask. "I always had the music, this world in my head filled with notes and melodies. At the worst points in my life, I would escape and hide there between the staves, bury my soul while my body endured their abuses. I had fairytale symphonies, but you... Your imaginary world was angels. I *created* it for you, and when my own life made me renounce such things years ago, I felt so blessed that you believed. ...If you shared my fate, there would be no angels."

Reaching determined fingers, she removed his mask and gazed at the tattered face beneath, smeared in tears and creased with an agony she couldn't fully comprehend. In a whisper, she demanded again, "But could you love me, Erik?" Clasping his shoulders, she gently turned him until he had no choice but to look in the mirror and see true faces, not masks. "If I looked like you, if I shared your face, could you love me anyway?"

Erik could not recall the last time he had seen his reflection. Typically, he refused mirrors unless they were doorways and showed him fantasies. To look now and see the heinousness of reality, a veritable corpse standing beside the most beautiful creature he'd ever known, it was a portrait he would have called wrong and unacceptable if not for the glow of affection in her blue eyes. They looked as well and saw the same image, and there was never disgust or avoidance; there was only emotion so blatant and unguarded that he could hardly believe it was his. If that look was the same always and affection bloomed bright and strong, nothing else could matter.

"I love you," he told the vision in the glass and watched her smile. "I would *always* love you, perfect or imperfect. My heart recognizes yours. You were meant to be mine."

Her reflection beamed with the brilliant glow of

her soul; he could practically feel its warmth upon his damaged flesh, and he turned to brush a tender kiss to her forehead, knowing she observed in the mirror all the while. Death laying a sealing kiss upon his beloved... And yet her smile only grew in its radiance.

"The Opera Ghost's mistress," she repeated with an idle shrug. "What does such a role entail, Monsieur Opera Ghost? What is my character? Brazen? Flirtatious? Coy? What would you have your mistress be?"

Provocative thoughts raced through his head, but he decided, "Devoted. My mistress would be at my side no matter what happens or who appears to sway her this evening. ...And I'll kneel at your feet in adoration if you eye me with desire at every chance."

"Like this?" she inquired with feigned innocence and gazed at him in unconcealed longing.

"Indeed." His palms set at the curves of her hips and drew her closer, and he couldn't help but peek at the image reflected in the mirror. This should have appeared as a horror story, but instead it was almost ordinary. A couple in love...

Blue eyes lifted in the glass and found his, and she asked, "What are you thinking?"

"That I am quite ugly," he stated bluntly.

"Look through my eyes instead," she commanded. "I look and don't see ugliness, Erik. I see *you*, and as your devoted mistress, I think my opinion should be the only one to matter."

"It is." He turned away from the vivid portrait of reality and found a better one in her eyes. Lips he refused to consider misshapen brushed grateful kisses to each lid before capturing her smile. A moment of indulgence was all he allowed before drawing back and insisting, "We should go."

Rolling her eyes, she added, "Into the den of insensitive patrons who think wearing a mask is a cause for jubilant celebration. Are you so certain you want to do this? I would offer no objection to remaining here and having our own ball without the rest of the world."

"And that's exactly why we are going. I won't let you become the recluse I choose to be. I want you to have the world as yours, Christine, and I never want to hold you back." As he spoke, he carefully replaced her mask, already eager for the moment he could discard it again. Putting on his own was less ceremonious, but as he lowered his hands, hers raised and cupped his masked face between them.

"You've *given me* the world," she replied, and though he glimpsed so many vows flashing in blue depths, she did not say another word as she slid her arm through his, guiding him out of the room with only the telling smile cast over her shoulder to mutter the words he still longed to hear.

*****

Christine wasn't sure if the nerves twisting her stomach were hers or Erik's. They built and suffocated her ability to breathe the instant the carriage pulled to a halt outside the opera house and left her to tremble as they made their way inside toward the resounding buzz of noise and music.

So many people, all masked and laughing delight, and as Erik briefly met her eye, she wondered if his apparent calmness was feigned. He was so accomplished at adopting the Opera Ghost's confident persona when he needed it, and she had the distinct feeling he hid behind its veneer now. Arrogant, uplifted posture as if to dare the world to attack and proclaim he'd win any battle. She recalled the impulsiveness of his temper, how simple it was for him to choose retaliation and assault when cornered, and she tightened her grip on his arm.

"Christine!"

Before she could assure in words, distraction came in the form of an exuberant, masked little ballerina, rushing to meet them and bouncing up and down.

"Have you seen this place?" Meg exclaimed with a shriek of excitement. "I've *never* seen this many people! The patrons are all trying to outdo one another this year. The costumes! It's practically a circus!" Meg jabbered on, but as she suddenly noticed Erik, words halted and green eyes widened.

Christine had an irrational fear that Meg recognized the resident Opera Ghost, and she was certain Erik shared it as he stiffened beside her. Hastily, she insisted, "Meg, this is-"

"Your husband?" Meg interrupted. "Oh, I'm sorry! I'm so rude! Bright lights distract me! And I sometimes forget to look beyond my own nose!" The little ballerina's warm grin surprised both Christine and Erik as she gave a sweet curtsy and said, "I'm Meg Giry. Christine and I are practically sisters, figuratively speaking of course. We were once ballerinas together in Christine's brief stint of toe shoes and tutus. I am just so thrilled to know you!"

Meg spoke so fast, one sentence barely out before the next began, and Christine giggled beneath her breath, pressing her hand to her lips in an attempt to hide it.

"What?" Meg demanded with an inquisitive tilt of her golden head.

"You certainly know how make anyone feel welcome, Meg," Christine replied, giggling further to observe Erik's flustered glare. "You've taken care of introduction, greeting, and half a life story without a breath in between! It's a talent!"

"I'm being polite," Meg insisted matter-of-factly and then matched Christine's laugh. "Oh, I must seem positively fanatical! Shall I begin again with less squeaks and manic behavior?"

"No," Erik decided and attempted a smile. "There is no need. Thank you, Mademoiselle Giry, for your hospitality. My wife is lucky to have such a wonderful friend."

Erik's first words had Meg gaping, and

Christine stifled more giggles. The voice of an angel, golden timbre and brilliance, it was as if he spoke in the lyrical legato of a melody, and Meg was star-struck.

"Will you say my name again?" Meg inquired with transfixed green eyes, and as Christine's laughter broke free, the little ballerina jolted out of enthrallment and blushed in chagrin.

Clasping Christine's free arm, Meg ducked her golden head close and whispered behind a hand, "Now I see how you could be swept off your feet so quickly! My goodness, Christine! I wish I could find such a gentleman, but alas, I am doomed to destitute stagehands who stammer merely to say hello!" Meg sighed. "And now I guess I shall go and seek out said stagehand and fluster him with a demand for a kiss. Do you think bravery can come from a costume and a mask?"

"Oh, I'm sure of it," Christine replied with a furtive glance at Erik. Though he seemed as if he surveyed the festivities, she had no doubt he heard every word.

"Well, I shall hope," Meg decided, and with a teasing, furtive point at Erik, she added, "Have a wonderful time, Christine."

Giggling, Meg rushed back into the crowd, and Christine imagined the number of eager ballerinas about to share the news of their arrival. She was on the verge of warning Erik that they would surely be stalked for a glimpse when she realized he was still rigidly poised beside her.

"Erik, ...are you all right?"

"For a moment, I thought sure she knew," he quietly remarked, staring the direction Meg had disappeared. "Meg Giry has always been the easiest to frighten of all the ballerinas because she is young and still so ignorant. Not much more than a child, and my instinct was to attack, to strangle life's vivacity out of her if it meant I was now in jeopardy and everyone would know you were in attendance with the Opera Ghost. I would have justified murder as protecting us." He shook his head with a rush of self-disgust.

"But you *didn't* do it," she emphasized the most important point, cupping his masked face in her palm. "Dear Lord, you *humored* her and were congenial about it! You are a better man than you consider yourself to be."

Leaning into her touch, he bid, "Perhaps this wasn't the best idea. I thought to proclaim to the world who you had wed as if the details were insignificant, but the truth is condemning, Christine; no one can know, and if there's even a chance I will be found out-"

"You won't be," she assured with the conviction he lacked. "Here we are in a throng of people, and no one truly knows what lies beneath our masks. *No one*, Erik. We could be anyone we wanted right now."

A small smile curved his lips, his fingers weaving in her loose locks as he corrected, "Well, perhaps *I* could. Between the two of us, I have the better chance. Your curls give your identity away, love. Masked or not, they make you obvious."

Mimicking his smile, she replied, "Next year, I'll have to try harder to blend in."

"No, you're perfect." Mismatched eyes bore into hers in further conversation, vows and promises, but all he spoke in husky tones was "Dance with me."

She smiled, clasping his hand and leading him through masked guests to a makeshift dance floor on the stage. A string quartet played a slow waltz as a sea of couples moved in graceful steps. Though Christine worried Erik would grow anxious, his focus was only on her, a mixture of desire and adoration etched vividly despite the mask, and it was just the two of them amidst the rest of the world. She never cared about prying eyes or rude comments as he drew her into his arms. Let them talk! Happiness never dimmed. She even laughed her delight as he guided her easily as if they floated on air instead of being resigned to the motion of corporeal bodies. No, she could almost believe they left earth and grazed the surface of heaven instead.

One dance and then another, and Erik called it torture to let her leave the protection of his arms. But he knew how imperative it was for her to grant a favorable impression to the patrons. The very point of this spectacular event was to make the largest donators feel appreciated and special as they mingled on the same level as their opera stars. Erik found it ridiculous. High and mighty society dubbed performers as scandalous and inferior, but a ball put patrons in masks and allowed morals and stereotypes to be loosed. It was a sad reality, and as such, Christine was forced to put on airs and play grateful and courteous like another opera role.

Erik remained at her side, apathetic through necessary introductions and relatively silent. He contented his unease by watching Christine. She inspired awe with her poise and gentility, with every elegant gesture and eloquently-spoken word. Of course he saw right through her pretense and knew how contrived her façade was, but it was constructed with confidence, the exact confidence she required to be the prima donna. Gazing at her, he was convinced she could carry the title.

"Oh, oh, Monsieur..."

Erik lifted annoyed eyes as the managers Andre and Firmin anxiously approached. It was odd to be face to face with those he preferred to torment through notes. Both gentlemen jittered in their places, their identities poorly concealed by mediocre costumes; certainly, in this den of the elite, they preferred to be recognized and acknowledged, especially if those in attendance came with bills in their pockets.

Still playing her role, Christine posed the unnecessary proprieties, "Monsieur Andre, Monsieur

Firmin, how wonderful to see you this evening!"

But the managers ignored her, their wide eyes on Erik. He was immediately on guard, prepared to be defensive before Andre suddenly gushed, "Oh, Monsieur, your donation was so greatly appreciated! We've never had anyone care about the arts *that* much! It is...bewildering!"

Firmin picked up where Andre left off. "And such an astonishment to be sure! We are humbled by your generosity!"

Every comment was overdone and dripping with saccharine sentiment, and Erik's expression never changed from chosen disregard. It was far too much to attempt hospitality with these two! He'd spent too long suffering their ignorance and blundering, questionable choices. He had no desire to seem cordial, so all he said in return was, "My wife deserves the best."

Catching Christine's arm, he guided her back toward the dance floor, feeling the flutter of her laughter shake the shoulder against his. "I was just abysmally rude to your managers," he reminded. "And you find such behavior humorous?"

"No," she commented back. "I find it humorous that your donation was described with wonder and awe as if it were a thing of beauty and revelry instead of only money! My goodness, Erik, how much of a donation did you give them?"

With a nonchalant shrug, he pulled her back into his arms and a dance and admitted, "It was technically theirs already. I simply 'donated' the Opera Ghost's collected salary. Years of monthly installments come to quite a nice sum."

Her laughter only grew and bubbled past her lips. "So you returned their own money, and they now see you as a god! Erik!" She giggled harder and clasped his shoulder as he spun her faster. "And what a patron of the arts you are! You've spent years embezzling from the opera you supposedly adore!"

"I only adore it when *you* are singing it," he corrected, relishing her amusement and granting her the first smile he'd known in hours of forced conversation. "Besides, I deserve imbursement for my skills of oversight and fixing their foibles. Those notes the managers so despise have given them the direction required to make the right choices. *They* do not run this place; *I* do. My part just goes unacknowledged. If it were up to them, Carlotta would have continued to be the prima donna until she was eighty and decrepit! They know nothing!"

Christine did not protest; she laughed without restraint and inched closer in his embrace as he beamed his adoration. *This* was his Christine without her elegant actress' façade in place and smiling with genuine excitement. How fortunate he was that she never played a role with him. Not even in days full of distance after his deception. She hadn't pretended even when the option was so much more appealing than reality, and now he reaped the benefits as she savored his presence and did not conceal an honest affection that ran to her very soul.

Erik wanted to linger in that place for the rest of the ball, holding her and dancing in their own little world, but abrupt and unexpected, his desire was stolen away.

"May I cut in?"

"Raoul." Laughter halted as Christine stared wide-eyed at the solemn Vicomte. "What...what are you doing here?"

"Asking for a dance," the Vicomte replied, glancing back and forth between Christine and Erik. "As a *friend*, of course. You look so suspicious. What do you think I intend to do in a room full of people? This is a ball; I have no intention of turning it into a raucous scene of mayhem."

"Yes, a *Masquerade* Ball," Erik coldly stated. "And yet the dashing Vicomte attends without a mask? Hardly fitting and definitely poor participation in such a festive event."

"I have no *need* for a mask," the Vicomte returned, the insult sharply flung. "It is juvenile to hide behind masks, Monsieur, and pretend to be something you aren't as if you have a right to do so."

Christine fisted her hand in Erik's sleeve, muttering, "Erik, don't."

"Don't?" Erik spat back. "Ah, you think to tug your leash, and your dutiful little husband will fall in line and preserve the welfare of your dashing Vicomte."

"This isn't the place for battle," Raoul retorted. "And I am not here to provoke. I am only requesting a dance. Do not presume to take out your jealousy on Christine."

Glaring aghast, Erik snapped, "Take out *my* jealousy on Christine? Why, you arrogant-"

"Erik!" Christine leapt in front of him and forced him to meet her gaze. This was the sort of rage she had once run from in terror, and here she was purposely placing herself in its path. "*Please* leave him be. *For me.* Let me dance with him as he wants, and then we'll go home."

"Home, Christine?" he tightly demanded.

"Yes, just you and I. All right?"

He seemed like he would argue further, but she lifted a hand and brushed a tender caress over his masked cheek, her eyes beaming with her adoration, unconcealed, undeniable. As she drew back, he only stated, "I will watch every second lest he try anything."

"In a room full of people?" Raoul questioned dubiously, but quieted as Christine caught his hand and dragged him a fair distance into the dancing throng.

"What are you doing?" she hissed as soon as they began to move in synchronized steps. "Why must you tempt him? Or is that your intent? To taunt him into attacking you? That is *cruel*, Raoul!"

"Whyever are you angry with me?" he demanded, blue eyes stern with annoyance. "I have done nothing worthy of your perturbation. All I asked for was a dance, not to run off together or some other absurdity. ...Not this time anyway. My last attempt had you appeasing him with marriage. God knows what it would have taken this time! A demon child, perhaps? Some other point of possession to keep you chained to him?"

"Is that what you think?" she posed back, shaking her head. She should have assumed as much. "If my only impetus was to keep him happy, I wouldn't be dancing with you right now, would I?"

"Then why did you agree if it will only incite your husband's wrath?"

"Because I will not let you to tempt him to some sort of spectacle." As she spoke, her gaze drifted between whirling couples and found Erik, scowling his anger and focused upon her. In somber softness, she insisted, "We're not hurting anyone by being here. It is not a scheme or manipulation; it is an attempt at acting ordinary."

"Ordinary? And how fair is it that he is allowed to walk amongst the same people who live in terror of his existence? It seems to me this is all some kind of game, and we are his pawns to steer and toy with as he pleases. Including *you*." That finally made Christine meet his eye, but before she could speak, he hastily defended, "You were afraid he would hurt me moments ago. He is unstable, Christine. Don't you see that? It seems to take very little to ignite the spark, and with the right incentive, he could go from an impulsive killer to a ruthless one."

Huffing her discontent, Christine retorted, "You've tried these arguments before, and if they made no impression then, why do you think they will now?"

"Because you know how capable he is of unleashing his vendettas on innocent bystanders."

"You are hardly an innocent bystander. You're too eager to goad him-"

"I feel I have a right!" Raoul insisted before remembering to keep his voice low. A glance about showed masked strangers observing and one in particular whose eyes shot daggers. "I have proof your fear is warranted," he tried again in quieter tones. "Christine, he sent me a letter, one of his Opera Ghost notes. Ask him. I'm sure he'll tell you, probably gloat over it as an achievement."

No surprise met his revelation, only distant sadness as she reluctantly inquired, "What did it say?"

"You already know. A threat on my life should I come near you again."

"And yet here you are."

Raoul shook a doubtful head. "I do not follow the wayward path of an idle madman to keep him sane and content. He expects everyone to work desperately to avoid the consequences of stepping out of his desired script."

"He loves me," Christine stated unarguably, but despair weighed down every letter.

"He probably does," Raoul concluded, "but then again love and obsession can look the same from inside. While you preserve his happiness, it is gifts and indulgence, perfect bliss, but what happens if you push beyond his prescribed fantasy, Christine? Then he cages you like a bird and tries to bend you back to his control. And if your argument is solely that he *loves you,* that is no argument at all."

The opportunity to devise another protest, *any* protest, was lost as the music ended. Within the second, Erik was at her side, grabbing her arm and pulling her away from Raoul before she even comprehended his presence.

"You drag her off because she has a free thought," Raoul taunted even as Christine met his eye and shook her head to stop him. "No," he told her, "you may walk on eggshells about his temper, but I *will not.* I already have his death threat; if the next step is attack, then let him have at it." Glaring at Erik, he insisted, "Tell her about your note, Monsieur. If I approach her or dare touch her, you will kill me? Well, now I've done both. Play your hand. Or do you just lay the threat with no intention of acting on it? Because that is the route of a coward."

"A *coward*?" Erik growled back. "You foolish boy! Have you no idea who you are dealing with that you so ignorantly flaunt your arrogance? Perhaps I should make good on the threat right now and put an end to every misconception in this room. How naïve of me to think I could play the part and exist among the masses! It's impossible when ignorance runs this rampant!"

"Erik, please," Christine appealed, but her attempt was devoid of the strength she was supposed to have. It had gotten lost somewhere in a dance and left her to falter.

Erik suddenly rounded on her, fire flashing in his glare as his hand pinched her arm in its brutal grip. "No more, Christine! I wanted to try; *for you*, I tried, but I'm through making the effort! Play the part to fit into the world! A world that would rather spit on me, if truth be told! And *you*!" His rage averted to Raoul and only increased to note the Vicomte's blatant concern for Christine plainly on his flawless face. "Oh, you think I'll hurt *her* for *your* insolence! No, the threat was on *your* life, if you'll recall. It was words, but I am a man of action. They were a warning you did not heed, and now they will be your reality."

Eyes were all around as the dancers halted and collected to observe. Masks on every side, and it felt like his nightmares come to life to swallow him. Erik dreamt of masks, of judgment and cruelty, of violence and heaved fists. He could feel the tension knotting in his gut with the need to lash out in retaliation. And the opponent he truly wanted was still more concerned with *his* wife than self-preservation.

"Christine, are you all right?" Raoul sincerely asked.

Only then did Erik glance at the shaking girl beside him, and he saw tears slipping past the trim of her mask. She wouldn't even meet his eye, her dark head lowered, the opposite of an earlier role of poise and grace. He immediately loosened the unrealized pinch he had on her arm and tried to make a caress instead, but she flinched and it only enraged him further. An attempt at ordinary, and as he should have known, it must end with confrontation and a broken heart. Happiness felt like a joke Fate had thrown his way only to laugh as it burst apart. All that he wanted standing beside him, and she was shattered and as destroyed as everything he ever attempted to touch.

Raoul glanced at the circle of observers and hissed at Erik, "Are you happy now that you've made her a spectacle? She deserves so much more than a monster on the brink of condemnation."

"More?" Erik retorted with a sneer. "You mean *you*. It kills you to know she chose me."

"She was *coerced* into choosing you," Raoul snapped back. "You deceived her from the first day, convinced her to care for what she should hate. If not for your lies, she would carry no feeling toward you save the same abhorrence everyone else does."

"Stop," Christine suddenly spoke up. "Please just stop."

"You know *nothing*!" Erik shouted at the Vicomte. "And yet you feel it your right to decide Christine's heart for her. It's an obvious sting to your ego to know she married a monster instead of you-"

"But she doesn't *love* a monster," Raoul accused. "How could she possibly *love* a creature like you? You, Monsieur, are an abomination and a disgrace to the plane of humanity. How dare you masquerade yourself as an equal to everyone here tonight. If they realized who you are, it wouldn't be laughter and dancing as your indulgence. They would spite you and for reasons far greater than your mangled face. Your actions have defined you as a monster, Monsieur, *not* your deformity. And Christine is so fixated on making amends for your physical deficiencies that she isn't seeing what is important."

As if a fuse suddenly sparked to life, Christine interjected, "How do you know what I feel? What right have you to judge any of it?"

Courage was new for her and left her to tremble with its surge, her voice wavering on every word, but her furious eyes showed conviction, tears no more than drying smears on her cheeks. One look at Erik showed surprise that became amusement and twinkled in mismatched eyes.

"Strong, Christine?" he dared to tease, and the hint of a nervous smile touched her lips.

"Devoted," she corrected. "My chosen character is my inspiration. I'm not going to let the two of you pose battle in the middle of a ball."

But Raoul wasn't through, and turning to Erik, he insisted, "Why don't you tell the truth? Let the world decide how to accept it. You've tormented these people for years without mercy, and now you toss your presence in their faces as if they are fools. They will not be moved so easily by a song and a voice. They will want vengeance."

"Raoul," Christine warned lowly, "stop it. Do you realize what you're doing?"

"I do. You will not see the bastard for what he is, but *they* will." He gestured to the growing throng, all gazing with curious and gossiping eyes. "He plays one role and then another, and everything is forgotten. The world is transformed to his desire. So now he'll put on the show as a rich patron, carve himself a new niche, and never be recognized for the damning acts he has committed."

Erik's hand released her arm, and in terror

where it intended to travel instead, Christine flipped about and caught his sleeves with gripping hands, staring into his rage-filled eyes without waver.

Everything blurred the next instant with no reaction until it was too late. Before Erik could conjure violent thoughts into reality, he caught a whir of motion in his periphery and didn't comprehend until his mask was hastily yanked from his face. He turned only to glimpse its protective shape in the hand of an equally furious Vicomte.

"Oh no," Christine whispered, but the words were swallowed in a collective response of horror all around them. Gasps and cries, terror and disgust, leering faces in masks, all attention locked on the only unmasked one among them.

Pain came in a brutal rush beneath Erik's skin, the remnants of past trauma erupting in unwanted reminiscence, and he abruptly chose anger, letting fury crease already abhorrent features and make an ugly face into an image of a demon. Only one glance was granted to Christine. This was not a story he wanted her to live with him, and he knew her intuitive eye had seen every emotion he wanted to hide. A threat in a demon's wrathful appearance, but she was not its target and did not look away from reality this time. To his surprise, she was the one steady constant in the room.

"Not a monster?" Raoul doubtfully posed. "Admit what you are, Monsieur Opera Ghost, and let the world deem how it will see you. ...How could Christine possibly love you? It is an insult even to consider such a thing."

Christine felt suffocated by the unqualified hatred permeating the air; it crawled along her skin and bit her with every overheard whisper of 'monster', 'demon', 'corpse', other words more cruel than she could have imagined or considered decent people could speak. Every letter burned as viciously as a hot poker and seared her though she was not their aim.

As her focus settled on Erik, she saw a broken man on the verge of vengeance, and she let impulse take over and guide her. Her shaking arm lifted as suddenly as she had the thought, and she pressed her hand to his mangled cheek, covering it as best she could from far too many bitter glares. No, this was *hers*; no one else deserved to look upon it. No one else could hope to understand it.

Erik was holding his breath. He didn't realize it until exhalation was necessary and shook his entire being with the violent shudder it brought. He wanted to cry and yet refused any urge. Pain and rage were dull in comparison to the emotion overwhelming him. *Love.* Love so great it made a monster and his anticipated revenge falter and crumble.

She met his astounded and desperate gaze, and he found no shame within her, no embarrassment for the demon corpse she had married, for the mere fact that every person in the room now knew his true horror. Her palm fitted to his cheek, but of course, she couldn't hide every flaw. Some were still on display to agitate a horror-stricken crowd further, the absence of a respectable nose, the pronounced eye sockets. Not even her tender gesture could make reality less shocking or less condemning.

Soft curses were muttered all around, and Christine coldly extended her free hand and cast a bitter glare to the unmoved Vicomte.

"His mask," she commanded, tossing her hand out again with more assertion. "Raoul, give it to me."

"Why? They've already seen. What difference will it make now?" Raoul insisted.

"Raoul!"

With a huff of annoyance, the Vicomte conceded. Once she had it in hand, Christine carefully replaced it over Erik's face, hiding the distortions from every cruel sneer and heaved insult. She had an unrealistic wish that manmade barrier could work like iron and keep every horrific expression around them

309

from penetrating. But it was only protection for a mangled face, and there was no protection for an equally scarred heart.

The mask meant dignity and the arrogant pretense of the Opera Ghost, and with it back in its rightful place, Erik growled into the throng, "You will regret this night. You have yet to realize who you have wronged. If you thought my crimes condemning, wait until you see what I am capable of. Death, destruction, pain the likes of which you can't possibly fathom. You've so eloquently dubbed me as damned; then what do I have left to lose?"

Christine wanted to shout at him. What indeed? Did *she* mean nothing when vengeance ruled, ...or was it only that he already considered her lost? She had her answer as Erik abruptly spun about and charged through a terrified, parting crowd without even a glance at her.

"No," she muttered, but before she could pursue, Raoul had her arm, restraining her as whispers from observers grew to flustered conversation. "Let go!"

"Christine," Raoul attempted, clasping tight. "Isn't it better this way? Maybe he realizes his transgressions and is releasing you. This could be a blessing!"

"And what will you call your actions tonight?" she retorted furiously, yanking to be set free. "What you did...," her voice choked over tears. "That was only heartless, Raoul, and I won't forgive you. Erik's face might be damaged, but *yours* is the face of a monster."

Her accusations finally rattled Raoul enough to loosen his grip, and jerking free, Christine pushed her way into the crowd, her heart rushing ahead in its urgency. Oh God, how could this have gone so wrong?

Erik's path had not been in the direction of the lobby and exit; it had been into the wings. She had an idea where he headed and quickened her steps for fear of being shut out. He had dozens of entrances to the catacombs, but she was sure of only one and burst into her dressing room already calling his name. He was gone, but to her relief, he had left the mirror doorway open.

She never considered she could be walking into danger, refusing to believe he could be beyond her aid. No, the Opera Ghost was bitter and merciless, but *Erik* was not. She was determined he would not fade to that madness again.

A lantern was lit and exuded its glow into shadowed passages. Pausing only long enough to close the mirror and lock out the rest of the world, Christine lifted the lantern and pursued with soft footfalls, her pale pink skirts trailing behind her in a whisper of silk.

It was cold and damp and reminded her how happy she was that they had a house up in the daylight. Erik would have only too happily resigned himself to live the rest of his days in this tomb. ...After tonight, she couldn't begrudge him that. Perhaps abandoning that world was not such a terrible idea.

Light met her from an open doorway. She hesitated only a breath, ridding herself of her lantern before creeping silently to the entry.

Before she even stepped inside, she had an idea of his frame of mind. Music came crashing out to meet her. Frustrated, violent in a manner she had never known music could be. The piano was taking a beating, its keys struck with wrath and vengeful fury until the instrument was hurting as much as its master.

Christine peeked inside, and the image she was granted enticed her first twinge of apprehension. Erik sat at the piano, mask-less, his disfigured face contorted into unpleasant shapes with his rage. His hands moved in a blur of motion along the ivory keys, music in cascading lines until he landed on one dissonant chord after another. It was the soundtrack to a tale of horror, and remaining sense called her ignorant to be stepping into the story.

Her footfalls were nonexistent, nothing to betray her presence as she crept toward the piano, staring at Erik's wild, unfocused eyes as they moved with his fingers, darting up to piercing pitches and down again into bellowing recesses that shook the floor with their bass.

She wondered how she was going to break his musical trance, and practically with the thought, he halted mid-phrase and rounded on her so furiously that she gasped and started. His hands went from clawing along the piano to clawing her forearms, fingertips digging sharp and painful into her skin as he jerked her close.

"*Afraid!*" he accused in a shout. "You're afraid of your husband! Little hypocrite!" He released one arm only long enough to grab her mask and yank it free with such brutality that she cringed. "There's my girl. I can steal your mask and uncover a thing of beauty beneath. How fortunate for you! I myself have never been so lucky. They take my mask and find horror and a reason for revulsion. Oh, I can't truly blame them for that, not when I am equally repulsed. Repulsed by my own face. I don't want to see it because it disgusts *me*, and yet I held you accountable when *you* were the disgusted one. It's a paradox in its way. I hate myself, but I expect *you* to love me. Ridiculous! I really should know better."

"Erik," Christine softly bid to the insanity flashing in his mismatched eyes as they bore into her. "Let go. You're hurting me."

"Oh? And will I leave bruises on your precious skin?" he taunted, only gripping tighter. "Bruises aren't enough; I really should damage you in some way, so *he* stops wanting you. If you weren't so damn beautiful, maybe he'd leave you be and stop making it his mission to save you from damnation. ...But then again I guess I've already damaged you, haven't I? You're *here*," he declared, emphasizing his point with a chuckle. "Into the den of the dragon all alone and unguarded. No sense of self-preservation, and even if you're afraid, you came willingly as if I pulled a string and tugged you after me. Yes, you're damaged because you *care*."

She nodded frantically. "I care, and I hurt. You didn't deserve any of this tonight-"

"It was *necessary*," he interrupted, and his body shook with agitation, jostling her merely with the intensity. "I needed to be reminded exactly what I was. It was foolish of me to consider it could be any different. A lifetime of such cruelty should have factored into my decision, but I had *you*. *You* are the variable that has broken my mind and suffocated sense. I don't listen to rationale anymore when my heart convinces me that everything has changed. As if love could transform the world!" he sarcastically exclaimed with another fanatic laugh. "The heart is an idealist. It seeks to rewrite history simply with a twist of feeling in its valves. I have ignorantly lived in its spell since I first saw you. I can make a legitimate argument that you were sent by God to punish me. As if my mangled face wasn't punishment enough! You are a temptation, a test to my better judgment that I failed to conquer. No, I fell like a masochist, practically choosing torture. I always knew you would bring pain, and I followed you anyway and let you contort me into knots of optimistic hope. How stupid I am! I wanted you so much that I convinced myself *love* existed! That it was real and requited! That you couldn't *pity* someone who loved *you* so much in return!"

"What are you saying?" she desperately demanded, never recoiling even as he leaned close enough that she felt every shallow, flustered breath leave his misshapen lips.

For all the ferocity of his rage, in equaled

heights surged agony, creasing unmasked features into obscure lines as he feverishly demanded, "How could you ever love a monster?"

"Those are Raoul's words, *not yours*," she insisted.

"But it's true."

"No, it's not. Stop this, Erik."

"Then say it!" he suddenly growled, shaking her hard. "You've never been able to say it! Never once! ...Do you love me, Christine? Do you? I am a murderer, a monster, the *Opera Ghost*. I am an abomination of a human being! I threatened your Vicomte's life, threatened violence and death. But do you love me anyway? *Do you?*"

Those mismatched eyes were urgent and furious, his body still lost to that vicious shaking she suffered with him by default, and as tears shielded her view, she admitted, "Yes."

"No," he immediately retaliated. "No, you can't. You don't! I'm *destroying you*. My existence is contaminating you. Every time you are in my arms, in my bed, I steal a piece of your soul and blacken it with my own evil. I am *poison*, Christine. What have I done to you...?" Tears poured over his malformed features as a sob choked words.

"Erik, please stop this." She longed to touch him, to press her hands to his face and *feel* him, but her arms were captive and she could not break free.

"*My love* is poison," he decided. "I don't know how to do it; I've never done it before. I must have loved you wrong, and now...now, Christine, what have I done?" Another sob broke his voice, but he diligently continued, "I should go and let you be, give you the life you deserve instead of condemnation. But...oh God, the thought of leaving you is unbearable! I don't think I'm strong enough! I'd rather chain you to the catacombs, never let you walk another day in the sunlight, sever us from the rest of the world. Oh, you were destined to abhor me in the

end! Why not take it now? Make you my prisoner?
Lock you in a room like a cell and keep you with me
always? You would curse and blight me. But then I'd
pin you to the bed and make love to you, and for a
little while with desire as my ally, you'd forget. Don't I
always make you forget reality when I'm inside of
you? Then you want me, and nothing else exists. I'll
make you desire so much and crave every second I'm
not buried inside you. Desire will dull the shrill edges
of hate. You'll hate, but you'll still want me."

"Erik, I don't hate you."

"You should! You *will*! I'll make you learn to
hate me."

"I don't *want to* hate you!" she exclaimed,
finally struggling free of his quivering grasp. He cried
out to lose her, hands flexing empty and urgent, but
before he could grab again, she did it herself,
wrapping her arms around him and hugging his
trembling body tight. "I don't hate you, and I *won't*."

"And if I wreak my vengeance?" he pushed,
hands fisted at his sides and not daring to hold back.
"If I murder every person at that ball tonight? Torture
your Vicomte in the most heinous ways imaginable?
Threats in words are not enough, and that is my
instinct. To *kill*! And yet here you are, holding me
when you should be running." His voice shook with
unceasing tears. "Christine, ...hate me please. It's so
much easier to be a monster if you do. I can't live with
the guilt of disappointing you. ...I'm a monster; let me
be a monster."

"No, no," she gently bid, "I won't. I won't let
you be a monster, and I won't hate you. I love you too
much."

One statement, one strung set of words, and
Erik sobbed as they burst through the haze and found
comprehension. Fists opened as he needed to touch,
and his hands caught her shoulders and clutched.

"You love me?" he stammered urgently. "You
should be shamed by me; you heard their vicious

remarks. You should be embarrassed my hands have been upon you, my deformed lips against yours, my abhorrent body atop you and inside of you. They were disgusted that I exist, but you... Oh, Christine, don't let me go. *Please.*"

"Never," she vowed, one hand drifting into his hair to cup the crown of his head as he bent and pressed his tear-streaked disfigurement to her smooth cheek. When he felt her shiver, he knew there was no disgust because she edged closer, molding her body firmer to his and softly gasping. She *wanted* him; it wasn't imagined or concocted. She *loved* him... That was harder to accept, so he let her voice replay its words in his memory, and cruel insults were drowned out by the only words to matter. She said she loved him, would never leave him; *she was his.*

Nuzzling her cheek with his, he stated, "The world recoiled from this face in disgust, but you...you held it in your hand. My brave girl."

A soft sound of delight escaped her lips as she turned to graze kisses to every scar. He shuddered at the delicious warmth of her mouth, the smooth softness, and a desire that had smoldered beneath the surface of trauma swelled into an inferno of flame and fury. He couldn't have controlled it if he tried. It was as necessary as it was potent, and he gasped above her ear, "I need to feel you, love. Please, *please* let me have you."

Any reply was lost to the shrill tear of material as his urgent hands ripped the back of her gown open from neckline to waist. But she didn't struggle, and he took that as concession. No, she *wanted* him, he reminded his doubting mind. Perhaps she could guess his addled thoughts; perhaps she knew he would question every detail after a night filled with torment because she drew back and met his stare as she shoved the damaged gown from her body, and he was relieved.

One layer after another fell free. Her hands

were as intent as his, tugging at his costume, fumbling with clasps and buttons when they were only another hindrance. She seemed to crave skin as much as he did, even scarred and marked, never the flawless perfection any of those other gentlemen could have given her. She seemed driven to the edges of desire by the abused torso she revealed when she pushed his shirt from his shoulders, pressing eager palms and racing taut fingers up and down his chest. *She wanted him*; he had to keep insisting it in his mind. This wasn't pity; it was love.

Jerking her pantaloons down her hips, he immediately sought an essential proof, slipping his fingers deep within her. She cried out, grabbing his shoulders to steady her sway as he made his motion as determined as lovemaking, thrusting fingers in and out of a wetness that grounded him with its reality.

He couldn't wait any longer and did not pause for flowery sentiment or gushing adoration. His strong arms collected her half-clad body, and forced her back against the stone wall beside the hearth. One yank of lingering barriers freed his throbbing desire. How it ached for the one place it longed to be! He wasn't about to deny it. Lifting her hips and pressing her to the wall, he plunged deep, thrilling in her shout as she clasped him with fisted hands.

Impulse yearned to punish *her* for what he had endured, to take out aggression in desire and let sensation steal him away. His first thrusts were harsh, crushing her soft body between his and the wall as if he didn't care about anything but release. His ears burned with her whimpers, and his remaining shred of sense wondered if they were for passion or pain. Pain...? No, how could he ever hurt her? Easing to a gentle rhythm, he felt her rock her hips to meet him, and with a sharp moan, he covered her throat in penitent kisses. *She wanted him*; she wanted *this*. He refused to doubt any longer.

Christine fitted her body as close to his as she

could get, cursing his haste with her chemise yet in the way as a silken barrier when she ached to feel the odd textures and planes of his every scar. He was so deep within her, joined, complete and inseparable. Why did they ever have to disconnect when these fleeting moments as one seemed the answer to every trial and tribulation forced upon them? This place was sacred; it was destined perfection.

Erik's thrusts were growing rough again, and desire robbed her of solid thoughts. She cried out, clasping his hips with her thighs. Pleasure came in a violent wave so intense she sobbed against his temple, arching firm against his hard body. Sense insisted that she would make them fall, but he kept her upright and fixed, pinning her to the sturdiness of the wall and riding out her climax with her, the hint of a smirk on his lips as he met her eye.

"You're mine, Christine," he hoarsely reminded, and she replied in a nonsensical cry, a passionate agreement when gripping hands clasped tighter as if they'd never let go. Pressing her hips into the wall with every driven thrust, he growled, "This body is *mine*. No one else will ever have it, not like this. No, this is for me alone." His words cut off in a fervent moan before he could utter a hoarse command. "Tell me you're mine. Say it, Christine."

"Yours," she gasped, forcing her lips to form letters. "I'm *yours*, Erik. ...I love you."

That was all he could take. Those beautiful words sent him over passion's precipice, and he clutched her fitfully as he exploded deeply within her, muttering her name in broken syllables.

Sense returned in fragments, and its first whispers were a fleeting fear she would push him away. He had been forceful and rough, claiming her so violently that guilt pricked his skin, but to his relieved astonishment, she wrapped arms and legs about his torso and pressed idle kisses to his scarred cheek.

"Christine," he weakly managed, "...are you all right, love?"

She lifted her dark head and regarded him through hazy eyes and a soft smile. "I love you, Erik."

Tears clouded his view of her beautiful face, but he smiled through their piercing emotion and whispered, "I love you, too."

Weaving his arms securely around her, he carried her to her bedroom, and as he laid her down, she refused to let him go, kissing his tears away and whispering soft adorations that inspired more. For the rest of the night, he was her willing victim, overcome by a love he had only ever dreamt of until by dawn's first light, doubt was a forgotten enemy.

Chapter Nineteen

Christine did not fall asleep until an early morning hour chimed. Erik lay beside her, watching her as coherency filtered in and the Masquerade's unsettling events fell into their proper perspective. Anger had died, swallowed somewhere in passion's possession, and with her warm body curled against his, pain was just as easily surrendered. He couldn't find the strength to carry vendettas, not anymore, and plotting revenge seemed a waste of precious time meant to be spent with Christine. There was only one point worth dwelling upon, and now that his mind felt like his own again, he devised a way to fix what had been damaged as methodically as solving a puzzle. Yes, there must be an answer, and within seconds, he found it.

Brushing a kiss to his sleeping angel's brow, he quietly rose and dressed, making certain to locate an acceptable mask from his wardrobe and hide his face. This errand could not be completed by a monster. One last peek into the bedroom and a glimpse of Christine to act as inspiration, and he fled the underground, knowing the sun would already be up and he'd have little time to act.

The opera house was dark and silent after a night of merriment, and Erik abandoned its sanctuary for the equally quiet city streets. Sunday, the only ones about were those rushing to early church services. Ah, religion and its servitude! He certainly would rather be revering life in a bed beside Christine than rushing into a building to bend at the knee and worship an invisible entity.

One brief stop was made at the local newspaper. He had an acquaintance that would take any story for a reasonable bribe. Erik was fortunate to arrive just before the day's paper was to be printed. Of course his addition meant a delay, but the right amount of money bought a Sunday print that would be delivered a few hours past its promised time.

He left the office as early mass was letting out and ducked into alleyways to avoid being seen. Until the paper was distributed, he had to be extra careful; its late-addition story was about to rewrite the gossip chain, but for the moment, nothing was changed and he was still a monster.

He had one final stop to make in order to be sure his plan went to par, and gliding as a shadow, he traveled the back roads until he came to a well-known estate at the edge of the city limits. This was a house he'd only passed on occasion with no desire to ever be within its walls, and yet stealthy in every motion, he scaled a locked gate and easily made his way onto the property.

The estate of the Vicomte de Chagny had no detail to announce it as special. It was as overdone and blasé as every other rich aristocrat's home. Considering the previous night's drama, Erik's only surprise came with the realization that no guards posted watch outside. In a way, it was insulting the arrogant Vicomte had not taken his threat seriously, not even enough to consider adding extra locks to the door, something to at least *attempt* to keep murderers out!

Getting inside was relatively simple, and as long as he avoided maids scurrying about in their morning chores, he had freedom to search. No one would dare disturb a Vicomte's beauty sleep, would they? Not a soul walked the hallway that led to the master bedroom, and when Erik could move like a ghost, nothing gave his presence away.

The curtains were drawn tight in the bedroom so that not even slits of daylight were allowed their rightful entrance. Erik glanced to the large bed and found his foe sound asleep. Oh, that wouldn't do at all! Hasty steps brought him to the tall windows, and Erik jerked the curtains open and welcomed the rush of sunlight that stretched to every corner.

"Still abed?" Erik loudly called. "Why, you are a lazy fellow, aren't you? Life and death threats hang in your periphery and yet you find peace enough to sleep? Most in your place would choose insomnia over being unprepared for impending doom."

The Vicomte darted upright beneath his covers, and as the haze of sleep evaporated, he locked his wary stare on Erik and stammered, "Monsieur, you take me unaware. ...Are you here to kill me now? Do you call it a fair fight to murder your opponent in his bed?"

"If I intended to murder you, you'd be dead already, but it seems murder is currently out of the question and your life is momentarily preserved." Arrogance was the inherent trait of the almighty Opera Ghost, and it exuded from every gesture, every motion, saturating his sinister steps as he approached the Vicomte's bedside. His eyes lit with condescending amusement to fully regard silk nightclothes and bedraggled hair, a less than pristine portrait for an aristocrat. "Actually, I'm here because of Christine."

Erik could not deny the flicker of fear Raoul did not conceal. The Vicomte cared, and that only made Erik hate him more.

"Is she all right?" Raoul anxiously bid. "So help me God, if you hurt her-"

"You need not trouble yourself worrying over *my wife*, but you are ignorant to believe I'd ever hurt

322

her, most especially when *you* are the one who deserves pain."

"So that's it," Raoul decided. "You can't kill me because it would stain your deceptive reputation. Must keep up the hero's image you've burned into Christine's head, right? So if death is not your purpose, is it torture? Revenge for unmasking you and displaying the truth to the masses?"

"Normally, I would argue that your actions are worthy of as much torture as the human body can endure, but in retrospect, I've concluded you acted purely out of jealous spite. You see, Monsieur Vicomte," he began as he idly leaned close and tilted his masked face, "I used to be rash and impulsive, used to attack with the merest provocation, but Christine has taken the place of my nonexistent conscience. She makes morality mean something to me, and she doesn't deserve to bear the backlash for *your* selfishness. Did you never consider you might have destroyed her career and reputation with your antics last night? How is she supposed to walk into rehearsal tomorrow amidst frantic gossip and heaved insults?"

"Perhaps *you* should have considered that before you decided to play ordinary," Raoul retorted coldly. "I would deem this as much your fault as mine. If you had just stayed away-"

"Why?" Erik shouted back. "Am I not allowed to walk in the world? Not even when a mask goes unquestioned?"

"You are a murderer."

"I am trying to amend my sins. I can't take them back, but I can strive to be a better man...for Christine's sake. She inspires me to want something greater than a life filled with pain."

A sad smile touched Raoul's lips. "Yes, she can have that effect."

Erik forced his temper to remain in control. It was difficult when this man loved his wife and blatantly put feelings on display. Erik had to remind himself that Christine was *his*, legally by marriage and law. She claimed love, but that wasn't enough to soothe him; only possession made him calm.

A clenched jaw was the only clue to his internal rage as Erik stated, "The reason I am here is not to hash out our differences or pose war. I have come seeking your cooperation *for Christine*. I refuse to let last night be *her* burden to bear."

"And what do you suggest then, Monsieur?"

"Not suggest, already done." Erik stalked a haughty pace as he revealed his covert actions. "When the morning paper arrives, God-willing by midday, there will be an article on the front page about the audacious scene performed at last night's Masquerade Ball. That is what it shall be: a stunt to garner publicity for the opera. What better method in a place of drama and overdone acting? A joke played on the other patrons as one of their own costumes himself as the notorious Opera Ghost." Erik spoke the fabrication with pride at his own genius. "They will all be convinced it wasn't real. No, it was the Vicomte de Chagny waging a battle with the supposed Opera Ghost for the hand of the new prima donna. Ah, a rivalry more brilliant than anything on the stage! You, Monsieur, will be acclaimed for your superb acting skills, and Christine will be able to walk into rehearsal tomorrow and laugh with the ballerinas over their gullibility to believe our scene as real!"

Raoul was unconvinced, arching a skeptical brow as he inquired, "Do you truly think that will work?"

Huffing softly, Erik halted and stared with annoyance. "I've come to learn in my years that people tend to believe what they *want* to believe. The murderous Opera Ghost walking amongst them is a horror story most would rather not live. And then to see his face...well, that is a monstrosity they'd rather attribute to makeup and effects, certainly not reality because something so ugly must not exist in their pretty world. They'll believe it, but I need insurance. *Your word*, Monsieur, that you will corroborate the story. I can't have you sabotaging my attempt and putting Christine in jeopardy."

Realization dawned as Raoul accused, "That's why you're not here to kill me. If I am found murdered, that certainly destroys your illusion."

"As I said, your life is *temporarily* preserved," Erik bitterly reminded, "at least until after the opera when the gossip subsides, and then... Test me and see how far you get. I will not play games with you anymore. Christine is my wife whether or not *you* agree with that fact. *She* made the choice willingly and eagerly. You are not allowed to be her hero just because you are the one with the perfect face and the title. Such things are not criteria for nobility. I have just as much right as you to love her and to have her love in return."

The Vicomte's animosity never softened as he sharply replied, "I'll go along with your little story *for Christine*. But this isn't over. I spent *years* in search of her. I had to love a memory for so long. Christine told you of our past together, didn't she?"

Erik eyed him dubiously, on guard with every detail revealed. "In scant paraphrases. I collected the rest when I observed your every encounter together." He hoped such news would shake the Vicomte and was pleased to see him waver a moment before he continued.

"It was never my choice to leave her. I had every intention of finding her again, but when I was finally able to pursue, she was gone, vanished as if she never existed. I searched for a long time, but I had little more than a name. And then suddenly, an article in the paper announced that Mademoiselle Christine Daaé was going to be performing in the place of La Carlotta at the weekend's opera. A couple of paragraphs upon the arts page. I normally don't

even read the arts page; it was purely luck that I
lingered to have a second cup of coffee that morning.
It was not some great coincidence I took up my
father's old box at the opera when I have no passion
for such things. I had to attend, to finally be with
Christine after all this time. That was how it was
supposed to be. But...the instant I appeared in her
life, I found someone else in my place."

Raoul regarded Erik coldly, and Erik matched
the expression right back as the Vicomte spat, "I will
not accept that I don't have a chance to win her heart,
not when it was stolen by deception and
manipulation. You never earned her affection; you
exploited it. And now you expect me to walk away
and allow your transgressions to be forgiven?"

"No," Erik snapped, "a *legal marriage* expects
you to do that. As far as I'm concerned, you are
coveting another man's wife, which is on that list of
sins en route to damnation if I remember correctly."

Scowling, Raoul replied, "You wouldn't be
trying so hard to deter me if you were certain I
couldn't win, but you're afraid Christine will
remember to fear you and run straight to me,
marriage or not."

A vision of Christine played in his head, her
eyes the previous night, her emotions flashing and
tempting him to leap heart-first after. He was solemn
and set as he reported, "She loves me. I don't care
whether or not *you* believe that, but if you wish to
keep my good humor intact, you will stay away from
her. Don't cross me, Monsieur Vicomte. I may have
been forced to act amicably and not *kill you* this time.
You can wager that won't happen again."

"On either of our parts. I have no intention of
dying by *your* hand."

"We'll see about that."

One final glare to keep the threat in place, and
Erik fled the Vicomte's bedchamber, suddenly
desperate to be back within the safety of the

catacombs. Too many excursions in the social world the past days left him craving solitude, no one but Christine as his ally and companion. After the previous night and its repercussions, he doubted he'd wish to play ordinary again for quite a long time.

Erik felt agitation the instant he entered the underground house. His gaze immediately sought the source and landed on Christine pacing fitfully before the hearth.

The moment she noticed his presence, she darted to him and threw shaking arms around his neck. "Oh, Erik, where were you? I have been sick with worry since I woke up alone. After you posed the idea of leaving me last night, I was terrified you had actually gone through with it!"

"No," he vowed, embracing her back and savoring the contentment that came merely with her closeness. "No, I'd never leave you. Please forget everything I said last night. I was beside myself, and you will not be the one to bear my trials." In his head were spinning corridors laden with doubts the Vicomte's words had inspired. He was suddenly afraid and clutched her tighter.

"It's all right," she assured, slipping fingertips along the nape of his neck, and he could not suppress an instinctual shudder as his body immediately ached for her touch everywhere.

"No," he said to both her and desire. "I acted foolishly, and I beg forgiveness. I practically hurt you, and that is one sin I would never forgive of myself. You mean more to me than anything in the world. I will not jeopardize losing you again."

"You aren't going to lose me," she replied, and for one blissful instant, he let himself believe her.

"No more dark thoughts," he abruptly decided. "I have to tell you where I've been and what I've done this morning. Let me put it this way: tomorrow at rehearsal, you are going to be applauded for being the greatest little actress in existence."

She drew back to meet his eye suspiciously, and he couldn't contain a chuckle. "What did you do?"

"Sit, love, and let me tell you a tale that turns a trauma into a strange blessing. Well, you did want to portray the Opera Ghost's mistress, didn't you? That role will now gain you praise instead of degradation, so I suppose it is a good thing you chose the right costume! You are about to be a star, Christine. You'll see what I mean..."

*****

Erik carried the optimism for both of them the next morning when she reluctantly returned to rehearsal. She still expected harsh words and insults behind her back. It was a sharp surprise when the only one to dare was Carlotta in her usual daily tirade. Everyone else eyed her a bit oddly but without hostility, and she was shocked they seemed to believe Erik's story. As the managers passed her in the hall, even they gushed over how they had been duped by her husband and the Vicomte's little joke, chuckling over their frantic agitation as she tried to match their enthusiasm.

As rehearsals began, it seemed all was back to normal with no more mention of a Masquerade and a disfigured Opera Ghost...at least until midday break. Meg rushed to her the moment they were released, clasping her arm and nearly dragging her outside into the brightness of daylight.

Once beyond the shadow of the opera house where sunlight seemed a protector, Meg halted and faced her with wide green eyes, insisting, "Talk. I want details, the *real* details. I may be gullible, but I'm not *that* gullible! A performance at the Masquerade? The Vicomte would never go along with that. So...? Is it true? Did you marry the Opera Ghost, Christine?"

Christine contemplated a convincing lie, but after a long pause and a sigh, she decided, "It's better I don't say, Meg."

328

"Why?" Meg shrieked in indignation. "Is it because of my insatiable need to gossip? Because if I truly try, I know I could keep your secret. Besides, who would I *want* to tell? This isn't exactly a pleasant topic of conversation among easily frightened and screechy ballerinas. ...Oh God, it *is* true!" Shaking her golden head frantically, Meg cast furtive glances about despite the lack of shadows. "Oh God, will he *kill me* because I know? And I can't *un-know* it and save myself, can I? Oh no, am I doomed, Christine?"

"No, no, Meg." Christine captured her arm and forced her attention. "He's not going to hurt you. He's-"

"A ghost!" Meg suddenly exclaimed, and her brow furrowed in deep wrinkles. "How could you marry a ghost? I mean *legally* marry. Isn't there some kind of law against that? Or a commandment or something?" She tilted her head, inquisitively contemplating. "And how does one work out the logistics of such a thing? I mean I saw the corporeal body, of course, and his voice...," her eyes glazed with the memory. "What a voice! But...if he's a ghost, doesn't that mean he's dead?"

"He's not a ghost," Christine explained, "not a real one anyway. He's just a man."

"With scars," Meg filled in and met Christine's eye warily. "Scars, Christine. Everyone saw. The story is it was fake and makeup, but...well, the Opera Ghost wears a mask for a reason. Ghost or not, the scars were real, weren't they?"

Christine grew solemn and silent.

"Oh, ...I'm sorry," Meg insisted, squeezing her hand. "I guess I sound shallow and callous, but it's just...his face was... And it was real...?"

A nod was her only answer to a question that seemed more intimate than any other. "You can't speak a word to anyone, Meg."

"I don't think anyone would believe me anyway," Meg concluded with a hopeless sigh. "The ballerinas are terrified of him, you know, and...they prefer the other story where it was all a hoax and you didn't *marry* him. It's an unpleasant truth to take." Realization began to settle in, and she muttered to herself, "It was real. The Opera Ghost and his face, ...and you touched it... I'd better quit thinking; it's making me nervous. But...do you love him, Christine? Or were you tricked?"

"I love him," she replied without waver and watched Meg try to register such a claim. "I've always loved him."

"Well, ...all right," Meg offered, still grimacing uncertainly. "But...if you need anything, ...a friend or a shoulder to cry on or an ear to listen, ...you know I'm always here, ...even if I'm relatively sure I'm afraid of your husband. That's natural considering everything. I don't think it can be any other way."

"You're wrong; it can be. If you'd look and see what I do, then you would understand."

"I don't think many people would *want* to look and see what you do, but I'm just being honest, Christine. One would have to ignore everything he's done to us, and...I can't do that yet. But if you love him, I promise to try."

And Christine couldn't ask for more than that. It was a start.

*****

"You were the one to insist on a lesson, and yet you are also the one to distract from any serious accomplishment!" Christine exclaimed, trying to sound serious, but a little giggle broke free and gave her amusement away.

Insisted on a lesson? Yes, Erik vaguely recalled it, but that was at the telltale creak of an opening front door with her return, before his eyes found her shape and those glorious curves. Since then, a lesson seemed a waste of minutes meant to be lost in her arms. With a conceding huff, he attempted to focus and devise an intelligible critique of the aria she had

330

just ended, but somewhere around the third line, his gaze had been caught and riveted to the motion of her lips, imagining their every vowel and consonant vibrating along the surface of his skin and he wasn't sure he heard a single pitch after that.

"*I* distract *you*?" he demanded in lieu of haphazard evaluation. "You stand before me, and your womanly graces and attributes call my name, and *I* am to be blamed for ogling them in reply?"

"This was *your* idea," she reminded, trying to control her smile. "And it isn't very professional of you to be ogling *anything* when I am solely your student."

It was torture to tear his eyes from her, but he fought to avert attention to his open score, glancing through the aria and scanning its passages. He could deduce only one point of criticism, simply because it was her most common mistake and likely as valid now as every time he'd heard the piece. "The high notes were too wide. You didn't round the vowel as you went up."

"I thought I did."

"No," he stated matter-of-factly and suppressed a smile. His teaching abilities might be lackluster at the moment, but he was determined not to let her know that. Trailing an impatient finger along staves and coarse paper as it dreamt of silken skin, he curtly reported, "Three high C's over the course of the aria, all different vowels, of course, but all should be executed with the same technique. So...a challenge," he decided. "Incentive to sing them correctly. For each high note you round and perform perfectly, I will grant you a kiss...anywhere you would like. Three high C's; that's three kisses you could earn to any glorious detail of your beautiful body. *However*, should you misstep and falter, I get the same. A kiss for each imperfect high note anywhere I'd like. Now don't you dare cheat and make mistakes because you want to kiss me. I'd grant the luxury without a challenge; the mere fun is claiming victory and demanding it."

Erik could read her delight with his proposition, her blue eyes twinkling above her grin. "All right," she agreed and lifted her posture.

"Round the vowel," he reminded before he began to play her introduction. As she began to sing, he paid careful attention this time and concentrated on every pitch.

The first C was perfect, and he wondered if perhaps she *had* done it right the first time. Maybe she had finally conquered her flaw, ...or maybe not. The second C didn't have enough support, and she pulled back, cringing at her failure. One for him, he concluded with the tinge of a grin beneath his mask. But that error seemed to ignite fire within her as she surged toward the end, and as if desperate to prove herself, she glided effortlessly up the scale to the last one and struck it with a power and brilliance that shook the bay window frame.

As soon as she finished, she arched dark brows and tilted her head, claiming victory in a haughtiness that made him chuckle as he corrected, "Two. You won two; the middle one wasn't right, and you know it. But...I *am* impressed. You've made such progress that I must be proud of you."

"Yes, and you also *must* reward me. Your pride is not enough when you promised incentives."

"With the utmost pleasure, my love," he declared. As he watched, she bit her lip impishly and reached for the clasps of her gown. Her nimble fingers unhooked one after another, but before she reached the last one or exposed skin he ached to see, she spun about and hurried toward the staircase. He hesitated only long enough to cover the piano's keys before following in a feverish rush.

By the time he arrived in the bedroom's doorway, her gown was a pile of sky blue and her petticoat a mass of ruffles beside it. She finished unlacing her corset, and it joined the layers with never a second thought as she lifted deceptively innocent blue eyes to his spying presence.

"Two kisses," she reminded, "anywhere I'd like."

"Anywhere," he vowed, watching in a fever as clothed in only her flimsy chemise and pantaloons, she approached in sultry steps that swayed her hips. How he longed to catch them in his palms and jerk her to his aching body! But he remained passive and waited for her instruction, hoping she would hurry when he could only be patient so long.

Christine reached for his mask first, discarding its hindering barrier and smiling so bright to glimpse his face. Had ugly scars ever received such a wonderful welcome? It made him love her so much that it swelled within and left him to tremble in its wake.

"One," she stated inarguably, and sliding her fingertips into his hair, she drew his head down until she could press his misshapen mouth to the flawless crease of her throat. He was only too willing to comply, his lips burrowing into that perfect curve and devouring as she cried out in delight and arched closer. One kiss had been the promise, but he lingered and stretched its bestowment, lapping teasingly at her skin with his tongue. Her hand fisted against his skull, gripping fiercely at his hair, and he almost smiled to hear a shrill moan of disappointment when he yanked free.

"One," he reminded in husky tones that gave his wanting away. "And where would you like the other, Christine?"

She blushed a pretty pink, and he chuckled beneath his breath. A blush yet! For all the voracious acts they had indulged in the past weeks, she still blushed! And how he adored its color!

Christine caught his hand in hers, grinning shyly and making him eager to take her lips as well.

But first, he had a vow to fulfill, and he burned as she guided his hand between her legs. He stroked first and felt her wetness seeping through her pantaloons to meet his touch.

"There, love?" he posed but did not wait for her answer. Sliding to his knees eagerly, he dragged her hips closer and kissed her womanhood. He could have rid her of her pantaloons without protest, but he chose to leave them on, running his tongue along rough material and tasting her through its thin boundary. She shuddered, her hands clasping his shoulders to stay upright, fingernails nipping him through his jacket. The sweetest torture!

Only one kiss was impossible, so he formed a dozen, teasing her with demanding lips and an urgent tongue. His gaze fixed to her desirous expression, every sensation she suffered unconcealed from his regard, and as his tongue made fervent circles around the epicenter of her passion, he let one hand wander to flick his thumb against the hardened nipple straining her thin chemise. She gasped, a sharp sound that thrilled him in its inhibition. He was anxious to turn it into a shout, and tempting, he moved his lips with intent, gaining the reaction he wanted as she cried out. Her hands left his shoulders to delve into his hair and clutch fitful and tense, but to her frantic dismay, he broke away and rose with a mocking grin.

"One kiss," he reminded, "and I'd argue I indulged you far more thoroughly than I should have."

"But, Erik...," she pleaded, edging close enough to arch her body to his.

"Oh, you wanted more," he taunted, and despite his resolve, he ran another caress along her wetness, searing his fingertips with her telltale desire. That single graze was all he allowed, and it left her muttering her indignation again as he drew away.

"Ah, ah," he chided, "you may not have fulfillment until you complete your own obligations. You owe me a kiss. Anywhere I'd like, Christine?"

"*Anywhere,*" she breathed, eyes beaming with a provocative glow he only saw when her wanting was so potent that it silenced the lingering voice of modesty. Without it, the blush faded from her skin, and he had glimpses of a sultry sensual woman, only just learning what her body ached for. How it aroused him as much as her every feature!

Sliding his hands into her loose curls, he gently tugged her downward, moaning when she went willingly with the hint of a seductive smile that drove him mad. His fingers were clenched taut and unable to relax, and so she was the one to unclasp his pants and drag them down with her descent.

"This was *your* choice," she reminded, arching a dark brow teasingly. "If you prefer I kiss you elsewhere, then-"

"No, don't you dare," he insisted with a harsh exhalation of a breath he hadn't realized he'd been holding. "Stop playing; I'm aching for your mouth."

Her smile only widened as she guided his undershorts off and replied with a bit of a giggle, "Yes, I can see that."

"Christine," he hissed impatiently. "Don't be cruel. This kiss was well-earned, and you must obey."

But she had every intention of that, and meeting his eyes for one more breath, she eagerly leaned close and pressed a long kiss to the tip of his manhood. His hands were rigid in her hair, and as her gaze roamed his face, she relished his complete surrender and every moan filling the air from parted, misshapen lips.

Christine knew she was torturing him, but she pulled away and insisted, "That was one kiss, and one kiss was all that was promised. Do you want more than that, Erik? Say the words, *ange*. Tell me what you want me to do."

"Must you?" he practically shrieked. "This is not the time to be brazen and test your authority over the Opera Ghost! You already know he is wrapped around your fingers...and preferably between your lips. *Please*, Christine!"

"Please what?" she dared to demand, one hand idly stroking a caress up the length of him. "Indulge me, my love. I want to hear you say it."

Without pause, he brusquely commanded, "Take me in your mouth."

She grinned her triumph before she complied. His groan was desperate, his entire frame shuddering from the instant she closed her lips about him. As she moved in a slow rhythm and teased him with her tongue, she cast glances at his disfigured face and savored the urgency of his wanting. Oh, how she longed to push it further! Gentle became fervent, and his strangled cry made her ache, his hands in her hair encouraging onward when words were nothing more than fragmented syllables and throaty moans.

His fists suddenly tugged fiercely enough to cease her seduction, but she did not give up without a final graze of her tongue, satisfied to feel him shiver in response.

"I wasn't through," she protested.

"No, but *I* would have been had you continued," he hoarsely bid, finally releasing her hair to catch her arms and help her stand.

"But...I would have anyway," she offered and could not control the rush of heat beneath her skin with her blush.

He shuddered at her words. "A tempting offer, to be sure, but nothing can compare to finding pleasure inside you. That's what I'm aching for, and I know you are, too." As he spoke, he caught the hem of her chemise and jerked it up and off.

Every other barrier followed, littering the floor around them with never a care when skin was so craved. Her palms pressed flat to his scarred chest, stroking its expanse with fingers dragged to trail behind like ribbons. She felt a strong heartbeat that sped its pace to know her touch, but before she could comment on such a phenomena, he stole letters from her lips, abducting them in his kiss.

His mouth was all fire, scorching her with its branding mark. He had her captured with his convicted hands and teased her with his hardness, rubbing its eager length along her skin as she arched closer and tried to get him to surrender.

"Christine," he gasped in a scant gap between eager mouths, "you want this body. How it always amazes me to know that! It is unworthy, and yet you want it anyway."

Her hands were still running desperate caresses along scars, her fingers tracing the meandering paths of damage and adoring every nuance as something more brilliant than perfection could ever be. Ducking her dark head, she pressed idle kisses to a mark across his collarbone and writhed against his desire, letting her body insist what she ached for.

A moan told his yielding. Clasping her hips between his hands, he guided her in small steps backwards until she hit the mattress and lifted her to sit on its edge. Her legs fitted to either side of his, her body throbbing expectantly, but he paused to meet her eye with glowing adoration.

Erik brushed a caress to her cheek and whispered, "I love you, Christine."

She was overcome, tilting into his touch, but before she could reply and make her own devotion, he thrust within her. Words of love became desirous cries as she arched her hips upward, anything to be closer and pull him deeper.

Hands resting upon her shoulders urged her to lie back before they made a path over her flesh. They lingered at her breasts, manipulating her hardened nipples and gently tugging them between fingers. Swallowing air into suffocated lungs, Christine tried to focus on every detail, to engrain it all into memory the way she caught him doing so often. Even now, his mismatched eyes were upon her, intent and studious, fascinated by her every reaction and searing her into his inquisitive mind. How many times she found him memorizing with a determination that almost scared her, as if he was still half-afraid he'd lose this forever.

No, no more. Christine grabbed his hands and pulled, drawing him down until he was pressed to her, skin to skin. Her arms weaved about his neck and hugged tight, her hips arching to entice him to more as she kissed his temple and set her cheek to his. His desperate moans brushed her ear, and she shivered her delight. Oh, to feel him and hold him and know he was hers! Nothing could mean as much as this moment, and she was convicted to savor every second.

But her body had its own agenda, and she could not stave off passion's swell, not as he moved harder and faster, delving so deep that she cried out and was dragged to an ecstasy so powerful that she felt tears prick her eyes and spill along her cheeks.

"Christine," Erik gasped as one crystalline drop tickled him with its fall, "what's wrong? Am I hurting you?"

"No, no," she muttered, turning to kiss her own tears from his skin. "I just love you so much... Please don't stop. Don't ever stop."

Erik found her lips with his, kissing with delicacy and cherishing her sweet words as he succumbed and sought his fulfillment. His moan of pleasure was captured between lips and no more than a vibration through his torso. Ecstasy didn't seem to matter because it didn't end in that one instant; it continued in kiss after kiss, evolving like the unceasing motion of a kaleidoscope.

He would have continued, but needed speech and declarations to make anchors to hearts, and as he broke a kiss, he vowed, "I love you. And this," he moved his hips to insist they were still joined, "is a bliss greater than any heaven or earth could offer."

She smiled so bright that he felt warm to his

soul, and brushing his fingertips along the curves of her lips, he dared to ask, "Are you happy, Christine?"

"Yes, of course," she immediately insisted, kissing his caress. "Of course, Erik."

But melancholy was too close, and had been for days, since a fated visit to a Vicomte, hanging like a curtain in the backdrop no matter how he tried to rip it down. "What if I set you free?" he suddenly demanded, fingers trailing her face. "What if I gave you up without consequence for anyone, without disaster or death for my loss?"

"Why do you ask such a thing?" she replied, smile dimming. He immediately missed it. "Are you going to leave me? You promised you wouldn't."

"I know, and I won't. I...I just wonder sometimes. If I offered you the chance to walk away, would you take it? Would you be brave enough to follow sense this time and leave me for good? Or would you again be yanked beneath the beat of *my* heart?"

"Neither," she decided adamantly "I'd follow the beat of *my own* heart and *love you* without regret." Her hands cupped his face and kept his eyes on hers. "Erik, why are you carrying such fear? Are you really putting credence to the Vicomte's words? Because if you think you will let me go and I will run to Raoul, then you are ignoring my heart completely. You're murdering it. I chose *you*, and I love *you*. Nothing is going to change that."

"Christine," he breathed, gazing at her in adoration, "you are the good part of me, and...I can't help but be afraid. If I ever lost you-"

"You won't," she insisted. "How can I convince you? ...Or maybe I can't, not yet anyway. Maybe after a decade's worth of years and a couple of children running about, you'll be able to look and see only my heart without questioning its beat."

"And until then?" he posed, humbled by her words and fantasizing that decade of time and sweet little children he prayed looked like their mother.

"Until then I will tell you as often as I must that I love you and that I am yours. And I will sleep in your arms and kiss you awake. And I'll adore every moment in your presence so much that you will feel it in your soul. Until then, I'll breathe with you and hold your hands in mine, and *I* will make *you* strong."

Her vows brought tears to his eyes, and whispering, "I love you," he sealed them in a vehement kiss.

Chapter Twenty

The next morning, as Christine entered her dressing room, she sensed something was wrong even before her eyes landed on an envelope resting unthreateningly on her vanity. Seal unbroken, ...no one else had seen its private words, and snatching it in a shaking hand, she tucked it into her gown to keep it that way. Oh, she had to be careful! She knew how often Erik lurked about, and she couldn't afford to share what could only be private musings. She recognized the handwriting of her scribbled name jotted across its center. *The Vicomte...* She was convicted to take care of things herself this time.

Her hiding place was in shadows; if Erik could conceal secrets in their recesses, so could she, and when he was more apt to seek her in the light, she had enough time to quickly scan the letter, squinting to make out every scrawled word. Oh Lord... And yet she was unsurprised; she felt she had been waiting for exactly such an advance. Now she just had to figure out what to do about it.

It was difficult to keep a convincing pretense and perform her best during rehearsal, but as the cast was given a reprieve for lunch, she nonchalantly caught Meg's arm and steered her outside to the crowded city streets.

"Christine, what-"

"Sshh," Christine warned and spoke not a word

until they were well beyond the opera house.

"What?" Meg demanded in an anxious shriek. "Oh God, did the Opera Ghost hurt you? Have you finally come to your senses and realized *who* you married? Oh, tell me, Christine! You know how my imagination runs away with me; I've already made all sorts of horrific tales. Does he want to kill you and make you a ghost as well?"

"Nothing nearly that melodramatic," Christine stated with a shake of her head. "It's not Erik; it's Raoul."

"Are you having an affair?" Meg squeaked.

"Of course not! Meg, just listen. Raoul left me a note, disconcertingly in my *locked* dressing room, but that may be the least of impending transgressions. He wants me to meet him tonight after rehearsal...*alone*."

"Affair!" Meg decided with a frantic point. "Or at least that's what *he* is hoping! What are you going to do?"

"Meet him, of course," Christine replied and watched Meg's green eyes widen. "This has to stop. He truly believes he has the chance to win my heart when it is already taken. I have to make him understand, but...I can't let Erik know about this. He'll want to play Opera Ghost, and even if his newfound sense of morality won't let him *kill* Raoul, hurting him wouldn't be out of the question if he foresees a threat. I owe it to both of them to finish this without violence."

"But, Christine, what if...? I don't know, but do you think the *Vicomte* would hurt you?"

It surprised Christine to realize she'd never considered it, and she suddenly called herself naïve. "I'd hate to think such a thing and ponder it as a possibility, but that will be another reason I need your help."

"My help?"

With an adamant nod, Christine explained, "I

cannot simply go and meet Raoul. Erik would know if I dared."

Meg eyed her oddly and decided, "Your husband is very paranoid, isn't he? And you don't find it restricting not to be allowed beyond his sight? I would go crazy if a man expected such restraint from me."

"You wouldn't call it restricting if you understood Erik the way I do. He's always worried something will happen and we will finally be forced apart. I love him too much to keep allowing him to be tortured that way."

"All right," Meg finally concluded. "Tell me how to help you."

"When rehearsal ends, I'm supposed to meet Henri, my carriage driver in the lobby, only today, *I* will not be the one to meet him; *you* will, wearing my cloak with the hood pulled close enough to smooth out any discrepancy."

"Pretend to be you? And then?"

This part was harder to say. "Return to my house in the carriage. That should give me enough time."

"Return to your house?" Meg squeaked, rigid and shaking a frantic head. "Return to the *Opera Ghost's* house!"

"It will be fine; he won't hurt you."

"No?" Meg inquired doubtfully. "Not even when I tell him that his wife is on a midnight rendezvous with the Vicomte?"

"Well, don't say it like that!"

"What am I supposed to say instead? Oh, Christine, he'll have me confessing my every sin since childhood with one look! You know how hard it is for me to keep my mouth shut!"

"Please, Meg!" Christine begged with her most persuasive smile. "I can't keep arguing my devotion with the Vicomte always a step away in our shadow. Erik would rather hide behind his Opera Ghost persona than be vulnerable, and I don't want the Opera Ghost. He will eventually use the role to push me away. I can't let that happen. Please, Meg, tell him...tell him that I promised to be strong and that is what I'm doing."

"But...he's scary," the little ballerina whined. "...Oh, all right, but only because I know how to use a toe shoe as a weapon. I won't go unarmed."

Sighing relief, Christine bid, "And that should give me the time I need to get to the cemetery and meet Raoul."

"Cemetery? Isn't that the cliché for some sort of horror story? Are you sure you want to do this? Because cemetery to most people with sense implies danger."

"Less so than if he requested meeting *alone* in his home," Christine proposed back.

"True, but you'll be careful, won't you? Sometimes a man in love will do desperate things if he thinks he has a chance."

Christine couldn't argue that. She recalled days when Erik had been in that role. He'd been just as desperate, but it was so different when love was requited. She didn't want to think how he would have been destroyed if she had pushed him away. He had called her the better part of himself; if she hadn't loved him, she wondered if he would have ever found that part.

*****

It wasn't difficult to switch places or trick anyone involved into believing them. Christine lingered in the shadows of the theatre doorway and watched Henri lead a silent Meg out. She was fortunate Henri never went beyond his duty, and a cloaked silhouette was enough. It was obvious why Erik trusted him when a mask and secrets were imperative, but he probably wasn't the best choice for a makeshift bodyguard.

The carriage rolled away, and as it vanished on

344

the crowded street, Christine disappeared into the night. She was taking up her alter-ego tonight. The Opera Ghost's mistress. Clad in black with her long cloak trailing in ripples behind her, she rushed in hasty steps, slipping into alleyways to avoid the cluttered throng on the main walks. Yes, she could be just as stealthy and just as omnipotent if she tried. Had the Opera Ghost himself not trained her?

With never a sound to betray her approach, Christine crept into the cemetery, curling into the protective folds of her cloak as she scanned the tombstones. Moonlight glinted on their stone surfaces, illuminating random names and bygone dates. The Opera Ghost's mistress, she called herself, and certainly, any ghost would feel at home in such a macabre setting.

Floating between headstones, Christine made her way deeper onto the sacred grounds. She had an idea where the Vicomte would be awaiting her, and as expected, she found him at her father's grave. His blue eyes lifted and lit hopefully as they regarded her.

"Christine, ...I wasn't sure you could get away," Raoul greeted with a tentative smile that abruptly fell. "Or is he here hiding in the shadows and ready to pounce?"

"No, you asked me to come alone, and I did. It's hard to believe you feel we must go to such lengths to have a conversation."

"A *private* conversation," he corrected. "Everywhere else, the walls seem to have ears, and here...well, the only ones listening are the real sort of ghosts, the kind that can't fly into rages and murder."

"If this is to be another lashing at Erik's character, I have no desire to stay," Christine threatened and fought to remain stern and unmoved. "I came because as you wrote in your letter, we are friends. We've shared things that not everyone can understand. A Vicomte and an opera singer... We are as much a contradiction now as when we were children. That has never changed."

"And yet I'm willing to ignore every retaliation it brings to be with you," he fervently declared. "Doesn't that mean anything?"

"Of course it does," she replied, careful to stay guarded. "I don't deserve your affection, Raoul. You gave it so willingly from the start, and I could never give it back."

"No, because you gave it to *him*." He cringed and refused to speak Erik's name. "He *tricked you*. But I've realized how futile it is to argue deceptions with you."

"Is that why you asked me here?" She almost smiled with a rush of hope. "To let this go?"

"No, ...I asked you here to once again request that you come away with me."

Christine felt her defenses rising and edged a small step back with her anxiousness. "And if I refuse? Will you force me, Raoul? Will you carry me off even though I'm another man's wife? This is my choice, and I'm not going to leave him."

"And can you say, here at your father's grave, that your decision is just and moral? Do you think your father would look past your husband's sins and grant his blessing? Welcome him into your family? Embrace that disfigured monster as his son?"

Merely the mention of her father struck a chord in her heart, and she tensed as she demanded, "Why must you speak of my father? He's *dead*."

"You must think of him," Raoul urged onward, and she fixed her eyes on the name etched into the tombstone. "How different your life would be if he were still alive! Do you think he'd be disappointed in you, Christine? You went against his every moral tendency. You married a murderer."

No," she abruptly insisted, meeting his stare again. "My father believed in forgiveness and penance. He would have seen the good in Erik's soul as I have."

"What would he have said to know how Erik manipulated his way into your life? Would *that* have been a sin worthy of forgiveness if murder is so easily redeemed? I can't imagine any father would accept such a transgression. Your father might have been the only one to break into your willing hypnosis. Pity he's gone." Steady steps brought the Vicomte closer, and though she kept guarded, she did not back away. "Christine, I know it's cruel to bring up your father, but he would have wanted you protected as much as I do."

"Protected?" she repeated doubtfully. "Your idea of protection is forcing me away from Erik and taking his place in my life."

"Your father would have blessed it! He was a good man, but like every father, he favored knowing a Vicomte was chasing at his daughter's heels. It was a privilege he knew you weren't entitled to." Before she could snap back, he grabbed her hand in his and continued in a rush, "Let me take you away from here, somewhere you can clear your head and make *your own* decisions without influences from the devil."

"You mean Erik," she coldly replied. "You want to take his voice out of my head and replace it with yours. You're so certain your words will change my heart, but I know what I want and what I feel. You could take me away, and I'd love him still. I've *always* loved him. I'm sorry you want me, but I can't be yours, Raoul." Christine tried to yank her hand free, but his grip was tight. "So you *will* force me to go with you," she concluded, shaking her head. "I didn't want to believe you'd do it, but that was your idea, wasn't it? If I refuse, you will take the matter into your own hands and dole out what *you* believe is just?"

"I hoped it wouldn't come to this," he argued as his free hand caught her shoulder. "Christine, I don't want to hurt you, but I need to get you away from him. It's the only way to save you."

Save her? She was just as sure she didn't need

saving. "I don't want to hurt you either, Raoul," she said. "That was never my intent, but if you don't let go of me, I will not apologize for my actions."

The Vicomte obviously did not take her threat seriously and began to pull her toward the cobblestone pathway. ...Well, she did warn him. But she was not about to be abducted against her will. Her foot darted out and kicked his shin hard enough to make him yelp.

"Christine!" Raoul shouted, but his distraction was enough for her to break loose. She backed between headstones, ready for another attack with fists raised this time.

"Don't you dare, Raoul," she warned, watching him rub his sore shin with a modicum of satisfaction. It was a victory, however minor. "Leave me be! You cannot simply drag me off as one of your belongings!"

"Christine, I'm not trying to-"

"No! No more! I am *not yours*!"

A chuckle resounded through the quiet graves, and then an angel's voice called, "Brava! Such fire! Such vehemence! I expect some of that later; I will not allow all of it to be squandered on the Vicomte!"

Wide eyes from both Christine and Raoul darted to Erik as he idly strode closer, and as the Vicomte muttered a curse, Christine asked with her own annoyance, "How can you be here? Meg is probably just arriving at our house to tell you where I am."

"Henri may be a fool, but I am not," he stated with an arrogant smirk. "Meg is about your size, but she carries a ballerina's grace when she walks, not like you. You walk in a singer's posture, unless, of course, you're shy or unconfident or being tormented by Carlotta. Then you drop shoulders. Either way, it was obvious *Meg* was not *you*, and I am determined to hire another guard or take you to rehearsal myself from now on."

Stifling a smile, Christine replied, "And I

thought the sound of her voice or her golden head would be the thing to eventually give Meg away. I should have considered that you pay attention to every detail, even the mundane."

"When it is concerning you, *no* detail is mundane." One more fond adoration was poured through his stare before he let it fade to bitterness and glared at the Vicomte. "Trying to steal her away this time? It's ironic that months ago, *I* would have been the one accused of the same, and yet I learned my lesson. You, on the other hand, have not."

"I told you I wouldn't just give her up," Raoul replied, matching his cold stare.

"I should kill you for this asinine attempt alone!"

"Wait one minute!" Christine shouted at both of them, holding up a hand to each. "I am no damsel in distress in need of rescue. Raoul," she faced him first, "I told you my decision, and it will not be changed. And Erik," her focus hastily shifted, "I don't want the Opera Ghost fighting my battles."

"Oh, I know that," Erik declared, his gaze glinting with pride. "You were handling yourself splendidly, and I am not solving any more dilemmas as the Opera Ghost. Have I not promised you that already? But," a smirk curved his lips, "I have far more productive tactics. Intelligence outweighs haunted torture, it seems; I get more accomplished by outwitting my victims. Monsieur Vicomte, I took the liberty of sending a copy of the newspaper detailing our Masquerade hoax to your dear old aunt, the Comtesse. You can imagine her surprise to learn you were cavorting about with an 'opera tart'." His gaze darted to Christine as he quickly added, "Those were her words, not mine, my love. I would have called you a sultry diva."

Christine bit her bottom lip to stifle a shy smile, but the Vicomte was much less amused. "You had no right to send that to her!"

"Indeed?" Erik posed. "Because she wrote back that you had arranged to bring your *fiancée* to her estate to stay a few weeks. Now, considering that fiancée is another man's wife *and* an opera singer, she is not welcome. The Comtesse sent you a letter of your own; it is likely awaiting you. She insists on your presence *alone*, Monsieur, so that she may remind you of your rightful place and that Vicomtes do not rush about creating scandals and kidnapping married opera singers."

"Why, you arrogant bastard!"

"Watch your language in front of the lady," Erik scolded, sharing a smile with Christine. "You already have enough sins on your plate, don't you? Now get out, and don't consider returning. You are an unneeded hero in this story; Christine already has one by her choice and her love. Your role is unnecessary."

Raoul scowled at him before he met Christine's eye a moment more. "If you need me, Christine, if you need *anything*, if this bastard hurts you-"

"He won't," Christine insisted, firm and certain. "He *never* would. Just go, Raoul."

The Vicomte was reluctant, but with a frustrated huff, he conceded and stomped a path out of the cemetery alone. He was barely beyond sight before Christine rushed into Erik's arms.

"Do you think he'll truly leave Paris?" she asked as she hugged him tight.

"At least briefly. His aunt is not the sort of woman to deny, and if he returns, we'll play a new hand if we must. It would be ridiculous if he doesn't give up, but obsession is a difficult bug to leave the system. Sometimes trying to deny its possession only makes you want it more. I have firsthand experience with its potency."

She shook her head and drew back to meet his eye. "It isn't the same; I've *always* wanted you, Erik." Delighting in the beaming grin he gave in reply, she laughed softly and declared, "*I* tried to fight with fists and kicks, with *violence*, and *you* were the one to solve the problem with words and wit. It's amusing!"

"Oh, but I won't devalue the joy of watching you kick and threaten the Vicomte!" he exclaimed, chuckling beneath his breath. "I don't think it possible to doubt you again when I can recall that memory and remember you literally fought to stay with me."

She laughed, imagining the scene, and then suddenly, her eyes widened with a rush of realization. "Oh Meg! She's probably sitting on our porch, terrified to asphyxiation by now! It was a panic enough to send her to *you* alone, and if Henri simply left her there..." Christine shook her head and insisted, "We have to get home."

"Oh, all right. Let's go and resuscitate the little ballerina. Wait until she hears your story, and *please* don't leave out a single detail. I would love for it to be the gossip around the entire opera house tomorrow. The Vicomte de Chagny, potential abductor, beaten away by the prima donna. We could keep him out of Paris simply by destroying his precious reputation with the truth!" Chuckling again, he slipped his arm about Christine's shoulders and began to lead her out of the cemetery.

But Christine halted one more moment and cast a look over her shoulder at her father's carved name, deciding, "My father believed in love first and foremost, and he knew better than to judge anyone without fairness. He wouldn't have been disappointed in my choice, not when it's clear I love you. He would have been pleased because I'm happy."

Erik simply nodded and continued to guide her away. He couldn't agree with as much conviction; to him, Christine was the exception to normal people because she had been able to look beyond the seemingly unforgivable. But then again, she had to learn to be that way from somewhere. Perhaps her father *would* have accepted him. As they left the cemetery, Erik silently composed a prayer of gratitude to her father's ghost for teaching Christine to have an open heart.

*****

The cast had three bows at curtain call to a house that would not stop cheering and praising their new prima donna. Despite her poised demeanor, Christine's cheeks flushed pink, and she fought tears at the overwhelming ovation, curtsying low and humble one final time before rushing into the wings amidst accolades from her cast mates. So many kind words, and yet there was only one opinion to matter, and she was impatient as she tried to maneuver through the crowd to get to her dressing room.

Finally! She eagerly locked the door and shut out a world that doted on her when it couldn't possibly be enough. No, not for her.

The mirror opened almost immediately, and without pause, she darted into the shadows and was caught by anxious and shaking arms. He didn't need to speak his pride; she could feel it radiating through his every overcome tremble.

"You are something extraordinary," he softly muttered above her ear, and she heard a catch of tears in his voice.

"I was well taught," she posed back, lifting her hand to remove his mask and touch his face with eager fingers. "Credit must be bestowed to my teacher's efforts and unceasing guidance."

He shook his head and pressed kisses to her brow. "Not even I knew you could do *that*. You were...amazing, Christine. I don't even have words to describe your brilliance. You moved me..."

She beamed as she kissed him, brushing tears with her fingertips. Drawing back, her smile only grew, "And I won, didn't I? Eight high C's in the whole opera, and every one executed correctly."

Erik fought not to laugh as he teased, "The one at the end of Act One was a bit suspect, if I recall."

352

"It was not!" she protested. "You just don't want to concede to my victory. We had a deal, *ange*. Play fair. Eight high C's, and if every one was correct, then *I* get to name the baby."

The word alone caused a shiver to race Erik's spine. It was still so new to hear it hit the air and sounded foreign in its syllables. He had yet to bring himself to use it, afraid in some illogical way that if he spoke the word, it would cease to exist, as if he could somehow curse something so pure and created out of transcendent love.

"Well?" Christine pushed, blue eyes bright with anticipation. "The privilege is mine, is it not? And you should truly learn better than to bet with such important details. Now you will have to wait until the next one to have an opinion over a name."

"Next one...," he muttered breathlessly. "I have yet to fathom this one, and you are mentioning the *next one*? Good Lord, Christine!"

"Well, start fathoming," she commanded with a giggle. "Because it isn't just going to go away if you don't think about it! ...You're going to be a father."

That word was even more astounding than 'baby', and it momentarily jarred sense as it sunk in, playing in the bewildered expression upon his face. Finally as if broken out of a trance, he stated, "I shouldn't bet *anything* with you. I should have known you'd rise to the challenge with such great stakes. And now our...baby," his voice trembled on the word, "will bear some flowery, sentimental appellation that will seem more a curse than a name. You will think with your emotions first and never consider the name will be pinned to our child forever."

"Think with emotions?" she snapped, and he cringed to remind himself how quick and easily her temper flickered these days.

Before she could continue, he kissed her hard and deep, stealing argument and devouring with lips that bore a smile at their corners. And that was why

353

he adored every emotion-laden outburst, because he knew she could not resist his eager persuasions as penance.

As he ended the kiss with a gentle nip of her bottom lip, he admitted, "Yes, yes, you won, and as your prize, you will choose the name. How could I possibly deny you after that performance?"

"May I have a further reward of being whisked home to a hot bath and a passionate night?" she inquired with a mischievous grin.

"Oh? You don't wish to greet your public and accept your accolades?"

"No, I prefer to remain a bit of a mystery. Let them all wonder where I disappeared. After all, the Opera Ghost's mistress doesn't need an excuse or an explanation. Let them think the Opera Ghost himself carried me off once again. I like that fantasy." Her fingers stroked the nape of his neck, her gaze insisting what she wanted, and Erik chuckled as he rested one palm against the beaded waistline of her costume.

"Do you hear that, little one? You are going to be born into an unusual family! With the Opera Ghost as your father and his prima donna mistress as your mother, you are certainly in for quite a life!"

"Well, of course," Christine gushed, covering his hand with hers. "That is obvious, and our child will love every minute of it! We're special, Erik, and that's better than ordinary. Don't you agree?"

"Very much," he breathed, and bending low, he brushed a kiss to her stomach and hoped the growing child within felt his love. It must exist in echoes when its mother radiated it right back.

"I love you both," Erik whispered and closed his eyes as Christine's hand stroked his scarred cheek. Perfect bliss in a happy ending and a future to come.

"I know you are not exceptionally fond of singing for me," Christine said, "but babies enjoy lullabies, or so I've been told."

"Then I shall begin composing a collection first

thing tomorrow, the most beautiful, lyrical melodies ever heard. Our child deserves the songs of angels."

"And an angel to sing them," Christine pushed as with one last kiss to her belly, Erik stood tall and eyed her with amusement.

"From Opera Ghost back to angel within a handful of words. Oh, of course I will sing for our child, but I will be writing you glorious harmonies to sing with me. Our child will have the best sung lullabies in existence."

"Our child," Christine repeated with an awed grin. "How I adore hearing you say it!" Brushing a kiss to his tattered cheek, she bid, "I love you, ...but I was hoping the Opera Ghost would drag me into the shadows and make me surrender again. I'm already starting to forget the last time we were so brazen."

"You mean yesterday during dress rehearsal's intermission?"

"Yes, well, you must refresh my memory," she insisted with a giggle as she released him and darted into the shadowed passageways, calling over her shoulder, "Are you coming? I thought you enjoyed chasing me."

"Catching you is the better part." His voice resounded into the darkness after her, and she tried not to laugh and give herself away as she ran. Never a step to betray him, and yet within moments, an arm grabbed her about the waist, and she was lifted off her feet.

The Opera Ghost's mistress, captured and yet eager to be his victim. Not all girls would wish for such a fate, but Christine embraced it with open arms and a thrill to call it hers. As he bent with a delighted chuckle and nuzzled his scarred cheek to her brow, she knew how completely love had transformed both their lives. Her husband, mask-less and proudly displaying to her the very thing he'd always been ashamed to own, choosing love over omnipotence, and she, touching the scars she'd once denounced, loving him more for their existence and strong enough to say so.

"The Opera Ghost shows no mercy," he breathed, his hand teasing the bare flesh above her neckline.

"Promise?" she tempted back and made a path of kisses down his throat.

"Oh yes, not an inkling."

"Erik..." Lifting her head, she met his mismatched stare in the scant glow of a dim lantern and whispered, "I love you."

With a soft moan of pleasure falling from misshapen lips, he rushed her into the shadows, eager to savor every syllable and cherish her with a million wordless adorations. Love, and how lucky he felt to have found it!

ABOUT THE AUTHOR

Michelle Gliottoni-Rodriguez wrote her first novel in high school. Fifteen years later, and she's up to 26 and still counting. Fascinated with Gothic romances, she would call her greatest influences the works of the Brontë sisters and then add in an adoration and semi-obsession for "The Phantom of the Opera" and Buffy the Vampire Slayer. In August 2011, she published her first novel, a Gothic vampire romance titled *Opera Macabre*. That was followed with the publication of the first of her angel series, *The Devil's Galley*; the second installment, *The Pirouettes That Angels Spin* will be following this winter. In addition to writing novels about vampires, angels, and demons, she writes and posts Phantom of the Opera stories online and has even had the honor of having them translated into German and Russian for worldwide fans. Due to the wonderful support of her Phantom "phans", she released a first collection of her stories called *Manifestations of a Phantom's Soul* this past summer and intends to follow it with a second volume sometime next year.

The other side of her life is a passion for music; she's also a trained opera singer with a Bachelor of Music from Saint Xavier University in Chicago. She's won various awards and accolades in the Chicagoland area and has portrayed such roles as Sister Genevieve in *Suor Angelica*, Rosalinde in *Die Fledermaus*, the Countess in *The Marriage of Figaro*, Yum-Yum in *The Mikado*, and the Queen of the Night in *The Magic Flute*.

From writing at 4AM to practicing for her next performances at 7AM and then onward to being a full time wife and mom with a 6 year old, a 3 year old, and a baby on the way, one would call her life insane, but she likes to think of it as "full".

For more information about Michelle Rodriguez and her other works, check out her website:

www.michellegliottonirodriguez.webs.com

Made in the USA
Middletown, DE
15 February 2023

24931080R00205